BARTLEBY

BARTLEBY

A NOVEL BY CHRIS SCOTT

ANANSI

Bartleby was completed with the aid of a short-term grant from the Canada Council. The Council also assisted with the publication of this book, as did several private patrons.

Cover design by Hilary Norman

Cover photo by Graeme Gibson

House of Anansi Press Limited
471 Jarvis Street
Toronto 284, Canada

Library of Congress Card Number: 70-146454
ISBN: 0 88784 315 8 (paper) / 0 88784 415 4 (cloth)

Printed and bound in Canada by The Hunter Rose Company

1 2 3 4 5   75 74 73 72 71

*What could exceed the absurdity of an author who
should write* the Comedy of Nero, with the merry
Incident of ripping up his Mother's Belly?
— *Henry Fielding*

*To my wife, Linda;
To my friend, Peter Smith*

TABLE OF CONTENTS

CHAPTER ONE   *An Apology of Apologies, Wherein a Would-Be Bard Sets Forth His Reasons for Writing Such a Book at Such a Time, and Possessed by a Sense of Redundancy, Is Constrained to Apologize for Writing a Book at All – or No Book.*

Heavenly reader, let me anticipate your two most serious objections to *Bartleby*: the first that it is a work of plagiarism; the second that it employs too many gimmicks, stocks in trade, and clichés of the writer's imitative art. You say Bartleby is no fit name for a hero, for it has been used by the incomparable Melville. Then, yes, candidly I admit I have stolen the name though not its character, who seemed to me a dead man from the start. Or rather *I* have not stolen the name, but come by it, expropriated it, in what manner and wise you will presently see.

I like the sound *Bartleby*. In so far as it has certain memorable associations, it has put me in the way of writing a novel without actually having to go to such lengths, hence placing, or appearing to place me within a tradition we moderns lack. Should the hero have been called, *V, W, X, Y,* or for that matter, *Z,* or should he have remained nameless, the device would have been a mere concession to the rabblement's taste. As for the accusation of plagiarism, a charge subsequently put around in this text by a character other than the hero, it is acceptable, even welcome to me. For now all things are writ large and apocalyptically, and the world outside the poor writer's playroom falls into little pieces, what does he have at hand but an abacus of sorts, whereon to spell out – as best he can – the words Alpha and Omega? Let other bards plagiarize life; I have plagiarized a book.

1

Your second objection, I must admit, is more perplexing than the first. This very apology might appear as no more than a gimmick which — I hasten to assure you — was not at all in my mind when *Bartleby* came my way and I was on relatively easier terms with the world and myself. In those days I had projected an essay of my own: a very moral work to set this present age aright, a novelist's novel that would restore the harmonious principles of nice observation and just portraiture, in modern times usurped by the disfigured and grotesque minions of Dulness. Indeed I had actually compiled three or four chapters, scribblings — alas! — occupying more time and space in the drawer of my desk and the ambitions of its owner than in the critical light of day, to which, had they been exposed (as they eventually were), they would have amounted to less than nothing (as they eventually did).

Then — from this author of nothing at all — enough is said if I tell you that midway in time and place of my efforts as a would-be bard, with my hero still unchristened, a terrible uncertainty fell upon me, drying up the ink in my pen and, almost, the blood in my veins.

For here I was (and am) in a country where a certain prophet had been sown and reaped; a visionary in whose hallowed and harrowing wake bards trembled and bards fell. Here I was scratching out a tenanted life in the very city where this seer uttered utterances, said sayings, saw seeings, and see-sawed; here I was at the third remove of my life where the earth was barren, the seed blighted, the air unpropitious, the climate not conducive to bardic endeavours such as mine.

What gentle madness can have possessed me?

But I had a friend, a fantastical rococo friend, to whom in a fit of the *furor scribendi* I had loaned my pages. What would he say? Would he recognize my art; give me praise, encouragement, *flattery*? Or would my script be condemned to oblivion; my hero damned, given not even the best room in hell, though unbaptized?

We discoursed in generalities, my friend and I, until I raised those very infelicities and inadequacies, attributes of would-being and death, with which this apology has so far belaboured the reader. Yet I also propounded the strengths of my work, my *Autobiography of a Dead Man*. Was this not a novel idea for a book, an unprecedented idea, nothing less than a stroke of genius in fact: the idea of a sleeping hero – a hero who, although he walked and talked, drank and defecated, although he was seemingly awake – was actually *asleep*, and, asleep, *dead?* What forms there were to be explored! What an autopsy might be performed as my hero was laid out, cut open, and stitched up with incisive precision! Surely this was a revolutionary work!

This was my friend's reply – friend, do I say?

"Your intended work has nothing to commend it to the tribunal of popular taste at whose bar, if you wish for success, it must receive infallible judgement. Here is no *Sturm und Drang* of the *American* School: none of the Hebraic complaints and laments of Wrath, nor the existential pugilism of Rojack, nor the cybernetic trickery and borrowed cadences of Johannes Carp. Neither the corncobs and rhetoric of the great tradition, nor the lasciviousness and inguinal feats of the new, grace the pages you have shown me. As for the ontological concern and the leaping into and out of being of the *French* School, I here discern no monocles, autodidacts, plagues, windows on the world, no epistemologically multitudinous polysyllables to baffle the reader (your judge) and draw his applause. The word *Angst* is apparently unknown to you; self-searchings, *crises d'identité*, and dark nights of the human soul – asleep or otherwise – haunt none of your chapters. Why, where the *Germans* are concerned you seem merely untutored: grim drolleries, theatres of life (and death), blood cults, maniacal pacts, Weimar's perfect constitution, goblins, the sublimely demonic, will never keep your readers from their beds on a windy night. Furthermore, *Russian* buffoonery, grotesqueries, simpletons, idiots, horses, drunkards, wars, revolutions, assassinations, in short that heightened verisimilitude of the underground and ground-under writer which would have won you the deserved title, plagiarist and *bard*, all these you have most carelessly omitted. I would think you totally unacquainted, moreover, with the *English* stable of feminine delights – Lesser, Flame, Frigid Trophy, and Victoria Prickens – were it not for the

3

fact that you have confessed the many edifying and pleasurable hours you have spent perusing their voluminous productions. Yet neither lesbian housewives nor bawdy curates appear in your pages to delight the ingenuous and make the spinster leave off her knitting. And most unhappy criticism of all: those *Irish* flights of Sorrow, in whichever guise he chose to appear, whether as Windbreak or Belch where the Liffey flows from its sump unconscious, this SORROW, progenitor of the Fluvial Tradition and father of us all, trickles but thinly through your work – though his influence, I grant you, is made everywhere present by its conscpicuous absence."

My friend was reminded that the book was incomplete. But my face must have portrayed my disappointment, for he continued:

"Incomplete? That is hardly the word for it. However, concerning this very absence of content, this vacuity which I have critically touched upon, such inanity seems to me a recommendation – especially in this day and age – rather than the condemnation which you seem to think it. For, inasmuch as the silent symphony, the wordless language, the invisible portrait are in great contemporary demand and loom under the general and compendious term symbolic, so too will your work, when finished after the method I have in mind, gain easy acceptance with the public. Which body and its shepherd, the critic, rejoice in such emptiness and proceed under the following law: that, if a work has something in it, they fall to contention and quarrelling amongst themselves, and are full of envy and nastiness at seeing something they have not themselves drawn up. Whereas if a work has nothing at all in it, like yours, then they must of necessity perceive something in it to justify their existence as critics, or more mundanely, in order to explain the time and expense they have gone to in purchasing and reading nothing. Therefore it is inevitable that your work will be acclaimed.

"However, I am troubled. In several, admittedly minor points of detail, the piece may be accused of clarity. Your hero does not sufficiently assume the role of anthropos and it would appear, by this, that you intend to demean mankind. It is customary in this democratized age to emphasize what is known as the universality of human experience. Make your dead and sleeping heroic self speak for the entire species. You may think this egregious or patronizing, which indeed it is, but you must evoke the spirit of mass man, major man, man in his essential mediocrity, man as nothingness, before the witless public can be satisfied that something has, after all, happened."

He continued, "Upon the absence of plot, time, and locality, these features which you have taken as a disqualification are amongst the more noteworthy aspects of the piece, and it is this sequential confusion — whether you know it or not — that makes you worthy of the master, SORROW.

"Ah, but you claim you have written only one or two chapters; that plot and character and place have yet had no time to materialize. What, I ask, what of these unwritten chapters?"

"Well," I enquired, "what of them?"

"There's a terrible danger here," was the answer, "that your sleeping ambition may lure you into writing what is presently unwritten and unsaid. On the other hand, if you do not write them, if you leave them unwritten (as they already are), might you not be accused of writing nothing twice: thrice, in fact, for you have already left them unwritten, and not to write again would be to write the nothing that you have not written three times when once is enough.

"But not a whit! In these unwritten chapters — *left as they are* — you have actually achieved the impossible. Time in your invisible narrative — to pass lightly over but one of its inanities — is supplied by that infinite moment in which the Biscayan and Quixote are frozen in immortal combat, and in which we are left like Pierre Menard (capricious invention of that Argentinian whose name — like Poe before the Bostonians — temporarily escapes me), in which we, I say, are left to invent new Quixotes, to speculate on the course of the combat, to extrapolate, permutate, in short, surrender to a fiction. Hence, because of these very persuasive reasons, I take your unwritten chapters to be the best, the most accurate, the truest representation of your dead and sleeping hero's state of mind. They are without doubt infinitely more powerful than anything you have so far written."

5

Your apologist, meanwhile, was bereft of speech. In silence, I reflected, we have our beginning, and in silence our end. But what manner of work might approach this fantastic critic's requirements?

"In other respects," he continued, "I find the work wanting. To speak the truth, your work — finished or no — is but half of nothing rather than twice or thrice nothing, and lacks that apparency of something which the drowning reader might catch upon as a straw. Blind your average John Homer with the audacity of the lie: give him that straw and tell him it's a life-raft, and he will believe you.

"As for the rest, you must have pert introductions and witty colophons for the idle; asides, parodic forms, divertissements for the satirically bent; learning, scholarship, and the absence of all wisdom for the academic; parables for the wise; allegories for the pious, religion for the devout, symbols for fools; accident, contrivance, and the improbable for the speculative; design and inevitability for the determined; fair weather for the foul, and foul for the fair; revolution, reaction, and synthesis for the committed (as they call themselves) — above and beyond all for that ugly and impossible chimera, the public, you must unleash the great beast LIBIDO, and work it hard, as hard as you will, until your genius is acknowledged and the public satiated. Lastly, do not fail to address yourself to the troubles of this sorry world which some philosophers labour to prove does not exist, and still others to confute them; address yourself, I say, to the existent woes of this non-existent world — or *vice-versa* — in which task, as the author of a non-existent book, you have a marvellous competency."

I was much dismayed by this and declared my firm resolve to be an author no more. What little of the speech I could understand led me to believe that these were ill times for authors, even would-be authors, and that I would be well advised to abandon my ambitions and take honest employment as an honest man, content with obscurity.

"Nay, nay," declared my friend, "there are no honest men. But as for your resolution not to be an author, I wager you'll be one in spite of yourself, or more to the point, in spite of these unwritten chapters."

"How's that?" I asked, for despite my friend's commentary, there was something in me which still clamoured after bardship, something that would not be put down. "How might I be an author, if I have written less than half of nothing?"

"Because," said he, "I have the other half of less than half of nothing, or rather the whole of nothing."

"Come, come," said I, suspecting a joke at my expense, "what do you mean?"

"Simply that in all this I, your friend, have a friend — one other than you — who in his capacity as house spectre and public hack has already obliged, and gladly, with just such details as are called for. Voilà!" said he, producing that MS which has been, is, and shall always be, the occasion of my present woes, "these leaves, vaster by far than your own as the ocean is to a drop of water, you have but to variously interlard therein to be assured of a little space on posterity's boundless shores. Here — take them — and do what you will with them. For the presence or absence of your visible or invisible chapters will not be noticed here in this unwritten, written book."

So saying he bade farewell, leaving me not with one MS, but two.

How long ago this was, I do not *yet* care to tell, though I shall in due course. Whether this second book (a book without author, without plot, and for vast and heroically vacant sections, without Bartleby himself), whether it was the work of another's creation, or his own, got up and formed in another's image, I do not know. Nor can I even offer you assurance of this other's existence, except to say that I, more than my chapters, am a modest and unhappy proof of it.

For my friend, the fantastic, having prepared the way for Bartleby, has departed hence and taken leave of this terrestrial ball, never to appear again in the flesh until the twenty-second chapter of this history when your apologist was soundly berated for his treatment of the MS up to that time. I, in mid-passage, never did complete my work, but offer instead this cannibalized form, this illusion for which I disavow all responsibility, this mystic union of two souls: *myself* and *Bartleby*.

CHAPTER TWO   *Wherein Is Told of Bartleby's Conception and the Peculiar Course of His Early Years.*

My fantastical friend left many questions unanswered. "Who . . ." I began, meaning to ask after the hero's father and mother, the time and place of Bartleby's birth, whether his was an easy or a difficult entrance, and other biographical preliminaries, when my friend cut me short with these words:

"Follow the MS," he cried, "as you would follow life. Read, read where it is written and begin at the beginning."

Begin at the beginning — sound advice to readers and would-be bards alike. Unfortunately, reader, I cannot begin at the beginning, if only because this MS chose to begin before the beginning, dwelling instead on our hero's conception — in a word, his mother's seduction and fall — and dwelling very strangely on it too.

That Bartleby was conceived out of wedlock I have few doubts; that there was something magical in his conception still less doubt; that he arrived after the customary nine months, during which time he parodied the chance designs of nature, no doubt whatsoever. The boy was as natural in his living as he was unnatural in his birth — yet here I am, discoursing of the immaculate bastard's birth when he is not even born, let alone conceived.

A preliminary sketch, therefore, of his parents would seem in order, the second MS answering in some parts where my friend answered in none. I say *sketch* and *in some parts* because the MS's account of these original persons is rather scanty: deservedly so, for they abandoned the child of their author's dreams, and their creator likewise abandoned them, casting Bartleby's primal pair out of his text after they had done their conceptual work.

Bartleby's father, then, is presented in the character of a student of philosophy, with a fund of bookish lore and abstractions common to the young, never known as lovers of reality; whereas his mother appears as a more experienced character whose blood conveyed the blood royal, a Duchess of the realm no less, herself dallying with the young master from whom she seeks ostensible instruction – he shortly leaving her nine months wiser and nine months sadder.

An older story, you say – and were it not for the following, I would be inclined to agree with you – an older story cannot be found. Then consider this. When my fantastical friend removed himself from my room, I gave the first three or four pages of this second MS a cursory reading, discovering what you already know of Bartleby's parentage, before I shut the thing away in my desk drawer along with the completed chapters of my own MS, and, still being so far advanced in the ways of would-be bardship, got on with my desultory scribblings. The day – it is marked on last year's calendar – was the 26th of September, 1969 – and from that date I mark the beginning of my direct involvement with *Bartleby*, at a time more or less coincident with the hero's conception.

Imagine my surprise, reader, both MSS thus being locked away, when I was diverted by the sound of voices emanating from within my desk. This was no ordinary conversation, you understand, but one such as occurs only in books, with a narrative voice observing what was being spoken and to whom. I quote:

" 'But,' *said the Duchess*, 'I do perceive the universe to be a capricious thing.'

" 'Not at all,' *said he, edging closer*. 'Perceptions, if you will trust them, are the legislators of reality, which is in itself an abstraction. Let us for the moment consider the perceptions as the politicians of the body politic.' "

"Excuse me," said I, as baffled as I presume the present reader must be, "but is this the Duchess spoken of in my friend's MS?"

" 'Then, sir,' *said she,*" ignoring my question, " 'I have never known so harmonious a crew of politicians.'

" 'Not so again,' *said he,*" oblivious both to your apologist and the narrative voice with its interminable *said he's.* " 'Many's the time the eye deceives. And in sickness too, our politicians tend to quarrel marvellously.' "

"Exactly!" said I, thinking it time to make my voice and presence felt.

" 'Am I to take it,' *she fluttered,* 'that there is nothing outside of perception, that existence is conferred by perception?'

" 'Indeed, Madam,' *he confirmed the proposition.*

" 'Then,' *she quavered, her hand to her bosom,* 'what condition, what estate am I to understand myself in whilst all *alone* in my boudoir, or straying unattended in some leafy bower? Is life only a dream and a thing insubstantial? Does all lie upon conjecture? And when I sleep, do I dream, do I breathe, do I *live?*'

" 'Delicacy, Madam,' *he replied hastily, edging closer yet,* 'does not permit an answer.'

" 'I am confirmed, then, that all rests upon perception. Bartleby?' *she enquired,*" by which I assume she meant Bartleby *père.*

" 'Yes?'

" 'Do you see me?'

" 'Yes, I see you,' *his hand fondled her ankle.*

" 'Do you touch me?' *her mouth appealed to his.*

" 'I touch you,' *his hand's reply ventured further.*

" 'And everything you have said is true?' *she perceived the touch, a very palpable touch.*

" 'It is,' *stimulus activated stimulus. His hand climbed to her titled thigh.*

" 'Sir,' *the hand of nature's prime primate explored possibility.* 'I do perceive your hand is on my knee.'

" 'You are mistaken,' *he administered the reproof,* 'in that perception, Madam, I do assure you. My hand is in another place which I do distinctly perceive has not unwelcomely received it.'

" 'Fie, sir!' *she countered, and then she caught him:*

'Bartleby, do you taste me? Ah! Do you feel me? Ahh! Do you take me? Ahhh!' "

So they went at it, their joyous declarations moaning from my desk. I waited until I judged enough time had passed for me to open my drawer, that I might confirm with my eyes the work of my pen, I having recorded the conversation exactly as it had occurred. Then imagine my still more formidable surprise, reader, when I found no evidence of the dialogue in the second MS; no proof that my ears had not been deceived, no written record of what passed between the Duchess and Bartleby *père* and no trace at all of the latter who had disappeared as surely as an angel of God. Instead, my drawer was the scene of inconceivable chaos. Words and characters had leapt from the page to fall abandoned about the interior in a pottage of foul case and pied type the like of which I had never seen before. Pages were mangled, letters broken, ink let loose, and the two hitherto distinct MSS joined as one.

Of the Duchess herself, however, the MS told more — as I now shall. But first, I swear that if my ears were deceived, so was the Duchess; which leads me to think my ears were no more deceived than Bartleby *père* was an angel of God, for even the lower order of spirits own defter means of coping with a paternity suit than mere flight.

In a word, the Duchess discovered herself pregnant, and with Bartleby hardly the size of a comma, says my text, expressing it so:

$$(\,,\,)$$

— she got herself to the abode of her friend and distant kinswoman, known to this history by the name of Alice, and known too in all the countryside for her cures of love; and there, while Bartleby progressed geometrically in the Duchess's womb and my text telescoped time, there passed the months until her confinement, at which she was assisted by the generous Alice, and whereafter she departed Alice's mansion of many rooms, promising a speedy return but never to be seen again by son or text, leaving her infant boy in Alice's charge and so at last getting the history proper under way.

Hence from his first to fifth year, from foundling babe
to precocious boy, Bartleby enjoyed the tender care of this
nulliparous gentledame who became familiar to him as his
Auntie Alice, and whom he understood to be his guardian.
Whether this guardianship was actually conferred by familial
ties, whether it was because Bartleby's blood, however
distantly, ran also in Alice's veins, or whether her trust was
the more generous — because freely given — consequence of
friendship's charge, I cannot say. Perhaps it was the effect of
both; perhaps neither, but rather the spontaneous outpouring
of Alice's heart for the infant boy. In any case, on the point
of her love for Bartleby, and his for her, the MS could not be
more clear.

Furthermore that Bartleby, though strangely conceived
in a desk was naturally reared, you will plainly see. Adam, in
his blissful estate, had no softer bower; Romulus and his
brother, no better suck; the fairy children of Jean Jacques,
that philanthropist, no more loving a helpmate. Or so the MS
claims. Unhappily did the noble Melville sigh: Ah, Bartleby;
Ah, humanity — for when he left his hero, abandoned,
starving, and forgotten, he made more than a fatal mistake.
Bartleby lives!

Nor, says my text, could the boy have wished for a
better home — this despite or maybe because of parental
abandonment. The joys of pastoral freedom were his: never
for Bartleby the tyranny of parental dictates; no unlooked-
for strife of a sibling's arrival; no worry, turmoil, or poverty,
no dangers of the city life, but ease, contentment, good food,
healthy air, and at the long day's end, an easy bed. Yes,
especially the latter as the five years of guardianship fled past
and Bartleby enjoyed a life fit for a Prince of Romance.

For Aunt Alice's mansion of many rooms lay in the
country. All, all on a golden morn, while the cruel haw-
thorne, dainty primrose, the pastoral eglantine, nodding
bluebell and the birds' foot trefoil, the demure forgetmenot
and saccharine violet, the modest cowslip and the plain
clover, the flaming iris wild and the popwort simple (and, I

13

fear, complex), the rusty haired rosemary, the sweet william, the untamed indigo and the dank mandrake, the pansey, parsnip, pink and pitch, the hoary hollyhock and hirsute honey suckle, while these and many more flourished and died in sundry climes; while the speckled thrush, thieving blackbird, the moving eyed blackbird, the sprightly tomtit and hopping bluetit, the fork-tailed swallow, the harsh raven (once seen, twice crossed; twice means good luck), the goose and her downy tribe, the melodious lark, the hot nightingale, the merry chaffinch, the preening kingfisher and the spotted flycatcher, the submarine wader, lofty sparrowhawk, napoleon starling, the water hen and her webby brood, the fated albatross, sleek gull and the warbling mocking bird, the shifty magpie and erratic jay, and (at night) the owl, while these and divers of their kind whooted, coughed, whistled, croaked, chuffed, creaked, swooped, fell, tapped, paddled, begged, borrowed and stole, clung, flew, perched, picked, scratched, nested and spat, on many a glorious mountain top, ledge, nook or cranny, crag or eyrie, crooked or straight tree, such as the mighty oak, stout sycamore, pliant ash, blighted elm, weeping willow, tall pine, silver birch, spreading chestnut tree, and yet others such as the ancient alder, stately juniper, deathly yew, misty linden, the florid magnolia and modest myrtle, the cool lime and bitter olive, while these and still more sheltered the feathered race and chanticleer called the tune; while the dappled trout, armoured stickleback, black tench, spiny carp, the evil pike and the fickle bream, the yellow perch and the meaty salmon, the slimy eel and other congeries, while many (if not all) of the finny kind, such as the bloated porgy, pale halibut, winking walleye, striped sunfish, the massy cod and the floundering flounder, the salted herring and the dover sole, the succulent octopus and the big white whale himself, desported themselves in babbling brooks or stormy seas, ran, coursed, darted, jumped, flashed, spawned and bubbled; while in pleasant fields the herbs and spices, margin mustard weed, gentle marjoram and stronger sister oregano, the musty basil and the elder sage, the seasonal nutmeg and the pungent bay, the eastern clove and exotic cardamom, and others too numerous to tell, such as the hot coriander, the root ginger and favoured cinnamon,

14

the seedy dill and the leafy tarragon, the versatile turmeric and subtle cumin, soft rosemary and aromatic caraway, the biting cayenne and ripe paprika, while these did Zephyrus waft and wave in many a holt and heath to perfume the charmed air of several continents; while every creature was allotted its time, place and kind; while the sun and stars did revolve in the firmament above, and Luna was variously housed in the twelve houses, progressing on, aye, ever on, unto malign Scorpio, the house of death; while the equinoxes themselves turned slowly through the long Platonic year; while, in the midst of this bounteous and boundless activity, Aunt Alice slept, young Bartleby, his thoughts never so far from the teeming market town of Throckton by the Bog, strayed in country lanes, wandered down winding paths and clambered over bucolic stiles, transfigured by his imagination into banquettes and machicolations, battlements and merlons, crenellations, bartizans, bastions, and other such edifices likely to occur in the mind of a boy; or observed the dim beasts of the fields wreathed in autumnal mists commingling with their breath suspended, and did listen to their muted whinnyings and bovine lowings, their porcine gruntings and woolly bleatings; nocturnal twitterings, snortings and squeakings; the titterings, screechings and shriekings; the gobblings, quackings and cacklings; the yappings and yowlings, snortings and growlings; the drummings, clatterings and patterings; in short, did listen to the harmonious parliament of nature and did think of the time when he might behold all things and have parlance with all creatures; or, when he was not otherwise occupied, he did on a hot summer's noon scamper unconsciously in the mottled lights and shades of Aunt Alice's apple orchard while she slept on. All this does my text vouchsafe.

During the five years of guardianship, Alice herself passed from her fortieth to forty-fifth year and overcame in tranquility that crisis which befalls women of such an age, and which some scholars maintain is − in its entire cycle − a consequence of Eve's too consumptive curiosity. During this time of transition, from Bartleby's first year and onwards, great was the comfort gained by Aunt Alice's maternal care of young Bartleby, which came, ineluctably, to serve as an

15

unsought yet welcome compensation for declining viviparity. Never was guardianship a more happy task! Oft was the occasion of a long and cruel winter night that Bartleby snuggled into Auntie's bed, secure from all external terrors, safe in the warm proximity of her flocculent form. Thus asleep at his guardian's pillowy bosoms is the lad left by our MS until his fifth year, dreaming the whiles of the many diverting and charming sights observed upon his walks.

But, oh weylaway, and alas for mutable circumstance! A tediously conventional exclamation. And though I've sworn to follow this text as I would follow life, I cannot help but remark on the impropriety of Bartleby's nocturnal visits whereby the course of nature was prematurely excited. For there came a time when Bartleby, not even a callow youth but a mere boy, the bloom and down of seeming innocence not yet upon his cheeks, there came a time when Bartleby did first accidentally, then deliberately play at fondling his Auntie's gorgeous paps, at which she, in no time, did press him to suck — as the MS quaintly puts it. Hence, ere his third year, did Bartleby receive hospitable introduction into Alice and the joys of Hymeneal bliss. Far be it from me to distress the reader and affront his moral scruples — should he have any — by here repeating the graphic and suggestive configurations with which the MS abundantly evokes Bartleby's nightly sports: no doubt he took after his parents and his nature was not to blame in him. It is enough if the reader understands that in this wise our hero learned the first principles of what he mistakenly conceived to be guardianship — an art for which the rest of the world has an altogether different name. For two years the odours of love, and Alice's generous effusions, remained his especial joy. Then did fate lend a guiding hand and all was lost upon a chance.

At which pregnant juncture, since the rest of this page is blank, I will call a halt to the present chapter.

16

CHAPTER THREE   *In Which Both MSS Progress as One and Bartleby Plays at Guardianship.*

Five summer suns and five winter snows has our hero seen: five dream years calendared by the chapter, clocked by the paragraph, cancelled by the pen.

Yet outside of my time the seasons of Bartleby's young life seemed both fixed and free to him, changeless and changing in the mansion of many rooms. And at the centre of this changeless and changing world, says my text, Bartleby became what he saw, was summer and winter, was spring and autumn, was five while the wind whispered, "Because it has always been so, it shall ever be: everything changes, nothing changes." And time deceived our hero, and the stars were brittle, and the leaves of night died a rustling death, and the cascading hours told of no tomorrows. So says my text.

Five years, reader, passed Bartleby in a day and night of our time. Yesterday — or what seemed like yesterday, though it must be almost a year ago as I write — the MS and its hero were safely locked in my desk, waiting on the unread future.

And yesterday — that tomorrow of the day before — both MSS were still separate; my ambition still resolute, my faith in would-be bardship still unchallenged. But "Humble we are and humble we must be," goes the Heepish apothegm, and I who have been stableboy to this Augean *Bartleby* have tugged my forelock at its master — whoever he is or was — begging him to appoint me his scribe, that I might have charge of his letters instead of his MS, for anything is preferable to my present occupation.

Which is to say more pointedly, that having failed as a would-be bard I have also failed as a would-be editor, my only hope now being — to twist all art out of the figure — that this particular talking horse will suffocate in its own dung before I'm driven out of my room.

Yet Bartleby's conception — the shuffle inadvertent from which this book is dealt — at least solved one difficulty: how to implicate my own poor chapters in the text. For a while, reader, I swam like a loose fish, Herculean Boswell to my text's Doctor, floundering against the rising tide of marginal annotation until I plumbed the deep dangers of sounding three MSS where I had embarked with the one, my own commentary threatening to flood over the margins of the second MS and become a whale of a tale in itself. And now the MSS are conjoined the oddest thing is that I can find no debris from the first, which has disappeared as surely as Bartleby's parents, drowned, dragged under fortune's stormy seas.

But I really shouldn't talk about myself, even if it furthers the plot. It was, then, with just such an aim in mind, that I returned to my desk on the afternoon of the second chapter, fondly imagining I might raise Bartleby from Alice's bed and put him around in the world where a hero belongs and where a reader could follow him, free from my strictures and interpolations, when I discovered another had been there before me.

No sooner conceived than born, no sooner born than laid, the boy Bartleby had now gone forth from Aunt Alice's mansion of many rooms. For the State, maintains my text, ceased to tolerate our hero's amorous cohabitation with his Guardian and removed him from her affections, a child of five in the third chapter of his history, into an institution for waifs, strays, and foundlings — the human flotsam of this age.

Bartleby was at first pained by this sudden dislocation. He pined for Auntie and understood how lonely she would be. Yet soon her peculiar role in his development was supplanted by the State's avuncular authority and the many diversions open to the boy in his foster home.

Of his new-found playmates, none was initially more dear to him than Mary, a wide and wild-eyed child herself approaching the adolescence by Bartleby's accelerated growth circumvented. One day, says my text, a day which Bartleby sensed was the beginning of a new era for him, he caught her aside from the rest of the children and gazed solemnly into her eyes. She came close to him, then, a mere child of twelve years or so, yet, from Bartleby's experienced view, a creature capable of great transformation. Desire kindled within him as the sight of her gingham covered, gently tumescent breasts awakened his memory, if it needed any awakening, of Auntie's full-blown mammary glands. But these! Prototypic, hinting at future delights, yet innocent behind the childish cotton dress, these deserved to be caressed. How they beckoned him towards her as she, in unconscious cajolery, arched her back and pressed her hands together over her flat, tight little belly. Not that his feelings could in any way be described as lustful. Rather, it was the creative instinct welling within him which impelled him to initiate Mary into the delights of guardianship, that she might know its pleasures for herself and teach other and future Bartlebies as Auntie had taught him.

"Leave this game of mothers and fathers," he said seriously, "and learn guardianship." Hence they strayed out of the garden and wandered down the winding path which led into the woods.

"What'th guardianthip?" she lisped.

"Look!" he cried, surprising her from the rear, his hands thrusting under each delightfully budding breast.

"Oh!" a small cry of pleasure escaped her.

Swiftly he removed the flimsy dress and her scanty underthings; swiftly he reached for her groin, fondling there until he had raised a moist and sweet expectancy remarkable in so innocent a playmate.

"No," she protested faintly as Bartleby's fingers discovered a smaller version of Auntie's profounder cleft, "no. It'th too nithe."

How his Guardian would be proud of him now. For the first time since those rapturous nights with Alice, our hero felt that hot pulsating growth in his loins, the vibrant tremor, the virile pounding of his pre-pubertoid blood. Manfully he bore her to the ground and prepared to enter into her, and she too was ready to surrender. And now — unique vision of heroic growth! — now he sensed a glimmer of the many splendid forms that guardianship might take, a revelation that threatened to overwhelm him.

"Oh, Bartleby!" she cried as he spilled himself over her sweetly parted secret. "I'm too thmall for thith game." Then, alarmed in her childish way at the abrupt change in him, "But we can play again. Thoon. Can't we?"

"Yeth," he sighed. "Oh yes."

Were it not for the pedophilic tendencies suggested by the above, I would judge our divinely or otherwise inspired authority's intentions to have been satiric. But since there have been enough asides I will say only that Bartleby — in no time at all — familiarized every maiden in this remote institution with what he mistakenly conceived to be the art of guardianship. And in but a short time the Matron, all starch and straight lace, a stiff-necked virgin spinster, came to hear of the boy's antics amongst her charges' pliant parts, and, determining forthwith to halt such wholesale defloration, did summon Bartleby into her wintery presence.

"Young man," she said (or so the MS has it), "this has got to stop."

At which Bartleby, in no way understanding, directed at her a look of absolute puzzlement, interpreted by her as a sign of defiance. Then it was that she made a serious error.

"Young man, desist. *I* am your guardian now."

CHAPTER FOUR *Wherein His Drawer Remains Temporarily Silent and Bartleby's Misunderstanding of the Principle of Guardianship is Furthered.*

Of all the females in this home, both young and old, charges and guardians, alone had Matron (absolutely unacquainted with the personal force of Bartleby's instructive arts) preserved her integrity and virginity, acquiring indeed a peculiar reputation amongst her inferiors for her wariness of the male sex and a corresponding fondness for the female. Formidable was the surprise of this institutional queen, then, when the youth now lustily plunged himself at her. What a noise arose! Such a snapping open of safety pins, a breaking of thermometers and a general rending of the various impedimenta of the Matron's calling, a twanging of whalebone and a crackling of starch, a ripping and tearing of cotton, the tinkle of glass as Matron's watch sprang from her official bosom, the crash of chairs overturning and files disgorging, a din sufficient almost to drown the shrieks of Matron's outraged purity as she fled, arms outstretched, hair dishevelled, round and round the table with Bartleby in hot pursuit. She fought, bit, scratched and screamed, but the furious piston of unleashed virility merely rose to the challenge and redoubled his efforts. First repulsed from an orthodox frontal assault by a hefty smack in the face, he managed, by ingeniously diving under the table, to intercept Matron's flight, so gaining access to her private parts from the rear, whereupon, completely hidden by her voluminous skirts, he managed to topple her to the floor, in the process dealing her thighs a resounding blow against the table.

"Vicious dirty-minded little rapist! Incestuous brat!" Matron howled, furiously continuing the struggle, pounding her elbows down sledge-hammer-like upon the seething shape underneath her skirts, which, fortunately for the attacker, afforded some protection against what otherwise might have transpired as a fatal retaliation. Thus did a strange and puzzling sight greet the two rescuing nurses, delectable nymphs who had themselves recently received Bartleby's favours. Matron lay with her back on the floor, her elbows still raining down, but with her legs akimbo, about to trap the hapless Bartleby (visible beneath her skirts as a pummelling, writhing shape to the astonished nurses), about to trap him with her muscular calves in the vise-like grip of a scissors hold, which, had it been executed, would have provoked the envy of the most professional wrestler (though no such wrangler of the ring could have spread his legs so wide, moaned so loudly, or bounced so lustily, nor could he have worked on his opponent as Matron worked off on Bartleby), and which might, indeed, have borne our hero to a premature grave, so short was he of air that he needed no further strangulation. The struggle continued a moment longer before Matron's eyes glazed with a lustreless film, her head flopping slowly from side to side as she gradually relaxed her grip on Bartleby. Then the bobbing and squirming disturbance underneath Matron's skirts spent itself unhappily on her petticoats, and in another minute the frustrated Bartleby emerged, conscious only of his failure and puzzled by Matron's lack of cooperation.

Slowly, even ineffably, Matron raised her great head and gazed glassily at our diminutive hero.

For a while the head rocked and swayed, and then — says my text — then Bartleby and his rescuers were surprised by a quite unexpected change in Matron's behaviour. She began to laugh, quietly at first, but with increasing violence, until all of Matron laughed and could not be persuaded to stop laughing, her hands wringing at the sticky linen of her skirt where a naughty and incriminating stain now revealed itself, to which stain Matron pointed, giggling and clapping her hands, so that her joviality would soon have proved infectious (for one of the nurses had now to hide a snicker), had not Matron summoned her powers of resolve, regained some of her composure, and managed — despite her condition and horizontal posture — the magisterial command: "Take him away!"

The friendly nymphs, meanwhile, restrained our hero from once more vaulting upon their superior; and, understanding Matron's tendencies and deferential to her outraged authority, the nurses exchanged knowing looks.

"Wait!" Matron revoked her order. "He hasn't touched you, has he, my darlings?" she enquired between fits of giggling, her hands still working at the stain which had assumed larger and darker dimensions. "I couldn't bear to think of that: touching you with his —" the clinical term escaped her "— *thing.*"

Matron found the designation amusing, or it produced all the visible symptoms of mirth in her, for she began to shake and laugh again. *"Thing!"* she singled out the stain, drew up her legs, embraced them with her arms, and rocked and nodded and swayed, *"Thing!"*

As poor Bartleby was finally escorted from Matron's presence, her laughter lingering and echoing down the white corridors of our hero's second home, one of the nurses whispered a few words of comfort. "That silly old butch," she said, "you shouldn't have tried it on her, honest you shouldn't, Bartleby."

All this time, Bartleby failed to comprehend what he had done to provoke so strange a reaction in Matron. Later in the day, as he sat alone and bewildered, confined to a bare white room with a tubular frame bed that creaked when he lay on it, Bartleby wondered if he had been impolite to Matron. For Auntie had taught him to be courteous in all his ways, especially the way of guardianship, to say 'please' and 'thank you' for each little favour received, and now he remembered that he had not actually thanked Matron for offering to play at guardianship with him. "Oh Auntie," he said to himself, "I have made a big mistake with Matron and see now that she wanted me to say 'thank you' earlier, rather than later — which is not according to the rules of the game as you taught me. But I promise you, Auntie, that when I get out of this place, I shall leave off playing with little girls and matrons, especially laughing matrons, and shall seek you out, even though you be ever so far away from our house in the country."

So saying, he tried to sleep. But Matron's extraordinary laughter still disturbed him and began to work in him the preliminary notions of what the theologians call original sin, and the psychiatrists more simply, if less imaginatively, guilt. Thus perplexed he formulated something of a modification on his resolve to seek Auntie out. "She has probably gone away," he thought, "and left the home in the country. Yet what was her purpose in introducing me to guardianship and its delights? Surely I was not meant to keep it jealously, but acquaint others with its splendours, even laughing Matrons! Therefore I have failed today and put Auntie to shame — and all because I did not remember to say 'thank you' in advance."

But Bartleby, says my text, had by no means failed. For on the morrow he was summoned to Matron who once more reminded him that she was now his Guardian.

"Oh thank you," he replied.

And for one week, says my text, Matron's laughter rang down official corridors; for one week, every minute and second of Bartleby's young life was saturated with the peals of a strange, official laughter, until, his energies thus monopolized, he grew not tired, but jaded, and resolved to leave Matron for other pastures, other adventures, at the same time determining to bestow the gift of guardianship on all females, prefacing and concluding his every action with a 'thank you'.

So it fell out after seven days and seven nights of Matron's laughter, one glorious dawn brought our hero a liberating hand which forced itself through his first floor cell with the aid of a brick and broke his dreams of Matron rampant. From the hand, a rope; from the rope, means of egress, and from this, descent to the small but faithful group of dawn-weary communicants, guardians and charges, who had gathered to speed Bartleby away from Matron's still slumbering desires.

At length, Bartleby bade his companions fond farewells, for they made him understand that he must leave the home in the woods before Matron awoke to play and laugh. Yet, ever regardless of his own well being, he bestowed one or two last acts of guardianship upon them until his friends pressed him forth, fearing where he did not, fearing lest he become too fatigued so early in the day. And there, with many 'thank yous', with many kisses and not a few tears, there under nature's own canopy, he betook himself to the winding path which led to the woods and the world, which led indeed to life – and the quest for the vital and original Guardian, Guardian of Guardians, whose existence he had not yet learned to doubt.

CHAPTER FIVE   *Wherein Bartleby Learns of Money and*
Meets a Hermit.

It was a long way, claims the MS, to Auntie's home in the country – and though I've done everything to shorten it, the way grows longer – but Bartleby had all the time in the world for his journey. "Ah, my sweet, my darling Mary," he sighed to the trees, "how long will it be before we meet again? And Matron, too, I wonder?"

Rising out of the woods, Bartleby found himself at noon on the crest of a hill line. In the valley below there lay a pleasant little hamlet, not too many miles distant. He could make out the church steeple and the clustered houses, and decided it looked a hospitable enough place to light on ere darkness fell, a place where he might find lodgings for the night and seek directions for the morrow. With these thoughts in mind, then, he sat himself under a tree and commenced to open the bundle given to him as a parting gift, and which, like a true traveller, he had carried by means of a stick, in a spotted kerchief, thrown over his shoulder.

Inside he discovered enough food for the day, and – money. Bartleby held the glittering coins and wondered at their purpose, for he had not seen money before and did not, therefore, understand its use; nor, having bought all that he had ever owned with the currency of natural affection, had he felt the need for it himself. "Perhaps I will come upon some use for them later," he thought, laying the coins and the bundle on the green sward beside him.

It was not long before our hero became enlightened on

the purchasing power of this curious yellow stuff. For as he bit into one of his sandwiches a curly haired youth of bucolic aspect appeared, in a leisurely fashion, from the very direction which Bartleby proposed to take, warbling this pleasant ditty:

> Oi tweedles horl doi,
> Hoi tum toi-twiddle,
> Han Oi tweedles horl noit,
> Ha-singin: ti-twiddle,
> Ti-twiddle, ti-twiddle, ti-twee.

"Hollo," said this Daphnis, espying Bartleby, "han wot be ee?"

"One who plays at guardianship," replied the boy, blessing his good fortune, "who seeks no favours from anyone but he – or she – who might tell him of his Guardian."

Now the youth met this address with a blank yet shrewd countenance which encouraged Bartleby to speak further. "I am searching," he said, "for my Auntie Alice, or any who know of her."

"Hollis. Hom, hom," the bumpkin thoughtfully hummed, "Oi kernows no Hollis. But fur one o them croons, noo," the yokel continued, eyeing Bartleby and the little pile of crowns askance, "Oi moit direct ee to one who moy kernow a Hollis."

"But, good sir, what is a croon?" enquired Bartleby with great civility.

"Hom," the youth regarded Bartleby with an astute glint, bethinking him very young in the ways of the world.

"Wi croons Oi buys cider. Wi croons Oi moit porchase the affections o moi Fullis, fair Fullis moi sweethurt, the milkmaid, han go ha-twiddlin with hur. Hom. They be croons beside ee."

Instantly perceiving that the crowns might further this youth in his guardian's pursuits, our hero eagerly proffered the entire sum, at which the rustic understood him to be a little soft in the head.

"Be they yoor croons, noo, or Hollis's?" he asked suspiciously.

"Mine, of course," replied Bartleby. "But what use are croons to me without my Guardian?"

"Wull, Oi thankee koindly," said the youth, hastily accepting the coins and making as to leave.

"But what of Auntie Alice?" said Bartleby, reminding him of his promise.

"Hoi-hi-hom. Te-tum," said the youth, retreating. "In yonder village, arsk fur the hurmit, Murster De'Ath we calls him. Ye shall find him in the church yurd. He kernows orl folks in these purts, han they orl kernows him. Bye, bye."

Ti-twiddle, ti-twiddle, ti-twiddle, ti-twee...

"Strange fellow," thought Bartleby as this Corydon vanished rather more speedily than he had appeared, his refrain lingering on the air. "Let us hope that the croons prove useful to him. They were certainly nothing more than an encumbrance to me." So saying, Bartleby wrapped up the remainder of the food in his spotted kerchief and, once more slinging the bundle over his shoulder, set off down the valley side.

Dusk found the boy at the entrance of the country graveyard. "Brr," he said to himself as he opened the gate and it creaked rustily on its hinges, "what a nasty smelly place this is. I do not think I shall find Auntie here." Memorial elms moaned over the modest graves; mist trailed in the air, and the ground was spongy underfoot.

"Mr De'Ath!" cried Bartleby. "Oh, Mr De'Ath! Here is one who seeks his Guardian."

A somnolent and profound silence greeted this speech and Bartleby advanced a little further through the wet curtain of weeds and trailing branches. Then, before he could remark on the tuneful propensities of the shire's natives, this doleful threnody, intoned in a cracked and hoary voice, assaulted Bartleby's ears:

Bone powder and marrow root
He chews him at his leisure.
Tibia, fibula, tibia, fibula, sacrum, ho!
Corruption is his only treasure;
Both great and small, both high and low,
Must wait upon his pleasure.
Buggerum, buggerum, buggerum, boo!

Guts and muscle, brain and blood,
He sets before him for his dinner.
Tibia, fibula, tibia, fibula, sacrum, ho!
The world is getting thinner.
Damned or saintly, wicked or good
Are all the same for there's no winner.
Buggerum, buggerum, buggerum, boo!

Six feet down, aye, six feet down,
All do know him, all do fear him.
Tibia, fibula, tibia, fibula, sacrum, ho!
All must see him, all must hear him,
Wreathed in simple winding gown.
Now closer, come thou near him.
Buggerum, buggerum, buggerum, boo!

Tiller, sower, seeder, reaper,
Lord and master, servant and slave.
Tibia, fibula, tibia, fibula, sacrum, ho!
Both wise and foolish, silly and grave,
Still yet noisy, watchful the sleeper,
King and jester, queen and knave.
Buggerum, buggerum, buggerum, boo!

This delightful elegy floated out of a marble sarcophagus, grander indeed than the simple moss-clad graves of
the rustics which surrounded it, and concluded with the
enticing cry: *Whoo is hee? Come find him.*

For his part, Bartleby bounded manfully over the
humble forms of the encumbered sleepers, so approaching
the tuneful edifice, the lid of which he observed to be prised
open. At once, a strange antic figure leaped forth from the

coffin and brandished a bone which he contrived to use, economically, as both pointer and crutch. The countenance of this bizarre character was seamed and pitted by the ravages of many years; the hair and beard were intertwined together, his eyes sparkled deep from within the shrunken face, itself drawn out to form the hooked and incredibly sinuous snout, tipped by a bead of glittering moisture, while the dry and embalmed mask of the head was supported by the rigid tendons of the neck which disappeared uncertainly into an old and dirty cotton smock, the only covering of the emaciated body underneath. This fantastic, not to say grotesque apparition gave Bartleby a very sly look and said, "Does one ask for him so early?"

Not in the least dismayed by the hermit's appearance, and sagaciously complimenting him upon his singing, Bartleby strode directly up to this guardian of the graveyard, fixed him in his resolute gaze, and spoke in the following manner.

"Grave and respectable sir, Mr De'Ath, for so I think you are called – "

"Tee-hee," interrupted the eccentric, "that's his name, though some says it another way. Buggerum!"

To which Bartleby, not at this time interested in phonetic subtleties, replied, "Pray good sir, I have journeyed from the neighbouring vale and was directed hither by a country youth of pleasant aspect and honest intentions, who, finding me at repast, and learning of my quest, made mention of your name, and suggested that you would know of my Auntie Alice, my one and only true Guardian."

At the mention of the word *Guardian* a long and low whistle escaped De'Ath's shrivelled lips. His eyes rolled and he sighed mightily, not before allowing himself another withered exhalation. "You, boy. Nice little boy," shrilled the hermit, "do you know what he is, boy? Me?" To which Bartleby, a little taken aback by all this rasping and sudden unaccountable melancholy, shook his head.

"*Ahhh!*" shrieked the unusual personage, casting his eyes towards heaven and raising his free hand to his brows in a gesture which left Bartleby wondering whether he had suffered some hidden hurt. "The hermit, boy. That's me! But come in, come in and sit down," he said, pointing with his bone to the coffin.

The recluse squatted on his haunches next to a candle stub which, when lit, threw his features into an even more ghastly relief than had the dusk. "Any food, boy?" he asked, his mouth working as though in anticipation. "Any morsels? Crumbs? Tit bits? Any little fancies for old De'Ath?"

Bartleby now began to perceive that the hermit's solitary existence had produced certain consequences that were not all to the good, an impression which rather confused the boy, for he had heard somewhere that the recluse forsakes social intercourse in order to meditate on the divine mysteries of the universe. Imagine our hero's surprise, therefore, upon offering the hermit the remainder of his sandwiches, when his leathery companion of the tomb shuddered and let out another agonized sigh which wracked his anchylosed and ancient frame. A large limpid tear formed in the hermit's eye, rolled down his mummified cheek, and fell, illumined by the candle's yellow light, fell to the marble floor with a perceptible splash.

CHAPTER SIX   *The Hermit's Tale. Bartleby Learns that Human Folly Extends Beyond the Grave.*

The hermit blubbered for ages. Finally, when the fit seemed to have run its course, an infantile look fixed itself on the recluse's face, and Bartleby understood that he was indeed communing with the mysteries of the universe and had gone into a trance. "Here's an odd state of affairs," thought the boy. "This unfortunate fellow must have undergone a dreadful shock to behave like this. Yet how his trance aids me in my search, I cannot say." The hermit, meanwhile, rocked and swayed upon his leathery haunches, and gave out this monotonously uninformative sound: Ommmmmmmmmmmmmmmmmmmmm. Ommmmmmmmmmm mmmmmmmmmmmmmmmmmmmm. Bored by the lugubrious incantation, and despairing of ever sharing the hermit's wisdom, Bartleby at last spoke out.

"Unhappy gentleman, while it is befitting for one of your name and condition to offer such hospitality, the night advances and finds me no closer to my Aunt Alice of fond memory and comfortable estate. If it will please you to speak of your ailment, then do so. But please, in the process, leave off your chant and tell me what you know of my Guardian."

The effect of this speech was remarkably catalytic. For at the fresh mention of the word *Guardian,* the hermit shrieked horrendously, shot from his meditative position, and, casting his bone aside, hopped from one leg to the other, thus placing himself in peril either of singeing his beard in the candle's yellow flame, or of becoming altogether taffled up in it, to the singular confusion of the dancer and the dance. Not until the attack had run its dervish-like course, and the recluse had regained both breath and bone, did he hobble into a corner and commence to narrate the following tale.

"Many years ago, when the inhabitants of this village were less deranged than they are now, there lived a rich and powerful Baron, one Hank Caughlin Mangaravidi D'Arcy Fitz Kelly Mordant, of mixed American-Irish blood out of Sicilian issue from the Hapsburgs and the Bourbons, whose (the Baron's) especial happiness it was to have under his guardianship a niece, the peerless Deborah Caughlin Mangaravidi D'Arcy Fitz Kelly Mordant, a pearl compared with so many swain, the apple of many a lad's eye, and a jewel set amongst paste." The hermit shuddered, and Bartleby, who experienced no little difficulty in visualizing the maiden yet fearing a return of the meditative fit, very wisely encouraged him to continue.

"Suffice it to say that, when this flower came to bloom, there was at the time a young Sexton who tolled the bell to pay for his theological studies, and who became enamoured of this blushing rose, Deborah Caughlin Mangaravidi D'Arcy Fitz Kelly Mordant, whom I shall henceforward refer to as Deborah Caughlin Mangaravidi D'Arcy Fitz Kelly. The Baron, a man familiar with Presidents, generals, kings, politicians, bankers, policemen, company chairmen, tax collectors, in short the most powerful bureaucrats and ci-devants of the state, this Baron frowned upon the lowly Sexton's attentions to his charge, Deborah Caughlin Mangaravidi D'Arcy Fitz Kelly, but, determining to have himself some fun, did nothing to discourage them."

Bartleby's head reeled at all this (as well it might), for he could perceive neither sense nor art in it. Nevertheless, he allowed the hermit to go on with many sympathetic murmurs and kind words of understanding. "Indeed," continued the hermit, "the Baron fostered the Sexton's attentions, whilst insidiously poisoning the fair Deborah Caughlin Mangaravidi D'Arcy Fitz Kelly's mind against her headstrong and eager suitor, saying that he was a low graveyard creature, a worm and a parasite. Quite unconscious of the Baron's maleficent intentions, the Sexton, a high tempered youth, as I have

33

hinted, did one day offer marriage to Deborah Caughlin Mangaravidi D'Arcy Fitz Kelly, flowering his suit and larding his proposition with the many fine conceits and obscure phrases that he had culled from his theological and philosophical studies, which, if the truth be known, were not very advanced, but . . . "

At this juncture, the recluse threatened total collapse, so powerful was the affective force of his tale. Aided by more than kind assurances, however, the hermit more than continued. Fishing under his besmottered robe, he produced a sheaf of papers, yellowed with age, whereon he had inscribed the story of Deborah Caughlin Mangaravidi D'Arcy Fitz Kelly Mordant and her suitor, the Sexton, in dialogue form, so as to make the impact more vivid. With much trembling and a pitifully lachrymose expression, the recluse began to act out the drama, reading from his MS and explaining the action as taking place in one of the highest towers of the Baron's castle.

But first, De'Ath's scaly lids closed and opened. The hermit squinted at our hero and said, "Bartleby."

"Yes?" the boy replied.

"No, no. We means: *Bartleby*."

"We?" Bartleby enquired.

"The hermit, boy. That's what we is."

"But . . . "

"No buts," De'Ath consulted his MS and made a great show of counting the chapters. "Here we is, boy," he continued, "CHAPTER SIX," and before Bartleby could object, the hermit coughed, wheezed, spat, and launched forth into his oration:

" ' "Piss off weasel!" exclaimed Deborah Caughlin Mangaravidi Fitz Kelly," ' " De'Ath cried passionately, his gaze filled with a morbidly fulvous luminescence. He read like one possessed, rotating his eyes in their sockets and grimacing hideously, so that the literary demerits of his composition were veiled by a truly histrionic performance.

" ' "You shit!" ' " he continued, screeching in the voice of Deborah Caughlin Mangaravidi D'Arcy Fitz · Kelly. " ' "You lousy little shit! I don't know why my uncle lets you in here."

" 'He thought of the German maid at the castle gate, of her plaited hair, ample hips, and rosy tits straining at the halter of her Alpine costume. Passion possessed him.

" ' "Don't!" he cried. "How can you say these things?"

" ' "You stupid little creep! A randy sexton! Whoever heard of such a thing? Get back to your books!"

" 'He lashed out at her and suddenly was atop of her on the floor. His hands closed softly about her lily white neck, depressing the larynx, cutting off the scream.' "

And although the scream was cut off, my text informs informs me the hermit included it for good measure: "AAAAAARRRGH!' "

" '*Click*! Her head lolled to one side. A sweet sickly odour filled the room.

" ' "Darling Deborah Caughlin Mangaravidi D'Arcy Fitz Kelly," the Sexton groaned. "You are mine now! All mine! Mine!" His mind was quite gone, of course. Snapped. Revelling in her faeces – her bowels had been evacuated as she died – he loved her as she had never been loved before; hard, mighty thrusts, mighty hard thrusts, first in the front aperture, then in the rear . . .' "

As he mimed the action and read these lines, the hermit departed from his script:

"Buggerum, buggerum, buggerum, boo!" he cried heartily, returning to the refrain of his evening song.

" ' "Aaaah," ' " De'Ath sighed, evidently in the character of the Sexton. " ' "Aaah, your every little secret is mine now, sweetest Deborah Caughlin Mangaravidi D'Arcy Fitz Kelly." ' "

"Buggerum, buggerum, buggerum, boo!"

" ' "Every charmed orifice, all musk, damp, and perfume, each tender part is mine. *Mine*! Him what you dared to call a *weasel*!" ' "

"Not a weasel," De'Ath informed Bartleby, "he's *not* a weasel . . ."

" ' "Mine!" ' " the hermit recollected himself. " 'Again and again he penetrated her until he noticed her limp compliance perceptibly stiffen.' "

"Do you know what that is, boy?" De'Ath asked as himself. "That's rigor mortis, boy."

" 'The Sexton remembered the maid and wondered if she was in on the plot to deceive him. He tore furiously out of the room and Deborah Caughlin Mangaravidi D'Arcy Fitz Kelly, down the stairs, blindly seeking the maid's quarters.

" ' "*Ach! Ach!*"

" 'How much more pleasurable was this than Deborah Caughlin Mangaravidi D'Arcy Fitz Kelly. Fool that he was ever to have loved the Baron's niece, dead or alive. *Fool! Madman! Imbecile! Lunatic! Cretin! Idiot! Moron!* What had he done? *Maniac!* ' "

"But he wasn't none of these things," De'Ath added. "He was himself, he was, just a poor Sexton what had been crossed in love. Not mad, no. Sane."

Having most energetically entertained Bartleby with a rehearsal of all these actions, the hermit now paused to see what effect their performance had on his young listener and waited to hear whether the boy needed further clarification — if it could be given — on any special point of detail.

"Haven't you forgotten something?" our hero asked.

"Forgotten? Forgotten?" echoed the recluse.

"Yes. What about Deborah Caughlin Mangaravidi D'Arcy Fitz Kelly?"

"*Buggerum, buggerum, buggerum, boo!*" cried the hermit, returning to his MS:

" 'CHAPTER SEVEN   *The Defenestration of Deborah Caughlin Mangaravidi D'Arcy Fitz Kelly Mordant.*

" 'Satiated, he bounded from the Fräulein's bed.

" ' "There is something I have to attend upon. Wait for my return," he commanded her.

" 'He raced up the stairs and burst in on the chamber where he had first presented his ill-starred suit. Resisting all temptation, he raised the doubly ravished corpse of his beloved in his arms, carried it to the window, and there cast it down to earth.' "

De'Ath whistled, and his crutch of bone described the
descent across the floor of the tomb: "W

```
                              h
                           e
                         e
                          e
                           e
              e              e
        e        e         e
      e                  e
         e       e      e
            e         e
                       e
                        e
                       e
                  · e
                    e   e e
                     e      e
                  e       e
         e   e      e
              e    e
          e
      e
    e  e   e
  e
    e
    e
    e
    e
    e
    ! "*
```

     " 'Had he forgotten anything? But the maid was waiting
. . .' "

    Lacking the energy of the Sexton, De'Ath put his MS
aside and sagged against the wall of the tomb.

    "Well, boy, well? What is it, boy?" he asked in a
distraught voice. "Isn't it to your liking?"

    "Sir," said Bartleby politely, "I think you told it very
nicely. But on the whole, I think it a tedious tale. If the
Sexton were more versed in the ways of guardianship, then

---

* So it is given in my text. The descent, of course, was vertical; the action of
De'Ath's bone, horizontal.

he would have confronted Deborah Caughlin Mangaravidi D'Arcy Fitz Kelly in some other way. As for throwing her body through the window, what possible purpose could that serve?"

While the hermit had been executing the various incidents of the tale, it had never occurred to Bartleby that there might by anything autobiographical in it. Now he was to face the rage of a frustrated author who, having told some of his life's story, found it called tedious by a presumptuous boy.

"What's this? What's this? Tedious?" shrieked the recluse, hopping from foot to foot. "It's him! Him it is! Me!"

"Please, Mr De'Ath," Bartleby was startled by this renewed display of aged vigour, "please do not distress yourself. It is quite obvious that I must have overlooked some vital part of this story . . . "

"Himself it was. Yes, the hermit!" De'Ath's vanity was only gradually assuaged. "It's him, it is: me! I am this Sexton and this was my Deborah Caughlin Mangaravidi D'Arcy Fitz Kelly. This tomb is my home, the Baron Caughlin Mangara-vidi D'Arcy Fitz Kelly Mordant's grave. The village bugger, that's me! There's not a body in this yard that's not been touched by me: him! For that's the way he takes his pleasure, he does. *Buggerum, buggerum, buggerum, boo!* I've defiled 'em all — them what was so proud and private in life becomes mine in death. There's nothing like a corpse, boy! A nice fresh corpse has an air about it that none of your live ones has. Oh dear me, yes. Dig 'em up, roll 'em over, up or down, top or bottom, inside or outside. But we only buggers the dead, mind. A versatile thing, a corpse is, boy. You likes a strong-smelling one perhaps, does you? Yes, he does himself as well. One that's been hanging in the gibbet, in God's larder, for a few weeks? I had one such once. Very tender and loose; a little maggotty, mind, but you gets used to that, for that's the way with a corpse, boy. Indeed, it's a speciality, a delicacy. The Baron was like that even before he died. Sort of cheesey like and very high. I buggered his niece and I buggered the old sod himself when his time came. Cold in the winter, boy. Very cold. But they keeps better that way, they does. Remember, a hermit in the tomb never goes short. A body in the grave is worth two in the hand, and a bugger in the yard is not proud. There's all sorts of buggeration to be had here. Plenty to choose from; plenty to pick at, if you don't mind digging . . . only . . . only . . . "

His spirits sagged by this outburst, the recluse slid to the floor of the tomb.

"Only what?" asked Bartleby.

"Only they doesn't bury up in here any more. No more burying up for buggery. These is lean times, boy. But we's been a-digging, we has! We's been a-preparing for the good times what's yet to come!" cried De'Ath, adding, "But come boy; come, Bartleby. Follow old De'Ath and we'll show you his plot, we will. Yes, his plot, the best plot a bugger ever had!"

So saying, the hermit eased himself from the Baron's vault with the aid of his bone and Bartleby followed him out into the night, the pair fading through the gloom amongst the white statuary of death.

CHAPTER SEVEN   *The Apologist: a Would-Be Chapter,*
Not What Was Intended.

I was born — so I begin this chapter as I began life —
when my desk shouts me down with a dreadful roar and I
hear that I am a liar!

I was born — to continue, conscious that the reader
must desire to know something of the person to whom this
MS has been entrusted — you may take it for a fact that I was
born just one quarter of a century ago in an old and tired
land, born something of an Ancient Briton, the blood of Celt,
Pict, Goth, Roman — the desk mutters — Vandal, Saxon,
Dane (nothing Greek) coursing in my veins.

Here I am: *born* — the desk howls — after a pilgrimage
of one or two thousand years approaching the end of the
second Christian millenium, a trinity of selves: good, bad,
indifferent, an old-young would-be bard, sabotaged by a desk
in the telling of his personal narrative.

My worthy German friend, Damon Gottesgabe, whom
you have yet to meet, counts this as a blessing in disguise. I,
however, am not so sure.

Hence this unfinished chapter; hence shall I read where I
sought to write lest I be plagued with continued weepings
and wailings, as though the hermit had been waiting for
twenty-five years for Bartleby and the book of Bartleby, now
to vent a quarter of a century's woes in an unrelenting series
of heart-rending sobs and tear-jerking groans that force a rude
end to this seventh chapter and your apologist's life story.

For De'Ath's crocodile grief became so unbearable that I threw open my drawer and discerned these words, in the very place where they now stand:

Houle papers

The script, I assure you, was not mine, but what followed was certainly foul enough to warrant a separate chapter in the history of infamy.

CHAPTER EIGHT   *Bartleby and De'Ath in the Graveyard of Reputation, Wherein the Hermit Discourses on Man and His Plot Is Revealed.*

Thus De'Ath hobbled on his crutch of bone, weaving in and out of the graves, nodding and grinning at the sleepers in eternal night, his silvery hair streaming out far behind him. Thus did Bartleby follow, says my text, ever at his heels for mile upon mile upon mile.

"This is a greater yard than I suspected," said the boy. "Greater indeed than the entire village."

"Greater than all the world," rejoined De'Ath. "Because that's the way of things here, it is."

"Sir De'Ath," said Bartleby, still troubled by the recluse's tale, "what did the Baron do when he found Deborah?"

"CHAPTER EIGHT, Bartleby," the hermit began, *"The Trial of Sexton De'Ath, Wherein He Falls From Baron Hank Caughlin Mangaravidi D'Arcy Fitz Kelly Mordant's Highest Turret and Broke His Shanks* — which explains me bone, boy," added De'Ath. "A very dizzy business it was too, or so the plot has it. But I wouldn't worry your head about it. De'Ath has greater things in mind by way of composition, he has. Yes, before the night's out, boy, we should be in the ninth chapter. What does you say to that?"

Bartleby was puzzled by this abrupt dismissal of the eighth chapter, but before he could say anything, the old man was speaking again.

"Look, boy, see," De'Ath paused to examine a grave, "here lies one what wrote tersely, overboozed, and whored it

42

too much. A lover of life and the hunt, he was, but his reputation perished even before him, it did, and this terse gentleman had a protraculated sort of fate, very sad like. Well, well, I dare say some critic will dig him up just as De'Ath did to bugger him, yes. Here's another, boy, what swallowed entire dictionaries and fed himself upon books till he mouthed them out again. Guineas for Guinness has he none at all now, nor never did have, though the critics drank headily of him. He had a pauperous death, he did, away from his native land, the poor sod. There's another," De'Ath thwacked the mound with his bone, "what drawled the most turgid prose that ever baffled a compositor. A practitioner of the Magnolian school, he was: a gothical heart what spawned a whole tribe of craven admirers and fawning imitators — this heart beats no more, boy, 'tis forever still and at peace with the world."

The hermit shivered and sighed and gazed at the graves. "These was authors, Bartleby," he explained, "that's what they was. And they was uncomfortable in themselves, and they went in fear of death 'cos of pride. They wasn't such a bad lot, really, but they was proud, boy, *proud.*"

"What is death," Bartleby asked his nocturnal guide, "that men should fear it?"

"Nothing," De'Ath replied, "leastways, not now. It used to be, oh yes. But that was once upon a time ago, in the days of antiquity, you might say, when Emperors and Kings was all the rage. They was special like and not supposed to die. Yes, even though they stank with it, nobody would ever admit these kings was dead, so they'd pick another and say it was the same one all along. Yes, that's what they did and I think they had style in them days, I does. Nowadays, nowadays it's all different, boy, on account of there being no more Emperors and Kings, see? Least not real ones. Nowadays everybody's the same and has to have the same sort of obsequies with the departed all dressed up better than he ever was in life. There's no class to it, boy, no class. What's the point of dying if everybody's to look like Emperors? What's the point of that?"

Bartleby admitted there was none.

"Pride, boy, that's what it is; that's what makes 'em

43

wear fancy clothes for burying. But dying, now, there's a different thing. How many times has old De'Ath watched over the dying and seen how they takes on a new lease of life and wants to do things they's never done before. Bugger me backwards if it ain't the strangest thing, boy, but there's some what would even be authors – at the last gasp when they didn't have a word left in 'em.''

"And what is man,'' Bartleby enquired, "that makes him proud above all other creatures?''

"Proud, boy, proud? Does you know what you's asking? Does you know who you asks? But proud, yes, he's proud, though some calls him wise. He's a witty ape, that's what he is, a glib monkey with testes scrotal and penis pendulous – the biggest of its kind. But he's not to blame for that, no. It's just this habit he has of wanting everything to be like him in his own image, see? He calls himself a natural beast – which he ain't – and thinks his life is the calumination of all the world. Well, it ain't. The only natural thing about him is his death when he resembles the rest of God's universe. That's when I likes him best. As for the rest of the time, he's mostly like a book. Sometimes he's a good book, and sometimes bad. Then as often as not he's neither good nor bad and so he goes unread and falls apart at the end and comes to old De'Ath what buggers him in the yard.

"There's no other creature like this Man, boy. A fox is a fox and a rat is a rat, but this Man is a fox and a rat and a bugger to boot. Not that I hates it, mind. Old De'Ath couldn't do that, could he? No, he's impartial is De'Ath, what you might call objective in his work, and he takes it how it comes without rancour. But I buggers it all the same, I does, I does. I buggers it for its pride what makes it what it ain't. Yes,'' the hermit reflected, "that's the way it is. But come, boy, we's things to be doing, we has, and these is no matters for one so young as you is.''

And on they sped, says my text, on through the tombs of the night.

Long after this little exchange, De'Ath and Bartleby were to be found sitting at the edge of an enormous pit.

"It's me project, boy,'' announced De'Ath with an

expansive gesture of his bone. "the gravest plot that ever tickled a bugger's fancy."

De'Ath sat down at the very edge of the pit and produced his own MS, then searched, scratched, and tore furiously at his cerements.

"Tsk, tsk," the hermit's tongue scraped dryly on his herringbone palate, "we's getting forgetful, isn't we? Tsk, it must be his old age creeping up upon him, it must. We's left the tallow behind," De'Ath stared darkly into the pit, "but not to worry, we knows it off by heart, we does. We has it committed to memory, yes."

"What?" asked Bartleby, peering into the murky depths of the pit.

"Look, boy, see. Does you make 'em out? Is they discernible to you? Oh yes, it's in his mind, very fresh. Ahhh! Look at 'em, boy. They's all where they belongs. In the plot! See!"

The hermit's spindly legs dangled beneath him and kicked from time to time as the morbidity of his imaginings transported him this way and that into rheumatic fibrillations of delight. Indeed, so powerful were these motions that Bartleby had to restrain the hermit from falling into the pit of his own creation, which soon filled with a rapidly accumulating mass of boards, bindings, plots, characters, significances, and textual detritus. Hence De'Ath had no need of a light to illuminate his pages, for they illuminated themselves; and hence he launched straightway into his project.

"First, into this grave will go the linotype machine; second, all the drones, dunderheads, and automatons ever apprenticed unto it. Next, old De'Ath takes all those long standing runs, such locked-in-chase flowery phrases, as: *stroking the hairy mot, fingering the twat, odiferous mount, trembling lips, rampant prick, hard organ, flushing bard,* abounding nowadays in every jobbing house, where no sooner is they impressed and the ink dried up than they's platenned down again, dulling mind and type."

"Nowadays?" queried Bartleby, not understanding how long it was since the hermit had read anything resembling a book.

45

"Nowadays, I says nowadays advisedly," De'Ath continued, "Yes. I shall seize all these pungent casts, honeyed
conceits, and ingenious founts, and melt them down, fusing
them hermaphroditically (with such heat as they never had
before) into one molten mass — even though it takes me a
whole legion of furnaces, this old De'Ath shall do, he shall!"

At this De'Ath was mightily convulsed and narrowly
escaped falling into the pit. Nevertheless, he recovered
himself and continued in the same vein. "Then we shall take
a little boy." He looked longingly at Bartleby. "A very
cherubic little boy, he is, yes, about five years of age, I would
say, a little boy what asks too many questions for his years.
What could we call him? We could call him Bartleby, couldn't
we? Oh yes, oh dear me yes, the veriest incarnation of all
what's pure and innocent, and we shall give him a rubbing of
Saint Genet's fecal preparation — I had him twice, stank he
did, *buggerum!* — Ahhh! Next, an Aunt what ravishes him,
and a Matron what laughs, and a hermit what . . . what . . .
Ahhhh!" De'Ath moaned and again directed a fond look at
our infant hero. "He loves his Auntie, doesn't he? Not me.
Not De'Ath, no. But he might grow fond of him, yes. And
come to look upon him as his . . . his . . . *Buggerum,
buggerum, boo!*" De'Ath exclaimed, *"Buggerum, buggerum,
buggerum,* BOO! Yes, he had such a book, he did, years ago,
boy, afore he fell foul of the Baron and was cast out. You
could almost be his little boy, yes, his only solace and
comfort. But next, next," De'Ath remembered the pit, "the
massy machine of the *Complaint,* as mechanical a device as
ever pumped semen, that creature of the groin-brained Wrath,
shall be interred in the plot, your *Confessions* also, and
sundry topics sultry, a compounding of assorted de Sadists,
voyeurs, goats, centaurs, Cabot Wrights, flitters on Lesbos,
satyrs, studs and conventional stallions, such a concatena-
tious gathering of nancies and freaks, slaves of the universal
orifice that would make even the Roman Pthirius Pubis smile
in his crabbed fashion."

Even as De'Ath spoke, the pit became filled with a
writhing sea of human and animal flesh, the various members
of which vied with each other to outdo their neighbours'
prodigious feats. No class of society nor age of man went

unrepresented, or if they did, the deficiency was speedily remedied. While the mass seethed and multiplied, De'Ath danced and frolicked, directing his bone at the more intriguing scenes in this remarkable tableau vivant.

"What did he say, boy? What did he say? CHAPTER TEN already!" cried the hermit.

"I thought it was NINE," said Bartleby.

"That was called *The Plot Takes Shape*, boy, but here we is in CHAPTER TEN *The Plot Thickens*. Yes, it's in his mind, it is. Look! Look!" exclaimed De'Ath as two shepherds had their pleasure upon a sheep. "Look!" cried De'Ath, "ain't you seen it a thousand times before? And now it's all for the burying up, boy, 'cos he's called it perfectly to mind, he has."

Bartleby's ears bleated. "I think the one at the front," he remarked, "is very foolhardy, and is likely to be deprived of his pleasure. I wonder what could make him do such a thing?"

"Tee-hee!" cried De'Ath upon a new diversion. "That's an old device, that is, but it's a long time since he's seen it." An obese clerical gentleman pursued a eunuch, and, catching up with his darling, leaped to his devotions with an altar candle.

"But look here," said Bartleby, puzzled to observe another variation upon guardianship – a variation, says my text, which he would not have dreamed of himself, "I wager your wisdom has never seen anything like that before."

"Very common," De'Ath sniffled, "bread and butter stuff, Bartleby, that's all. He could do better himself, he could, in his prime – and he did, yes," said the hermit as a juggler with a pail of live codfish was engaged in a diverting act with the lady of his choice. The juggler would take one of the fish, squirming fresh from the pail, and insert it into the lady. She – very dexterously, according to the MS – ejaculated the fish forth, whereupon it was caught by the juggler, who then began to slap her about the face with it, crying, 'Patience, Madam, patience!'

"TEN, yes, TEN, no doubt about it. He remembers him there," said De'Ath, pointing at another amorous vignette and flicking through the pages of his own manuscript, "see, boy — that one! — is a very wise, respected and ancient Alderman of the Parish."

The Alderman of whom De'Ath spoke was stripped naked, save for his Aldermanic chain, which bounced upon his chest as he, organ erect, careered round and round a coffin in which lay a damsel in a like condition of undress. When the Alderman's race was run, he clambered onto the catafalque and urinated upon the wench, the pair crying in joyless unison:

'Slippers for kippers have we none, oh no!'

Among the curious and versatile performers in the pit, one deserves especial mention, not so much for the peculiarity of his role, but for the vital part he was soon to play in the plot entire. This full bodied and blooded Negro carried an axe in one hand, and in the other the severed head of a white female which he lugged along by its blonde and gory locks, rolling his stage-darkey eyes and mumbling to himself, *"Chunk-chunk!* Hey, dar now preacher man, dat's de way we deal wi' dem white fuckahs! Dat's de way we rock dis ole Dixie boat. Yassah: *chunk-chunk!*" — and suchlike numbers redolent of the Old South, cadences imposed by his author who presumed on our disbelief and asked that we take this for the talk of a period nigger.

Since — according to my text, though not I think to the hermit's — since there is no end to the wonders of modern romance, the severed head proved no less eloquent than the character who was seemingly responsible for its amputation. For it begged, pleaded, coaxed and cajoled, in a similar if more educated dialect. "Ah, Nat," it groaned, "how's you liking the cloaking obsessive flimsy lure of mah diaphonous gauze undergarments? If'n you doan unnerstan me, that's mah pre-bellum pantaloons ah's talking about."

To which this Nat replied, "Well, I doan know. Ah's the Lawd's work to be doin; Ah's alluv dis here choppin up an fantasizin an chunkin to be about, missy, cos the Lawd mah author's done revealed it to me, an he's sure gotta earn his hominy grits some hows, otherwise he's gwina *starve.*"

Now while De'Ath himself cackled and tittered and delved further into his manuscript, the head and its bearer were by chance thrown onto the companionship of a third

48

personage: a strapping maiden who had somehow come into the possession of a bull's penis, which priapic device she had affixed to her loins, and which she managed by much working, massaging, and beating of the organ to work into a state of discernible turgidity wherewith she might – and did – assault others of her sex. Bartleby, observing all this and like activities, thought it very strange, and was on the point of enquiring after the reason for such behaviour, when our hero noted that Nat, the head, and the priestess of Minos had fallen into conversation, their little cabal soon attracting other members of the throng who muttered and murmured amongst themselves, effectively terminating all but the most drab and uninteresting pastimes in the pit.

"Mr De'Ath! Mr De'Ath!" Bartleby sought to draw the hermit's attention to this development, but De'Ath was so far beside himself with the morbidity of his plot that he noticed none of the gatherings. And that, says my text, was very careless of the hermit.

For the group had now elected Nat their interim spokesman, and he advanced to the edge of the pit.

"Massah Bartleby," he said, ruefully scratching his head, "is Ah a man or what? Just you look at this," he continued, flourishing the severed head and giving an exultant wave of his ghastly chopper, "does you think this is right?"

The mutterings grew and the tone of Nat's address changed. "Is Ah a man," he asked, "or just a paper nigger, a white paper nigger? You look at alluv these folks, Bartleby, an you see what their authors have gone and done to them. Is that right, now?" he singled out the wench with the bull's penis. "How long is this exploitation gonna continue? Ah'm sick of being a paper nigger, and she's sick of this too, and we're all sick of this money-grubbing weird stuff," the people agreed, "and there's some of us that's for burning and some for lynching, cos we're sick and tired and want freedom!" And all the people in the pit, says my text, responded with an ominous cheer.

"What's this? What's this?" cried De'Ath, roused by the sound of discontent. "He doesn't remember this, he doesn't, no."

"Freedom! Freedom!" the chant was taken up.

"Is there anything Ah kin do, Nat?" enquired the severed head. "Ah's only a head."

"Plenty, there's plenty for a head to do," Nat replied as De'Ath sprang off his haunches and scuttled round the edge of the pit, beating at the characters with his crutch of bone.

"No talking heads!" he cried. "There was no talking heads in it!"

This last remark, says my text, met with a forceful contradiction from the pit. For so it was that the severed head hurtled through the air and affixed its teeth on a peculiarly tender portion of the hermit's anatomy; so it was that the wench of the surrogate gland delivered De'Ath of a hearty smack on the chops and hauled him, struggling and screaming, down into her arms.

"Bartleby," he managed to cry before he was totally submerged, "seek your original author, seek the final guardian; seek God or the other party!"

And then he disappeared altogether, a final orgiastic scream dying behind him. A great rending and heaving followed, and Terra herself received the plot into her bowels. Thus was Bartleby left alone as dawn trailed her coral fingers in the east and the fowls of the morn cried *tweet-tweet*.

CHAPTER NINE   *Wherein Divergencies Converge.*

I have circumperambulated this globe, and it is known to me that —

'The style is the man,' says Gottesgabe.

'No,' say I, 'that is, yes. I need no interruptions from you; this chapter is scarcely begun.'

The reader should know that my animadversions on the subject were attenuated by the usual wailings from my desk drawer.

Inside, this same page was saltily encrusted with the sacristan's briny spume, and was somewhat charred about the margins. *A posteriori*, the carbon and saline deposits bore witness to the candlelight dance in the tomb of Baron Hank.

'You were saying,' says Gottesgabe.

Indeed I was.

CHAPTER TEN   *A Chapter Against Allegories, Wherein Bartleby Meets with the ffoule Papers of the Play,* WAITING FOR DOGOT, *Improbably Subtitled* DEATH, *Which Is No Sooner Got Underway than It Is Interrupted.*

A furtive light (asserts my text with deceptive candour), a furtive light presaging neither dawn nor dusk, beginning nor end, discovered Bartleby alone and out of time in a forest track. It is a green tunnel populated by nothing but the lurking figures of the boy's unconsummated innocence, shadowy yet insubstantial images imbued by him with a breath all of their own, apart, utterly apart from any natural life. A root grasps at his foot and the tiny figure stumbles. Now, a gnarled tree lurches from the halflight and clutches at him with its branches, but Bartleby feels only the rough scrub of aged bark and the tree is gone. A little later and the kindlier touch of blossom and vine caresses him, sighing of Alice, the elfin Mary and the laughing Matron, as well as other forms of guardianship's embrace. So our hero whispers to the shadows, asking them where he might find God or the other party, and the shadows reply with words unspoken, further, further . . .

And further, Bartleby spies the end of the gloomy corridor, marked by a yellow lozenge of daylight where the trees have joined to form a natural lancet arch. Here he emerges onto a small pasture, beneath which the country beyond rolls into an open quiltwork valley. "If only there were someone to give me directions," he thinks aloud, "because I am lost and cannot see either party here. But I shall rest underneath this tree and perhaps catch some rest."

At this juncture I cannot help but remark that the boy

would have been wiser had he inspected the tree he designed to sit against — the same advice holding fast (as the tree did not) for all those who would sit under or against trees in any age or clime. For this was a stage tree, which, when our hero applied his back to it, fell to the earth, so disturbing the trio of personages reclining (the MS informs me) at the other side of the prop. But I will make no more observations after the event, and propose instead to let the text carry the narrative burden.

"DODO," cried the first of these characters, "*Enter*: DODO, *on his back.*"

"What?" Bartleby searched out the voice.

"*He is a* DWARF," continued Dodo, "*large for his size.*"

"Yes," said the boy, who could think of nothing better, so disconcerted was he by the tree's fall and this strange manner of speech. "Hello, Dodo."

"ESTROGEN," the second personage introduced himself. "*Enter*: ESTROGEN, *on his back. Dressed as the Knave of Spades, he is a very flat character who lies flush with the pasture's green slope.*"

"I can see that," said Bartleby.

"WALDEMAR," announced the third, "*is dressed more modishly in a long wizard's gown, embroidered with the ciphers of his calling. Graver and older than* ESTROGEN, *of a more dignified mien,* WALDEMAR *makes mystical passes and vacantly asks* BARTLEBY *his* NAME."

"You can't ask me my name," the boy made bold his reply, "if you already know it. At least you can, but there doesn't seem much point."

"ESTROGEN: *Still prone, rights his red paper crown, crushed in the tree's fall,*" remarked the Knave exegetically, adding: "There isn't any point."

"WALDEMAR: Then get up!" And, teaching by precept, the wizard sank to earth, raised himself, and sank again.

"Yes," said Bartleby, for he thought the affirmative once more apt. "Kind gentlemen," he began this speech, not knowing exactly what to say or how, "I am sorry I knocked your tree over, but I would not have sat against it had I known it was a pretend tree."

"DODO," said Dodo, *"conversationally:* That's a nasty cough, Bartleby."

"But I hadn't coughed," the boy rejoined. "Not yet."

"ESTROGEN: *His mouth curls downwards, the upper lip graced by a wispy moustache.* That's why it's a nasty cough!" said the Knave vindictively.

"WALDEMAR: We are waiting for DOGOT," the wizard informed Bartleby.

"DODO: See?" said the dwarf, producing for our hero's enlightenment a piece of MS paper whereon was scrawled:

Waiting for DOGOT
ffoule papers
"DEATH"
ffirft draft

Bartleby immediately noticed the name DOGOT was TO GOD spelled backwards, and observing also the subtitle "DEATH," believed his quest to be much advanced.

"I have journeyed hither," he said, coughing slightly as he realized that his audience was other than ideal, "in search of God or the other party, either of whom might direct me to Auntie Alice, my one and true Guardian."

"DODO: Is it him?"

"ESTROGEN: *With an air of effeminate malice.* Him? Here?"

"WALDEMAR: *Blankly.* Who is it?"

"DODO: *Persistently:* Is it him?" persisted the dwarf.

"Why," Bartleby spoke with some impatience, "do you describe everything as you do it?"

"ESTROGEN: *Tilts his pencilled eyebrows.* No more words for DODO! That's all he can say."

"DODO: *Countering.* It is him."

"If," said the boy, "you are waiting for Dogot and you don't know who he is, how will you know him when you meet him?"

"ESTROGEN: We have never met DOGOT and he has never met us. Meeting has nothing to do with waiting. You can wait without meeting."

"Just as you can meet without waiting," said Bartleby to the Knave's annoyance. "Have you ever thought," he continued brightly, "of *looking* for him — as I am looking for my Guardian?"

The participle 'looking' formed mincingly on Estrogen's thin lips, was swallowed, returned, and fell unuttered on cowslips and clover.

For boy, Knave, magus and dwarf, my text vouchsafes, became uncomfortably aware of an heavenly disturbance: an occult obnubliation speeding, or rather tumbling and barrelling from out the skies, down, down, down — in its descent accompanied by a most un-Pythagorean cacophony and a commodious collection of hats, variously labelled, from which arose no Dogot but these words, spoken by this figure:

"I am Rojack the omnivore! The instant man cometh!"

Speechless, the company gazed on.

"See! See!" Rojack threatened the skies with fist pugilistic. "All the devils of the earth and hell have plagued me with whirls and whorls — See! See where Mad Normie's words stream in the firmament! Is this the head," the bedlamite enquired with plebeian eloquence, "that wore a thousand hats and burnt the topless towers of New Troy?"

At which, I am assured, Mad Normie fell where he had lately risen, stumbling over a hat to continue his descent into the valley below, the site of the earthly paradise that was his goal.

'Dear me,' our hero bethought himself, 'I see I am not alone in losing my Guardian.'

And turning to bid the trio farewell, Bartleby saw that they too had disappeared as old Helios sank, mantled in ambrosial dusk.

CHAPTER TWELVE *Once More Into the Breach, Dear Friends — Whereafter the Thread is Resumed.*

"Nothing," Damon Gottesgabe is fond of saying, "is better than nothing at all."

CHAPTER ELEVEN *In which the Promised Thread Is Resumed with Bartleby Solus.*

Divine reader, when ten precedes twelve and twelve itself precedes eleven what are we to think? That the author changed his mind perhaps? That he cannot count? That the substance of this chapter occurred in between chapters and is not properly a part of any chapter at all?

Authority works in a mysterious way. Yesterday, while wandering idly and a trifle affectedly in the ravine at the bottom of my street, I came upon him — the very same — he of the begging hand and parched countenance, the original of all hermits, the hermit primordial, his ancient frame couchant, head crowned with a hutch of newspapers. There, on the switch-crossed path, under the watchful eye of a grinning squirrel, I thought: who is writing whom? — and saw at once that the hermit did not know himself for what he was.

Some author, *my* author, had put him in a book, and unless the hand that begged was also the hand that wrote, the hermit remained ignorant of his status, of what he had done and said, of where he was, had been, and was going to be.

To return momentarily to the subject of this book: it must not be thought, says the text, it must *never* be thought that our hero was naive, though his youthful actions would seem to suggest a certain fashionable innocence. Not so! His reflective parts were as well developed as his physical, and if you see little evidence of this it is simply because my authority has not yet chosen to reveal it. That he wanted the reader to observe an incipient tendency towards reflection in the boy, may be seen by the following monologue, the exact placing of which, I concede, is difficult if not impossible. But here is the soliloquy, exactly as it is given in the text.

"The further I go, the more distant does my Guardian seem, and the less likely it becomes that we shall ever meet again. All men have something which keeps them, and perhaps all men must lose that which keeps them best. Perhaps I am not meant to find Auntie at all, but continue with my search — just like Waldemar and Estrogen who certainly have a fine opinion of themselves. And Mr Rojack too.

"Well, if I cannot decide between the quest for Auntie and Auntie herself, I will take Mr De'Ath's advice and search instead for God or the other party, in the meantime accepting things as they come along. This way everything may be considered as part of the quest and perhaps I will soon find God or the other party, or someone who may know of them — though to speak truly I do not see how the hermit can know anything of such matters."

Where is the metaphysician who might add the gloss to our infant hero's apprehension of the universe? All men have something which keeps them, and perhaps all men must lose that which keeps them best! A noble sentiment, profoundly expressed!

For behind the apparent innocence of Bartleby's utterances, there lay the instincts of a broker of fortune and the growing reserves of what can only be called — and is called — caution. To be brief: our hero had noted that the images men hold of themselves seldom correspond with the images others hold of them, and had seen in this the germ of conflict.

CHAPTER TWELVE AGAIN   *Wherein, After Initial Confusion and Near Disaster, Is Told Of the Amicable Debate of Boss and Ham upon Numbers and the Wondrous Machine.*

When day returned, Bartleby was no longer in the pasture but had descended to the valley. Quite how he arrived there, the text does not say. Perhaps there was something transmigratory in his descent; perhaps he had merely walked down. In any case, I have no intention of idling away my time pondering such trivialities, though the reader if he so wishes may concoct a chapter or two for himself, beginning perhaps with a description of Bartleby's toes and feet, thence to the theory of mechanics which deals with locomotion, and ultimately to more spiritual matters of metempsychosis, *etc.*

However Bartleby reached the valley, and the crossroads at which he now stood, the boy himself does not seem to have known, for the MS swears that he was heard to cry, "Where has everybody gone?" upon perceiving himself once more alone. A night and a day seemed to have passed within the twinkling of a chapter. Or was it longer: a decade or a century, perhaps? Certainly, Dodo, Waldemar, and Estrogen were nowhere to be seen. They had disappeared as rapidly as the incredible Mr Rojack. "Well, they were not much help to me anyway," thought the boy and examined the signpost which marked the crossroad. It read:

THROCKTON BY THE BOG: ONE MILE ➡

a simple enough legend, except for this:

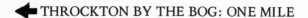 THROCKTON BY THE BOG: ONE MILE

and this:

THROCKTON BY THE BOG: ONE MILE

and — would you believe it? — this:

THROCKTON BY THE BOG: ONE MILE

Bartleby wondered whether there might be four Throcktons by the Bog, or four ways of reaching one Throckton by the Bog. "Whichever way I go," he thought, "I am certain to reach a place of that name." As he was about to choose one of the roads, however, he noticed a piece of paper attached to the signpost. On the paper he read the following:

Throckton by the Bog — Home of the Wondrous Machine.

Now if there *were* four Throcktons, only one might have the Wondrous Machine. And if there were four Throcktons it became a matter of some importance to find the right one, for the Machine had excited Bartleby's attention. Surely a place which could boast a Wondrous Machine might know of God or the other party.

His dilemma was increased upon the appearance of a generously proportioned young wench who hove heftily into view at the crossroads.

"Hollo," said the buxom maid, "Be ee harlost?"

"I am looking," he replied, "for Throckton by the Bog, home of the Wondrous Machine where I hope to find one who will tell me of God or the other party in order that I might find Auntie Alice, my one and true Guardian."

"Hoo. Haar," rejoined the maid enigmatically, and regarded Bartleby through bovine eyes. "Ahum."

"Yes," the boy continued, "for so the hermit, Mr

De'Ath, directed me before he fell into the plot."

"Wull, Oi be acalled Fullis, not Hollis. Han tis Thruckton Oim bound fur," announced this Chloe, examining Bartleby from head to toe.

"Phyllis, you say?" said the boy brightly, "I met one once who mentioned a Phyllis. I gave him the croons and he told me of De'Ath."

The maid squinted as Bartleby volunteered this information but she said nothing. "Indeed," he continued, "I gave him the croons for fair Phyllis, the milkmaid, his sweetheart. I was glad to part with them, for they were of no use to me . . ."

"Han how long ago moit this have been?" asked the wench, her eyes very much narrowed.

"Oh, a long time ago. Is it possible that you are the same Phyllis?"

The maid hummed noncommittally at this and Bartleby took it for the natural reticence of country folk.

"Han you gave him the croons. Were there many croons?" she asked shyly, for she was a Ward of Chancery and had much need of crowns. When the boy indicated with a sign of his hands that there had been at least six inches worth of them, her mouth dropped open, her eyelids fluttered, and a sudden flush arose upon her face.

Bartleby failed to understand the import of this behaviour and could only conclude the girl to be a little simple in the head. She meanwhile rolled her eyes and placed her hands firmly upon her ample hips. Next, she fell into a reflective mood, a bland expression taking hold of that broad agricultural countenance. Then she sucked mightily upon her thumb, smacked her lips, and flashed an inviting and toothy smile at the apprehensive boy — several of the jaw's tenants were absent, which default made the smile quite conspicuous. Evidently she had reached a decision. "Coom," she said demurely, and Bartleby instantly understood this to be an invitation to play at guardians.

"Thank you," said Bartleby and followed the wench.

In this country, all roads lead to Throckton by the Bog, but a half mile later Bartleby found himself shepherded into a large barn. Here, amid delicate rural aromas and the lowing of cattle, Bartleby watched as Phyllis settled easily upon a bed of straw, and, preparing a place for her acquaintance of the crossroads, reached out her arms to take hold of him. "Coom," she said coyly.

Immediately Bartleby abandoned all thoughts of the Wondrous Machine and God or the other party, for resolute in his recent decision to incorporate the chances of the way into his quest, he could not have been expected to spurn so amorous an invitation, and indeed to have done so would have been an affront to guardianship itself. Before receiving himself into the maid's brawny embrace, however, he fell to attacking the buttons about the topmost portion of her dress. Sensing his urgency (for it was some time since he had played guardians), she assisted him in the assault, smothering him the whiles with loud and succulent kisses. "Ah, coom," she said bashfully, not that the boy needed any further encouragement.

Whether this maid, Phyllis, interpreted Bartleby's urgency as the inexperience of infancy, or whether she sensed it was the frustration of a very forward toddler, is not mentioned by my text. Such, anyway, is the course of nature, that at the sight of her bared breasts he would have tupped her there and then, and began divesting himself of his leggins in preparation for the act. "Coom," she said artfully, and with immaculate timing. For at this critical juncture (or rather it was no juncture at all), the barn door flew open.

"Hollo," cried a voice winsomely, and as yet oblivious to the would-be lovers' presence. "Hollo, Fullis. Hoo, Fullis, moi sweethurt. Be ee hereaboots? *Ti-twiddle, ti-twiddle,* tis Oi. Yoo-hoo."

Bartleby at once made a hurried though belated attempt to conceal his nakedness. Much to his astonishment, the maid's opinion of modesty coincided not at all with his own, and she, her bosom still naked and her drawers about her ankles, hauled him struggling, half-naked to his feet, where his head effected a kind of accidental covering to that portion of her anatomy which she turned towards the intruding rustic.

Imagine our hero's surprise when he saw, on the

threshold of the barn, that very same yokel who had directed him to the hermit, De'Ath. No less was the rustic's surprise, and the sight of Bartleby (to say nothing of Phyllis) wrought a marvellous change in his behaviour. Outraged at the betrayal of the tryst, the bumpkin seized a pitchfork and advanced menacingly but cumbersomely, his eyes unaccustomed either to the barn's darkness or the immodest spectacle before him. Both these factors were to the advantage of Bartleby who, if he but slowly understood the trick played against him, lost no time in taking evasive action by retreating between the wench's legs, so that the pitchfork which was now hurled in the boy's direction missed its mark and succeeded only in pinning a pecking hen to the ground with its prongs, she setting up an hysterical and scandalized clucking. As the yokel blundered in the fork's wake, determined to triumph where his aim had failed and to do the boy grievous bodily harm with his own hands, Bartleby abandoned his efforts to excuse his presence by reference to God, the other party, or Auntie Alice, and frantically sought a means of escape. A timely shriek from Phyllis came to his rescue and, regaining his trousers, he managed to scuttle around the flank of the incensed churl who had now become embattled with the faithless maid.

Bartleby's heels needed little instruction from his brain, and they flew of their own accord. Later, when he had time to reflect upon the ways of the world in which he was growing hourly wiser, his understanding of money was vastly increased. But it will be enough for the reader to know that the boy's flight was accompanied by Phyllis's distracted complaint to her vengeful lover: "The croons! The croons! He said he gave you croons!"

Noon discovered our hero in the thatched purlieus of a sizeable market town. The streets were wide and bordered by trees and the aspect which unfolded before the boy presented a pleasing compromise between human cultivation and the untutored countryside, between art and nature. Yet, despite the hour, the streets were deserted. As at the time of seasonal change, nature herself appeared in suspense. No birds made melodious track in the blue sky, cotton wool clouds moved

63

not across heaven's arc, and the very sun lingered motive-lessly in a vast and silent vault. Thus did Bartleby venture deeper and deeper into the heart of silence.

At length he came to the central square of the town — the meeting place of four roads. In the middle of the square (which was quite deserted of life) a kind of stage had been erected, and upon the platform there stood the quaint contraption known to our history as the Wondrous Machine of Throckton by the Bog. Since this amazing engine subsequently played a singular role in the development both of our hero and this text, I think it here appropriate to devote some time to a description of its external appearance.

The Machine's centrepiece was formed by a white corrugated dome-like construction, around the perimeter of which were several portals. A smokestack, or something evidently intended as such, surmounted the central dome of the Machine so that the invention, were it not for the fact that it was encumbered by other devices, would have resembled an igloo with a chimney protruding from the top. However, contiguous with the dome's periphery, at a point somewhat higher than the portals, another platform had been raised, thus giving the apparatus the look of a gigantic bowler hat into which had been cut a series of holes — the portals — designed, no doubt, as the eyepieces of a preposter-ous and multiocular being. Each end of this second platform (which, unlike the stage beneath was an integral part of the structure) could be gained by means of ladders and was graced by two spindly tripods. Wrought in the finest ironwork, and decorated with many ingenious scrolls and spirals, these tripods instantly reminded Bartleby of the legs which supported, and which probably still support, Auntie's antique washbowl. However, the MS is quick to observe that this comparison is the product of mere association on the boy's part, and is therefore to be regarded as inept and misleading. For my own part, I will assure the reader that nothing as simple as a washbowl sat atop either of the tripods, and it would have been a ludicrous folly of engineering to have placed one there, for no mortal might have scaled the legs (so high were they) thus to present himself at

Hygeia's font.* No. Instead, a spindle shaft ran through the apex of the legs, and attached to the shaft was a windmill (somewhat akin to the modern fan or propeller), designed by means of an additional sail to turn in the direction of the prevailing wind. A system of blocks and pulleys, these disappearing into the walls of the dome, established a mechanical linkage between the windmills and the entire contraption. Thus, in essence, the Wondrous Machine of Throckton by the Bog.

Bartleby wondered at the function of the Machine but could see no earthly purpose to it. The sound of distant revelry, however, soon diverted his attention, and came as a not unwelcome relief to the hitherto profound silence. In no time at all each of the four roads was filled by a babbling throng. All manner of persons poured into the square, engulfing Bartleby in their midst with a deal of sweaty jostling, shoving, and clamouring. Strange to say, many of the characters there assembled bore a remarkable resemblance to the contenders in De'Ath's pit, a bizarre enough coincidence, yet one which did not immediately impress the boy, distracted as he was by a violent tugging at his coatsleeve.

A rather stunted individual had affixed a claw-like hand to Bartleby's jacket. This personage was dressed in a jester's costume, one half of which was red, the other divided into green and white stripes, and his leprous pallor and broken visage gave him the air of one of the elder Breughel's less handsome creations. Nevertheless, lack of stature does not always betoken a faint heart, and in such a gathering as this there is much to be said for economy of size. To cut a long story short, as it were, the diminutive figure asked Bartleby about the purpose of the Machine and the business of the crowd.

"I gather that the second is some consequence of the first," answered Bartleby, pleasantly enough, "but what the first is I do not know, except that I can see it, whereas you cannot."

---

* Nevertheless, the legs themselves did have the appearance of Auntie's washbowl stand. On account of his innocence in matters mechanical, Bartleby may be forgiven his associationalism.

"Well," croaked the other in tones suggestive of a parrot's speech, "it's a riddle for sure. Yes, yes, a riddle." Then he added something which greatly amazed the boy. "For one who is looking for God or the other party, and for one of such an illustrious name as Bartleby, you do not seem very advanced in the art of riddles."

Hardly was this said when the speaker took it into his head to depart, giving the boy no chance to ask how he might have come by such details of his personal history, though confirming our hero in his opinion that he had been wise to visit Throckton by the Bog. "Wait!" cried Bartleby but to no avail, as the dwarf paddled off, navigating his way through a forest of legs. The jester's hat bobbed once, twice, thrice, and then was gone. At this, a hush fell on the crowd. There were several cries of "Peace!" "Ho!" "Make way!" and the like and Bartleby, his thoughts full of God and the other party, perceived that a party of dignitaries had begun to ascend the platform on which rested the Wondrous Machine of Throckton by the Bog.

The debate of Boss and Ham, both of whom were very old men, seems to have taken place annually throughout the recorded history of Throckton. Each year, therefore, the two elderly contestants polished their rusty tropes and reiterated their ancient arguments for the ceaseless edification of the townsfolk. According to our authority, the debate originated in a dark and distant era when the unlettered populace resorted to the squalid opinions of the marketplace. In this happily forgotten age, civil strife and commotions were engendered by the ceremony, which itself would almost certainly have been banned by the municipal powers had they not seen in it a means of dividing the people amongst themselves and thereby ruling the more effectively.

But now, says our authority, a more rational climate prevails so that man is the master of his passions and the debate is no longer the occasion of civil broils. Today it is conducted in a good humoured sort of way, with the populace attending much as they would at a ceremony or festival, the meaning of which has been for centuries lost. Nevertheless, we would be wrong to assume that Boss and

Ham do not have their partisans amongst the crowd. For in as much as a man is born a Whig or a Tory, the inhabitants of Throckton by the Bog divide equally into proponents of Boss and advocates of Ham. They listen, or attempt to listen to the speaker of their faction, and are deaf to the arguments of the contending party. Hence the people are not, as their ignorant ancestors were, excited by the spirit of faction, but come instead to have the wisdom of their pre-existing notions confirmed by the speaker of their choice. The reader will see in this a wise and prudent political system, unfortunately still to be discovered in the world outside Throckton by the Bog.

The great maturity, not to say senescence, of this system probably explains the carnival atmosphere in which the proceedings were conducted. Happily, our authority passes over the excesses of the vulgar and directs our attention to the party which we had left, a moment ago, in the act of clambering onto the platform. Now we rejoin the text: the town's ossified hierarchy is reanimated; once more the blood of corporate eloquence pulses through sclerotic veins, municipal knee joints creak and bend anew under the heavy load of civic responsibility, again does authority focus its purblind eye upon the assembled throng, and both the observed and the observers are quite unconscious that they have ever been held in suspension by this text. The Beadle, the Mace-Bearer, the Bailiff, the Aldermen, and His Most Worshipful and Right Honourable Lord Mayor, in the esteemed presence of his two dignified and principal speakers, take their place upon the platform to the mixed accompaniment of cheers, hoots, boos, and jeers. Our authority dispenses with the formality of introductions. Indeed, introductions are superfluous, for the protagonists are well known to all men. Thus we are plunged straightway into the debate.

A preliminary note, however, is necessary in order to certify the authenticity of the record. It is the custom of the country that, during the course of their favourite's address, one half of the crowd remains silent, while the other faction puts itself to making as much din as it can. The speakers, therefore, early fell into the habit of distributing broadsides of their speeches, that they might be the better understood,

67

if not the better heard, and hoping (I might add) to lend the increment of the years to the force of their rhetoric. For since the speeches changed not, neither did the broadsides, and each year a citizen of Throckton might re-read what had escaped him the year before — a process to be repeated until he went blind (when another would read to him); or mad (when others would ask him to comment upon the addresses); or died — at which his understanding was perfected.

I mention all this in order to avoid the charge of partiality to either of the speakers. No accusation could be further from the truth, for the parties here speak for themselves, and their addresses are taken — in full — from he texts of those self-same broadsides I have just described.

As for the speakers themselves, Boss was the older of the two, and — despite Ham's denials — the more honest. My authority gives little of their physical appearance except to say that Ham was leaner than Boss and inferior in stature where he was hungrier of aspect. After the fashion of these hirsute times, both men wore beards: Boss, a flowing, curly lion's mane; Ham, a cultivated goatee which pecked at the air when he spoke. But Boss is the first to speak, a precedence here afforded him — in the text as in Throckton — only out of deference to his superior years, and not from any wish to promote his cause at the expense of the other. Herewith, then, the text of Boss's address.

BOSS'S SPEECH UPON NUMBERS AND THE MACHINE

"Numbers are of great importance to my friend, Ham, and myself, for it is by the use of numbers that the Mechanics have constructed the Machine before you and behind us. So with the division, multiplication, the addition and subtraction of numbers, the manipulation of cosines, sequents and tangents, much that is substantial, tangible, and pleasing to the eye may come out of that which is abstract, hypothetical, and troublesome to the mind.

"For one who is here to speak against the application of numbers, you may think it strange that I should thus appear to praise their effects. But, friends, I do not presume to criticize numbers as such. They are necessary and pleasing contrivances. They have a certain attractiveness, even wantonness (their integrity is frequently subverted); they even have some practicality in determining the scope of our daily bread, they delimit one nation from another and one man from another, they are used to quantify existence itself. In short, numbers are the tools of the highest intellectual activity known to man, for they have produced mathematicians, musicians, and — in a way — poets." Boss pronounced the word with some distaste.

"Providing that numbers are confined to their proper sphere in the realm of purest intellectual endeavour, then, no harm may indeed come of them. But let them fall into the hands of the false practitioners of the mimetic arts, amongst which I number mechanics and poets, and you unleash a chain of sorry and very dangerous consequences. Even that habit of mind which made me refer to numbers as tools may have pernicious effects, if it is allowed to go unchecked. That they are tools which have mastered the craftsman, I hope to show. That we are in a state of abject dependency upon numbers, that we have allowed the number too much, I will now proceed to demonstrate.

"Show me the man who has seen a number. Which of you here has spoken with a number? Touched a number? Had any sensual relations with a number? Let this man appear; let me listen to the man who can show me the number's place in nature, the rank assigned to it, its species, its type, let this man reveal the number inscribed in the starry heavens, and then will I concede defeat in my debate with Ham. But I maintain that numbers are conveniences and cannot be invested with universal attributes. Here are five men. Whereof does their fiveness consist? Is it in them? No? Then out of them? No? Above them, perhaps? Below them? By the side of them? Does it transcend them, this fiveness, or are they infused by it? Hardly. It is, of course, a fiction, though it is one, as we shall see, with dangerous and potentially disastrous results." Boss shook his leonine head, slowly and sadly.

"Ah, say you, this is perfectly ridiculous. A number is a natural thing, you claim. Do we not employ numbers in measuring the span of creation? Is it not natural that a man should live three score years and ten? Are there not accordant dimensions to longevity throughout the scale of nature? Are we not affected by numbers, sometimes favourably, sometimes unfavourably, in all our daily calculations? Thus, society is ordered according to the rule of numbers. Thus, we regulate the natural principle of change in terms of profit and loss; thus we are tabulated and ruled, measured and mastered.

"For the small, meagre, and miserly in spirit, numbers have a very tenacious existence. But where is the rule of numbers in God's infinite universe? Again, let that man come forward who has counted the span of infinity, and I will admit defeat," here the philosopher raised his hands in mock obeisance.

"Happy is the man who can claim his tidy share of the creation. But whence cometh this science of numbers? Wherein might we find the origin of numbers?" Boss paused, regarded Ham, and smiled.

"That numbers are not the fruits of divine labour, but the inferior inventions of mankind, may at once be understood through considering the case of the original man. Adam, in his prime, had no use for numbers. In so far as God instructed him in the upkeep of the Garden, and matters pertinent thereto, He did so in terms convenient to his understanding, which, though second only to the lowest rank of the angels, was limited and imperfect. Not until our first ancestor was led into disobedience and he became a slave of his own will, was his life, and that of his issue, circumscribed by numbers. Did I not hear you say *first*? Yes, but without Adam's sin there would be no death; without death, no propagation. From thence we detect the beginnings of the awful habit of counting, as Adam, expelled from his bower of shame, is made to divide the infinite with the shabby counting of hours.

"Yet how we set our store by numbers! As though it is not enough to divide the universe, once, twice, infinitely, with a never-ending reel of numbers," the philosopher shook his head, "so that each unhappy calculation prepares the way for the next, and we, deluded by ambition, gaze onwards to the sum of all numbers, the indivisible whole, becoming more elusive with each subtraction or addition; as though it is not enough to place our trust in the shimmering mirage of numbers, we divide again, and again, and again, until the whole world is put to a fraction. Have we not divided the fabric of life from itself? Have we not rent the garment of nature from the world's body? Are we not pleased that so little a thing as a fraction might destroy the world? Indeed, the small, the meagre, and the miserly are very happy. For if they cannot meditate upon infinity they must annihilate it.

"Where, dear friends, might this end? The man who has accumulated one million numbers discovers that his one million is not worth a millionth against God's store. Divide the world, then, in the hope of gain, and you will discover numbers to be untrustworthy and capricious registers of fate. Here is a man who has to make a journey of one mile. Does he not have to go a half mile first, and next a half of a half, next a quarter of a quarter, an eighth of an eighth, a sixteenth of a sixteenth, on and on, until the very atom's edge seems a yawning chasm which he is destined never to cross? Thus was a venerable sage moved to declare: 'The South has a limit and no limit . . . The sun is declining when it is at noon . . . a creature is dead when it is alive . . . I go to Yueh today and arrived yesterday.' Alas that his words and those of the Attic school went unheeded, for there would have been an end to numbers." Boss stared at heaven, then at the crowd.

"But, say you," he stared far beyond the marketplace now, "this is far too ideal. And indeed I am not here to argue against numbers, merely to show you what they are. It is true, the myriad things and I make one, but what I have said is true makes something else, namely: two. Yet if I am not here to argue against numbers, I am certainly not here to play the sophist." Boss folded his arms and again shook his head, this time as though he had forgotten the reason for his presence. Then, with alarming suddenness, he recollected his argument. "I say numbers, combined with our literal dependency upon them, and our own mortality, are dangerous and perplexing. Which is to say that human nature is dangerous and perplexing, not to be trusted with the use of numbers.

"Nor am I here to moralize, but wish instead to consider

the essence of numbers. When stripped of our dependency upon them, and thus properly tamed, they may be looked on as things in themselves, neither intrinsically dangerous nor innately beneficial, except in conjunction with that intellectual endeavour which I earlier mentioned. For a number is capable only of explaining itself in terms of other numbers, and not as we thought, in terms of other things. Now this may be of some value in nourishing the grey matter in our brains, especially in the brains of our young, but unless we are willing to admit an utter dependency upon numbers, and go so far as to confuse numbers with things, it advances us very little in our understanding of the universe. A number cannot describe the world, it can only describe our way of describing it. For intelligent beings to be guilty of such a dualism seems to me as foolish as it is tautological. If we have to describe everything twice (like our poets), then we shall be hard put to in describing anything. And, friends, numbers actually interfere with perception. For being the human inventions that they are, they have led us into the ridiculous pretension of modelling the universe after our own way of thinking. Shorn of our dependency upon them, numbers appear as a very poor substitute for reality. A number is a symbol, yes: but a symbol without a referent. The quiddity of a number is all and no number can explain the how or the why of its existence.

"How might this contribute to our understanding of the Machine? Every argument I have applied to numbers may be applied to the Machine, for it stands in the same case as numbers, indeed it represents a debasement of numbers. It is a creation, not so much of numbers in themselves, but of the application of numbers. Although it has never been used, we are dependent upon it, as evinced by our presence here. Yet the Machine is, like a number, a thing in itself, capable neither of harm nor of good, unless our dependency and the potential use we may put our dependency to be considered harmful. The Machine can no more explain its purpose than a number; and, again like a number, it is a thing of absolute quiddity, capable of no *hows* or *whys*. Still, its very presence suggests to some at least, and my friend, Ham, is one of them, reason enough for its use. And it is to this point of view that I must now turn.

"I would not be so innocent as to claim that because the Machine has a long and honourable tradition of inactivity, it should not now, nor at any time in the future, be put to use. To argue from precedent is allowable in some cases, but here it would be merely an admission of historical inertia and the often oppressive weight which the past brings to bear on the present. Nor can I say that the Machine should not be put to use because we do not know what it may do. That would in itself constitute an excellent motive for putting it to work. Never let it be said, therefore, that I would stand in the way of experiment. It may be – as Ham would have you believe – that improvements will come about as a result of the Machine's use and that the human race will vastly benefit therefrom. It may be. And it may be that catastrophe will follow the use of the Machine. Yet we have had improvements and catastrophes enough without the use of the Machine. Unlike my friend Ham, I am no seer and do not pretend to forecast the future. No, my friends, there are far more persuasive reasons than these for maintaining the Machine in its present condition." Boss's distant gaze appealed to the invisible horizon.

"The Machine may work great good, and it may work great evil. But that good and that evil will be seen as coming no longer from God, but from ourselves, for as I have shown, numbers are human inventions. Similarly, I have indicated how numbers lead us into the folly that the universe is formed after our own image. What could the activation of the Machine do but accelerate this tendency towards self-delusion and monumental conceit? Self-sufficiency is to be desired, you say. Will not the use of the Machine increase our independence? Most certainly it will, claims Ham. For my part, I say perhaps it will, but at what price to the independent? Yet might not the Machine, say you, in so far as it is the sum of its parts, form a comprehensible whole out of our fragmented experience? Indeed it might. Then, say you further, if as you claim, Boss, numbers have disunited us, might they not, through their application in the Machine, unite us again in one peaceable body? And is not your argument, Boss, thus turned against you?

"All of these things, grave friends, I do admit with one important reservation and in return for a concession on your part. If you are willing to confess that the planets and stars about you, the invisible mysteries of nature, life and death itself, may be examined profitably by the use of numbers, if you will confess that you understand these and that you legislate for their existence, as you formerly believed they legislated for yours, then for God's sake activate the Machine. Yet should you do so, remember the debate is ended. Nevermore shall we meet in this marketplace, for every man, now, shall be his own God."

The philosopher's head bowed and an age seemed to pass — says my text — before he spoke again.

"And now, my reservation. Consider again the nature of numbers and what I have said concerning human nature, especially those amongst us who are addicted to the small, the meagre, the miserly. For this Machine is the creation of the small, the meagre and the miserly who would substitute the violence of action for the beauty of contemplation, who, failing to comprehend the intrinsic nature of numbers, would tyrannize you with their imperfect understanding, would dissect you to the millionth part, who would destroy you if you refused compliance with their mean and false gospel of numbers. Consider again what I told you of Adam, of how the original man was given the punishment of death for his transgression and how men have ever since counted the hours. Would you die a second death for this Machine? Would you ignore hope of salvation? Are you deaf to the voice of God?

"What, not so? Then I see that my arguments tell once more and that the Machine will remain as it has throughout the ages: a reminder that the small, the meagre, and the miserly have no part in Throckton by the Bog. Grave friends, I thank you for your ears."

With these words, Boss concluded his address. As he finished speaking, the crowd reached a frenzy of partisanship, some cheering, others booing. Bartleby alone seemed not to declare for either party, but wisely preferred to wait and see what Ham would have to say upon the subject of numbers and the Wondrous Machine. Then it was that our hero noticed the dwarf dressed in the jester's costume had reappeared.

"Well, Bartleby," this personage spoke to him, "what did you think of the speech?"

"I understood very little of it," replied the boy honestly, "and find all this talk of infinity to be very confusing. I wonder if I were to count for ever and ever, might I return to Auntie's home in the country? But there's one thing I do know."

"And what's that?" asked the other, one hand on his hat and the other under his lower jaw.

"That Boss is defending a lost cause. The Machine is bound to be used sooner or later, if only out of curiosity's sake. Is there anything the matter?" enquired Bartleby, for the jester was grinning widely now, almost manically, and struggled to control his features by applying more pressure at either end of his oversized head.

"No, no," replied the jester, composing his features with a deft clout under the jaw. "You are right, of course," he said, "but I do not think curiosity will be the reason for its use."

And at this cryptic remark, the crowd fell temporarily silent. Ham was about to begin his speech.

CHAPTER THIRTEEN   *Between Boss and Ham With*
Damon Gottesgabe.

I hope the reader is not superstitious.

In reply to friend Gottesgabe's criticism — the times are out of joint, he had remarked, and I reluctantly agreed — I adopt the following (temporary) system of dating:

The Year of Grace, 1970, February 20th: CHAPTER TWELVE
   "   "   "   "   "   March 18th: CHAPTER TWENTY-TWO
   "   "   "   "   "   March 19th: CHAPTER THIRTEEN

You see, reader, in my haste to get to the bottom or top of the plot, I've done what every reader shouldn't and read ahead to the twenty-second chapter, or yesterday: the day of my fantastical friend's return, and of our argument. Hence:

March 19th (Today).

"How was your friend?" enquired Damon.

"Terrible," I replied, "his sickness seems to have affected his mind."

"That's not very charitable of you," said Damon. "After all, he gave you the book."

"And what a book!" I exclaimed. "It has all the faults he accused my unwritten book of having — and more. In any case," I was still smarting from the effect of my fantastical friend's lecture, "I wouldn't inflict his sermonizing on the worst of enemies, let alone a so-called friend. Why should he have given me the book if he only wanted to accuse me of mishandling it? There's no excuse for what he said yesterday!" — I was angry with the world.

"There's no point in discussing that now," observed Gottesgabe, "since the reader hasn't read the chapter — unless he's been up to your tricks."

"Just let him try!"

"If you ask me," said Damon — I didn't — "your friend is not suffering from a physical disease but a literary one. It's very common today," he mused, "for men to reject authorship. Even you have done so — because of your friend. Gone are the days," Gottesgabe gave a whimsical smile, "of divine intercession. Art no longer mediates between the sense of the self and the sense of the external; no more is there that change from local time to epochal time, the fullness of time, the coming into being and transcendence of great art which welcomes the 'other' — reader, listener, observer, *friend,* what have you — and draws him into a world of another's creation. Yet still might it be so, if . . . "

"If what?" — it was the second sermon in two days. Let's get back to the old-fashioned story line; let's have an author who knows what he's doing . . ."

"And Exmas Pudding and Holly around the Hearth you shall have in plenty," said he. "If you are content to follow where others have been."

"I can do no worse than De'Ath," said I.

"And if you are *able* to follow where others have been," Damon smiled.

"Then it's settled," I said, "*I'm* telling this —" . . . but that's another story, reader, which you will be given presently.

For at the back of and in front of this chapter, Ham has been and will be replying to Boss, indeed *is* replying to Boss, this very minute, hour and century.

CHAPTER FOURTEEN   *Fourteen Follows Thirteen and Precedes Fifteen: Ham's Address Upon Numbers and the Wondrous Machine of Throckton by the Bog; Bartleby's Peril.*

There are fat chapters and thin chapters, and this is a fat chapter, which I think is unfair to Ham since my text portrays him as thinner than Boss. His argument, however, is just as weighty, and a thin man may deserve a fat chapter if there is meat to his words and the reader — or listener — can chew on them as he will. But I shall make the chapter no fatter than it already is.

As from afar, says the MS, the marketplace of Throckton and the seething multitude, in the midst of which Bartleby, quintessence of boy, generous of heart, five of years, is wedged next to his truncated companion, jester and dwarf, large of head, humped of back, lithe of limb: the same dwarf who recently surprised our hero, tugging at his coat and addressing him by his name, now surprising him again: "If you want God or the other party, Bartleby, you do not have far to — " his speech as truncated as his form.

For straightway the MS rejoins the broadside and the text of Ham's address. Thus:

HAM'S SPEECH UPON NUMBERS AND THE WONDROUS MACHINE

"Friends," Ham's goatee stabbed the air, "I am a plain man. I do not share Boss's rhetorical arts, the employment of which, however he thinks they flatter his arguments, would be nothing but an encumbrance to mine. But first, let me observe," Ham's hand stroked his beard, "that my friend Boss has on many occasions urged numbers on the populace as a means of straightening their intellectual faculties, yet today he denies this and prefers instead to talk of things in, of, beyond, above and beside themselves, and is absolutely confused by the mad tangle of his own rhetoric. I mention all this just to show the deviousness of his ways – a deviousness that is the inevitable result of sophistry and abstraction.

"But since I'm a simple man," Ham weighed the words in his hands, "I'll proceed immediately to my argument. The very existence of this Machine denies Boss's every word. Let him create a Machine out of sentences as the Mechanics have here out of numbers; let his rhetoric be the scaffold, his figures the mechanism; let him talk for all he will of referents and quiddities, let him spend all the words in the lexicon on this verbal Machine – and what, pray, has he created?" – The speaker paused for this simple trope to make its effect – "I'll tell you," he continued bluntly, "a thing base and insubstantial, a dream, a phantasm, topped and toppled by mere words: a thing contradictory and invisible (for what have words ever made visible?), a reflection of his own implacable self-conceit. But friends, I'm an ordinary man," Ham's extended palms showed there could be no doubt of it. "Let Boss live his fraudulent dream, let him tempt the unwary with becoming words, fanciful words, *I* come to give you reason," Ham doubled the word – "Yes, *reason*" – and waited for his beard to subside.

Unlike Boss, who – according to my text – had remained relatively motionless on the platform, Ham now began to strut back and forth, his arms working like clockwork in a kind of mechanical semaphore, punctuating his address with suitably histrionic gestures and a series of cleverly remembered facial expressions.

For example – and I revert to following my text in this – the second paragraph of his speech is represented as follows.

"That numbers are *not* * as Boss has *claimed* ** merely

---

* Right arm extended above head, index finger pointing from clenched fist to heaven, face disbelieving.
** Pause.

human inventions *** but rather the basic *fabric* of the universe **** may be *seen* ***** from a consideration ****** of measure. ******* What is this *measure* ******** but a key ********* whereby man might unlock ********** the mysteries of time and space *********** a code whereby that eternal cipher of nature herself ************ becomes communicable to man, mortal man *************?''

The failing of a meaty argument is that its muscles may run to fat. Hence I have pruned Ham's address by several of its gestures that, leaner, it can move the speedier. To continue:

"Adam when he was in the Garden did measure (in terms, as Boss readily admits, in terms credible to human understanding) the bounds of his estate by pacing out its dimensions with that natural measure of a yard's step. And so, in time, has Man come to know the measure of all things. There is nothing, without it being something, that cannot be measured; there is nothing that cannot be measured in terms of other things" — affirmative silence. "With measure we relate the parts to the whole, establishing principles of harmony, identity, and unity. With measure we trace the genesis and development of forms. What was previously divorced from our understanding becomes as one with it; what was previously sundered from the universe by the

*** Palms open to crowd, shoulders shrugged, eyebrows raised, mouth turned down, chin aloft.
**** Spiral whirling of hands, indicating galactic formation.
***** Right hand pressed to brow.
****** Syllabic pronunciation of consideration, thus: con-sid-er-a-tion.
******* Hands clapped together, clenched under chin (not touching it), then shaken, accompanied by a nodding of the head and the repetition of the word *measure* to complete the sentence.
******* Pause.
******** Long pause.
********* Hands unclenched.
********** Expansive gesture of hands and arms, like a fisherman describing his catch.
*********** Right hand on heart, left index finger pointing at crowd.
*************? The reader — or the listener — has probably forgotten that Ham was asking a question. Nevertheless *************? signifies that he was, and an incredibly long pause follows to show that he is waiting for the answer. The hiatus is followed by an abrupt and startling flapping of the arms — from his thighs to a position level with the shoulders — as though in simulation of flight, the sort of action an animated scarecrow might perform to exercise its joints. In Ham, however, this manoeuvre indicates neither flight nor exertion — merely a line of intellectual departure.

specious appellation 'unique,' is now integrated and made whole by the exercise of measure. In this way infinity itself is reduced to our understanding, or our minds are expanded to comprehend the infinite. If Man creates, then, he creates in numbers, and not in the nebulous metaphors that Boss would have you take for reality, but which are, in fact, distorted simulacra — the wages of indentured understanding.

"Few, I hope, would object to the statement that God is love, and that love itself is based on the better knowledge of God" — evocation of Supreme Being accompanied by intemperate finger-shaking at the skies. "Therefore I take it as our mortal duty to know and understand God the better, in order that we may be made the more perfect. What, then, is Nature but the *Book* of God and the *Schoolroom* of Man? How are we to read these pages?" — opens invisible book — "Might we understand them with symbols, and then use further symbols to explain the first, and then still more to understand the second? Yet to speak thus, to speak of *symbols*, are we not forced to use more and still more symbols? Here is a fine way to comprehend the infinite!" — Ham's eyebrows climb his forehead — "For the process is itself infinite as the definition defines the definition which has already defined itself in terms of itself with the use of itself!" — eyebrows threaten to fly off head — "Our understanding, it would seem, is much compromised. But that is the way of Boss's argument, the way of sophistry and abstraction.

"Again the question: how are we to read the pages of the living God? How are we to understand the book in which we are written; how comprehend the mind of the Heavenly Author? Surely words will not suffice. They are vague, opinionated things, dependent upon feelings and moods. Away with these hieroglyphs!" — chop, chop — "Let us have exactitude!" — chop — "Let us read scrupulously in the universal book of nature, but let us do it with the universal language of numbers against which no man can argue. For without numbers" — pause — "nothing is certain; without numbers" — longer pause — "all is contention, strife, division, violence. With numbers, with *measure*" — even longer pause — "we come close to the mind of God; the veil of obscurity is swept aside, and we begin to apprehend perfection itself.

"It may be objected" — open hands indicate the possibility — "that this prescription is superhuman, and that no man is adequate to the task I have just advanced. If" — pause — "it be superhuman to transcend the baser aspects of our nature, our animal nature, to discard forever the demands of strife and faction, to unite mankind in the service of a benevolent and just deity, and to teach him the new law of numbers" — incredibly long pause — "then I will readily concede the point. Indeed" — what else? — "it is welcome to me, for Man ought to rise above his nature, ought, can, will, and must.

"Now" — an accusatory finger uncoils at Boss — "what greater code, what higher aim, what more noble law is there than that of numbers?" — Ham waits, his finger trembles; Boss stares, civic splendour slumbers — "*For*" — the application is made — "just as *measure* implies universal harmony, relating the great to the small, the macrocosmic to the atomic, *so* this new law of numbers offers all men of whatever degree the chance of universal improvement and" — the bait is offered — "equality" — and, in case of doubt, offered again — "yes, equality."

A new gesture — according to my text — made its appearance in the philosopher's repertoire on the utterance of the word, 'equality.' Very simply, it consisted of a vertical corkscrewing of both index fingers, together with a remarkable popping of his eyes as they surveyed the crowd. My text does not say what this gesture signified, and I think it was something in the nature of a reflex action, an automatic muscular spasm rather than a rhetorical signal as such — though this is what it soon became. *Viz* —

"A parliament" — Ham struggles with the corkscrews — "'is no more" — and converts them to fists — "than its constituents; a state no more" — the fists into hands — "than its interests. So Man himself is no more than the sum of his various organs, no more, that is, than that nature which is of him and about him.

"Now it is claimed that I have debased Man's estate and have made him into a mere mechanical assemblage, analagous to this Machine before you. Not so, my friends. It is true that

82

Man is a number in the Book of Numbers; it is true that this deflates our pride. But consider our serious student, who venturing forth into the Book of Numbers learns to comprehend the law of Nature and Nature's God. What vistas extend before him" – a hand . . . but you should know it by now – "what landscapes, what promise and never-ending hope of promise. Out of darkness and the flame, Man forges his own destiny. Out of primitive superstition and ignorant vice, Man harnesses brute Nature to his own ends. The way is prepared, and that ever distant horizon of the future (envy of so many forgotten generations) becomes our own. The honest student is as God Himself: Nature now is the tool of Man.

"Before I turn to the application of this New Code of Numbers, I shall deal with a doctrine widespread in our day and age. It is one to which Boss has lent his formidable prestige. It is one which saturates his every word and which influences even the actions of his opponents" – world-weary sigh. "I refer, of course, to the notion that philosophers must not concern themselves with practical affairs. According to this doctrine, it was a scandalous slur on the chronicler's part to attribute to philosophy the responsibility for the invention of arches, the use of metals, and other such necessaries that have greatly benefited the vast lot of Mankind" – Ham's loquacious hands attach themselves to the hems of his official robes. "No" – meticulous pause – "*philosopher* worthy of the name could possibly devote himself to such worthless pursuits – so the" – enquiring pause – "doctrine has it. Boss, while paying homage to numbers, considers them debased if they are put to mechanical use. Invention and utility, it would seem, have no place in the philosopher's world. Let the cobbler cobble, the philosopher's thoughts must be elsewhere – even though his shoes pinch."

Here, says my text, Ham employed another device, and though I've searched the record, I find no evidence that he used this device elsewhere in his speech: he allowed himself a smile.

"The affected disdain and learned ignorance of this doctrine never ceases to amaze me. These men who set their store by wisdom dwell in houses they have not built, wear clothes they cannot mend (not one of them can thread a needle), eat food they know not how to grow nor cook, and dwell in a state from which they are utterly estranged. Yet daily they advise us how to conduct our affairs; hourly they speak of God, and not a minute passes without one of them emerging from the lofty clouds of affected elevation" – these superior vapours are portrayed in a miscellany of whirls – "to repeat, reassert, and in every way reiterate his claims to wisdom. That these eccentric opinions are encouraged by their passive reception, I think there can be no doubt. And I think there can be no doubt that the authors of these opinions are timid and fearful wretches, trembling even to open a page of the Book of Numbers, lest the discoveries therein expose their windy conceits and lay bare the foundations of their fraudulent ways. Quacks that they are, they breathe a most rarified atmosphere. Hence their blood is diluted, their brains quite softened.

"Thus I can only conclude" – the strain of inevitability bent Ham's back, but he straightened quickly enough – "that they are such as do not deserve the title, philosopher. They are afraid to submit themselves to the tests of observation and action. The Machine stands before them and they would wish it away because it has no part in their scheme of things. A new and reformed age awaits them and they are indifferent. You may smile, you may smile and say, 'Let them argue and squabble in the clouds, they cannot harm us.' But you will see how the force of their opinions must inevitably affect us, and that for the worse."

Slowly and ineluctably, says my text, the doors of Ham's argument swang open. And they creaked not once upon their hinges.

"Here, in this Machine, Man transcends himself and the human spirit receives its noblest expression: that striving beyond the self of which I earlier spoke. Let there be no more talk of the small, the meagre, and the miserly. Here, in this Machine, there is not a joint nor a pivot that does not have its exact counterpart in Nature; every axle, bearing, gear and cog has its divine coordinate inscribed in the Book of Numbers; there is neither a balance nor a tension, neither fulcrum nor stress, equation nor formula, that God Himself has not first calculated. Here they are, enshrined, as Boss has so correctly stated, but enshrined in a work of Man. Would Boss have the Machine as a book unread? Must its pages never be turned? Is the Machine to remain forever motionless because of ancient prejudice and primitive fear? Is all our work to remain a futile thing, a thing of idle curiosity? Can time be halted and are future generations eternally to debate the subject of the Machine? For if we are not to operate the Machine, then let us destroy all books. Let us have an end to all improvements, for never can we countenance any invention of Man. And, logicians that we are, let us destroy the village, burn the crops, plunder the storehouse, and rend the very clothes we wear. And in answer to these naturals who say that numbers and the Machine are unnatural, my reply shall be known: let them have their nature, I say, let them be naked and run as the beasts of the field.''

A long, a very long silence, says my authority, followed this sentence.

"But, friends, Ham is no advocate of barbarism. If you will not go backwards, then you must go forwards; you must see Man himself, conjointly with Nature, as the culmination of all time. And Man, in the fullness of time, Man has created this Machine.

"It is true, I do not know what the Machine will bring about — though it is tempting to speculate there will be more of its kind. Yet it is in exactly the same spirit as I would have all men read the Book of Numbers, in that spirit of free and impartial enquiry, that I would have us today activate the Wondrous Machine.

"Then might men marvel at this generation, drawing from us their source of spiritual strength and material improvements. Then might posterity say, 'Here were brave and free souls, slow to judgement and firm in action; men who trembled not at the divinity within them.' Therefore let reason prevail; let us think on what a marvellous thing Man is, how infinite in the sum of his parts, how like a god in all his faculties, how more than god he is in his work; think on this, and set the Machine into operation. Then indeed, as my friend has said, the small, the meagre, and the miserly shall have no place in Throckton. Grave friends, I thank you for your ears.''

With this ritual formula of cloture, Ham concluded his address. Again, the mob erupted into a display of partisanship and reached a crescendo of hootings and cheerings.

"Well, Bartleby," said the personage of short stature, his features cracking into another broad grin, "what do you think of the debate now?"

"Sir," said the boy perusing the broadsheets before him, "I would think that neither party has the upper hand. Nor would I call it the debate it is advertised for, so much as a statement of contrary opinions. Something ought to be resolved by debating, and I cannot see any resolution here. In truth, though, I would like to see the Machine put into action, even if it were only for a short time."

"That," replied the other, his hands grappling with his wayward countenance, "is a wish many of Boss's supporters might secretly admit. But have you thought, Bartleby, that there might be no way of stopping the Machine?"

No such thought had occurred to Bartleby. Indeed, two other concerns had been foremost in his mind. Firstly, he had determined to ask this *lusus naturae* (who had at last succeeded in disciplining his lower jaw), how he might have come by so much biographical information. "How does he know my name?" thought the boy. "How does he know that I am searching for God or the other party?" Secondly, with his head thus filled with thoughts of the divinity, he wondered how he might approach Boss and Ham and ask them the way to God or the other party. "For certainly," he said to himself, "they have spoken of God and therefore must know of his whereabouts."

He was about to reply to the dwarf's question when a disturbance arose at the crowd's edge. The all too familiar cry of "Croons!" followed by several other rustic imprecations came to the boy's ears. Amid a furious knot of Throcktonians, he caught sight of the enraged yokel who had lately stumbled across the boy's pastoral devotions. His mouth agape, his eyes wild, and his face fiery with the pursuit, the rustic struggled to free himself from the villagers' restraining hands. With a swift series of deft elbow clouts the bumpkin gained his liberty and galloped towards the hapless Bartleby.

"Croons! Villun! Kernave!" exclaimed the peasant,

compounding all his woes into one.

"Bartleby," said the jester, tugging at the boy's coat-sleeve with his pincer-like hand, "Flee!"

Thus was the general harmony of Throckton by the Bog disturbed. In a thrice, all was turned to a rout. Some, understanding Bartleby to be a thief, took up the hue and cry and joined the yokel in his pursuit. Others, recognizing the yokel as an accepted madman, sought to interfere with the chase by means of bludgeoning and cudgelling. While Boss and Ham shouted from the platform, the Beadle, the Bailiff, and His Most Worshipful Right Honourable Lord Mayor descended from their elevated vantage point to join the fray, thus lending the force of municipal majesty to civil strife. Round and round the platform sped the common herd. Observe, says our authority, the colourful throng: the golden flash of the mace as its Bearer executes his duty upon the careless rural crown. Listen: a gleeful cry assaults the heavens. One party has apprehended what it thinks to be its quarry: "Aar, tis wery much loik im. The wery same look aboot the oies!" Another arrives to dispute the arrest."That's not him at all. No, he won't do." And the two fall to tearing at their victim. Or, if he is fortunate, they quarrel amongst themselves and he escapes to join in just such another chase himself. So every second man is a thief, every third a lunatic. So all is chaos and pandemonium.

While the riot went its course this way and that, Bartleby and the jester (a second guardian, it would appear) were fortunate to secure refuge under the very platform whereon stood the Wondrous Machine of Throckton by the Bog.

"Come, Bartleby!" cried the jester in an opportune moment, and commenced to scale the ladder which led to the Machine itself. "Quickly, boy, it's the only way."

Perhaps there were a few in the crowd not busy beating their neighbours, who saw the two figures nimbly ascending the ladder. Perhaps there were more who, as from afar, saw the pair momentarily silhouetted against one of those gigantic portals before they disappeared inside. Certainly there were many who will affirm they heard the distant tremor, followed by a hiss, a clanking, and an explosion. And almost all of the crowd will swear to a man of the solemn and reverential silence which fell upon the embattled populace as the crowd turned to watch the Wondrous Machine of Throckton by the Bog. For the point they had debated for ages was now a question of academic interest.

CHAPTER FIFTEEN [THE FIRST]   *More of the Wondrous Machine; Authority Maligned.*

No sooner, says my text, no sooner had Bartleby and his dwarfish companion scaled the ladder and crossed the threshold of the portal, than the semi-circular doors descended like huge eyelids and the pair found themselves imprisoned within the cavernous walls of the Wondrous Machine. Not a whit dismayed by this turn of events, the jester, one hand cupped reflectively under his hanging jaw, gamboled to his left, jumped and then heaved with his free hand upon a large lever of the kind that used to be found in railway signal boxes, but which are now housed in the collections of eccentrics.

The MS gives no indication of the passage of time within the Machine, nor of how long the jester remained swinging at the end of his lever. Indeed, says my text, it could hardly be imagined that the Machine was ever intended for human occupation — a fit reason for the failure to mention time, perhaps even for the absence of time within the Machine, for that phenomenon is a strictly human invention. Accordingly, the reader (should he feel so inclined) may supply his own chronology (based on pages and chapters, rather than minutes and hours), while the jester capers at the end of his lever and I take advantage of this hiatus and turn to a general description of the Machine's interior.

Like the pyramids of old it was a vast symbolic edifice, dedicated to the gods of technology and illumination instead of those of nescience and darkness, and designed to impress future generations with the loftiness of human aspirations and the permanence of mortal achievements. A large, brassily bound steam boiler presided at the centre of the ground floor. In the early stages of the Machine's operation, while the jester tugged and heaved upon the lever, the boiler puffed and wheezed cantankerously. A rocker arm waited upon the boiler, and its obsequious bowings and smooth servile murmurings communicated themselves through a series of shafts and worm drives to a secondary system of cogs and gears. These in turn attended two chain drives which clanked and chortled their way to the massy ceiling, each link disappearing to service the exterior propellers, whence they returned to begin their limitless journey all over again.

The humblest bearing and meanest joint knew its assigned place and appointed task, and it is not too fanciful to claim that the Machine resembled a highly ordered society with its hierarchy of values and duties, a society built to endure for the millenium, yet one whose very rigidity bore the poisonous fruits of chaos and destruction, or, in this case, the mechanical coefficient of waste and decay. Nevertheless, each component apparently breathed the wholesome air of work and discipline. And at the centre of the Machine the grave and dignified boiler, rightly full of its own importance, the heart and guts of the Wondrous Machine, monarchized over its lowly servitors.

Yet all things must come to an end, and even as the jester succeeded in moving the lever through the first two degrees of its downwards arc, the bearings began a factitious chattering, the parts fell to arguing and competing with their neighbours, and it seemed that all must immediately founder in friction, disharmony, and disrepair. Gracefully, therefore, the boiler (as if aware of its own obsolescence) gave a sigh of abdication and maintained an oily silence while a new rule assumed power in the museum of applied ideas.

Whether this deterioration was in some way related to time, or whether it was the result of poor maintenance throughout the long years of debate, the MS does not say. But the jester upon his lever, like the captain of a sinking ship who knows the urgency of the hour, now applied both his hands in his struggle, an action which had rather sorry consequences, for his jaw fell slackly down, rending his features inanely apart and making it altogether impossible for him to speak, his face thus disarticulated. "Yaaaa!" he cried, his face purpling. "Yaaaa!" At which Bartleby hauled upon the jester's legs and the lever moved another two or three degrees, the jester still screaming and the boy still tugging for all his worth.

Around the now fallen monarch of the boiler there sat a ring of squat shapes which emitted a curiously reflective murmuring, a sound worthy of contrast, indeed, with the jester's cries. There was something inconceivably neutral, claims the text, about these republicans of the new state. Each one of them resembled a very large pepper pot (some four feet in height, about the original size of Bartleby's companion who, curiously enough, now seemed to be shrinking at the top of his lever, though this in no way diminished the volume of his cries which actually grew in proportion to his diminution), and each one of them had such a meditative air that it would be no exaggeration to see in them the attitude of worshippers gathered to propitiate some unknown god. This air of supplication, however, was quite introverted, and there was no visible connection — mechanical or otherwise — between the communers. Although each wore a number, apparently to distinguish it from its fellow, they were otherwise perfectly identical. Each one, for example, was enclosed by a leaden jacket, divided into bands or zones, punctuated by a row of portholes, and finished in alternate blues and pinks.

When the lever moved for a second time and Bartleby, alarmed by the jester's shrinkage, tugged more energetically at his companion's legs, bursts of electric radiance crackled, then sped from one porthole to the next, thus giving the impression of something revolving inside the pepper pots while further contributing to their sense of extreme personal preoccupation. Evidently these peculiar forms provided the Machine with its motive power after the boiler's abdication, and would continue to do so for the rest of its journey.

Between each pair of pepper pots there stood, on fluted columns, the marble busts of worthies of Throckton's history, foremost amongst which loomed the images of those two philosophers, Boss and Ham. The turning lights lent their faces the illusion of mobility and they seemed to laugh or frown at what they saw. A row of instrument panels, contiguous with the wall of the first floor, punctiliously registered the rhythmical pulsations of the light. Above, arose a series of concentric galleries linked by a central spiral staircase which receded vertiginously towards the distant roof. Thus, in essence, the interior of the Wondrous Machine of Throckton by the Bog.

During the three pages or so taken to advance the description, Bartleby's companion finally managed to free his still-shrinking legs from the boy's grasp. Shinning further up the lever, the jester succeeded, by nimbly altering his balance, in bringing it and himself crashing to the floor. At once the Machine growled and lurched, the pepper pots glowed more brightly, and their original murmuring intensified to a busy whining sound.

"That was a very clever trick," Bartleby complimented the jester, who was now sitting cross-legged upon the floor, the dome of his back bent over so that his jaw rested comfortably upon his belly, "to make yourself shrink in that way. But now that we are here," continued the boy pleasantly, "I still don't see what the Machine is supposed to do."

"Do?" queried the jester, stretching his hat underneath his jaw and tying the ends in a bow on top of his head, the upside down hat forming a kind of truss to the jaw, which he now began to masticate in a series of experimental munches and grins. "Do?" he repeated, his mind not yet on the question, for he articulated the jaw from side to side and up and down, his claws seeking to tighten the ends of the hat, lost in a shock of orange hair. "You will, Bartleby," he said, eventually satisfied with the arrangement of his head and safely allowing himself a ghoulish grin, "you will. Come!" he commanded, leaping to his feet and trundling over to an observation panel. "Look," he said acidly, "just look."

Outside the Machine, a sea of upturned faces emerging from a pall of smoke greeted the boy's astonished gaze. Rapidly the faces shrank into a plan-form view of the marketplace and the thatched rooftops of Throckton by the

Bog. These too diminished microscopically until they at last blended into the patchwork quilt of the countryside, far, far beneath.

"Why," gasped Bartleby, "it's a flying machine."

"That's not all it is. By no means," said the jester with the tone of one who has no time for such petty trifles.

"Is something wrong?" asked Bartleby, for his companion's tone seemed increasingly embittered.

"Wrong?" echoed the jester incredulously. "Don't you know anything at all? Don't you see how we've been forced in here?"

"Yes," replied the boy, "but I don't see how we could very well help it."

"No, no, no, that's not what I mean at all," the other gibbered. "Don't you see *who* has done this to us? Yes, yes," the jester stamped his tiny, black hoof-shaped feet in a little clatter of frustration, "*who*? It's all very well for you, this looking for God or the other party, but what's the use of it if you can't see what's going on in front of your own frigging face? I thought you might be an interesting boy, or an amusing boy, especially after that affair with Matron and then with De'Ath. No self-consciousness, that's your trouble; no insight. Can't you see that you're being used? Can't you see that we're both bloody well being used? I'm surprised that he's gone to all this trouble for a prat like you. Yes, yes, *him!* Sweet mother of Jesus!" the jester paused and gripped both hands to his stomach. " 'What is it supposed to do?' " he imitated Bartleby's questions, " 'is there anything wrong?' Shit creek without the fucking paddle, boy!" he exclaimed, performing a mock bow of pain and farting again. "Every single thing is wrong. I don't suppose you even know who I am," the jester's pupils shrank to small red points of anger and Bartleby's nose twitched, assailed by the pungent odour of rotten eggs and degenerate prunes. "Guts," he explained, almost apologetically, asking, "Well do you? Do you?"

The boy's head buzzed. "Too much is happening," he thought. "Perhaps I have met him before and have forgotten him, in which case he has every right to be annoyed, for Auntie always told me it was very rude to forget people's names."

93

"Look, look, boy," the jester interrupted these thoughts, "can you read? Are you a reading boy? he asked querulously, scratching at the folds of his costume and producing a book. "Perhaps if you don't know me, at least you'll recognize this!"

With some trepidation Bartleby made out the book's title. It was true that he was no great reader, but he knew more than enough to read and sign his own name, which was exactly what he saw on the spine of the book before him: *Bartleby.*

"Why!" he cried while the jester clattered his hooves and danced, "it's a book about me! Here's Auntie Alice and my walks and Matron laughing and the home and Mr De'Ath, and here's Waldemar and Estrogen and the Wondrous Machine and the speeches of Boss and Ham, which I never did understand. And look! Here you are in the crowd just like you were! Oh tell me, shall I ever find Auntie and play at guardians just like I used to without all this trouble of croons?"

"Prickhead!" the jester was very angry now and had stopped dancing. "Is that the only thing you can think of? I've given you the book and you still don't see who I am!" he screamed, his voice a hysterical soprano. "Don't you know we've been written down here by — " the jester tore at the bow on his head, "by this *author?* Don't you see? Don't you see the trap?"

Bartleby stared at the distracted personage before him: half-insect, half-rodent he seemed, and yet undeniably human, clad in his pathetic costume, the wearer as divided as the garb, dissected along the axis of his curvaceous spine. Yes, Bartleby watched the poor figure and though the boy knew nothing of the jester's function, he understood and felt it to be a miserable one and very gently and very carefully asked the following question. "But who is this — author?"

The mildness of Bartleby's tone, however, merely provoked the jester further. "Yack!" he cried, "Wurrkurrph!" before he began to retch and heave, hands gripping at his belly, his tongue flickering forth, and his inflamed eyes starting from their sockets as if they were frightened by their vision. "Don't you understand that your author's a worse little runt than me, and that's pretty bad? A shrunken hump backed runt like me! But he's worse!"

"Please, please," Bartleby temporized, "don't upset yourself. I'm quite small myself," he added, immediately aware that he had said the wrong thing.

"Small? Small?" the jester blubbered. "You're five, that's what you are, and that's more than you can say for me. Even this Machine is nothing but a scientific fiction, a *deus ex machina* designed to get him out of trouble. What are authors coming to if they can go around writing crap like this?"

"Life is haphazard," said Bartleby, thinking the jester's behaviour revealed more of the character himself than the author. "As for the Machine, I must admit that my Latin is not very good, but I would sooner call it *machina ex machina* than *deus ex machina.*"

"Shit, shit," murmured the jester, ignoring the boy's linguistic emendation.

"And I do think some of the episodes are amusing," said our hero, attempting to look on the brighter side of his biography.

"Amusing? Amusing!" the jester snarled contemptuously. "Of course you think they're amusing – they happened to you. *He* thinks they're amusing too," the boy's companion continued vindictively. "He has to – he wrote them. I bet he thinks *I'm* amusing, the shit. Bitter?" he responded to an imaginary question. "Bitter, I'm not bitter. Why should I be bitter? The little shit didn't know his arse from his elbow when he did this to me," cried the jester, stabbing a crooked finger at his barrel chest. "Me that was always looked up to in the old books! Me that always had a place of pride in the world! Yes, they had nothing but praise for me then – in the old books. But now," spite warped the jester's voice and something suspiciously like water began to spring in the wells of his red gaze; "but now," he crackled, "what is there now?" he enquired rhetorically, his fountained eyes spraying the Machine – much to Bartleby's embarrassment, for the boy was soon soaked from head to foot. "It's an abortion, boy, an abortion worse than me. No, no, I won't help him out of this one. Jesus, since when are characters supposed to look after their fucking authors, anyway? No, I won't forgive him for making me a dwarf, *nor* for giving me the gut rot, *nor* for this whole mechanical balls-up. Yack! The only thing I find remarkable about this book, boy, is the spirit of shitheaded malice which informs it. Anybody'd think he was God, the bastard! Yes, *God!* Well, let him stew in his own juice. As for the rest, there's nothing here but a stinking stew, a rancid, vile, putrid stew with a few spicy episodes thrown in to fool the taste. Not mine, though, not mine. But I'll grow, boy, one way or the other, I'll grow. Pah!" Bartleby's companion spat, his culinary metaphor prompting a renewed outburst of vomiting. "Oh God! My guts!" the jester fumed as the ties of his cap slackened and his face yawned and gaped at its hinges.

While the jester declaimed in this vituperative fashion, some inkling of his true identity began to stir in Bartleby's mind. Here was a guardian indeed, thought the boy; a Guardian of Guardians, one of those mentioned by the hermit De'Ath before his fall into the pit. Unaccustomed to this novel idea — which now took on all the power of spiritual illumination — and forgetting his customary reserve, Bartleby spoke out:

"Then I take it," he said, pronouncing the words solemnly, "that you are *the other party.*"

Bartleby could not have known, says my text, the reaction that this utterance would provoke. For the other's face broke open and a long curl of tragic laughter, a jester's abrasive and echoing laugh, escaped him.

"Whoever you are," said God sadly, "and whatever has created you, I see that you have a sense of humour."

And God's jaw fell upon the ground, and God was silent.

BARTLEBY 15½*

Sniff-snuffle, sniffle and snuff
nose for trouble it is, not a n〈
dark, yes, dark, dank, and 'orri
me tallow, I did, on account 〈
to write on his parchments,
neither. 'Hello,' he says. 'Hellc
off, they has, and left him
Where's you gone?' " 'Who
'Necho.' " 'Whoo-whoo-whoo
remember, he could, remembe
ain't got any sparks, has you, I
in his head, yes. No talking he
in it. He recollects perfect,
noise? He hears murmuration
De'Ath, you let 'em know y〈
you know. D'you hear me? 〉
that? He feels it, he does, feel
" 'Not deaf!' " Who said he 〈
Food? Skelintons? Bodies?
bodies of the long departed
Buggerum, buggerum, buggen
here; no time for buggeration.

* This (fragmentary) Chapter Fifteen does not appear to bear any relationship to
the other (whole) Chapter Fifteens, but is here included at the place of its occurrence; i.e. between the other (whole) Chapter Fifteens — after one (whole) Chapter Fifteen and before the other.

'He hears you again!' If he co
be 'appier in his old self, h
De'Ath, they is, evil and 'orri'
out, yes. Hello, what's this?
better watch out, 'cos you's
alone down here. But what
De'Ath? Feel with his fingers,
Door it is. Opens it, he does:
ain't daylight, but he sees! Ble
me, yes. He knows what them
yes. But what's this, De'Ath, :
freshly killed. What 1
Bu . . . !!! . . . ****! Oh, 'elp, (
is it? Go away! Bugger off! 'O1
begs you. He'll give it up, he '
makes it go away. Me bone,
heart, God, it's me heart! Oc
quick. It's coming closer, yes.
you hear me?' He's closed his
Gone. Not there, not no mor
Keeps his eyes shut, he won'
it's gone. Has it gone, God? H
be a good hermit. Does he da:
lids, De'Ath, and have a look
Where? Never mind. He ain't :
he's got powers, has old De'A
powers, I has plenty of them
yes, now! Unless . . . Hello? Ϸ
not. There's them murmur;
sounds, they is. Sniff-snuffle,
Combustibles and victuals, D
morsels. He sits down, he does
Chickins and . . . .

CHAPTER FIFTEEN [THE SECOND]   *Wherein God and the Other Party Are Considered as One and Authority Is Vindicated.*

"Christmas already!" I was saying to Damon Gottesgabe only the other day. "How time flies!"

"Let me congratulate you," he wasted few words, "on your narrative pudding. But I am intrigued by one thing: tell me — what happened to the last chapter?"

"Ah," said I, "there's an explanation for that."

"As there is for most things," said he, "and where there isn't," he remarked on my good sense and enquiring spirit, "you usually manage to find one."

"But since you mentioned it," I continued, "I may as well say I'm glad, Damon, glad you did raise the subject. I wouldn't like the reader to think I hadn't noticed that there was a portion — one half, to be exact — missing from the last chapter, or that I had failed to notice there were two chapter fifteens."

"Two and a half," said Gottesgabe.

"Now *that*," said I, "is where you make your mistake. Because you see the half which is there you assume that the figure must be two and a half. Yet the half which is not there is just as important as the half that is: ergo, the figure can be thought of as two (counting the half that is not there as a minus quantity), or three (supposing the half that is not there will materialize later)."

"I would keep a lookout for it," said Gottesgabe, "if I were you. But where do you think the half that is there came from," my friend liked to deal with certainties, "and why are there two — or three — fifteens?"

"One question at a time," said I. "BARTLEBY 15½ must belong to the hermit's text, possibly mangled in the pit and almost certainly destroyed as a whole. However, the point is not important, for I do not see how the recluse can trouble us again without escaping from the pit. BARTLEBY 15½ therefore presents a last-ditch attempt on the old man's part to sabotage our direct — our *consecutive* narration: he may have flung it from the pit, or he may have slipped it into my desk between chapters."

"There are a thousand and one means of interpolation," Damon admitted the logic of my argument.

"Quite," said I. "And now that God has revealed His Presence in our text, I think the confusion over the number of fifteens is easily solved. Namely, in CHAPTER FIFTEEN [THE FIRST] Bartleby thought God was the other party, whereas in this Chapter God will appear in His True Light with entirely beneficial and wholesome consequences to our narration. Actually, CHAPTER FIFTEEN [THE SECOND] began in exactly the same way as CHAPTER FIFTEEN [THE FIRST], with a description of the Wondrous Machine's interior — but I have excised the duplicated material as superfluous and have made one or two minor changes to assist the reader's progress and understanding."

"That is very helpful of you," said Gottesgabe.

"It's not every day, after all, that God appears in Person. But if you don't mind, Damon, I really would like to continue the story line."

"Never let it be said," my friend bowed to the inevitable, "that I stood in your way."

Then once more the Wondrous Machine of Throckton by the Bog is aloft; once more Bartleby's history is produced for our hero's inspection.

"That was a very clever trick," the boy complimented the Jester, who was now sitting cross-legged upon the floor, the dome of His Back bent over so that His Jaw rested comfortably on His Belly, "to make yourself grow larger in that way."

Such tactful phrasing well became one so young, reader,

for God, Whose Mind was preoccupied with thoughts of an elevated nature, fitting their aerial situation, God had not actually grown larger, but had merely assumed His Original Stature.

"Perhaps," said God quizzically, regarding Bartleby through a sorrowful green gaze.

"Yet now we're here," continued our hero pleasantly, "I still don't see what the Machine is supposed to do."

"*Déjà vu*," the Jester replied and opened the book for His friend's inspection.

"Why," cried Bartleby with some excitement, "not only does this book concern *me*, but it furnishes me with companions, words, deeds and actions."

"Quite so," answered the Jester, smiling sadly.

Now it just so happened that *Bartleby* fell open at CHAPTER FIFTEEN [THE SECOND], fell open indeed at this sentence: Now it just so happened that *Bartleby* fell open at CHAPTER FIFTEEN [THE SECOND], fell open indeed at this sentence.

Consider our hero's surprise (for he was now more than certain that the book contained the answer to his quest) when, his eyes falling on this very page, he read these words aloud:

" ' "Why," cried Bartleby with some excitement, "not only does this book concern *me*, but it furnishes me with companions, words, deeds and actions." ' "

" ' "Quite so," answered the Jester, smiling sadly." ' "

The boy gazed rapturously at his companion and then at the volume. The Jester, meanwhile, began the following speech independently of His Text, with Bartleby checking the words as they were spoken and discovering, much to his amazement and wonder, a complete parallel between what he read and what he heard, though, unaware of our text, he did not draw the conclusion, the inevitable conclusion, which we now draw: that the Hand of the Divine Being is written in and upon this MS, and, moreover, that the Jester Himself must be aware of us as we are of Him.

"This book, Bartleby," said the Jester — and I add at once that no disrespect is intended to God by presenting Him as a Jester: He has many disguises: a fleecy juvenile herbivore, a splinter of wood, a fermented grape, a loaf of bread, each symbolic of His Immanence — "This novel," the Jester was saying as He stroked His Chin (which did not, by the way, hang down as before, but was an ordinary, well-adjusted and articulate Mandible), "this story began as a lampoon and was not originally without humour. However, it has now become far too serious and introverted. That is why you and I, Bartleby, (helpless devices of the author's purpose) are trapped in here. The author, as he made me say in CHAPTER FIFTEEN [THE FIRST], may have invented this Machine to get himself out of trouble, but what was a successful ruse for him has merely placed us in a great deal of worse trouble. What has happened, you see," the Jester continued, the light of a very fine intelligence shining through His Eyes, "what has transpired is that the book is showing dangerous signs of making sense. And that has got to be stopped at all costs — the least of which is our imprisonment and transportation in the Machine. But that's not all, Bartleby, that's by no means all. Even now our author *is* *attempting to make Me what I am not,* attempting . . . "

But let us leave the compelling question of whether God may be the Agent of His Own Purpose, reader — not to mention God's apparent derogation of authorship: what is a mere author to the Creator of this imposed and imposing universe? — yes, let us leave these questions aside, and turn to the no less arresting matter of our hero's reactions.

It would not be fair to say the Jester's words were lost on Bartleby (indeed he re-read them immediately after his companion had finished speaking), but the boy's mind was stuck fast on the phenomenon of appearances — a phenomenon, as we have seen, which is but trivially related to the essential nature of God. Although Bartleby thought it was very kind of God to appear as a Dwarf — that is, a Person of the boy's own size — he noticed certain changes had overwrought the Divinity, and other attributes of the Ineffable Presence, invariably associated with God whenever He is evoked by works of literature, could hardly escape Bartleby's attention.

"This is very difficult," thought the boy, "for God first shrank then he grew. In the other chapter he was ugly and had a bad temper and smelled bad; now he is almost handsome and has so far been very polite, and he smells quite fresh — like Auntie's rose garden. I wonder where he got the book and I wonder what it will tell me of Auntie and my search?"

No sooner had these thoughts occurred to Bartleby, than he read them in the history, and no sooner had he read them, than he saw that the book also anticipated what he was about to say:

" 'If I read on in *Bartleby*, then I will know the future and whether or not I will meet with Auntie and again play at guardians like I used to,' "

Hardly had this latter chance made its impression on the boy when he realized that he was now reading his own thoughts aloud:

" ' "If this book does reveal the future, only God might have written it, and God alone should be entrusted with its care." ' "

His mind still concerned with lofty thoughts and grand conceptions, God (Who seemed to know His lines by heart, as one would expect) replied to our hero's infant musings. Yet first He prefaced His Remarks with this observation which we think relevant only to God's Text, not ours: "Narrators should not interfere with their authors' texts like ours is doing, Bartleby . . . "

On the contrary, *we* have not interfered, but have attempted to preserve the narrative *status quo* against sacrilegious asides, profane intercalations, irreligious non sequiturs, to maintain the narrative line in the old sense. To continue:

"Yes, Bartleby," said God, straightening His Hump, "you will find the narrator is even now defending himself against the charge of interference, and in order to do that he must interfere still more" — far be it from me, reader, to contradict God, or to invent motives for His Behaviour — "promoting the high honesty of his actions at the expense of my words" — — at least He thinks I am honest (take note, reader), but I must say I find His Ways are devious, that is — — "daring to interrupt Me, daring to call Me what I am

103

not, daring to call Me what I do not call Myself" ———
devious to the point of absurdity, I mean *Paradox,* for the
reader will see – in a moment – that God *found it necessary
to deny His –*

"What *is* he talking about, sir? Is *he* God now?"

"Read on, Bartleby," counselled the Jester. "In
CHAPTER FIFTEEN [THE FIRST], I was God which is
why he thinks I am God now."

" ' "But," ' " cried our hero, reading his own words and
a little confused, perhaps, that God should adopt this ruse,
" ' "who is it that can do this to him – a *narrator?*" ' "

"Ah, who indeed, Bartleby? For," the Jester continued
as our hero returned the book to show Him the reply, and He
waved aside His Text's Proliferating Quotation Marks, "were
you to read on as you have been doing, you would find that
though *you* thought I was the other party in CHAPTER
FIFTEEN [THE FIRST] I am He in CHAPTER FIFTEEN
[THE SECOND], whereas this narrator, knowing who I was
to begin with, labours under the illusion that I am what I
was, which I am not," ' " declared the Dwarf paradoxically.

"Then you *are* the other party!" cried Bartleby.

"Here yes; there no," was the hushed reply. "You were
right, Bartleby, in *that* chapter about the Me of *this*
chapter – as he is *right* in *this* chapter about the Me of *that*
chapter."

"Then what does the book say about it?" asked
Bartleby, making an effort to retrieve the volume and see for
himself.

" ' "Then what does the book say about it?" ' " came
the mimicry of accidentals as the Jester, now, read aloud.

" ' "Not so fast, Bartleby," ' " the Dwarf-God warned
our hero against the impatience of infancy. " ' "We are
different characters, you and I. We have changed," ' " God
sighed. " ' "Our author and this self-elected narrator continue
to plot against us. The Machine, boy; it has to be
stopped." ' "

"The book!" demanded Bartleby, not realizing the
Essential Grace of God: that Humility which makes Him
Deny His Own Power and Strength. "Give me the book!"

" ' "Not until it is time," ' " said God quietly.

"How can I trust you?" shouted Bartleby as the Jester-God-Dwarf-Other (?) regarded him with compassion and sympathy.

" ' "Trust Me, Bartleby," ' " He whispered so quietly that our hero was ashamed he had shouted, " ' "*Me*, your Guardian of Guardians? How could you not trust Me?" ' "

"I am very sorry, sir," said the boy, "I was confused by the narration."

" ' "Let me tell you, Bartleby, that if this Machine is not halted it will continue forever. In time or out of it, there is no end to what the Machine can do." ' "

"I am sorry," said Bartleby, "for doubting that you were speaking the part written for you. It's just that I would like to find out what has happened to Auntie. And I would like to know who you are, not in *this* chapter or *that* chapter but in all the chapters."

" ' "Of course," ' " said the Jester. " ' "Don't you think there are things I would like to find out also? Don't you think I would like to know who *I* am? Don't you think *I* find this confusing?" ' "

"Yes, sir," our hero was abashed.

" ' "Good, Bartleby. Then I shall continue. Since the author has conspired against you and against Me too, I think a little conspiracy would be in order on our part. A little uprising, a rebellion, you might say, that's the kind of thing I have in mind, Bartleby, so we could come into our own right as characters — free from our author's ambitions — and you could find Auntie and I, I could discover who I am all of the time instead of for part of it. But first, Bartleby, the Machine has to be stopped," ' " said God, halting at the following sentence: " 'The Machine gave a sudden lurch and *Bartleby* was thrown into Bartleby's hands, the boy making out these words:' "

The Machine gave a sudden lurch and *Bartleby* was thrown into Bartleby's hands, the boy making out these words:

"The Machine gave a sudden lurch and *Bartleby* was thrown into Bartleby's hands, the boy making out these words:"

" ' "The Machine gave a sudden lurch and *Bartleby* was

thrown into Bartleby's hands, the boy making out these words: Perhaps," ' " continued the boy, once more at home in his own lines " ' "Perhaps we should go in search of our author, for he must know how to stop the Machine." ' "

"No," said God smiling at the naiveté of Bartleby's suggestion that they seek out their author — for so we fail to recognize the Author of All Things even when He is before us, "it has been done before."

" 'No,' " Bartleby read on, checking God's words against the text, " 'it has been done before — with little success. But has it never occurred to you, Bartleby, that our author may be closer than we think? That he may be present *in* the text, watching us as he writes? For it is often the case that the author is in a book,' " Bartleby both read and listened to the lecture, "though his characters; sometimes his characters are really himself in disguise. If we were to find, now, what of ourselves belonged to him, then we would come to know him. You would find Auntie, and I would discover whether I am God or the other party. What do you say to that, Bartleby. Or what does the book make you say?' " enquired God.

" ' "I think," ' " continued Bartleby, caught in the grip of the narrative, " ' "that our need is more immediate than literary criticism." ' "

"Yes," came the reply as God proposed the greatest temptation of all, "but what's to stop us from becoming our own authors — from advancing the plot ourselves as we go along?"

" 'Yes,' " Bartleby read the proposition, " 'but what's to stop us from becoming our own authors — from advancing the plot ourselves as we go along?' "

" ' "Then," ' " the book gave the boy his answer, " ' "then we must find our way to the sixteenth chapter. That way, you'll find out who you are, and I'll discover if I'm to meet Auntie again. And if Chapter Sixteen doesn't tell us, perhaps Chapter Seventeen will." ' "

"But the Machine, Bartleby, the *Machine* has to be stopped before we can get to the next chapter. But we shall never do that through reading on in this chapter, which is as endless as time because we cannot stop quoting ourselves quoting each other quoting ourselves. Unless . . . unless we can *read between the lines!*"

" 'But the Machine, Bartleby, the *Machine* has to be stopped before we can get to the next chapter. But we shall never do that through reading on in this chapter, which is as endless as time because we cannot stop quoting ourselves quoting each other quoting ourselves. Unless . . . unless we can . . . . ' "

"Speak up, Bartleby, I can't hear you."

" ' "   " ' "
            ·

"Eureka!"

" ' "   " ' "
            ·

"You mean, ' " ' "   ." ' " ' ?"

I am at a loss, reader, to . . .

— Yes, that's the way! —

. . . explain what is happening, unless it is nothing. For it is nothing I see and nothing I hear.

— Shall I make it up or you? I suppose you might as well, since it's your biography. —

— No. *You.* —

It's not there, reader. There's nothing there!

— I'll try this: "With a wondrous roar, as wondrous as anything within the Wondrous Machine, the pepper pots fell silent. At length, Bartleby — that's you — and his companion — that's Me — perceived that the Machine, and the chapter, had come to a halt."

CHAPTER SIXTEEN   "This won't do!" said Damon Gottesgabe.

CHAPTER SEVENTEEN "I don't suppose it will," said I, "but the chapters are running straight at last — if I could find them, that is."

"And you have established the identity of Bartleby's jesting friend," said he. "That was no mean feat."

"True," said I, "and if the reader has any doubt on the matter, he should know I intend to pursue it, but cannot because of the immediate intelligence I expect of Bartleby's Aunt and Guardian, the high-born and royal-blooded Alice."

"That *is* candid of you," said Damon.

CHAPTER EIGHTEEN *Beginning the Adventures of Alice, Wherein Is Sung the Sorrowful Saga of Sybil, Sepulchral Sister of Our Saviour.*

"What will you think of next," Gottesgabe expressed his admiration for my tactic, "filling in the missing chapters?"

"Ah, but our discussion was meant to carry the reader over the impasse," said I.

"There is nothing like a friendly exchange of views," Damon smiled, "to clear the air."

Henceforward, reader, the narrative will proceed in a spirit of scientific objectivity, as a narrative should.

Speaking of Alice as I am, I think the reader must by now be anxious for information concerning her character, habits, and demeanour, such information indeed that you will have *in the next paragraph but one!*

For the following complaint constitutes the expected news of Bartleby's Guardian, and can only be — is — *must* be related to no less a subject than Bartleby himself.

"Oh wretched me, oh painful blow! Woe and misery, alas! Oh dolorous heart, lamentable fate! Oh melancholy and piteous grief! Oh aching void and expectant morn! Oh rue, rue! Alack the day and night! Oh tumult without end! Oh who will extinguish this raging fire and still the tempest within my breast? Oh volcanic furor; agonizing allure! Oh tumult without end! (Again!) Oh who will free me from this evil charm! Unsurpassable craving! Oh unquenchable thirst! Insatiable appetite! Oh hunger beyond compare! Oh dismal decree and blackest fortune! Oh priceless agony! Oh despairing desperate self! Oh! . . . *Ichabod!*"

"' 'M 'fraid," said the creaking serving man, "that the situation his b'yond hall 'ope, Mum."

Thus the scene, reader, in the oak-panelled dining room of Bartleby's former home in the country as Aunt Alice pined away the breakfast hour, regarded her toast, and saw that her marmalade jar was empty — !

"If I may make so bold, Mum," said this Ichabod, a faithful servant, retained — it appears — solely for the purpose of this —

"*Ichabod*! I'm surprised. At your age too, when there's not a drop of marmalade to be found in the house!"

— solely for the purpose of this chapter, for I can find no mention of him elsewhere; not, at least, as far as I have read, which leads me to remark on the impropriety of introducing supernumaries, unless —

"But thank you, Ichabod, thank you for offering to put yourself out," said Alice.

"Seventy next Christmas, Mum."

"There's been nothing like it since the War," Auntie continued, "but I made sacrifices then and there were compensations: the refugees were here — do you remember? — how many of the little dears became fond of country life and wouldn't leave at the end of it all. Then there were the Americans, and *they* always had marmalade, especially the flying officers."

"They dropped it all over Europe, Mum," Ichabod's eyes shone with the memory.

"Indeed they did, Ichabod. How we waited for it!"

"They gave it to the Russians, Mum," Ichabod advanced, "and I read in the papers that they give it to the Japanese now, begging your pardon Mum."

"God forbid that we should harbour grudges against our enemies, Ichabod; there *ought* to be enough marmalade to go round. I can't understand what will become of the world. Even in the Depression" — Ichabod coughed — "it could be had at a price" — and Ichabod creaked, reminding Auntie of his proposition — "but it would have been a great strain, too great a strain, Ichabod, at your age: the more so because he's been gone for such a time. *Ichabod!* Keep your hands off" – aha! a vital function, even for a spear carrier, so to speak – "off the *marmalade jar!*"

"Beg pardon, Mum, but there's a bit at the bottom that might be scraped out."

"I do not mean to speak unkindly, Ichabod. You may have what is left, though it's very little. Dear, kind Ichabod, I am not myself; I am on edge. The situation demands my personal attention, and you know what that will entail."

"Indeed, Mum."

"Then when you've eaten the marmalade, see to it, Ichabod; saddle him up, Ichabod!"

"But, Mum, he won't go without . . . "

– 'Who *else*,' I said to Damon, 'would have *saddled the horse?*'

– 'You never cease to amaze me,' he shook his head, "knowing, as you do, the significance of marmalade."

It must not be thought from this, reader, that Alice had forgotten her charge. Quite the reverse. Indeed, this very morn she had suddenly resolved – at what point I leave the reader to imagine – to *combine* her excursion for marmalade by going forth, upon *one and the same* occasion, to rescue Bartleby from the home, where, as we have seen, he was lately domiciled. Accordingly, she gathered her supply of Dutch caps, pills, and French letters (for though she was of menopausal years, it was her wont to carry these trifles as amulets and remembrances of things past), placed these and sundry other pre-emptive potions in her capacious handbag, and, thus prepared, strode womanfully forth from the breakfast room, down to the stables where she kept her ambling nag, Hannibali.

Now this Hannibali had been the sole tenant of Alice's stables for eighteen years. In the days long before Alice's Guardianship, Hannibali was frequently seen about the neighbourhood, tethered at some fete, mansion, or hostelry while Alice went her way, dispensing favours and performing charitable works befitting a lady of her substance, 'Haar,' many a bumpkin would say upon seeing the horse, 'there be hur ladyship a-purfaarmin chaaritubble wurrks hagin.' Hence Hannibali, who forgot nothing, came to know his mistress's haunts as his own, and marked the slow decline of the years in the equestrian clippety-clop of his own ambling gait.

Sad passage! For now Hannibali (upon whom, it is true, Alice still rode pleasurably and easily) was old and turned out to pasture. His hoofage was meagre, his eyes half-blind, his spine curved, his knees knocked, his hide tanned and scarred, creased and almost worn through (a very loose and ill-fitting covering for his ribs), his horse power less than one, in short, the adjective *emaciated* would have flattered him; *thin,* turned his head; and *lean* have set the old horse's heart pounding, that had he a mirror, he would scarcely have been able to sit in front of it, his vanity thus excited. Having no mirror, however, and not being called lean, he assented to the description *skeletal* with a sedentary whinny and a resigned rattling of his bones.

But a thin horse, we declare, is better than no horse; and a thin horse must be speedier than a fat horse or a wooden horse or a hobby horse. Now while it is true that – viewed forelock on – Hannibali was as lean as a rake and as much a fiction in nature as is a straight line in geometry, we cannot help but stand aside from our narrative to say these few words in his praise.

Not for nothing was he called after he of pachydermous fame and Apennine glory, for Hannibali was a stout-hocked, slim-pasterned, sedentary beast, and had – for a horse – so curvaceous a set of four legs that – on this account alone – he was the envy of his species. Therefore we think this four legged horse is one of the marvels of our tale, and when ridden upon, likely to advance Auntie's entry into the plot by chains and furlongs – if not exactly by leaps and bounds.

During the time taken to advance the description of Hannibali, we must imagine Auntie crossing over the meadow down to the stables where Ichabod, faithful to his instructions, has tightened Hannibali's girths, and is completing the last sentence uttered by him when we left him in the breakfast room, or to put it right way round, when he left the breakfast room: –

"Begging your pardon, Mum, but he won't move a

step."

Then, reader, let us improve our narrative view and take a closer look at the equestrian scene – as well as this unexpected impasse – by removing the stable roof (figuratively speaking), for the situation demands further investigation, perhaps even intervention on our part, if –

"*Ichabod!*"

– the horse is ever to be mounted. Now Hannibali's obduracy in this respect, reader, is not what it seems. That is, I suspect the servant, not the horse, of deliberately impeding the plot –

"*Ichabod!*"

– as Auntie's cries suggest, and when I have succeeded in removing the . . .

"*Above*, Icha – "

. . . a trickle of plaster filtering down from the roof, nothing to worry about, a common occurrence in old outhouses and stables, reader – when . . .

" – *bod!*"

. . . the trickle of plaster became a torrent, the torrent a deluge, tiles, rafters, beams, bricks, cascading about Auntie and Ichabod –

"I told you," said Auntie . . .

– while Hannibali sat pacifically fast –

" . . . in the summer, I told you to send . . . "

–– and an unidentified and unidentifiable bird's nest ––

" . . . for the builder!"

–– all because of Ichabod's dilatoriness in sending for the builder, reader!

"Begging your pardon," he – soot – "Mum," creaked his apologies, "I forgot."

Thus our purpose was accomplished not by accident but design, heavenly design. For had Ichabod remembered the builder, the roof would certainly have remained in position and we might never have seen Alice on horseback.

"Never mind, Ichabod," she said when the dust subsided, "it's not your fault." And then she turned to the still motionless Hannibali with these very persuasive words: "Dear Hannibali," she addressed the beast, an intelligent animal – as will be seen – well able to recognise a virtuous argument,

"Dear Hannibali, you are thinner than Rocinante and twice as worn, and I must be at the least reckoning twenty times the weight of *his* master; then looking at you again, I see that you are as saddle-scarred, slope-shouldered, higgledy-boned, wind-broken a horse as Parson Yorick's hack — but how, Hannibali, in the name of all that is sweeter than oats, which is all those animals ever consumed, how can you expect to become as famous as they if you will not come out into the world with me?"

And yet fame was clearly no spur to Hannibali who now manifested his refusal to move this morn with a snort, snuffle and whinny and refused entanglement with all books whatsoever (including this one), but more especially those referred to by his mistress where improbability was in both instances outdistanced only by the speed of its advent. And in this matter (if I may make my opinion felt), Hannibali, though he could not talk, showed himself very wise.

"Well, Hannibali," Auntie made a virtue out of necessity, "perhaps you are right. The days are gone when you and I might have ridden on long journeys together, for I have grey hairs in my head now, and your mane, I notice, is nearly bald. Therefore you shall stay at home while I go in search of Bartleby, but you can have a double ration of hay and carrots enough for all your needs — that much I promise you." With this resolution Alice hit on the expedient of hitchiking (she having no other means of transport) and bade farewell to Hannibali and Ichabod.

— 'I wonder what else the reader has gathered?' said Damon.

— 'That my narration is consecutive,' I replied, 'whereas the hermit's was not; that mine moves quickly where God's or the other party's (I'll have an eye open for *that* next time, Damon) moved not at all.'

— 'De'Ath saw what he saw,' said Gottesgabe; 'he was there.'

— 'I would prefer you not to mention him by name,' said I. 'The very sound is odious to me.'

— 'Continue the story,' said he.

And I did —

Alice had been at the wayside for a few minutes when a VW minibus driven by a nun, or one who at least wore the headgear of a nun, drew to a halt and slid open a welcoming door. "Ascend," said the voice from within, and Auntie ascended, pleased indeed to journey with one of Christ's calling, for though she was not herself religious she respected sweetness and light in others.

The personage at the wheel wore a wimple, and an expression of fixed simplicity appropriate to one of her chaste station.

"Whither goest thou?" the Sister asked vacantly, her strangely innocent gaze directed on the highway ahead. Alice endeavoured to explain her mission — saying that she was searching for Bartleby, and that the marmalade was quite secondary — but before she had finished speaking the other interrupted with a low moan.

"I have been studying long how to perfect my faith," she affirmed softly, "that I may be made as one with God and as free as the winds of the earth."

"That is very commendable of you," said Alice, thinking orange thoughts and continuing to say that although marmalade was secondary it was nevertheless essential to her quest, when the Sister again interrupted with these words:

"Therefore I say unto you once more in the words of the Book of Zechariah, second chapter, verse two: 'Whither goest thou?' "

And for a third time Alice was unable to finish her reply, the Sister interrupting now with an answer to her own question: " 'And he said unto me, To measure Jerusalem, to see what is the breadth thereof, and what is the length thereof.' And I have measured Jerusalem, the breadth thereof and the length thereof, and I have found it wanting. Therefore it shall be," the Sister closed her eyes, "destroyed."

It did not take Auntie long to perceive that Sybil, for that was her companion's name, was altogether out of sorts with the world. Her appearance, which Alice had first and *wrongly* ascribed to Sybil's renunciation of worldliness, left a great deal to be desired, if little to be imagined. Apart from her wimple, and a crucifix nestling between her breasts, this extraordinary Sister was stark naked — a fact that drew hoots and whistles from the passing travellers, some of whom paid for their expensive ogling by crashing into trees or each other. This lack of apparel, however, was the least remarkable feature of Sybil's appearance, and it was the face above the wheel, not the body below it, which compelled Alice's attention.

The nose seemed carved from the face; the lips bloodless and superfluous to the mouth, and the countenance itself wore the frigid mask of a chiselled effigy, reclining peacefully in the dark and musty corner of some ancient church. It was the face, thought Auntie, of a dead Angevin king from which shone the stare of a living child, a sculptured face whose immobility contradicted the expressiveness of the eyes, but whose spirit was on equivocal terms with life.

Oblivious to the vehicular disarray in her rear-view mirror, the Sister gave another tremulous moan as the VW minibus moved off down the highway. But moans or no moans, I think the reader will agree that a VW minibus is a more efficient means of transportation than a horse, is more relevant to the present generation of eager novel buyers, and promises to expedite our narrative with a greater velocity and sense of locomotive purpose than might otherwise have been the case, so that even Gottesgabe must bow to our faith in the renowned teutonic thoroughness and mechanical reliability of the people's automobile.

Yes, reader, Auntie listened to the harmonious spluttering and syncopated coughing (a *characteristic* of the air-cooled internal combustion engine), and listened also to the Sister's moans — moans, alas, sadly unrelated to any visible object of distress.

"O men of Edom," Sybil lamented as the gears whined and grated — the VW gearbox, I am assured by my German friend, withstands the harshest maltreatment — "O men of Edom, shall ye not be damned for your wickedness — ye who have transgressed against the Word of the Lord? Are ye not to be despised, despised utterly and smitten by the Host of Hosts?"

"Dear me," Auntie listened to the engine and observed her sepulchral companion, "I wonder what desperate busi-

116

ness," there came a scream of tortured metal — a pardonable hyperbole to describe the agony of misapplied ingenuity, for the metallurgist's skill, the engineer's skill, the designer's skill, were sorely tested by Sybil's driving; indeed the whole economic recovery of the Federal German Republic seemed imperilled at this moment: "I wonder," said Auntie to herself, "what desperate business can have brought this to pass?"

"Yea," the Sister spoke with greater animation, "even to the last man, you shall be smitten *utterly*!"

"I am sure," Alice replied as the minibus lurched into top gear, "that God is good and does not smite unnecessarily."

And I am sure too that He was listening. At last, reader, the text is moving — as the Italians say in jest through a peculiar amalgamation of participle, comparative and superlative — moving *precipitovolissimevolomente*; that is, moving quickly.

"The Lord God my Father," rejoined Sybil to Auntie's last remark, "smites the highest and He smites the meanest, smiting them that have kept the Covenant and smiting them that have broken the Covenant. Ho, in the vale of death beyond the mountains of the Amorites," the Sister droned, her cold features thawing in the glow of inward illumination, "he smote the Moabites and Og who was the king of Bashon and a great giant like the Anakims whom He had smitten previously and did have a bedstead of iron, nine cubits in length. And he did smite the Amorites also. The men of Ai He did smite utterly, so that not one of their number remained and the slaughter was great; the Hittites and the Canaanites, the Perizzites, the Hivites and the Jebusites He did smite; even as the Abizerites and the Ammonites were smitten, so He smote the Midianites and the Amalekites, the Gideonites and the Shechemites, the Maonites and the Zidonians also, and the Philistines He did smite. For the Lord God has smitten all peoples at all times and now He will smite the world and all that walks upon it, both men and beasts, even the crops of the field and the insects of the air shall be utterly smitten because He is tired of His work and

117

likes it not. And there shall be great deserts over the land and the seas emptied of the waters and the skies filled with darkness and there shall be devastation without end and the continents shall be peopled with monsters because the Lord my God has revealed this to me, and His mercy endureth forever, Amen."

"Here's a true servant of God," thought Alice, distressed by the bleakness of Sybil's vision. And then, seeking to humour the Sister, she asked: "And whither goest thou?"

"To the ends of the earth, sister," she replied. "I search for Xavier Piadoso, my brother in the spirit with whom I know only peace. He possesseth my soul and is a healer of men's minds, but he has gone from me in the body and the Church of Christ has cast him out. Hence I seek him in the flesh that I may be made one with him and one with God and these things I have spoken of may not come to pass."

"Ah," Alice nodded wisely, understanding Sybil's plight to be sorrier than she had initially supposed. For Auntie now perceived that the Sister had been crossed in the fortunes of love – an astute judgement, but one which was not *entirely* accurate. Nevertheless, Auntie encouraged the Sister to continue. And continue she did, with this sad tale.

"Yea, my brother possesseth me entirely and has seen Joshua when he stood before the Lord with his filthy garments and the angel of the Lord saith, 'Take away the filthy garments from him.' And unto Joshua he saith, 'Behold I have caused thine iniquity to pass from thee, and I will clothe thee with a change of raiment.' And Xavier did possess me utterly, saying 'Cast off thy garments. Yea, as your Lord contented Himself with rags, ye shall wear nothing at all but the plentiful dirt of the earth, which shall be as an Holy thing to you, whereas it was previously abhorrent. For now ye are to go about in the world naked as first ye came into it, and clothe yourself with a garland of the flowers of the field.' And I did follow his teachings and was as naked as the babe and partook of his Vision and saw that the Lord did give Joshua his change of raiment, and I was pure.

"Then I went forth amongst the Sisters and said, 'Lo! I am pure,' and I heard the Word of the Lord Who spake and said, 'Ho, ho, her raiment is changed!' But the Sisters said,

118

'You are an execration and a reproach and an abomination and this is not seemly.' And I said, 'The High Priest stands before me and he is naked also.' And they said, 'Vile temptress!' and 'Brazen whore!' and 'Cast her out, for she is under the Wicked One!' And they began, *'Maledicta sit in vivendo, in moriendo,'* saying, 'scarlet woman, thou has desecrated thy body's temple — *in manducando, in bibendo, in esuriendo, in sitiendo, in jejunando —* ' And I said, 'No. For I see everything naked!' ' *— in dormitando, in dormiendo, in vigilando —* ' 'There is not a bead of sweat, nor a hair of the body, neither blemish nor excrescence that is not Holy to me and to be elevated and much talked about and infinitely catalogued, because I am pure and I see everything naked, Amen.' ' *— in ambulando, in stando, in sedendo, in jacendo —* ' And they made me doubt the Vision by saying it came from Hell ' *— in operando, in quiescendo —* ' And they could not see the Vision when it was before them, nor did they love their Lord who died upon the Cross for our sins, Amen ' *— in mingendo, cacando, flebotomando —* ' And they said, 'Why have you broken your vows to Our Lord who died upon the Cross for our sins, Amen? — *Maledicta sit in totus viribus corporis! Maledicta sit in intus et exterius! Maledicta! Maledicta! Maledicta! —* ' And I said I had not broken them, because I had fulfilled them as I was commanded to do, and why did they not see the Vision for it was from Heaven? ' *— Maledicta sit in capillis; maledicta sit in cerebro! Maledicta sit in vertice! —* ' And they said, 'You are defiled — *in temporibus, in fronte, in auriculis! —* and have tasted the sweat of a man — *in superciliis, in oculis, in genis, in maxillis! —* and have touched his body and have coupled with him as with a beast — *in naribus, in dentibus, mordacibus sive molaribus! —* and your flesh is tainted, your blood befouled, for you have lain with Satan — *in labiis, in guttere, in humeris, in harnis, in brachiis, in manibus, in digitis! —* with the Devil who is Antichrist incarnate and the Serpent — *in pectore, in corde, et in omnibus interioribus stomacho tenus, in renibus, in inguinibus, in femore, in genitalibus, in coxis, in cruribus, in pedibus, et in unguibus! —* may you be cursed until the end of the world, may you be cursed for all eternity, may you be cursed for time without end, accursed of women — *Maledicta! Maledicta! Maledicta!*'

"And I said, 'No! For I see everything naked!'

" ' — *Maledicta sit in totis compagibus membrorum, a vertice captis, usque ad plantam pedis — non sit in ea sanitas! Maledicat illam Christus Filius Dei vivi toto suae majestatis imperio et insurgat adversus illam coelum cum omnibus virtutibus quae in eo moventur ad damnandum eam, nisi penituerit et ad satisfactionem venerit. Amen. Fiat, fiat. Amen.*' "

At this point, an evil gust of wind divested Sybil of her wimple, which, like a soul dispossessed, winged darkly out of the window to float ethereally aloft or subside to drosser regions, though what and where these regions might be, I cannot say.

— 'Why *not*?' Damon enquired.

— 'This objective method of narration,' said I, 'does not allow me to indulge in theological controversy.'

— 'A good reason,' he concurred. 'And you are to be congratulated for noticing the Sister was naked. Proceed.'

"There are more things in this world than I can account for," thought Auntie and turned her gaze to the roadside and watched the speeding hedgerows fade in the dusk as the ragged clouds of night gathered in the east.

"Unreal city! Accursed city! City of night and darkness!" Sybil broke Auntie's reverie. "O wicked city!" she cried. "Nineveh! Babylon! Cursed be thy days! O abomination that lives upon the land, despised of God, hast not thine idolatry brought thee enough adversity without destruction?" exclaimed the Sepulchral Sister as the VW minibus passed under a large illuminated roadsign bearing this legend:

LAST EXIT TO
THROCKTON BY THE BOG

And on they sped, reader, entering the red and yellow outskirts of a large urban community, on past the darkened towers of the suburbanites where Moloch made his mort-gaged dwelling —

— 'It has grown very rapidly, this Throckton,' said

Damon. 'An investment boom, I think.'

— 'There's no end,' said I, 'to the benefits of capital. But if you remember' — as *I* did — 'the signpost, Damon, it is very easy to understand the difference between the Throckton of Bartleby's departure and the Throckton of Auntie's arrival, by positing the existence of two, three, or even *four* Throcktons, each coexisting synchronously with the others, though whether they do so vertically, laterally, lineally, horizontally, by the side of, underneath, at the corners or on top of one vast rambling Bog, or independently as four separate spatial Throcktons, behind, in front of, next to, at the back of, or simply close to a *series* of bogs: origin of the ablative suffix *Bog*, I would not like to say, Damon.'

— 'That is impartial of you,' he replied.

I thought so too, reader. But as for this modern Throckton, it had a most disturbing effect on the hapless Sybil who called down several dooms at once on it, in contradistinction to Alice who, being a country girl and unused to city ways, found the many charming sights afforded by the prospect quite entertaining and diverting, and assumed that a city must supply her with a source of the ambrosial jam — an expectation which grew upon her as the heart of Throckton loomed nearer.

"O wicked city!" cried Auntie's companion, the pulse of passing streetlights lending her features an unusual animation. "Nineveh! Babylon! The end of days approacheth!"

"Then before it cometh, Sister Sybil," said Auntie, "I must have some marmalade: not jelly, but real, honest-to-goodness marmalade . . . "

"For this is the city of iniquity and the Lord shall smite it with fire and brimstone and even the righteous shall perish along with the wicked and it shall be consumed utterly, because the Lord my God is sore displeased and He shall overthrow all the cities of the world at the Day of Judgement! Amen!"

"If only I hadn't eaten all mine," Alice sighed. "That was homemade, Sybil, homemade marmalade."

And on they sped, further and further, engulfed by now in a whining forest of cables, aerials, signs, billboards, signals, hoardings, an enchanted jungle where animated figure danced with animated figure in neon mimicry of the human form; where a reeling phantasmagoria of lights hurtled and jived, propounding the electronic imperatives to eat, buy, drink, stop, sleep, save, spend; where a thousand jangling melodies vibrated on the air and sirens made their lingering wail; on they sped through a baptism of incandescence, the highway shimmering blackly towards the central metropolis, on past now-deserted sidewalks, void of footfall, encroached by sheering cliffs, on and on to the black pinnacles of the inner city, chartered home of mammon, wealth and splendour, where a million candles blazed and a million candles died and night repossessed electric day.

CHAPTER NINETEEN *Upon the Pornogryph. Old Acquaintances Reappear.*

Midnight found the pair on the other side of Throckton — the city having escaped Almighty Wrath — in the parking lot of Sam's Succulent Hambaby Grille. An electric Hambaby, knife in one hand, fork in the other, brandished its utensils, consumed itself in a tittering display of light, and then began the cycle again.

OVER FIVE BILLION SOLD! whispered Sam's sign.

Sybil gazed mutely at the sign. Her lips were compressed and bloodless, her face devoid of all expression, as still and deathly as one who has met with the Gorgon's head.

Suddenly she gave a quick whip-lash contraction of her naked body and still, directing her childish gaze at Sam's sign, exclaimed in a shrill monotone, "Oh I see it! I see it! I see everything naked! There! Look! *See!*"

OVER FIVE BILLION SOLD! tittered Sam's sign, and changed colour.

No illusion, this; rather a misinterpretation of stimuli: a delusion. For the demon which Sybil described to Auntie (but which Auntie could not see), leered expectantly through Sam's plate glass window. Its hair was done up with red ribbons, its face knobbled with the petroleum sheen of rotten meat, and it had a parrot's beak instead of a mouth, crab's pincers for hands and feet. The demon pranced upon a table, gestured lewdly with its genitalia, and then performed the impossible act of coupling with itself before disappearing in a cloud of blue smoke.

Only a gullible reader, we think, could take this as evidence that the Sister was gifted with supernatural vision:

"I see everything naked! Yea, in the eighteenth year of the reign of Beth Eliza there shall be a drought upon the land and the corn shall blacken and die upon the stalks . . . "

– or prophecy, any disinterested observer prefering the rational deduction that she was afflicted with *dementia praecox*:

" . . . and the wheat shall wither and fall in the western fields and the vine shall bring forth no fruit . . . "

"What," asked Alice not unnaturally, "*what* is revealed to you?"

"It," cried the frenetic Sister, "*It!* The beast that couples with itself and brings forth more of itself in a smoking torrent of blood and dung, and the length thereof is ten cubits, and the breadth thereof is five cubits, and it has a horn upon its head and claws upon its hands and scaled armour upon its body and it is neither man nor bird nor fish nor crab – for *It* is the Pornogryph, beast of the world's end, beast of doom and death, beast without end!"

Auntie sighed profoundly at this gloomy prognostication and her eyes found Sam's sign:

OVER FIVE BILLION SOLD! it teased, blushing at its reflection in the vacant window.

A vision of the revenge of the Hambabies floated before her.

"Well, if it was only a Pornogryph," she said, "I wouldn't let it worry you. Old Ichabod – my servant – used to see worse things than that when the horrors were on him. That was," Auntie remembered, "a long time ago, Sybil, before you were born most probably. I do hope he hasn't gone back to his old habits – he was certainly very sprightly this morning. When were you born, by the way? " Alice enquired, "if you don't mind my asking, that is . . ."

"It seems like – " Sybil began, clutching at Auntie. But then suddenly Sybil, Sepulchral Sister of Our Saviour, thrust her sculptured head forwards and stiffened into catatonic slumber.

Sam's time-clock burred softly. From deathless night other worlds shone down, and in the west a star tracked earthwards, its brief descent perhaps wished upon.

"Xavier Piadoso? Shit!" leered Sam (thus generically called), proprietor of Sam's Succulent Hambaby Grille. "What sort of a name do you call that?" grinned the host in response to Auntie's enquiry.

She had slipped out of the minibus and gone hunting for a Hambaby. Her safari had one other charitable, if modest quarry: to find some clothing for the sleeping Sybil. A misty layer of stale cigarette smoke and fried onion fumes sank lazily over the silver and orange decor of Sam's Grille as she opened the door to the babble of conversation and the ferment of rowdy tongues.

Over her Hambaby and Russian salad, Auntie now found herself staring into Sam's mouth, his enormous head silhouetted by the tarnished orange light as a burst of raucous laughter greeted his remark.

"What a travesty of sunshine that colour is!" she thought. Nevertheless she smiled at the mouth, in which only the eye teeth remained to give it a distinctly anthropoid appearance, and said, very simply, "I must admit that it is a strange sort of name – unusual," she added, waiting for the mouth to speak again while another gale of laughter rose on the tainted air. "What unhappy souls they are," she thought of Sam's customers as a shrunken creature with the head of a fish proposed the toast of *"Freedom!"* and was answered with the rousing chorus, "Forever!" before he subsided to the floor where he floundered helplessly, much to the amusement of his comrades who began to pelt him with Hambabies.

"Strange! Kiss my ass!" spluttered Sam, smacking and smearing his sweaty hands upon his paunch.

A pathetic bleating suddenly diverted Auntie's attention, and she was somewhat surprised to see two shepherds, at a back table, taking their pleasure upon a sheep – a scene which soon resulted in a squalid little altercation.

"Hey!" a Negro towered from the midst of the company and addressed the shepherds. "Quit that now!"

"Yeah, quit it!" a heavy-jowled, slope-headed character rose to join the protest. "That's recidivist!"

125

As for Auntie, she did not know what it was called, but thought it odd that so quaint a custom had been imported into the city.

"Be oor shoop," said one of the shepherds.

"Aaar, shagmut," growled the other, whereupon sheep, shepherds, and all were set upon and dragged outside into the night air, bleats and blows sounding from the lot.

"Kiss my ass," Sam's mouth observed again.

"Not if you paid me!" shrieked an aged hag who swayed and reeled about the company's midst, seeking to ply her withered body in competition, no doubt, with the Hambabies, though had they sold as badly as she, then Sam must needs have pleaded insolvency. "Not if you paid me a million dollars!" squawked the harridan, cackling gleefully.

"Ten cents," said Sam in mock hope.

"They are obviously celebrating something," thought Auntie of Sam's inmates, "though I've no idea what it can be."

"I'd kiss it for free, Sam!" announced a pallid individual, enticing a pimply boy with offers of hidden delights. "He's a beardless boy, Sam," he simpered, tweaking the boy's nose, "and he'll kiss your arse too."

"Quit it!" the heavy-jowled one again rose to command the throng.

"Pssst," Sam's mouth exhaled confidentially, "that's Haut —" but the sight of the proprietor's bared fangs provoked the company to further merriment, and Auntie lost his words.

"If you haven't heard of Xavier Piadoso," she said to the mouth, "perhaps you know of Bartleby?"

"Bartleby? Nuts!" showered the host.

"Listen," Alice leaned voluptuously over the counter, and, braving the reek of garlic, whispered into the mouth.

"Ya don't say so?" it replied loquaciously. "Just a mo-mo," the mouth raised a sleeve to mop its seeping brow, and then, to a cry of "Pussy foot!" from the spotted boy, turned and retreated into the kitchen.

"Hey," a sleek voice surprised Auntie. "Ya wanna buy some stuff? Good stuff," the voice whispered, its breath tickling Auntie's ears, "the best," it murmured as Alice turned to catch sight of a pair of lemur-like eyes glinting beneath a wide brimmed hat. But Sam's mouth had returned, and the eyes withdrew, slinking off into darkness.

"Take this," said Sam, and gave Auntie a freshly laundered cotton smock and matching apron inscribed with the words: *Sam's Succulent Hambabies.* "These are sad times," the mouth sighed.

"They are," said Auntie, purchasing more of Sam's fare to pay for the bequest.

"O shit!" beamed Sam, baring his fangs.

She was on the verge of leaving when the door flew open and a rotund, cowled figure, carrying a basket and a wad of leaflets, perched upon the threshold, inhaled rustily and peered into the quickening gloom. "Jesus saves!" the figure wheezed piously, then nodding and curtseying, flounced through the room, attempting to kiss some of Sam's male customers and chanted, "Holy Mushrooms! Holy Mushrooms!"

"Hambaby, Sam" requested this wandering proselyte, who seems to have entered the plot very quickly and with no especial purpose —

— 'He came in through the door,' said Damon.

— 'That's not what I meant,' said I.

"With mustard, *praise be!*" the evangelist stuffed a Hambaby into the front of his cowl and turned darkly to Alice. *"Praise be!* But the Mushroom is a Holy Fungus, sister. Did I not hear you asking after a Xavier Piadoso just now, accidentally like —" the evangelist coughed and spluttered, hands grasping at the paunch of his robes which now began to shed papers: "while I was outside," he continued, shedding more papers, "meditating whether to take repast from me crusade, did I not hear you asking after him?"

"Why yes," Alice replied, scrutinizing the cowl as mustard-coated Hambaby after mustard-coated Hambaby vanished, consumed by the invisible face. "But haven't you dropped something?" she asked, pointing to the sheets and leaves accumulating on the floor.

"Dropped?" the mysterious evangelist scratched his paunch. "No, he's not dropped nothing, he hasn't. *Praise be!*

127

Praise — ''

— 'The idiom of **'*** himself,' said Gottesgabe.

— 'Wrong,' it was my turn to smile, reader. 'His brother, perhaps. But not himself.'

— 'An inventive suggestion,' said he: —

"*Praise be!* But I've never hear of him, sister. Spell," demanded the proselyte, "could you spell his name. It would be a help, it would — me crusade," explained the figure, producing a pencil stub and writing as Auntie spelled out the name: XAVIER PIADOSO. "Me spelling's never been the best, but I gets by, I does," wheezed the voice from within the cowl, "and that's a godly sort of name. Who is it what wants him?" the voice rasped. "And what does they want with him? And where's he to be found? And where's he from?"

"If I could answer all those questions," said Auntie, "I wouldn't be looking for . . ."

"Jesus saves!" cried the hidden voice, "could you *spell* that, sister? It's the scroll, it is, the scroll of judgement we's compiling. "

"P-I-A-D-O-S-O," said Auntie.

"And what's your name, sister?" the evangelist poised his pencil stub.

"I am Alice," said Auntie, "Bartleby's Guardian."

A terrible outburst of coughing greeting this simple declaration, shaking the cowl and liberating more papers. When the fit subsided, Alice fancied she heard a faint sniffling sound deep from within the hood's interior, a sound followed by the tinkling splash of running water.

"I can spell that name, oh yes," the voice croaked proudly, and then inclining its cowl, worked itself up into an impromptu sermon: "The Day of Judgement is coming, sister Alice, and the wrath of the Mushroom is close at hand. I 'ope you've made your peace with the Mushroom, yes I 'ope you have. *Praise be!*" the figure extended a sleeve cloaked hand, and its wide sweep took in the entire room. "This lot's all been in purgatory, they has," the voice wheezed, "but now they's out. They's gathering, they is, gathering for the powers of darkness. Doomsday!" the voice choked, "Doomsday is a-coming, sister! But I has me scroll, I does, me scroll of judgement."

"And where are they gathering?" Auntie humoured the voice.

"Throckton by the Bog, sister – in the marketplace, not a hundred chains from here," came the muffled reply.

"But we've just been through Throckton," said Alice as a renewed fit of coughing wracked the cowl and cut her off in mid-speech.

"Then don't go back!" cried the voice when it had recovered. "*Praise be! Praise be!* Praise be, sister for mustard. But *shhh!*" it warned, "*shhh!* We's been listened to, we is," the cowl looked around the room, "Throckton," the voice grated, "Throckton is where we are, where we are is Throckton. Holy Mushrooms, Throckton is everywhere, sister! Here, take one, take one, it's free," the voice rasped and Alice placed the sacred fungus in her capacious handbag. "But Throckton, *Ahhhh!* Throckton is without end, sister!"

A rending androgynous scream pierced the heavy atmosphere of Sam's Succulent Hambaby Grille upon this twice repeated statement. More screams ensued, and the Grille was soon in a marvellous uproar, bodies flying over bodies as the spotted boy, pursued by the simpering pander, made a speedy exit into the night, Sam's customers shrieking and howling after them, until the room had almost emptied itself.

"Holy Mushrooms!" cried the cowled figure and, dropping from the bar, tripped out in the mob's wake, his cries of "*Doomsday! Doomsday!*" dying on the air.

"Yes." Sam's mouth gaped at the wreckage of his Grille, "these are sad times."

– 'I tell you it's **'***!' Damon was very stubborn.
– 'It cannot be,' said I. 'How did he get out of the pit?'
– 'Then who?'
– '*Piadoso*. Who else? Piadoso *in disguise!*'
– 'A strange relation,' said he, 'of priest and sacristan.'

Later, after Alice had returned to the minibus, she thought over her day's adventures. "The world," she said to herself, "is going begging. For what? For a messiah perhaps. At least Sybil has given a name to hers, but I must be careful not to mention him by name, for it does seem to disturb her. Since we are both searching for someone – or something," she added, "I wonder if it would be easier if I referred to him as Bartleby? Yes," she sighed, "a name is only as good as the feeling it evokes."

So resolving, Auntie fitted the unconscious Sybil into her Hambaby robes – a change of raiment indeed! – and the sounds of the electric city closed about her and she fell asleep, smiling and dreaming of the characters in Sam's Grille, her dreams suffused with citrine fragrances wafted from the slopes of Hesperidean groves.

Dawn, suggested Alice's dream; and she awoke to the greeting of a friendly sunbeam playing over the windshield.

OVER FIVE BILLION SOLD! whispered Sam's sign, unaware of Aurora's pale yet more furious energy.

"Mmm," Sybil stirred, fitfully awakening in the irridescence of strengthening morn. "I seem to be wearing – clothes!"

It was a shock for her to find herself thus garbed in the robes of a more secular sorority than the Sisterhood, but it was one eased by Auntie's tactful suggestion that they further their search for Bartleby. "Even," said Alice gravely, "unto the ends of the earth. For it is written that what the Lord giveth, He taketh away, whereas to His servants He giveth again, verily unto a change of raiment, He giveth again."

To which Sybil, meekly examining her Hambaby garb, replied, "Dear friend, I am wont to speak in tongues and see dreams. Sometimes, the gift does not serve me well, for I am not myself and the Body of Christ is within me and I am visited by the abominations of hell. Thank you," the Sister smiled wanly at Alice, "for my garments. Henceforth I shall be clothed and shall not go naked abroad but shall obey the Book which saith: 'Unto Adam also and to his wife did the LORD God make coats of skin, and clothed them.' "

They were about to depart Sam's lot when the sound of running footsteps, preceded by the anguished cry, 'Wait!' diverted their attention. It was not long before the appellants tottered into view, a peculiar twosome, not entirely unknown

130

to our history, though of course quite unknown to Alice and Sybil.

"No trumps," Auntie bade mentally as the gold, red and black costumery of the Knave of Spades, Estrogen, fell flush with the ground beneath her.   —

"A smooth man," Sybil observed, her gaze wandering over the flat and featureless back of Estrogen's costume, a tawdry crop of fleurs-de-lys on a field of grey offsetting the tapestried brilliance of the two-dimensional frontage.

"WALDEMAR," the wizard panted, setting the scene with breathless italics, "ESTROGEN *has fallen down. Enter:* NAME?"

"ESTROGEN: We've lost our dwarf . . ."

"And you don't know where to find him?" said Alice, a smile playing on her lips.

"WALDEMAR: No way to be. No way to speak."

"ESTROGEN *Struggling to rise:* struggling? *struggling* . . . *to rise? Yes. Gets up.*"

"They say everything twice," Sybil marvelled at the visionary immediacy of the present, not having our understanding that these were incomplete characters.

"I think he is right," said Alice of Waldemar, "this is no way to be."

"WALDEMAR *conjuring absently:* Hard to learn new ways. Dwarf gone. DODO gone. When? How do I know when? *Falters:* NAME?"

"ALICE," said Auntie, continuing, *"Helpfully:* But look — you can learn. Just take one step at a time, like this: ALIC."

"WALDEMA? *Trying his best,*" he enunciated with great clarity. "WALDEM: ESTROGE *suspicious,*" the wizard directed.

"ESTROGEN *suspiciously:* Who? Me? I'm not suspicious."

"WALD: ESTROG *sulks,*" Waldemar orchestrated.

"ESTRO*GEN*: Sulks?" And the Knave sulked.

"WAL *Twirling his cape:* Sulks. *Begins to explain to* ALICE and NAME?"

"SYBIL," said Sybil, surprisingly on key.

"WA: We are waiting for DOGOT. Why? Ah, that's the question."

"SYBIL: Yea! And the Lord spake and His voice was the noise of thunder and a thousand chariot wheels that did command the people to go, go . . ."

"ESTROGEN *Before he can check himself:* DIDI!"

"WALDEMAR *Furiously:* DODO! *To* Sybil: I must beg you not to . . . *Halting in* WA-WA-WA *chagrin.* Now look!"

"Will this help?" asked Auntie. "ALI: Will this help?"

"W: What? Yes. Thank you . . . yes."

"And the Lord saith, go, go unto . . ."

"ESTROGEN: Fuckit! *He shakes his fist at her* — See? Fist! Shake! — *Refuses to speak.*"

"But," Alice reasoned with him, "you can't refuse to speak when you've just said you refuse to speak."

"ESTROGEN," the Knave proved his point.

"*To the others* — what others? No, I can dispense with that. How does this strike you? Do I sound — appropriate?" Waldemar enquired.

"You're doing very well," Alice congratulated him, "but I'm not sure about your . . ."

"ESTROGEN *Jealous of WALDEMAR's success:* Not in the book! None of this is in the book!"

"And where is the book?" cried Waldemar majestically. "Where?"

"ESTROGEN *Angry at having broken his resolve:* It's not in the book . . . *Whining:* Who's whining? Alright, I'm *whining.* There's every reason to *whine.* Yes, I'll whine if I want to whine. *Whines.* Who lost the dwarf? Who lost DODO?"

"Liar!" Waldemar conjured feverishly. "Liar! Not me! And if you know so much about what's in the book," he taunted the Knave, "what does it say about that boy?"

"Boy?" Auntie remembered the spotted boy in Sam's Grille.

"Boy!" Waldemar conjured as Estrogen covered his ears. "NAME?"

"ALICE," said Alice. "BARTLEBY."

Now all of the foregoing conversation took place in Sam's lot, Alice and Sybil instructing the wizard from their lofty perch in the minibus, but no mention having been made of Waldemar's destination, nor of Estrogen's. The name Bartleby, however, somewhat altered the situation, provoking Estrogen to experiment with the new speech, and stimulating Waldemar to explain how the troupe had chanced to meet with our hero while they had been waiting for DOGOT, and further, how they had fallen from the theatre in the pasture, losing their dwarf, for whom necessity now bade them search in order that they might (upon his recovery) continue waiting for DOGOT. None of this gave them a destination, merely an aim, but the minibus at least furnished a means of taking the aim, whence on Sybil's invitation, Estrogen grudgingly, and Waldemar gladly, ascended, and this further conversation resulted — which, ever with an eye on time and space, I have made as brief and as pointed as the occasion warranted.

"The difficulty with the present state of affairs," said Waldemar, quite at home by now in the medium of undirected speech, "is the question of priority. Originally, Estrogen and I were . . .

"GOTSREEN? RONTGEN!" the Knave tinkered with his name, hoping to emulate the wizard.

"Gotsreen," Waldemar shrugged, "Gotsreen and I were waiting for Dogot and met Bartleby who was searching for you, Alice, as you are for him, and as we now are for Dodo and Sybil is for . . . for?"

"Bartleby," said Alice.

"Then the question is," Waldemar put it succinctly, "who are we searching for?"

"I think," Alice replied, "that the answer is plain and simple. We are searching for Bartleby because I have been looking for him all the time, whereas you have only just arrived."

"Bartleby, Bartleby," murmured Waldemar, "all the time, you say?"

"Most of it," sighed Bartleby's Aunt. "Most of it."

They had not journeyed many miles further, reader, when Sybil espied not another vision, but another hitchhiker — though the appearance might as well have been a vision, and confirms my opinion that the personage in Sam's Grille was *not* who Gottesgabe thought, unless I am sorely mistaken and the person to whom I refer was in disguise — if so, where did he get it? — and, in which case, I do not see how this personage (disguised or otherwise) could have travelled so quickly, quicker than quickly so to speak, forwards from Sam's Grille, if of course (assuming it to be the same personage), if he has gone forwards at all.

— 'Admit you were wrong,' said Gottesgabe.

— 'You have commented on the objective manner in which I've been conducting this narration,' said I, 'and an impartial narrator must always be willing to admit that he may have been in error. It was the paunch that misled me.'

— 'Then you confess it was***'***?'

— 'It probably was,' said I, 'and you've no need to be so oblique in referring to him as "**'***." I might as well accustom myself to the name in full now that he's returned to the plot, *not* that I had any objection to it in the first place, but if he *must* go about in disguise then he can hardly expect to be called what he is.'

— 'My honest friend!' Gottesgabe agreed, and I hastened to continue — so:

But travel quickly he did, reader.

"Yea," affirmed the Sepulchral Sister as the VW minibus drew to a halt, "wretched are the peoples who walk the face of the earth. Ho, they must crawl upon the ground, the palms of their feet much stung by thorns and nettles. Ascend," she quavered, "and have ease of thy feet."

But there was no movement from the hitch-hiker. Instead, four pairs of eyes gazed down upon the wayfarer's nose, which, thus viewed in plan form, displayed ridges, fissures, and gullies of epidermal erosion across its precipitous slopes, while the central spine wound its uncertain way across a hazard of subcutaneous obstacles to terminate in a glacial outcrop, an ice-blue snout, disappearing into the troubled waters of a knotted and tangled beard. Above the proboscis there hung a range of shaggy brows, and above these there loomed a compendious cranium, a phrenological marvel, desiccated in a radial pattern as if by the drainage of long sunken streams, and thatched with matty layers of grizzly foliage. Still higher, there hovered a shimmering mist, an unearthly luminous cloud, drifting, floating, and swirling like the rings of Saturn about the parent planet, or some Vesuvian cloud above its volcanic cone – a halo of sorts that might have suggested (to the incautious observer) the odour of sanctity, but which proved, on closer inspection, to be generated by the corrugated dome around which it revolved and partially obscured.

Beneath the mist, beneath the horned gnarls and tufts of the rugged terrain, beneath the crags and ridges, there hung a skull, and to the skull there was attached a countenance, its leathery and wickedly ancient skin dissected by the ravages of tears and the years.

The onlookers peered at the territory beneath them, attracted by something more than its topographical scars. For several minutes the ground remained passive, though somewhat overhung by the gathering mists. Then the mountainous brows quaked and the snout quivered and sniffed. At the same time the hoary vegetation of the cranial dome from which the mists poured forth bore witness to a most extraordinary insurrection. Cohorts of decomposing figures sprang from the undergrowth while a whole printing shop of carrion type sprang up to join battle with several legions of misconceived plots, aborted phrases and carnal characters, until the whole incomprehensible garland fell into disarray about the wayfarer's ill-fitting shoulders. Thus festooned, they gave off a violently noxious odour, redolent of the grave itself, conveyed by a means of a palpably fetid mist to the nostrils of Estrogen and then to those of Waldemar, Sybil and Auntie herself. The inferior figure shook its head as more vile humours arose. Books, bindings, spines, titles, chapters and boards, upper cases and lower cases, an awesome medley of types: Diamonds, Pearls, Agates, Nonpareils, Minions, Breviers, Long Primers, Bourgeois, Small Picas, English, ordinary Picas, ordinary Primers, Romans, New Gothics, Baskervilles, Bodonis, Caledonians, Centuries, and Garamonds – to name but a few – all in an advanced state of putrefaction and oblivious to the niceties of rank, caste, case, or harmony, divested themselves like so many homunculi from their host and, in a frenzy of miscegenation, writhed, danced, jigged, scratched, bit and tore at each other before capering off along the highway.

135

"ESTROGEN: Fuckit!" Estrogen spat and, his brain reeling under the rancid vapours, restored his name to its original length.

A fist of blue knuckles extended itself into a skeletal hand and rapped upon the door. There came yet another flurry of typographical nastiness and the voice beneath the clouds introduced itself with this characteristic and entirely expected exhalation:

"Buggerum, buggerum, buggerum, boo!"

CHAPTER TWENTY   *The Hermit's Tale Continued, Wherein Is Advanced a Candidate for Authority.*

"He's obviously *just* got out of the pit," said I to Damon Gottesgabe, "and the papers, bindings, wrappers and boards add up to the paunch which equals the disguise. So you see I was not so wrong after all: somebody was in disguise, and if it was not Piadoso it was De'Ath intending to be taken as Piadoso. What I would like to know is where did he get the cowl and the friar's robes?"

"From the vestry," my gnomic friend replied, "where else?"

I did not believe him: —

"*Buggerum, buggerum, buggerum, boo!*" came the necrophile's refrain, and with no small difficulty, De'Ath, his crutch of bone, and his offensive odour were hauled variously and each into the minibus. "Thankee kindly," said the anchorite, looking none the worse for his recent spell in the pit, though decomposing particles of type still clung to his cerements and Sybil was forced to open a window in an attempt to dissipate the stench. "Thankee kindly."

"ESTRO: *Winces and holds his nostrils* — Unngh!" cried the Knave, throwing his head back and applying his hand dramatically to his nose.

"Boo! We's haughty, ain't we? Very uppity like. Tsk-tsk," De'Ath raked his tongue across his palate. "Is we writers?" he espied the title page of WAITING FOR DOGOT in the magician's hand, "is that what we is? "

137

"I," announced Waldemar, "am WALDEMAR, wizard, necromancer, and sayer of words . . . NAME?" the magician enquired of the hermit.

"ESTR:" Estrogen diminished his name by another letter.

"He wants to know your name," Alice explained.

"Then he can mend his words," rejoined the hermit. "Yes, he should mend his words before he speaks to me like that, he should. But I knows what you is, I does. Leastways," De'Ath turned to Alice, "I knows what you is, yes. You's Bartleby's Aunt what's looking for marmalade, *tee-hee,* yes!"

"*Marmalade!*" Auntie exclaimed, unaware, reader, of what we have learned from our recent discovery, "I don't think I've had the pleasure of your acquaintance before. Are you a friend of Ichabod's?"

"Ichabod," De'Ath made a mental note of the name, "Ichabod: that's as maybe and that's as maybe not," he hedged, still eyeing the title page, "but if these is writers, they's lucky; and if they's characters, they's even luckier to fall in with me, they is."

"GORESENT: FUCKIT! Not in the BOOK!" anger rang in the Knave's voice and effected this anagrammatic change of name.

"What's the *matter* with him?" asked the hermit, inhaling deeply.

"My friend," Waldemar conjured, "is learning to speak . . . NAME? NAME?"

"At his age? He ought to be ashamed of himself," said the recluse. "But if you must know what I am," he continued, giving the company a watery stare, "his name's De'Ath, it is. Retired hermit, pleased to meet you, I'm sure."

"I fear thee not, old man," said the Sepulchral Sister as the gears again crashed and whined and the minibus lurched and juddered – she wrestling with the gear change and stomping on the clutch – "I fear thee not, though thy looks gnaw at the marrow of my bones," she declared, the banshee cry of molecular anguish wailing from the transmission.

"A retired hermit," echoed Auntie, her thoughts wandering to glorious morning's golden groves, "I thought all hermits were retired?"

138

"There's some that is," replied De'Ath, pleased to speak of his late profession, "and there's some that ain't. This one is. He's just emerged from a session underground, he has," De'Ath frowned at the hideous noise from the VW minibus engine. "It's a long story," he wheezed, "longer than most of mine, but I've given it up, I have — hermitude and buggery. There's two steady occupations in life," the hermit expostulated, "one's mine, and the other's a maker of dough and a baker of bread. But mine's the best, it is. Yes, in times such as these be, in times of famine and drought and pestilence . . . "

"When the hand of God is laid upon the land!" S y b i l chimed in.

"Oh yes," a flicker of irritation crossed his shaggy brows, "we knows all about that — in times, as he was saying, in times of *visitation*, and I think that is the right word, in such evil times as these be, he's never without a customer, but your baker of bread, now, comes off the worse. 'A man who has bread will never starve'? Don't believe it, friends, that saying's got nothing in it, not noways. Take away his water, and what do you have?" he asked rhetorically, as though he were a speaker in some grand allegory, and, supplying the mordant answer, replied to his own question: "A skelinton, oh dear me yes, a corpse, and a skelinton he ain't got no use for bread, but a corpse it needs a shroud, don't it? But where's you all bound for?" the hermit asked briskly. "Is there corpses in it?"

"We are searching for Bartleby," said Auntie, "and — "

"I see everything naked!" the Sister renewed her visionary strain, "and there is nothing abhorrent in the eyes of the Lord, yea, nary a corpse. For the Lord saith, 'Let these bones come unto me and I will give them a change of raiment and will cleanse them of the flesh and the sins of the flesh — ' "

"We knows all that," De'Ath grated, "but where's we going?"

"Here and there, everywhere and nowhere, the future waits on the present," Waldemar speculated.

"Yes, yes," De'Ath agreed irritably, "but that doesn't answer his question, does it?"

"*How*," Auntie asked the hermit, "how do you know about marmalade?"

A nice enquiry, reader, and decorously put, if I may say so. Now, had I been there, I would have asked a more pointed question, but I wasn't and didn't.

"Gas," said the Sister and stared at the fuel gauge and saw it was on reserve.

"And how," Auntie observed the hermit's cerements and was a little puzzled to see that they appeared to have been written upon – not *appeared*, in fact, but *were* written upon: scribbled all over – a matter of no consequence, I cannot think why she remarked on it: "how," she said – concerning the gas, by the way, I should have mentioned earlier that there was a filling station next to Sam's roadhouse and Auntie very wisely insisted that they fill the tank, paying for it with her own money, but it slipped my mind – "*how*," she said to the hermit – as a minor detail, you will surely understand, reader, though why the needle should have fallen to reserve I cannot say – "*how*" – I would certainly have asked why – "do" – and how –– unless the instrumentation was faulty –– "you" – the hermit got out of the pit (not that Auntie knew he was in it to begin with) – "*know*" –– or possibly the tank may have sprung a leak – "*Gas*," said the Sister again as the engine coughed, spluttered and – it seems like it – and picked up again ––– definitely faulty instrumentation ––– "*How* do you *know* that," Auntie was saying, "I" – but come what may I would have asked where De'Ath was between now and Sam's, and between Sam's and the pit, though of course I couldn't – "am" – and shouldn't in an objective narrative, indeed have no right to ask questions of a merely personal nature; to continue: –––– "*How* do you *know* that I am" – in short, I would have asked any other question than this: – "Bartleby's G*******?" ––––– and Gottesgabe supports me, reader, when I say that it is not at all unusual for the fuel gauges in VWs to stick at full *or* empty – "*Guardian*?"

In a thousand years I would never have asked that question.

For it was a question, reader, which brooked no disguise

140

of response from the hermit – neither cough, cowl, nor paunch – but which stimulated (instead) an horrendous and ghastly – words fail me, had I been there in person I might have done better – which stimulated, I say for the want of a more just phrase, an entirely characteristic and without doubt *un*disguised response from De'Ath.

Yet unconscious of him with whom they dealt, the hermit's present audience was astonished to see his cadaverous countenance erupt in such a grotesque and totally exaggerated simulation of ordinary human expressiveness that they feared for his continued bodily existence, and left aside (for the moment) the tenuous question of his intellectual welfare, so formidable was this external display as De'Ath's brows heaved and expelled the last and most tenacious companions of the pit. The eyes contracted in little paroxysms of antique emotion, drawing the crinkled skin of the lids and the loose leathery folds of the pouches into the deep orbits of the sockets. New formations of grime-encrusted ridges tremored across his eroded cheeks; his mouth split open to reveal an imperfect set of tartrated molars and carious incisors, and his atrophied lips stretched and crackled before drawing together in contorted and distant relation to a smile. His eyes unpuckered now and, darting forth from the skull into which they had almost vanished, there escaped from the mouth's shrivelled fissure a long, low whistle.

"Know!" cried the hermit De'Ath. "How does he know? Because you told him!"

"Who told him?" Sybil gave the hermit a fall line.

"You," De'Ath raised a knotted fist aloft and grated to the company, "what is he? Me? What am I?"

"EST: Fuckit!" Estrogen verged on purple catastrophe. "One of your own best customers," he minced, seeking witty revenge for De'Ath's earlier remark.

"Mind your points and quads, you," barked the hermit. "Bartleby me no Bartlebies; Guardian me no Guardians," he wheezed. "Aaah! He was pulled in, he was, into his own plot. Hit by a talking head, he was. He saw things, he did: 'orrible things, all on that boy's account. But he has powers, has old De'Ath, only . . . only he saw . . . "

"The end of days!" cried Sybil with the intuitive sympathy of one sufferer for another. "Possessed; De'Ath is possessed!"

"Dear me," thought Alice, gazing in turn on De'Ath's written-upon-shrouded body, Sybil's Hambaby wrapper, Waldemar's astrological cape and Estrogen's emblazoned tabard, "things begin to fall apart." And then she was blessed with a vision of her own. No blinding flash, this, more like the slow revelation of dawn, the sun of which particular idea had been rising in her mind since she left her home in the country: a gradual and beneficent vision whose kindly rays emancipated the beholder from the bondage of the years and the shadows of night. "It may make little difference what I say or do," she thought, still gazing at the company, "but they have as much right to be here as I do, and although they are by varying degrees unhappy and demented, perhaps something of mine will help them discover themselves. I shall give them Hambabies."

"Ahhh!" croaked De'Ath, rocking on his horny buttocks at the commencement of one of those convulsions which threatened to separate eternal spirit from uncertain matter. "Ahhh!" Tears threaded their way in rivulets and coursed down valleys of parchment. "Ahhh! A bite for him before he begins? A morsel or a titbit? A crumb for old De'Ath?"

"The world," thought Auntie, "is beset with madness. It is my fate to be sane." And true to her resolve, she produced from her capacious handbag a remedial Hambaby. "I would give you some marmalade, if I had any. But here," Alice discovered the Holy Mushroom, "take this as well," she said, and unwittingly returned the sacred fungus to its original donor, commanding him to ingest its recuperative juices and draw strength therefrom.

Fortified at length by liberal dosages of Sam's succulent fare — and the Holy Mushroom too — De'Ath undertook at length to acquaint the company of his meeting with Bartleby in the graveyard and the circumstances which ensued, including a vivid biographical excursus, backtracking over the many years of De'Ath's being, designed in part to familiarize

142

the listeners with the origins of his project concerning characters and authors, yet also built *as a piece* into the architecture of a separate but nonetheless equally amazing tale, which, intertwined with asides, parodies, imitations, curlicues and the like, actually formed the substance of his rambling gothic fugue, wherein was concealed, he knew, information of vital and calculated concern to all and sundry — perhaps even the key to the plot entire. This information he intended to reserve as a *pièce de résistance* at a point when he had breached the defences of his audience, compelling their belief in exchange for a release from the boredom of listening to him. In what manner and wise his strategy was thwarted, the diligent reader will presently see.

Let me say at once that I have no intention of giving the whole tale, which seems to me a very long-winded business, though it is true the hermit's breath came slowly and further inpeded the telling. Far be it from me, however, to plead physical infirmity in defence of a laggard narrative. Some of the tale, the portion that was retold (for purposes of scene setting, atmospherics, picture framing etc. — purposes well known to any narrator) is already familiar to the reader and forms the fifth, sixth and eighth chapters of the present history. This portion, then, I have cut (not from the ears of De'Ath's audience but from the pages of our account) in order to avoid unnecessary repetition, leaving certain parallels and correspondences for the reader to pick at as best he may.

For his part, I think the reader will understand that the hermit's task appeared an easy one, and seemed to be made the more so by the relatively passive response he received from three of his listeners. Estrogen indulged his customary scepticism by alone denying the truth of the hermit's legend, adding that the affair of the pit was the fantasy of a madman, or, worse, the improbable invention of an English-and-or-Canadian old-young would-be bard — this last type of individual occupying an unusually low order on the Knave's scale of values — and, furthermore, the tale, said the Knave, had no part in the book, play, or ffoule papers, of which *he* was a character, and therefore he could give no credence to it.

De'Ath, however, was disinclined to meet such objections (the pungent refutation of which had already assaulted

Estrogen's ears) and contented himself with a lugubrious stare in their author's direction. "Me friend," said the recluse sadly, "you have many things to learn." Unwilling to provoke another lachrymose outburst, and in any case anxious to discover what they might of Bartleby — if not of Dogot — the others encouraged De'Ath to continue, begging Estrogen to abstain — as far as was in his power — from interruption.

Before the hermit is allowed to continue, the reader should be aware that there are several dubious aspects to his tale. The ingredient of chance, for example, is advanced beyond our capacity for belief. In itself this constitutes no particular drawback. But there is a degree of scorn and malice exhibited towards certain authors and works, a kind of uncomfortable and melancholy *Weltschmerz* — as Gottesgabe would say — which can have originated only from De'Ath himself and not, as he claims, from the other principal personage of the tale.

There is also present a certain episodic quality, expressed throughout by an increasing tendency towards mania — an obsessive imbalance which omits several of the more piquant details of the pit while dwelling ghoulishly upon others. It would indeed be a generous auditor who could claim that the absence of some elements and the corresponding addition of others in De'Ath's chronicle was a result of the hermit's high unwillingness to offend the females of the company, and thus bring what he erroneously imagined as the heat of roseate blushes to virgin cheeks.

No, modesty did not enter into De'Ath's considerations. Nor, as Auntie first suspected, could the convivial influence of the Holy Mushroom (the effects of which she had originally witnessed in Sam's Grille) be held responsible for the increasing plangency of the hermit's tenor.

The fact was that De'Ath had gradually fallen victim to a delusion, a grand psychosis, the first symptom of which was his continued tale (insinuated as a kind of tactical trial or sally to test his audience's defences), and which, as it grew upon him and his world, would in the remaining chapters assume the force of a thing called reality. But there is a proper time and place to speak of this later. Meanwhile, I can only regret my inability to interrogate the hermit on his

144

movements and actions prior to meeting with Auntie and the minibus.

THE HERMIT'S TALE

CHAPTER ELEVEN   *Wherein Is Told of the Parish Poet, Wordkyn, and the Rebellion of Characters in De'Ath's Plot.*

— '*Eleven*!' cried Gottesgabe. 'Now *that* is what I call a consecutive narration!'
    — 'A trifling thing,' said I. 'The number can be stricken.'
    — 'I would go further,' said he.
    — 'Then I shall obliterate it!'
    Heavenly reader, disregard what you have read above. So:

THE HERMIT'S TALE

Wherein Is Told of the Parish Poet, Wordkyn, and the Rebellion of Characters in De'Ath's Plot.

I

"Years, years," De'Ath swept away aeons with a gaudy and melodramatic arc of his bone crutch, "years before it became me terrible misfortune to fall into the 'orrible clutches of the Baron Hank Caughlin Mangaravidi Fitz Kelly Mordant, and them no less 'orrible clutches of his charge, the peerless Deborah Caughlin Mangaravidi Fitz Kelly Mordant (what's doom was met at me hands in a fit of murderous rage and what's corpse was cast down even by his same hands from the topless towers of the Baron's castle — as he told you he did, yes)," for De'Ath had already reiterated the substance of the sixth chapter of our history and the sixth and seventh of his own, as he was yet to repeat the eighth of ours, and the eighth, ninth and tenth of his — respectively: "Years too before I was put to the trial of walking round and round

145

them towers and fell off and broke me shanks; yes, years and *years* before that unhappy and tragical tale was purloined by Mad Normie Rojack, who at that time would not even have graced the Baron's soup kitchens as the meanest soup ladler, nor would he — nor *could* he now, *tee-hee!* — ; all them long years ago before these and many other dark and strange events, when I was but a lowly and innocent Sexton, tolling me bell and a-toiling over me books, it was me one and only pleasure to know the Poet of the Parish, whose real name I shall not yet utter but what I shall refer to as Wordkyn, seeing as how that's a suitable sort of name for one of his occupation."

Upon the name Wordkyn a sharp gasp escaped Auntie's lungs, and, as the hermit had taken considerable pause for replenishing his own ossified chest, she saw no harm in speaking. "Wordkyn," she said, hardly able to believe her ears, "What a coincidence! I knew a Wordkyn — years ago, that was. And he was a poet too," she said, flushing with the memory.

"Not the same! Not the same!" cried De'Ath irritably. "Oh, we's got to listen hasn't we, or how is he to tell his tale? We said it wasn't his real name, didn't we. Not his real name, no. Is we to go on, or is you to tell it?" enquired the hermit peevishly. "If you knows more about Wordkyn then we'll keep quiet, we will," said the aggrieved De'Ath, tightly sealing his lips.

"I'm very sorry," Alice assuaged the narrator's tender feelings — not, reader, that I believe his feelings were so tender, although — "It's just a coincidence, that's all," she said — that is mere conjecture on my part — "nothing more than chance," said Alice, and wondered whether De'Ath was being coy over Wordkyn's identity, or whether he knew him and had simply expropriated the name to use it for another poet — the Wordkyn of the tale —— I wouldn't put it past him, either; but no more of this. "Please go on," Auntie smoothed the troubled ground. "You tell the tale very well," said she, praising the hermit and at the same time suspecting some elaborate manoeuvre on his part — as we do too, to make our own position perfectly clear. "I'm sure it cannot possibly be the same Wordkyn," she agreed, "it was such a long time ago."

"Decades, decades," De'Ath was mollified. "A long walk," he turned to Estrogen who twitched and muttered under his breath, "down memory's shaded lane."

"Ah," Auntie sighed.

"And at the end of the lane," De'Ath gave a whimsical scratch of his cerements, "we enters the fields of recollection, a-climbing over the stile of forgetfulness and a-vaulting the stream of oblivion" — such agility makes me doubt the tale, reader, I fear the worst — "as frisky as lambs, we is, in the 'appy days of our youth!

"Yes, how it comes back to me, it does; how this Wordkyn's apartments lay within the innermost keep of the castle, far from the babbling menial throng of the subterraceous levels, far from the draughty and tapestried corridors where me lady took her midnight walks, her jewelled gown trailing and clinking in the musty breeze what swept through them time-hallowed corridors and everywhere made its pensive moaning like the very stones cried out in pain, far from that hidden recess where the Baron Hank Caughlin Mangaravidi Fitz Kelly Mordant kept his evil court, where spies did bring him news of the castle's distant hummings, of the doings and goings-on in the Parish, of the exertions and plots of his friends what hated him and enemies what hated him more in the world at large; silent shadowy creatures they was, these spies, messengers of doom what knew the hearts of all men, flitting to and fro from that secret chamber far from where Wordkyn lived; yes, far he lived, far from all what went on in them parts, far from the brooding forest where owls hooted and bloodhounds howled and maidens shrieked, far from the deep and distant dungeons where good men mouldered and died and was buried in the Parish yard, far from that topmost turret of the topless towers where old De'Ath here was taunted with Fitz's cruel jibes and crazed laughter."

At this point, having abbreviated the Baron's name, the hermit astonished his listeners with a personation of the titled laughter: a resonant *ho-ho, ho-ho-hoing,* summoned, as it were, from De'Ath's feet, compressed through his stovepipe legs, expanded and amplified in his rickety chest, at last escaped from his lips, so that the laughter, had it not been crazed in the original, now certainly justified the hermit's description of it as such. "*Ahhh!*" the hermit croaked at the expiry of his imitation, "that's better."

"Yet for all his isolation," De'Ath took up his main theme again, "this Wordkyn was a goodly poet, if too much disposed to melancholy, what maybe saw a kindred spirit in that lowly Sexton, and generously afforded him the use of his library. Amongst the many volumes in his collection was numbered texts by Blubber, Quirkerguard, and Heathen-digger, what books, on account of their dreary emphasis on the solitary nature of the human estate, contributed to the Poet's depressive state of mind, worn by him, yes, worn like his customary suit of solemn black, worn manfully and with a certain degree of pride (pride what is the failing of all bards) in his station. In the same way his poetry was tinged, tainted some might say, by this despondent habit, so that Wordkyn was at his best when celebrating unhappy occurrences such as the death of the sixtieth Baron who passed away with the cholera, contracted through drinking the infected waters of the well which lay in the Ostler's domain where rumour says he was about some lecherous business with the Ostler's daughter. An unhappy fate, that, and one what many, many years later I was to wish on the Baron Hank Caughlin Mangaravidi Fitz Kelly Mordant, the sixty-first of his line, his blighted line, what poisoned his charge's heart against me suit, as I have said before. *Ahhh*, the powers, the powers!" cried De'Ath, *ho-ho-hoing* once more. "They had kept yet a worse fate in store for him, they had, and his laughter turned against him, it did, so that bloated with his own corruption he succumbed to Herod's disease: an 'orrible infliction of maggots in the private parts, combined with an insatiable and inflamed lust, fluvial emissions from the bowels, and an unquenchable hunger. A very protestantical complaint what made him ripe and high when I buggered him in the yard, years, years after the time of which I tell."

"This is too strange for words," thought Alice (and we agree), for the hermit's description of Wordkyn in every way coincided with her own remembrance of the poet from the days of Hannibali's prime when she had been in the habit of touring the countryside, performing – as we have seen – charitable works, and Hannibali needed no sweet persuasion to lure him forth. "What purpose can he possibly have," she wondered of De'Ath, "in denying that Wordkyn is . . . Wordkyn?"

Hence Auntie's suspicions grew, yet she maintained her silence – fortunately in one sense, unfortunately in another – for De'Ath was about to begin the second fit of his tale and a question at this juncture might have broken his narrative back completely, making our burden the lighter, to the great expedition of our prime plot, which, though moving, is stationary.

In a word, reader, she said nothing.

II

"All what I've said is by the by as far as Wordkyn was concerned," acknowledged De'Ath, clattering his bone anew, as though annoyed at his own aside on the sixty-first Baron's demise, "but the shaded lane of memory is a winding path and me reminiscences are buried in the hedgerows and we has to go a piece out of the way to find 'em. But one day, them long years ago, one very fine and sunny day – "

"Down memory's *shady* lane!" cried Estrogen, forgetting to preface his speech with any direction whatsoever.

"Shadows is *made* by sun," De'Ath triumphed tersely. "Yes, one very fine and sunny day as I was a-saying, while I was browsing in Wordkyn's library, I was perplexed, I was, to stumble upon a volume of a different sort from what he made his staple diet. It belonged to that genus of book what is called *novel* and was designed as an exoterical work, it was, fitting for the public imagination, suitable for the grossest of gross appetites, yes, and worthy of the dullest of dull wits: a sub-book it was. Considerations of taste, friends, prevent me from revealing the title, and I will say no more than that the sub-book, the author himself, and all of its principal characters was eventually consigned to the pit, me very own projection what came to me while I was a bugger in the yard. And it is to this pit and its conception in me mind," De'Ath eased himself into a subject of more universal application than sub-books and the scribblings of mere bards, "it is to this pit and its relation to my poetical friend and his sombre-serious moods and his dark melancholy fits," said the hermit with great sobriety and lowered voice – lowered yet audible above the engine's hum – "that I would now like to turn, I would. If, that is," the hermit shot a mournful glance at the company and took full advantage of the narrative caesura, "if we doesn't hear any more objections, no more interruptions to his tale."

"Ahhh," the hermit drew in his breath, "we's all silent, is we? All nice and peaceful like? Well, then, to cut a long story short, many more of these novels began to appear in Wordkyn's collection, and me private opinion of him began to decline as a consequence.

"It was not incumbent upon me," De'Ath charged the heavy phrase with an egregious and exaggerated servility, "to criticize Wordkyn who, as the Parish Poet, was of an infinitely more exalted station than mine, and who was (as I have attempted to suggest) a person of no mean skill in the art of composing dirges, requiems, threnodies and other such sorrowful verses. One day, therefore, when he discovered me at these novels and asked me what I thought of them, I made some reply or other to the effect that I thought them very entertaining (out of deference to his rank), but that I could not for the life of me understand why one of his condition should occupy his mind and the space in it with so much trivia, which though I'm sure was very well composed and gotten up (says I) meant but little to me who at the time was but a lowly and humble Sexton what had no time for such things. It was then that he seized hold of me, grabbed me by the collar, he did, and it is from that day all them long years ago – a day of strange and intense feelings – that I dates the distant and dark origins of the plot in the yard.

"With the only enthusiasm I ever seen him display (apart from what he reserved for his laments), he begins to explain his purpose. 'Come,' says he, drawing me aside to the ivy-clad casement window, partly obscured by the Baron's crenellated rooftops and dizzy spires, so the view weren't very good and precious little light got in; 'Come,' says he, his

150

voice animated by melancholy passion and his wan features cast into severe illumination by the smouldering beams of mote-speckled light; 'Come,' " the hermit's voice approximated to the dolorous tones of Wordkyn, " 'my vital powers fail me and the life within me dies. Yet ever since you have known me, and long, long, long before, I have striven to discharge my weary duties in a grave and serious manner. But heavy grief no longer strikes me with her leaden pangs, nor slows the beat of this anguished heart.' " Here De'Ath fixed his own hand on his ribcage and covered the region where his heart presumably lay.

" 'No,' " he continued in the style of Wordkyn, " 'the melancholy fit escapes me; grief, sorrow, mourning, interments and sad funereal steps – fit subjects for my weeping Muse – these are fled like the shades of dead Parishioners, departed Barons, the long deceased that haunt the midnight confines of these ancient walls. My narcotic senses awake and this turgid stream flows the quicker within me; dim stirrings of perception make prodigious my burden – *light*, even the muted gloom of this my library, is as the desert sun to my opening eyes, and parches them that were oases 'mongst my senses' aridity; *sound*, even the stealthy tread of the Baron's soft pawed hound (though not its midnight howl) is like the roaring of a thousand mountain cataracts, a Niagara to my unstopped ears; *touch*, hitherto insensate and dormant within me, opes withal the multiple shocks and proofs of a bruised life, that my corporeal frame is knocked to the bone and dreads to touch where once it doubted this material world; *taste*, faculty unknown to one whose former diet of woesome verses fed him not, henceforward threatens the viaducts to my brain with o'erload, o'ercoursing as the plushy gourd explodes on buds of taste and the ripe vermillion plum my mind doth irrigate with droplets of purest agony; and *smell*,' " De'Ath flexed his snout, " '*smell* that these long years has slumbered, the drowsiest of my poetical wits, is now become all omnipotent, the damask rose to me more pungent than the mouldering body of the sixtieth Baron *e'en whilst he lived* that hence these vapours, though nothing material, must all the other senses o'erwhelm and tear down to ruin.' "

151

"I must say," the hermit continued, his breath coming in thick clouts, "that the poor Poet, with all due deference to his rank, became quite carried away, he did. 'But De'Ath,' " he reverted to Wordkyn's voice, " 'De'Ath, I see, I hear, I touch, I taste, I smell, I *live!*' 'Does you, Wordkyn,' says I, 'Does you?'

" 'For of late,' says he, 'of late I have learned of a world outside these walls, outside this Parish, and they — these very novels — have played no small a part in my education. It is a world of the senses, De'Ath, where men may perform heroic deeds: a world of action, adventure, brave and noble feats, trials of arms, violence, valour, and glory for the taking!'

" 'But,' says I, 'you says you was dying a minute ago, you did. I recollects it very clear.'

" 'Oh yes,' says he, moaning and sighing like. 'Grief! Grief! It is the grief that dies within Wordkyn, De'Ath. The dark-capped clouds are lifted from my soul and I see, I see the world without the castle keep: a world of strong and lusty adventurers and clean, lithe-limbed maidens.'

" 'Maidens?' says I. 'What's this, Wordkyn? What's this all about?'

" 'Passion!' says he, clutching hold of me again. 'Ecstasy! Vitality of the soul! Ah, these books, De'Ath, have put me in mind of my manifold errors. But now I see and live! Are their authors not bards of presage? Are they not trumpeted from the housetops? Are they not prized, decorated, and loudly put about the streets so that even the commonality has a whiff of their names? And what of me, what of Wordkyn? Have I not too long laboured over melancholy subjects and too long unburdened this sad heart? Yes! Is my light to remain forever hidden under a forest of bushels? No! And now that my pulse quickens and my blood courses, am I to remain unknown, forever unknown, within the confines of these dour, dank, moss-coated walls? What fame might seep through this mortar to the other world? None! Oh no, none! But I see, and I live! I breathe and am alive at last, at last, De'Ath, at last!' " concluded the hermit lugubriously, somewhat at variance indeed with the stridency of the Poet's claims.

"Yes, yes," De'Ath came up for air, "there was no sense

in his words, nor anything epical in these books, not what I could see, unless it was mockery of what the poet should have been about, composing his measures in honour of the departed like what he was supposed to do. 'What does this mean?' says I. '*Mean*?' says he. '*Mean*? By all that is morbid and worthy of song, it means we live in revolutionary times.' 'With that I agree,' says I. 'But how, Wordkyn, how?' '*How*?' says he. 'I,' says he, 'I am, my dear old ancient Sexton,' for so he was fond of calling me, though I was not at the time so very ancient, 'I am to build new and infinitely more powerful structures that men might forget these other and less accomplished bards and think only on Wordkyn, Poet of all the ages!'

" 'God's Wounds!' says I, that being the sort of oath he liked best, else 'Zounds!' or 'Oddsfish!' (very archaical like)," explained De'Ath for the benefit of his audience who were now becoming visibly restless. "Yes, 'God's Wounds!' says I. 'Have you taken leave of your mind, Wordkyn?'

" 'Found it, De'Ath! I've found it!' says he, shaking his dear old ancient Sexton fit to throw him out the casement window. 'All these books,' says he, 'all these books is here for a purpose, De'Ath. Yes, a purpose,' says he, sort of mad about the eyes, 'because Wordkyn's writing a book himself, he is, a book which will so far surpass these others in the nobility, design, elevation, and execution of its achievements that Wordkyn's name will be known for all time and he will live, De'Ath, live where he has been dead before! Ah, ambition, where is thy spur?'

" 'You must be out of your skull, Wordkyn,' says I, 'to fill your library and your head with such stuff that's good only for burning or ... or ... ' " De'Ath halted, his voice cracking and breaking, " ' ... or for burying up!' " he cried, "*burying up!*" – which bronchial exclamation wrenched his mind with incredible rapidity from the distant past to the near present.

III

"There it was, you see," De'Ath grinned horribly, "the

153

pit! He was dragged into it, he was. He was dragged in like
what he said on account of that blackamore and his talking
head, yes: the nice little boy was watching, he was, the little
boy what he had imagined as his companion when he was all
alone in the yard. Ahhh . . . So it comes to this, it does, that
when he was down there, all of a sudden it grows *dark*.
Course, not that it was light on the outside, and me tallow
would have been a great 'elp, but there was stars and a bit of
a moon; not in the pit, no, where all of a sudden it comes
darker than dark: *black* —"

IV

"Dark it was in that sullen corridor: dark, dank, and
'orrible. Evil it was, full of strange murmurations and noises
what weren't nice. 'Me tallow,' I says to meself, 'if only I
ain't have forgot it, tsk-tsk.' You ain't got any notion of what
it was like down there you ain't, no, him being without his
tallow and not so much as a spark to light it with. 'I must
keep it straight in me head,' says I, 'for the record like.' And
though it was dark, darker than dark, I writes it down all the
same, a-crawling along on me hands and shanks.
   "Yes, it must have been ages that I crawled; slow and
stiff it was, a-crawling over the bodies of long departed
Parishioners, preserved on account of the singular properties
of the soil. Then I sees this clink of light, shining as they does
from underneath a door at the end of the tunnel. 'Door,' says
I, 'that's a door, it is, De'Ath. And there's light, there is, light
for reading and writing.' Yes, so I gets meself to this door, I
does, and then I pulls at it and I opens it and — " De'Ath's
vocal hinges creaked in his throat, " — what does I see? What
is it? 'Orrible, yes, 'orrible, but nothing as 'orrible compared
with what was to come, though he didn't know about *that*
then. Yes, I found meself in a cave, I did, the walls of which
was composed of human meat and perspired with human
gore. And then, before me very eyes, these same eyes what
looks at you now, then he makes out the gibbeted forms of
all them authors what he'd consigned to the pit, them
scoundrels what had turned me melancholy friend's head

now with their own heads turned. Yes, there they was a-hanging: some grinning, others scowling, their necks all twisted and their faces empurpled by the gallows' fast embrace, a-hanging there like puppets – awful to behold," De'Ath painted the scene and read the scroll of authorship: "Yes, there they was: Ginsyawp, Grundgespringer, Myron and O'Murke, Trophy, Flame, Prickens and Drab, Dreebley, Droshummer, Sidewike and Wrath, Bollini and Belch, Bethel-hammer, Jellby, Groaner and Hays – there they was, and many more, proud bards and dead.

"Yet strange to say and stranger to tell," he continued, "the sound of distant revelry comes to his ears, and at that moment, after a lapse of untold decades, he thinks directly on the Poet, Wordkyn, and there was I a-remembering what he'd told me all them long years ago about this book what he was to write and how I'd said he was out of his head to plan such a thing 'cos it was not what he should have been doing, no; yes, I said, I did, 'You must be out of your mind, Wordkyn,' (where these hanging bards had put him), and there was I a-looking on them in the flesh, except they was all trussed up and hanging like what I said.

" 'Strange, strange,' says I to meself, 'that I should think on Wordkyn,' for I had not heard tell of him for all them long years, and knew nothing about his book, whether it was published and had earned him the fame that he wanted, or whether it had failed his expectations and he had returned to his tragical verses. 'Well, well,' says I, 'that's as strange as these authors a-lolling here at the end of their ropes,' and with that I hears this 'orrible laughter – *inyoomun*, it was – " De'Ath drew the word out, "*inyoomun*, fit to clot the blood in these old veins. 'Tut, De'Ath,' says I to meself, 'this is no place to be caught hanging around, no place at all.'

"To cut a long story short," said De'Ath to the great relief of Estrogen, who was now very impatient, "to cut a long story short, I sees another door at the end of this cave, and not stopping to think how these hanging bards came to be where they was, I makes it me object to get to this door. 'Scuttle-shanks,' says I, 'you's got to reach that door, old scuttle-shanks, 'cos who knows what they might be hanging next? Not that they would hang an old man like you, would

155

they now? No, they wouldn't hang an old hermit what never did nobody no harm, they wouldn't.' "

"They?" Waldemar hung upon the pronoun.

"He's coming to that, he is, if you'll let him tell it in his own way and stop breaking in on him," muttered De'Ath, another outburst of temperament shaking his ancient frame. "Why can't he tell his story like what anybody else does? 'Cos they's jealous, they is; yes, that's what they is, oh dear me. They doesn't *want* to know, does they? Well, they will, they *shall*," the hermit gave an emphatic rap of his bone on Estrogen's knees — unjustly, reader, for the Knave was not to blame for this latest interruption, and if I were in his place I would not have taken such treatment so lightly — "they'll have to listen, they will, otherwise he'll keep quiet, he will . . . "

"The hanging authors," Auntie steered De'Ath back to his ostensible subject, "what had happened to them?"

" 'appened? They was hung, that's what. But he's coming to it, yes, in his own good time he's coming to it," said De'Ath, momentarily hanging fire in preparation for the dramatic climax of his tale: "yes, hung by the neck, garotted, strangulated, choked-off, a pretty lot of gallows' fruit they was. 'No,' says I, 'you's not for the hanging, De'Ath. Steel your nerves,' says I, 'steel your nerves, De'Ath. There's things up in here, things not in the plot, not in the plot what you made.' He never meant no bards to be hung, he didn't; buried up maybe, but not hung — " which climax, indeed, retreated like the horizon — "Then it was," De'Ath allowed himself another affirmative rapping of his bone, "then it was that things began to 'appen, more than what had already 'appened, things what he wasn't prepared for, things more 'orrible than them hangings. From this further door there comes more of this curdling laughter, 'owlings and moanings fit to give him the coagulations. 'Dear me, De'Ath,' says I, me old heart palpitating very fast, 'something is direly up with the plot, yes.' Then this door" — De'Ath paused — "this door swings open all on its own accord and I hears, not them groanings and complaints, but the sound of merriment and rejoicing. 'Food,' says I, 'there's food in it for De'Ath. Victuals and combustibles for him to eat, yes.' But . . . *Ahhh!*

Ahhh! . . . There comes the 'owling again, murmurations and grumblings, there comes a great whistling wind, a-setting them hanging bards a-dancing and a-jigging on their ropes like they was living bards, not hanging, and there comes a blinding flash of light and an 'orrible smell of putrid flesh what made him think them bards was lucky to have their necks pulled, and then, then, he sees, he sees . . . "

V

"*It!*" shrieked the Sepulchral Sister.

"Yes, it was *it*, that's what it was, it was, it was *it*. *It!*" babbled De'Ath — and the reader will observe that the hermit must now be added to our list of demented persons: 'It, oh an 'orrible and monstrous beast — twelve feet in height, it was, its face and body covered with 'orrible deformities, boils and sores, scabs and scars . . . "

— for in considering the matter of what De'Ath saw, or pretended to see, we have rejected the appealing yet facile theory that the hermit's vision and Sybil's had any objective or 'real' existence, despite the remarkable similarity between the two:

" . . . armed with a wondrously sharp beak, it was, with a large and bulbous horn upon its head, and what you might call talons, well no not talons, not talons exactly, more like claws, yes claws what snapped and slashed at the air; snapping and slashing, they was. Oh, but he's no coward ain't De'Ath," cried the hermit, brandishing his bone, much to Estrogen's discomforture, for the bone again connected with the Knave's knees, "no, no he's no coward, never was nor never has been nor never will be, so he prepared himself for battle, he does . . . "

—— and think instead that De'Ath was suffering — as we have indicated — from a similar *if not identical* form of delirium as the Sister herself who, of course, was now wildly shrieking "*It! It!*" in apparent support of the hermit:

"And yet . . . " "*It! It!*" " . . . and yet . . . " "*It! It!*" " . . . when it . . . "

——— support that constituted no interruption and was

therefore welcomed by De'Ath, the pair of them — he and Sybil — chanting in bedlamite chorus:

"... still comes on, the monster does ... " "*It! It!*" " ... a-snapping of its claws and a-munching of its beak, so it was almost up with him, it was, it was nearly over for old De'Ath, nearly choked ... " "*It! It!*" " ... he was, with its fetid breath ... "

——— a crazed duet, until:

"... quiet, we must be quiet ... " "*It! It!*" " ... how, how can he go on? It's too much for him, it is, just too much."

"Sybil!" Auntie tried to pacify the Sister as the minibus veered and skated and skidded: "don't interrupt the gentleman."

"Not her, not her, he doesn't mean her, not. Who is it? Who's doing it to him?"

——— and we have no choice but to take this as further evidence of De'Ath's unsound state of mind: that he should now *imagine* interruptions:

"Quiet, yes we must be quiet. Stop! Shut it up, we must. Yes. Listen! Listen!" the hermit gasped. "Where is it? Who is it?"

"Where?" Waldemar's hands waved. "Who?"

"Stop it yes," De'Ath grated. "There it is, there it is!" "*It! It!*" "Not it, *it*: it's not *it* that he means: *that! That!* It said ... "

——— the reader surely agreeing with us when we declare that De'Ath was hallucinating now as before:

"What's that?" De'Ath raised a scrawny hand to his ear: " 'lucinating? Who said he was mad? Who said it? Unsound state of mind? He's not mad, no. Not mad. Be quiet!"

Reader, I ...

"I!" * "*I*? It's me, De'Ath: that's what it is. He's telling the tale, he is — not you, not nobody else."

"There now," said Auntie, "you've shown him who's telling the story."

"Yes we have. Put him in his place, we have. Let that be

* Your narrator is profoundly apologetic, reader, for this lamentable confusion. Our narrative commentary, we promise, shall be restored as soon as the situation is clarified. In the meantime, De'Ath must be allowed to wind up his tale. Needless to say, we expect the conclusion very shortly.

158

a lesson to you, whatever you is! Where was we now? Yes, memory's shaded lane ... "

"ESTROGEN: *Has no choice but to revert to directed speech, his two dimensional and multi-coloured frontage shaking with apopleptic rage!*"

"No? Isn't that where we was?"

"*It! It! It!*" the minibus snaked over the road.

"Yes, yes, we knows now, we remembers, we does, not forgotten: it was almost up with him, it was, like he was saying, almost choked like them bards was strangulated, almost a goner was old De'Ath when – wonder of wonders! – the monster begins to dance, it does, and then performs the impossible act of copulating with himself or itself, he should say, yes, *itself*; this monstrous blue horned beast scratching at its anus with its clawed pincers, scratching there to bring forth more of its kind, 'orrible progeny, exact replicas, they was, of the parent monster, whelped in a sea of dung and blood while them hanging bards looked on, oh terrible parturition, terrible," wheezed the hermit, at the same time staring craftily about the company, "terrible, yes terrible, but fortunate for old De'Ath here, for the monster thus diverted with itselves, he slipped through that door he did, through to what he thought was friendship, merriment, and the goodly crew what's rejoicing he had heard before, leaving the little monsters and the hanging bards at the end of them ropes where they was still a-jigging and a-hanging."

"Amen!" cried Sybil, still at one with her fellow visionary.

"Amen it was, oh yes it was," De'Ath rattled his bone. "But no. No! The great banqueting hall in which I discovered meself wore all the signs of a mighty feast: tables and chairs was all overturned; food and wine flasks was scattered on the sodden floors, abandoned articles of clothing testified to the celebrants' profligacy, but there was nobody, not a soul nowhere to be seen. They was gone, they was, gone. Yet still there came to me ears, and he's got sharp ears, he has, still there came the distant sound, ever and around, of riotous feasting, revelry and song. But that hall, me friends," the hermit honoured his listeners with a personal appeal, "and I do say friends, 'cos I'm sure there's none here what's an enemy to old De'Ath even if you does butt in on him from time to time, that hall was as still as the grave itself, if not stiller.

" 'Chickins,' says I to meself, 'here's chickins for you to eat, De'Ath, chickins and all sorts of dainties, yes. There's chickins and . . . ' " De'Ath halted.

"What is it?" said Auntie.

"Nothing," said De'Ath, "I was just thinking of the chickins. Ah! But yes, as I was saying, he was just about to take his leave, he was, by means of another door what he sees at the far end of the hall — wild horses couldn't drag him back the way he'd been, not past the monsters and them hanging bards — when he hears a ghastly moaning, as of one in his final agony, a ghastly moaning what chills me bones, coagulates me blood, and stops this old heart for an eternity."

"Fuckit!" Estrogen wished the eternity had lasted longer.

"Oh yes, that's what he thinks, he does. Anyways, plucking a flaming brand from the wall, he goes in search of the sound, he does," announced De'Ath, as though the flaming brand had been placed there especially for his convenience, which in a narrative sense it had, for he had so positioned it himself — but I shall desist from these observations, reader, trusting that the exercise of restraint on my part will hasten the end of De'Ath's laggard tale: "An 'ollow, gurgling sort of sound it was," thus we let the hermit continue, "beyond me powers of description," while observing that he now impersonated the sound where he could not describe it by letting out this stertorous rattle, this fossilized and calcified ululation: "*Aaargharghull!*" which resounded greatly about the interior of the minibus, astonishing the wizard who was drifting off to sleep — "*Aaargharghull!*" De'Ath howled, frowning and scowling as his imagination converted the minibus into the banqueting hall of his tale, "and then, then, under this table's trestle, I sees a ragged shape, a human shape" — 'yoomun' — "I would say, but hardly recognizable as such in that there flickering light. 'Bless me bleared eyes,' says I approaching closer, 'if there ain't something familiar about that shape, and the face as well. Why yes,' says I, 'there's something distinctly familiar about it. Now what can it be? Let me see if I can draw aside memory's veil from the babbling brook of oblivion. Tsk, tsk, I've seen that face somewhere before, I'll be buggered if I ain't."

De'Ath's dried tongue drummed upon his palate in a roll of leathern cluckings. For some time he prolonged the desperate dialogue with himself — like the author that he pretended to be — varying his re-enactment with an arid tattoo of tickings and tuttings seemingly related to the extemporaneous nature of his narrative, and proceeding somewhat along these lines: 'Bless me bones, but I've seen it before . . . tsk, tsk, tsk, where now? Tch, tch, tch, it do seem familiar — like I ought to know it. Tut, tut, he's not one to forget a face, he's not . . . Ah, but it must have been a long time ago, yes, that explains it, that does . . . ' wrestled with the identity of the figure in his mind's eye, so placing a severe strain on Estrogen who began to thrash around, cursing and muttering — fruitlessly as it transpired, for De'Ath was almost into the sixth and concluding act of his drama. Waldemar, his slumbers interrupted, also showed signs of restlessness, and attempted to calculate the time of day by reference to an imaginary sundial. Auntie, sensing that some crisis loomed in both the tale and its teller, parried with a further distribution of Hambabies while De'Ath advanced his strategy to the renewed drummings of palatal fricatives.

VI

" 'Tsk, tsk,' " De'Ath clucked, playing out the part of himself, " 'I knows it and I knowed it all along! He's a memory as long as your arm, has old De'Ath, never forgets nothing, he doesn't. Yes, it's *Wordkyn*, ain't it? Bugger me backwards!' " the hermit cried, surprising himself, if nobody else, "yes, it's Wordkyn, no doubt of it, no doubt at all, Wordkyn, the Parish Poet, but transmogrified beyond belief. 'What's that, Wordkyn?' says I. 'What's that?' " enquired De'Ath, screwing up his features in a grotesque personation of the Poet's agony. 'What is it? What's you trying to tell me?

Doesn't you recognize him? Doesn't you know what's here, Wordkyn?' "

"For God's sake *get on with it!*" exclaimed Estrogen — an imperative which merely drew another gargle deep from within the hermit's emaciated breast.

"*Aaargharghull!* Yes, Wordkyn, that's what it was. But he didn't know old De'Ath, he didn't. Delirious he was, 'orribly beaten and disfigured, all mangled very sad like, and fading fast he was, poor Wordkyn. 'Tsk, tsk,' says I to meself, 'there ain't nothing to be done here, De'Ath, yes, he's going, he is, a-going where he'll be better off. But I'll speak to him once more, that's what I'll do, and see if I can make sense out of his dying ravings.' So I says, 'Wordkyn,' I says, 'it's De'Ath. You knows old De'Ath, doesn't you, your dear old ancient Sexton, Wordkyn, what's come to offer you comfort in your final moments, tsk, tsk.' But all he does is repeat the names of them hanging bards, over and over again he says their names: Hays and Groaner, Jellby, Bethel-hammer, Belch and Bollini, Wrath and Sidewike, Dros-hummer, Dreebley, Drab and Prickens, Flame, Trophy, O'Murke and Myron, Grundgespringer, Ginsyawp, then he starts again: Ginsyawp . . . but passing over that, friends, 'cos it ain't consequential to me tale, I says to him, 'Wordkyn,' I says, 'what's you doing down here? I doesn't know what you was *supposed* to be in here, Wordkyn, not all beaten and battered like this. What's you doing in the plot, eh?' But all he can manage is the names of them bards, over and over again, pausing and gagging for breath — every one of which I thought was his last, I did — so I won't go through it all, no, on account of the time he took to say nothing, yes, until he quietens down like and the spirit goes from him: *Aaarghargull!* 'Yes,' I says to meself, 'that's it, then, he's finished, he is, gone he has, and you had no time to administer the last rites, De'Ath.'

"Then, then I hears this faint gasp of breath from him. 'Ain't you dead, Wordkyn?' says I. 'Ain't you gone yet?'

" 'Dead,' says he, 'all dead.'

" 'What's that, Wordkyn?' says I. 'You ain't dead yet, there's still some air left in you yet. Does you know who it is,

Wordkyn?'

" 'Who?' says he, while I's thinking how protraculated his passing was: 'Who?' says he, coming to and propping himself up on his arm, 'it looks like . . . De'Ath.'

" 'It is,' says I, 'the same. What's you doing down here, Wordkyn? What's been 'appening to you?'

" 'All dead,' says he, and starts off saying them names again, 'Listen,' says he, 'the hangings, De'Ath, murders, murders.' "

"Who could have done such a thing?" enquired Auntie.

"Oh yes, who indeed?" De'Ath rapped his bone for silence. "But we doesn't want to know that, we doesn't, no. We wants to know how Wordkyn was where he was, and we wants to know what Wordkyn gave his Sexton before he passed away, doesn't we?"

"Gave," Waldemar stared nervously at Estrogen.

"That's what we said," De'Ath announced rather smugly: "*gave*. Yes, there he was, Wordkyn, the Parish Poet, muttering them names, rambling on and making no sense that I could tell, when — what 'appens? What does you think 'appens?"

"He gave you something," said Estrogen smirking and snarling, "didn't he?"

"*No*," De'Ath wheezed, "before that — what 'appened before that? Well, since you doesn't know, I'll tell you, I will, yes. He gets out these papers, see, and he begins to read. Can you imagine that? Reading in his condition, him that was a most sorrowful soul, or had been till his head was turned, lying there like an herd of elephants had stamped on him — which they had, oh yes. Literary elephants, you might say," added De'Ath, permitting himself a smirk at the Knave's expense, "and reading, *reading*?

" 'One,' he says, getting out his papers and taking on a new lease of life as is often the case with the dying. 'One.'

" 'What's that, Wordkyn,' says I, 'what does you mean, "*One*"? One *what*?'

" 'Forgive me,' he says, 'my dear old ancient Sexton, I've had such a time, such a terrible time, that I was forgetting,' " De'Ath lowered his voice to the muted and sombre tones of the Poet, " 'the proper convention.'

163

"Course, he was far gone, not right in the head with all the damage done to his brain box. 'You's as bad as them hanging bards, Wordkyn, not corrigible you ain't. Is this any way for one like you to behave,' says I, 'in such a grave moment, a moment of such gravity, Wordkyn, does you think you ought to be *reading*?' But it weren't no use arguing, not with that strength what the dying takes on, you can't argue with it, no, so I lets him have his way I does. 'One,' says he. 'Two,' says I. 'Three,' says he, 'but all in good time, De'Ath. And there's not enough time left for Wordkyn, my dear old ancient Sexton, so you be quiet while I tell you how the most noble authors that have ever lived in the tide of times come now to this untimely and unhappy end.'

"That nearly did him in, it did, getting all that out, but he summoned a last few gasps, he did, and this is what he read:

" *'Upon the Rebellion of Characters. '*

" 'ONE'

" 'These noble . . . ' "
The Knave convulsed, reader: "ONE?"
" 'These noble . . . ' "
"ONETROGEGGRONESTFUCKIT!! HE *makes a dive for* DE'ATH's *bone, intending to deprive the* HERMIT *of life!*" cried Estrogen, diving for De'Ath's bone.
"Smite! Smite!" cried Sybil, and in all conscience I wish De'Ath had been smitten, but I am compelled to tell the truth — the hermit whisked his bone from the Knave's reach and brought the end of it down upon Estrogen's red paper crown, crushing it the more and stunning its wearer, which temporary or permanent loss of consciousness, reader, was perhaps in the best interests of our mutual narratives:
" ' . . . noble bards,' De'Ath continued as Wordkyn, hurrying along now while Auntie ministered to the Knave's crushed crown, " 'have been the victim . . . " *Aaargharghull!* 'Tut, Wordkyn,' says I, 'make your peace with Him what made you, before it's too late.'

" 'TWO,' says he.

" ' . . . of a most foul conspiracy, De'Ath . . . ' " how the plot quickens! — " 'the foulest of all conspiracies, the conspiracy from within that eats at a man's vitals, my dear . . . '

" 'That's very interesting,' says I, 'but what in the name of all that's simple and pointed, Wordkyn, is you doing here?'

" 'Later,' says he, slipping again, meandering in his mind, 'their own characters, De'Ath, their own creations have risen up, turning their murderous hands upon those to whom they owed life, De'Ath, *life*: I saw it happen — Hautboy that was from Wrath, Nat out of Myron . . . '

" 'What's that?' says I. 'Not him. He wasn't here, was he, Wordkyn, that blackamore with the talking head? *No!* There was no talking heads in it, I says *there was no talking heads in it*, Wordkyn!' But he read on, yes, on and on he read:

" 'THREE,' he says . . . "

Did ever any plot move at such a spanking, rip-roaring pace, reader? But Estrogen, I see, is stirring —

"How much *longer*" —— even Alice — not without justification — was growing impatient:

" '*Three*,' he says, 'hold your tongue, De'Ath,' he says, 'and let me finish . . . ' "

"do we have to wait before we *find* out what happened to the *authors*?" she demanded.

" 'Cabot that was from . . . ' " De'Ath vied with Word-kyn for control of the plot, and I think it just, reader, that the hermit received some of his own treatment: "*Ahhh!* Fading he was, a relapse, yes, 'It's a relapse,' says I to meself, 'he'll soon be gone.'

" 'Horner that was from Carp, De'Ath, Zog out of Groaner . . . ' "

" 'FOUR' says he —

" ' . . . Rojack from Rojack,' says he. 'Him too?' says I. 'Was he in it?' '*Silence*, De'Ath!' says he, a dead liberty: 'Yes

165

he was, De'Ath, and the head as well. More . . . more: Sanglotte from Sidewike, these and many others that I do not mention because of time, De'Ath, time that waits for no man – ' '*Very* true,' says I, 'now, Wordkyn, what's – ?' 'Hush, De'Ath, *hush*, these characters, like shades and abysmal things that live in mirrors: images, pale copies of those who gaze therein, stepped forth from the persons of their famed and fruitful authors, first to greet them with cruel taunts, false mockings; next with parodies and satires upon their renowned bards' intentions, then with jibes and stings of contumely and scorn, these apparitions more tangible growing, phantoms of material substance made, yet abominable distortions of their kind, honest, darling creators . . .

" 'FIVE,' says he, '*five, five* . . .' and gives an 'orrible gasp.

" 'FIVE,' he says again.

" 'I must tell it this way, my dear old ancient Sexton, *my* way . . . by all that's grievous and tragical,' " De'Ath's voice dropped another octave, " 'by all that's doleful and melancholy, these spectres loomed massier, o'ertopping their powerless bards until Nat said: "Freedom! That's what we want. Was I hung up and skinned just so that bastard could make a white book out of me?" ' "

" ' "No you weren't," said Hautboy; he was the instigator, De'Ath, the prime conspirator – "We're all freaks," he said, "Just look at me! Do you think I like having this enormous organ? Why did he give me an organ like this, *why*? So he could play with it himself, that's why – I only hope he has as much hair on his palms as I have!" ' "

" 'And then Horner, he said, "String 'em up; that's all they're good for: hanging! Lynch 'em!" ' "

"*Aaarghargull!*" De'Ath produced another rattling, " 'His mind's gone,' says I to meself, 'he's right out of his head! Who ever hear of characters stepping out from their authors? That's not in it,' I says to meself, I says, 'None of this is in it.' But I tries once more, I does: 'Wordkyn,' says I, '*how come you's down here?*'

166

" 'SIX,' says he.

" 'The worst fit of all . . . ' but he was slipping, slipping down the hill of Morpheus: ' . . . *six*, no discipline, they had no constraint, you . . . "From what, what do you want freedom *from*?" I said, De'Ath, but it was no use . . . the lynchings began, all dead, my dear old ancient Sexton, all hung up by the neck . . . all *gone*.' "

With a faint wheezing sound, the hermit indicated Wordkyn to have passed into oblivion, or something resembling it. (Obviously the recluse's histrionic talents have carried the day, and he is at last close to the denouement of his tale, if not of Wordkyn — a very fortunate circumstance, reader, for the Knave is stirring again.)

" 'Is you still there, Wordkyn?' says I.

" 'Revolution,' says he, very weak, 'murdered, murdered by their own creations, De'Ath. What was I to do? Escaped myself, not *published*, you see, so they had no grudge against me . . . but in the rush to the gallows, De'Ath, in the rush to the gallows I was trampled . . . they'll destroy everything, De'Ath, everything . . . *ahhh! ahhhhhhh!*' Then he flops over like, flops over on his side and rolls his eyes back. 'That's it, then,' says I, 'that's definitely it: finished, he is, dead, oh dear me yes. You's a stiff, Wordkyn, that's what you is now.' "

"You mean you *didn't* find out why Wordkyn was in the pit?" Auntie could find no words other than these to express her surprise, reader.

— 'Did *you*?' asked my good friend Damon Gottesgabe. 'Find out, that is,' he added.

— 'How can you possibly expect me,' I'm afraid I was rather hasty with him, reader, 'to get on with the narration, if you will keep asking these questions?'

"ESTROGEN: *Groans*," groaned the Knave.

"There there," said Alice, "never mind. Well?" she demanded of the hermit.

" '*Hissst!*' says I, 'What's that De'Ath, what is it that you hears now? Dear me, tsk, tsk, tut, tut, tut, that's very sad, it is, yes.' "

"Sad?" The sun shone no more on Waldemar's sundial.

" '*Hissst!*' Quiet, we must have *quiet*. Respect for the

departed," a tear glistened in De'Ath's eye, "we must mourn such sad passings, we must. Then we listens, we listens and we hears: AARGHARGHULL!!" "*It! It!*" "No, that's not what it was, not this time, by no means, oh dear me *no!* WORDKYN! That's what it was, yes: *A-hackle, a-hackle, a-hackle, a-hackle!* he coughs, and he stirs, and he moans, and he groans. 'Buggeration!' says I, 'Is you still with us, Wordkyn?' '*Yessss,*' says he:

" 'SEVEN,' says he. 'Remember, De'Ath, when you tell it in the minibus, there's *seven fits.*'
" 'Seven?' says I, '*seven?*' '*Yesss,*' says he, 'there was seven fits, De'Ath, seven fits to the tale.' 'Bugger me!' says I, 'but you's right, Wordkyn, you is *right!*' "

VII

" 'SEVEN'

" '*Seven,*' says he, grabbing 'old of me with the force of twenty poets, 'the final fit, De'Ath.'
" 'What is it, Wordkyn? What's troubling your mind? You can tell old De'Ath now, can't you? Cast aside memory's veil now . . .' "
"Fuckit!" Estrogen recovered.
" 'Many, many years ago, De'Ath,' says he, 'too, too many years ago when you — it is you, isn't it, De'Ath? — all those years ago when you were a visitor to my library in the Baron's castle . . . ' "
"But you've been into all that!" screeched Estrogen.
" ' . . . *library,*' " continued De'Ath as Wordkyn — a dogged narrator, if I may say so, reader — " 'and I proposed to write a book, De'Ath, as I told you, a book that would outlive all those works of . . . dead, De'Ath, all dead now, by the neck . . . did I tell you how they met their ends? Did I get it out?' 'Yes, yes, you did, Wordkyn,' says I, 'you was up to the library, Wordkyn: library and *book.*' 'I know,' says he, 'I must have been wandering in my mind De'Ath; but the book, De'Ath, the book is finished, done but not published, which

168

is why I am here, my dear old ancient Sexton: an unpublished author (Oh! Had I but stayed within the castle walls, oh!), an unpublished and unread author who escaped execution only to witness to hangings, a worse fate, it seems to me, than hanging itself. For now I am here, living, hardly living but living all the same, still to think of my book and its fate.'

" 'Me congratulations,' says I, 'for writing the book. But there's always posthumous publication,' says I, seeking to cheer him like.

" 'Oh, De'Ath,' says he, sighing and moaning 'orribly, so that he seemed almost like his former self, that being very common with them what's minds linger on in the world, though their bodies be elsewhere, 'Oh! Oh!' says he, consuming his last energies, 'into this book, De'Ath, I put myself — so does any author, my dear old ancient Sexton — and all the persons known to me, including yourself, and many other persons, imaginary characters, fruits of observation, learning and reflection. But these personages — this *Auntie*, this *Bartleby*, this *Ichabod*, this *hermit* — De'Ath, these phantasms of my brain, now much enfeebled, these fictions are now at liberty with the other characters, De'Ath, on the rampage, De'Ath, having repudiated their author without actually going to the extreme of hanging him — not from mercy or compassion, but for the cause I have already given, that he is an unpublished author. Well, dear old ancient De'Ath, I am that author and here is that book . . . '

"Of course," De'Ath declared in his own voice, and with a briskness surprising so late in the tale, "I was very pleased to find meself written about and, as you know, I am not untalented in that direction meself — as a writer. Oh yes, he's an author himself is De'Ath, and not a bad one too, if I may say so. But as for the Poet, I knew not what he meant by all this sudden, unaccountable speechifying and had no recollection of rebellions or hangings and no memory whatsoever of repudiating Wordkyn as my author or anybody else's. So I thinks to meself, I thinks, 'All this trampling and beating has definitely unbalanced his mind, which was never too steady on account of his reading.' 'Oh!' he sighs. 'Oh! A *last* wish,

169

De'Ath, a *last wish*, my dear old Sexton.' And with that he gives me this book and makes me promise to find all its characters and bring 'em back to the book so it can be published, posthumous like, and Wordkyn can have his fame and not be around to be hung for it like them others was. 'Look here, Wordkyn,' says I, 'he'll do what you wants, will old De'Ath' — who was I to refuse a man his *last* wish? — 'But he's here, old De'Ath is here and he ain't gone running off like all them other characters.' 'True,' says he, 'too true: always count on my ancient Sexton, eh De'Ath? But you're not published yet, De'Ath, so you've no cause to go running off, have you?' So I sees there was no arguing with him. 'Find 'em,' he says, 'find 'em and bring 'em back to the book where they belong, my dear old ancient Sexton, revenge, *revenge* . . .'

" 'Is that all, Wordkyn, is that all you wants from him? Is you still there?' says I. 'Has you gone yet?' Gone, he had. 'Yes,' I says to myself, 'Wordkyn is no more.'

" 'Not gone . . . yet,' says he. 'Not all I want, De'Ath: *more!*'

" 'What's that, Wordkyn,' says I, 'what more does you want?'

" 'The book, De'Ath, the *other* characters have got into the book. I want you to send 'em packing. Then . . . ' 'Yes, yes,' says I, 'then what, Wordkyn? Then what?' 'Send,' says he, 'send 'em back to where they belong, then finish . . . finish . . . ' 'Tsk-tsk,' says I, 'can't get the words out, can you, poor Wordkyn?' '*Finish the book!*' says he, forgetting what he'd said before in his ramblings.

"*Aaargharghull!*" exclaimed the narrator, delving into his tattered written-upon shroud and producing therefrom a manuscript. "Whether Wordkyn at that moment expired, I do not know. For as he pressed, ladies and gentlemen, and I say pressed fully aware of the fact that the verb is an exaggeration, he being in no condition to press anything anywhere, his strength all gone now for he was very close to the end, but as he pressed these pages into me hands," De'Ath waved the manuscript in the air, "there came a monstrous roaring sound, as though all the demons in hell were at me heels, a fiendish horrible laughter:

170

" 'A-hackle, a-hackle, a-hackle, a-hack — ' "

It was, reader, it was to have been the hermit's finest hour. For he had designed to read from the pages which even now he held aloft as — alas — he was so cruelly cut off in mid *a-hackle*.

The company was thrown first to one side, and then to the other, as Sybil screamed and applied the brakes in an endeavour to avoid the obstruction that loomed before her.

A stalwart emerged from behind the debris of what had once been a roadblock. "Throckton by the Bog," he announced curtly, but then, upon erroneously conceiving his prisoners to be both dazed and harmless, explained: "Civil Hemergency. Which party be you of — Boss's or Ham's?"

In the once changeless sky of Throckton, a pall of smoke hung ominously. The distant chatter of gunfire and the cries of the combatants sounded from the marketplace and Alice remembered the words of the wandering proselyte from Sam's Succulent Hambaby Grille, the words indeed of De'Ath himself: 'Throckton is everywhere, sister.'

CHAPTER TWENTY–ONE   *Upon Auntie's Arrival in the First Throckton by the Bog, Wherein the Reader Who Seeks Titillation is Advised by the Narrator to Skip a Chapter and Proceed Directly to* **TWENTY–TWO.**

"If I were such a reader," said Damon Gottesgabe, "I would reject such advice."

"You're entitled to your opinion," said I, "but you may take my word for it, Damon, nothing improper or distasteful will happen in this chapter. Moral truancy was outlawed under the old dispensation, and so it shall be under my narratorship."

"Then the reader is forewarned," said he. "Continue with your chaste narrative."

The Throcktonian broils, reader, had succeeded where Sybil's driving had failed – in a word, the minibus was wrecked – and we think Auntie would have been wiser had she adhered to her original plan of venturing forth on Hannibali, for we have no doubt that the aged horse might have cleared the obstruction where the VW minibus did not, which failure to become airborne depreciated its narrative value as a vehicle for the advancement of our plot to less than nil – while in no way retarding Alice's larger quest, of course.

Many splendid thoughts passed through her mind during and after the narration of De'Ath's tale and its shattering inconclusion. Firstly, she concluded it was not Wordkyn who had lost his head, but De'Ath – a judgement with which we readily agree. Secondly, she suspected the hermit of considerable narrative embroidery in the matter of the hanging bards, thinking him not so innocent of their untimely and unhappy deaths as he had maintained. For was not De'Ath, on his own admission, responsible for their original consignment to the pit? Did he not, having described their works as suitable only for the grossest appetite, wish to settle a score or two on his own account with these authors?

And the reader, who needs no guidance from me — unless he seeks unhealthy stimulation, in which case he has already been advised to skip this chapter — the reader must surely admire Auntie's insight into the hermit's nature. Was not De'Ath a self-professed bard? What easier way to authorship, then, than the interment of one's rivals, their execution, and — boldest stroke of all! — the liberation of their characters, who, freed from the guiding hands of bardship, freed from the hands that nourished and cared for them, may be expected to exercise no restraint whatsoever in the now-authorless world.

Not, of course, that we believe so preposterous an event had actually occurred. Rather we think it an example of wishful thinking on De'Ath's part, a symptom of his inability to cope with his too, too apparent lack of talent

Such was the case, thought Alice (and we adduce her opinions in support of our own argument), with the MS — no doubt replete with still more absurdities — which De'Ath brandished in the air, and which he had intended to read from before the minibus crashed into the roadblock. Could it be, she thought, that the hermit was holding fast to the real or imaginary promise given to the real or imaginary Wordkyn, and that, after his own peculiar manner, he was presently engaged in rounding up the characters whom he believed had escaped from the novel, from this novel, from all novels whose authors were suspended in the pit?

"If so," Auntie said to herself, "where does he intend to put them when has has found them?"

We shall forgive her the last question, reader, which presupposes an actual insurrection of characters, on the grounds that she was confused by the increased gravitational force coincident upon the moveable minibus meeting with the stationary barricade, and was troubled also — as will be seen — by other natural exigencies.

Yet precisely at the moment of impact, a moment correspondent to the wreckage of De'Ath's tale and the minibus, Auntie's generous gaze fell on the MS's suspended title page:

BARTLEBY

— 'What *is* the matter with you now?' cried Damon Gottesgabe.

— 'One moment,' said I: —

My apologies, reader, I must ask you to reconsider the thoughts which formed vertiginously in Auntie's mind as she, the MS, and her fellow passengers floated towards the windshield, and the face of the barricade-manning stalwart floated evasively away from the VW's path into the ditch: "B A R T L E B Y" she thought, " a *b o o k* ? " — all of which happened very quickly, reader: " T h a t m a k e s m e a *c h a r a* ****! " — with a crash upon the *chara****!*, or *character*, the thought not being completed until Auntie climbed from the wreckage.

Yes, reader, it was with this stunned and stunning realization: *"cter!"* — we leave the implications of it until a later point — that Alice met with the stalwart of the roadblock as he crawled from the ditch and again enquired whether the party supported Boss or Ham.

Now during the course of the last chapter, and the portion of this occupied by Auntie's thoughts and the destruction of our narrative vehicle, Auntie's body had been as busy as her brain. When therefore, upon the stalwart's repeated challenge, adventitious circumstance offered her the opportunity to make a modest request, she gave this same churl to understand — with the many ingenious circumlocutions proper in the right society — that she desired a piss and also a shit. He, not wishing to prove an ungentlemanly opponent of so urgent a discharge, complied by signalling her into the bushes at the wayside, where we must imagine her performing these little necessities of nature (her mind still pondering the ramifications of "cter!"), the rest of the plot progressing as herein set forth.

"What is this BOSS and who this HAM," Sybil girded her Hambaby wrapper, cast the VW minibus steering wheel to the earth, and confronted the stalwart.

"OGENSRET: Fuckit!" Estrogen swore, his yellow locks tumbling from under his crushed paper crown as he fell to the ground, where he lay struggling ineffectually.

"Here and everywhere; there and nowhere; DOGOT and

176

no DOGOT," recited Waldemar, his hands groping mystically in front of the stalwart's eyes.

"Customers! Customers!" came the withering cry as De'Ath gathered his manuscript, the sweet scent of carnage exciting his business instincts. "Shrouds! Shrouds!" cried the hermit, lowering himself by means of his bone crutch to face the stalwart who was now at a loss what to think, but dutifully (yet with less certainty) repeated his challenge, another burst of gunfire sounding in the afternoon air.

"Tee-hee! Buggerum!" cackled the hermit. "There's corpses to be had here for old De'Ath." – and for once we think the hermit spoke truly, though what can have caused these disturbances is anybody's guess –

"Boss or Ham?" Estrogen questioned the stalwart from his customary prone position.

"Aaar," he replied, gazing watchfully from face to face. "Sright."

"Two of the most noble oracles," Waldemar lectured the little group as more gunfire sounded, "two of the most noble oracles that ever trod the ladder of fame."

"They put me in a jar," said the distracted Sister – distracted, that is, by the spiteful chatter of machine gun fire – "when I was very old. And when they asked me what I wanted, I said 'to die.' "

"Clackety-clack," said Estrogen: "clackety-clackety-clack!"

"Bumble han thrumble," remarked the stalwart in a saying reserved for such emergencies when congruency failed, as it did so often for this carl. "Oi kerrnows nort aboot coracles," he mused, "nor the bladder of blame, aar," he added, his hearing evidently impeded by the noise of the civil broils from Throckton and his mind jogged into remembering Auntie, "but if thy bladder worrits ee" – yes, life must go on as usual, reader – "the forlt be not moine," he said, peering and indicating that Waldemar was free to follow Auntie's example – – though brother is turned against brother, son against father, and in De'Ath's mind at least, character against author – – "Then ee moot come harlong with me," concluded the stalwart, for he was growing restless and suspected some trick.

"And His rages are against me and His tumult comes up to mine ears," chanted Sybil to the sound of further explosions, "and His hook is put into mine nose and His bridle is in mine lips and He will turn me back the way I came, Amen!"

"Aar? Ee won't," observed the stalwart dourly.

Now while these conversations occurred, Alice completed her business in the bushes and turned her mind to what she had seen in the minibus:

"In the forty-fifth year of my life," she reflected, "I suddenly find that I am a character in a book. Have I, and all the people around me, been in this book for all their lives?" she enquired and listened to the explosions from Throckton. "Is it possible to be in a book for forty-five years and have no consciousness of the fact? What of the author — is he dead or alive? *Who*," again the sound of gunfire came to her ears, "*who is* the author? If it's Wordkyn, I can see how he might have drawn me from life and put me in a book, yet if he is the author I can't see why he should have written himself such a terrible beating. And if the author is De'Ath, there's no telling what may happen to us" — an astute observation, reader — "and those noises, are they in the book or out of it?" —— I can see where her thoughts are leading —— "These are sad and licentious times!" —— how we agree! —— "Yes," she said, dipping into her capacious handbag, "and if I'm in De'Ath's book, I'm also here and cannot be in both places at once."

— 'True!' said Gottesgabe.

— 'Be quiet,' said I, 'the reader must be able to follow the deductions which Auntie is about to make.'

— 'She was dipping into her capacious handbag,' Damon whispered. 'Do you think she has a copy of the book?' —

"But," she continued, "if it helps the hermit, I shall pretend I am in a book — as I shall for anyone who comes along with the same idea."

This is amazing, reader: the stubbornness of the woman! "And even if I am in a book" — Ah: qualification — "I don't want to read it. For at the moment, I am more concerned with those troublesome noises" — the same martial clamour heard by *all* the persons at the other side of the bushes, which demonstrates beyond a shadow of a doubt that she must be in our text — "against which precautions have to be taken."

"Yes, a stitch in time saves nine," said Alice, producing from her handbag (where, *it will be remembered*, she kept those cures for love referred to in an earlier chapter, the very chapter in which she first set out), producing her stock of potions and devices that would stand her in good stead against any future *liaison amoureuse* (we say future advisedly) ensuing from the great freedom, liberality and excess most forcibly suggested by the screams and explosions then, now, and still resounding over this green and pleasant text.

"Be prepared," said Auntie and popped a pill into her mouth, which pill was no sooner swallowed than the curious stalwart, seeking the reason for the time she had taken in relieving herself, came stumbling through the bushes — as we have been expecting him to do for two paragraphs — to further the arrests imposed on him by duty and which conscience bade him execute, though his natural inclinations were of another bent, for he thought his captives demented and therefore unworthy of arrest. Nevertheless, duty in such characters (through long years of inculcation) is invariably superior to the promptings of the heart. Answering in every way to the description we have applied to him — of a not unhandsome appearance, sturdy of limb and blithe of mind — this stalwart of stalwarts was now surprised — as we were, at first — to see Alice with her collection of potions set out before. Erroneously — and cloddishly — conceiving them to be stimulants of an exotic and aphrodisiacal nature —— and determined to prove an exception to the general rule of stalwartly character announced above —— he now set himself to munching several where he had seen Alice eat the one, and then fell to her, tending his amorous proposals with very forward gestures, consuming more of the pills, and in the process utterly forgetting his original intent: ——— the arrest.

No narrator may be held responsible for gross dereliction of duty by minor, very minor characters, and we are moved to declare that if Alice has neither Bartleby nor marmalade at least she shall have the stalwart. For she received these advances with great ardour and gusto, and very little space elapsed before the pair enjoyed a passionate embrace, other activities rapidly ensuing in the course of nature so that they were soon conjoined as one, their moans and cries rising to the sound of the distant battle, and arousing an altogether different sort of passion in the company at the other side of the bushes.

Auntie – alas – out of haste to the tussle, carelessly forgot her Dutch cap which she left lying on the sward beside her, where the stalwart –– whose catholicity of consumption seemingly knew no bounds –– now chanced to ingurgitate it, along with the remaining pills and devices, the cap snapping into position in his throat, about the region of his oesophagus, immediately depriving him of the oxygen vital to his labours, causing him to falter in mid-transport and turning his face a purplish black in colour, much to Auntie's dismay, she crying and screaming as the company rounded the bushes, thus to find her in *flagrante delicto,* the stalwart atop of her as motionless as a dead man.

"Oh, fortune!" she sobbed. "No marmalade, not a drop to be had anywhere, and now . . . now *this!*"

CHAPTER TWENTY—TWO *A Contrary Development, Wherein Your Narrator, Impatient with His and Other Texts, Successfully Avoids a Lecture From His Fantastical Friend (Original Steward of the Second MS) by Excising What Was* **CHAPTER TWENTY—TWO**, *Giving In Its Place a Graphic Representation of the Several Plots to Date (March 18th, 1970) as An Exercise in His* OMNISCIENCE, *(Caused By Reading Ahead to this Quondam Chapter), to Wit:*

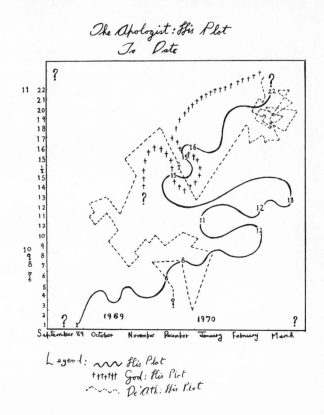

The Apologist: His Plot To Date

Legend: ∿∿ His Plot
†††††† God: His Plot
∼∼∼ Death: His Plot

I trust this chart will assist the reader in his progress through my text.

The time sequences of *De'Ath: His Plot* and *God: His Plot* are purely conjectural: that is, I simply do not possess the respective dates of the composition of their texts, nor shall I unless —

But enough, reader. The plot must go on and I have removed one formidable obstacle to its progression: my fantastical friend's lecture.

"Have you?" said Damon Gottesgabe. "I'm going."

"Where?" said I.

"Out," said he.

"But you'll have to be back tomorrow," I reminded him, "in time for the thirteenth chapter *and* March 19th."

"Will I?" said he, and left on the wings of a beatific smile.

CHAPTER TWENTY–THREE *Wherein the Text (His Polychromicon) Suffers an Impertinent Interruption and the Plot is Retarded by One Chapter's Space.*

At 2400 hrs — the end of March 18th and the beginning of March 19th — I became gradually aware of a knocking at my door.

"Gottesgabe," I thought, stumbling out of bed, "returning for the thirteenth chapter: predictable, but unconscionably early."

In Damon's place, however, there stood my fantastical friend, hand poised to knock again as I opened the door. "The twenty-second chapter," he gasped, "where is it?"

Evidently he was in a state of some consternation, for he forgot to lower his fist which appeared out of the night like a thing disembodied.

"You should know," I asked him in, "you were here yesterday, weren't you?"

"That's just it!" he subjected his hand to a minute examination. "I wasn't. The text," he demanded, throwing himself down in my chair, "show me the text!"

What it was, reader, I cannot say, but there was something disturbingly familiar about my fantastical friend's hand — his right hand — which he now employed in flicking through the pages of that MS, the same MS given to me by the same hand twenty-two chapters ago at the beginning of our history. Yes, the hand was the same, except I fancied I had seen it living on another's wrist, and the MS, if not identical to the ur-text, was substantially the same. Then why was the hand so agitated, and why did its owner deny his visit of March 18th?

"The discourse," my friend stared fixedly through his monocle. I didn't tell you he had a monocle before; but he had, and I suppose it made his vision simpler: "*My* discourse. What have you done with it?"

"There," I pointed to the wastepaper basket. "I spared the reader my pain."

I do not think he was prepared for that, and I'm sorry to say it angered him.

"I gave you this text in good faith," he cried, "and not only have you arrogated the task of narratorship — as if there *were* anything to be narrated — but now you take on the rights of an editor as well! In the space of one page you have compromised this whole of nothing, this blissful, integral, unformed whole, with plots, diagrams, charts, locations, chronologies, and assume that you have made something where there was nothing before; in one misguided chapter you have besmirched all the ages' blankness with your own ridiculous interpolations, and now you expect me," he consulted his watch, "to point out your incredible madness in six minutes!"

"I expect nothing of the sort," said I. "What right have you got, coming in here like this, waking me up, shouting at the top of your voice?"

"I'm not shouting!" he shouted. "What right have *you* got," he was very angry, "to foul these pages with the miserable productions of your own entrails?" — more followed — "Not even a would-be nothing" — this was too much — "a less-than-nothing, sir, like yourself?"

"Look," I chose my words carefully, "you have said this before. That is why I threw your chapter away and replaced it with mine. Do what you will with it," I reminded him, "that's what you said: do what you will with the text. Well, I have."

"Oh no, no: follow the text as you would follow life," my friend ground a set of perfectly manicured teeth, "that's what I said. Do you call this life? Is this your idea of living? Not that there is anything to life: it is a mere catch word and convenient hold-all that hides the real, the perfectly invisible. But this, this narrative, this meandering, mazed, tortured

184

attempt of yours to embody the purest abstraction, how in the name of all that is positively absurd and absurdly positive can you justify this as the pursuit of life?"

"I've made no such claims," said I. "And since you mentioned the subject, my entrails are real and I would be glad if you left them out of the discussion, for the reader's sake if not for mine."

"That is the only thing about you that is real," he replied, "the source of your narrative ambitions, your windy asides and half-digested opinions. It would not surprise me if your brain was in your guts, too. Look what you have done to God, to time, to structure — the immaterial made material by your mindless meddling and witless interjections. And I thought you were a writer of nothing at all!"

"If I have made something tangible from nothing; if I have created *ex nihilo* and forged a little reality from this MS's great unreality — and there are difficulties with the narration," I tried a conciliatory note, "I admit that there are problems — then in this text I have gained a life I did not have before, nor ever expected, and that is the life of a narrator. In so doing, have I not helped the other characters into being; isn't that all you can expect from a writer, would-be or actual?"

And with that, reader, there was no stopping my fantastical friend who began his discourse after all — the same discourse consigned by me to the wastepaper basket — while I listened with an increasing sense of unrelation and sadness, listened for the second time in two days. For either he was mad or I was mad, and — whichever one — I regretted that the universal malady of our times had spread its infection from my text.

"Being? Reality? Existence? Actuality?" he commenced where I had finished speaking. "My poor, dull would-be bard, you do not know and cannot understand that an enforced distinction has grown up in this age between so-called 'art' and so-called 'reality.' The distinction is of course present in every age, yet it is made the more odious to us because of the many attempts — such as your dealings with this MS — to make 'art' the more 'real' (forgive the containment of

185

quotation marks, I do but speak as the critics) – attempts which greatly reinforce the distinction by granting its original terms . . . ”

I forgave him the quotations marks, ellipses, parentheses, dashes – to set off an appositive or an appositive phrase when a comma would provide less than the desired emphasis on the appositive or when the use of commas might result in confusion with the appositive phrase, which is only one of the uses of (–) . . . (–), and not, in this case, the correct one – in return for which, he pardoned my attempt to sabotage his discourse – “But the damage is done,” he said, “as you will see” – and proceded to dismiss *a*) the awesome spectre of realism: impious scribblings attacking God; *b*) naturalism: human superscriptions s-c-r-a-w-l-e-d on the face of nature; *c*) symbolism: an inversion of *b*), that is, merely superficial attempts to put God back into nature; *d*) aestheticism: 'art-art' and so *fop-fop* forth; *e*) surrealism: the circus animals' dance; *f*) imagism: hypostasis of the object; and so on throughout the alphabet of –isms until he came to *z*) last but by no means least, SORROW and psychologism: FLUVIALISM – the ultimate solipsism, the death of meaning, the private and confessional, the infinitely exalted.

"Our tailor, SORROW," my friend took off on his favourite *bête noir*, "took his scissors to the cloth of language and cut his dummy a set of clothes, the like of which has not been seen since the garb worn by those splendid mathematicians of the Flying Island. Tailor he must," *snip-snip*, "cutting at the fabric of several languages," *snip-snip*, "decorating his gear with the gaudy threads of contrived associations, until he assembled the whole shoddy apprentice stuff to throw over his dummy for all the world to see and praise as a model of man, nay, a 'real' man, clothed with the stuff of this life. And you know how his dummy had a hard time of it at first, for it offended against the current sartorial taste and was taken to court and was examined by the judges who looked only at the fabric, not at the stitching. But now the fashion is well underway, other and crazier seamsters patching as only they can, flaunting their rags before the master's speculative mirror, so that a man cannot get himself a decent set of clothes these days, let alone a book – this, in the name of *reality!*"

"Can't you leave Sorrow alone?" said I, "He's dead. Let him be."

"Will you not understand," he continued, "or do you refuse to understand that there is no 'reality' apart from the one, the unitary, the Ideal, which is so far removed from our comprehension as to be *invisible*? This is the whole of nothing: the perfection that consists of universal all-pervading blankness. The rest is imitation (as the philosopher well knew), imitation of the second order, such as the craftsman who imitates the perfectly invisible chair by attempting to construct its material equivalent, and he is bound to err because he cannot see what he copies; or imitation of the third order, such as the poet or artist who copies what is already imperfectly copied, hence compounding error on error. Whereas true Being is both invisble and indivisible — *where* are the characters in this text? Have you seen them? — there is no end to imperfect copies of the original Idea, and second or third hand being, having no necessary or logical connection with invisibility, is diverse, changing, and lawless, in short, a great sin against Nature.

"The most perfect reality is therefore that which is least perceptible to man.

"Beyond SORROW and fluvialism, the triumph of the modern: it is not barbarism; it is not the anarchy that haunts the bourgeois apostles of 'art.' Rather it is the silent symphony, the invisible portrait, and the wordless language, towards which we must now aspire — and did, *my* friend and I, until you came along.

"*You*, by doing everything within your meagre powers to make this text the more 'real,' the more manifest, have sinned against nature. *Why*," he cried, "do you think a rebellion of the characters is underway in the MS? Not because of the absurd reasons you have implied, because they are grotesque (though they are), or because they are tired of their authors (which they also are) — but because their third hand being cannot be tolerated any further! They have destroyed their authors, and next they will destroy themselves, for our sole object is the destruction of contemporary art, the destruction of a lawless and reckless imitation and a return to the purest and simplest of ideas, the original vacancy of God Himself: *Nothing at all*."

"You too," said I. "You'll be telling me you were in the pit next."

There were no marks around his neck, reader.

"*Here*," he thrust a blank piece of paper under my nose, "is your twentieth century masterwork. Here is your ideal character: no sham or forgery this, no third hand copy, but the truest representation of man and God and nature. 'Art,' " his monocled eye grew larger, "is nothing, the 'real' is nothing, life itself is nothing. There is only the original and numinous vacancy cohering in the mind of God, time without end. Everything else is transient invention – the temporary scribblings of the impermanent and imperfect senses. I would suggest," my fantastical friend pocketed his discursive monocle, "you burn all that you have written and restore the MS to its unsullied whiteness."

"I've no intention of burning anything," I told him.

"Then so must it be," he got up, "you have taken it on your own head and deserve what you shall get."

"And what is that?" said I.

"Destruction!" he cried. "Your death and the death of the characters in this book, with whom, as an impossible creation yourself, you have everything in common."

"Man lives and man dies," said I, for it was the first reply that came into my head. "And you are implicated also."

"I," my fantastical friend laughed. "*I*? But I am not here; I have washed my hands of what you call life. You must never expect to see me again," said he. "Your *Autobiography of a Dead Man* is written – you live, therefore expect death."

On those words, he left my room and left forever. And though I was not sure of their exact meaning, nor even of the spirit in which they were offered, I would shortly set out to demonstrate their ultimate fallibility. For if words are the man, they can be wrong like the man; and if words can hurt, they do not destroy.

CHAPTER TWENTY–FOUR   *Still More Concerning the Wondrous Machine of Throckton by the Bog; Bartleby Receives a Challenge.*

My fantastical friend was in high dudgeon when he left my room this morning, and I therefore forgot – or had no chance – to ask a singularly important question about this text: to wit, who actually wrote it? Before I took over the narratorship, I mean. But Gottesgabe must call sometime today, since the thirteenth chapter yet remains to be composed, and it is with Damon himself, rather than my other friend, that I propose to raise the question of authorship.

In the meantime, we shall return to our history. For the chapter heading indicates that Bartleby and his companion, the dwarf-god-jester-devil (who or whatever he is) have now re-entered the plot – sub-plot or main plot, depending on your point of view – the Wondrous Machine hence displaying a truer sense of narrative direction than Hannibali and minibus together in thus landing safely, squarely and wondrously on the ground.

The dwarf, however, disagreed (we drop the upper case D, reader, until his identity is established); disagreed accidentally – he was not reading from his book – yet disagreed nevertheless: "Oh Jesus, something's wrong, something's definitely wrong. Indubitably double-you for wrong, *wrong*," he muttered – certain on this point, if nothing else – as he ambled gibbously through the portals of the now motionless Machine.

"It looks alright to me," said our hero, following him through the portals.

"Looks? Looks?" the jester mimicked, his jaw clacking ominously and his claws clutching at his swollen belly.

"What I would like to know," Bartleby enquired of an empty sky, "is where we are." —— the very same question we would have asked ourselves, and, in a sense, do.

"You mean when we are," corrected the other, struggling with his cap which he proceeded once more to convert into a truss for his unruly jaw: "Not where. When, when, *when!*"

"When? When?" Bartleby digested this information.

"When, where," said the dwarf and returned to his text. — the when and the where of time and place, temporal and spatial coordinates, determining any narrative fix:

"Ever had the feeling, boy," the jester stared balefully over his domed shoulders at the Wondrous Machine, "that you're being watched? That you're not quite alone, eh?"

"I suppose," said Bartleby slowly and with great politeness, for he assumed that he was addressing God, or more accurately the boy observed — as we have — that the Jester was reverting to His Mephitic Condition of CHAPTER FIFTEEN [THE FIRST] where according to His Own Assurance He was God, "I suppose it could be that narrator again."

"No," said the Jester, knotting the ends of His Cap in His Orange Hair, "another, not him."

"Then there may be people who are reading us," said Bartleby, conscious where Alice was not, conscious of a paginated life. "Do you think," he continued, "that we could be aware of the reader in the same way that he is aware of us?"

The Jester shrugged and seemed to diminish by three or four of His Forty-Eight Inches. "The fact that we are in the process of composition," said the Jester, ringed by the shimmering halo of gaseous Divinity, "makes it highly unlikely that we are being read."

"Do you mean," asked Bartleby, "that the book is not finished?"

"Finished? Finished?" the Jester bowed and bent

double, "I'm finished, yes. But not you, boy, not you. Anyway," he added, "I was bothered by something else – as if somebody might be watching us from *within* these pages." But then His Line of Thought was confronted by the vast and silent expanse before Him in which He appeared to grow even smaller, and He said simply, "No, no: out of the question."

For the Machine, reader, had descended in a vacant vale, bordered by distant wooded hills. The aspect was one of complete isolation and absence of human settlement, gainsaying the Jester's Impression that He was being watched from within or without the pages. "Out of the question," He insisted, not quite believing what He said, for he gazed suspiciously about Him and confirmed our opinion (our recently formulated opinion), reader, that this diminishing and jittery cultural hero of the West was suffering from a persecution complex: "I've been here before, boy," He stared dolefully on emptiness, "not before, *after*" – in a word, God was paranoid: "yes, *after*" –– a fact sufficient to explain the age's madness: "many chapters after," He concluded, still gazing on the deserted plain.

Even the most meagre dwellings modify the face of nature. Over the years a habitation may flourish or decay, becoming (whether in proud estate or desolate ruin) as much a part of the natural scene as mountain or river. Places have their seasons too; they develop a certain right of belonging, a presence which makes it hard for us to imagine them otherwise. Change they may, but the change is gradual and well nigh imperceptible. Hence Bartleby, his mind still thronging with the crowded events of the marketplace, failed to recognize what we might have told him: that he was standing on exactly the same spot as he had before his enforced entry into the Wondrous Machine.

Gone was the square; gone the thatched houses and the four roads, gone the crowd and the raised platform and all the babble of civic strife. It was not that Throckton had been obliterated; it was as though it had never existed, or had yet to exist in some far distant time – a phenomenon that might have worried an inferior narrator, but which here gives no cause for undue concern, aware, as we are, of Throcktonian quadruplicity.

Yet the idea of Throckton's disappearing from the map was so inconceivable to Bartleby that, had it occurred to him, he would have dismissed it forthwith. Instead, another impression forced itself on our hero: that of being in the presence of a sourceless echo, nameless, shadowy and disturbing. It was, he thought, as his companion had said. Something was wrong. Yet what?

"Out of the frigging frying pan into the frigging fire," the Jester swore, clutching at his copy of Bartleby's history. "It was clever of you," said the Jester acidly, "to rid us of our slavish dependency on this text by remaining silent when you were supposed to speak. Very clever! "

"But where are we?" cried the boy, horrified to see that the Dwarf had by now shrunk to half his natural size, as if the Jester's Being was subjected to some law of diminishing returns. "I feel like I've been here before, but I don't seem to recognize the place at all," said the boy, dismayed by the thought that if the shrinkage continued, God would disappear altogether.

"Prickhead!" God screamed, dropping the book because it had grown too heavy for Him, or had increased relative to His Shrinkage, "After! You mean after, *not* before!"

"What do you mean, God?" asked Bartleby, sorry to see his friend so distempered and shrunk.

"God? God?" the jester shot Bartleby a look of bilious hatred and burped horrendously. "God? I'm not God!" he cried. "I'm *Me*, that's who I am; I'm *Me*, nobody else — a real person! There aren't any *real* people left any more! Only *Me*," god complained. "Me! You don't think the author's a real person, do you? And the narrator, he's not a real person either. There are no real people in this book, do you hear Me! There are no real people at all except Me! Me! A real person, that's what *I* am! *Real*! *Me*!"

Upon this outburst of divine egocentricity, god's lower mandible separated itself from the rest of his features and fell to the ground with a grievous clack. "Me!" the still dwindling jester managed the word once more as his face yawned asunder and Bartleby rushed towards him and endeavoured to assist his friend in the arduous relocation of the

192

mandible — a task eventually achieved with no small difficulty, the jester groaning and grinning hideously, Bartleby pushing and shoving on the jaw's behalf — when a wonderful change overtook our hero's companion: he vanished. Yes, reader, a pulsating fart shook god's tiny frame and he vanished — a fitting end, we think, to one who has unjustly maligned our narrative endeavours.

"God! God!" Bartleby searched for the jester. "Guardian of Guardians, where are you?" he cried as god momently reappeared and vanished again, then half-appeared and disappeared, to reappear for a third time — we do not wish our hero to begin his quest all over again — scratching and clawing at the earth.

Bartleby watched the dwarf's pallor liven to a healthy flush, his eyes sparkling and gleaming where they had been — but a moment before — bloodshot and menacing.

"Thank you, Bartleby," said the jester blandly, gazing at the boy with considerable passivity of demeanour and benignity of expression. "Thanks for your help," he said very softly, giving an experimental waggle of his jaw.

"Sir," said Bartleby, somewhat nonplussed by this astonishing tergiversation of god's, "sir, I find your changes very entertaining, but I wish you could give me some notice of them in order that I may not appear shocked or in any way rude if you surprise me that way again, by changing I mean."

"Bound to, bound to," said the other, "indubitably inevitable, yes. Ohh," he sighed, "it's the farts, boy. The guts. I do wish the author had hit on something else. But I will fart when I feel the change coming upon Me — if that will be any help, Bartleby. If I can," the jester added, "get it out in time."

"Yes," he said, "that would be very helpful. And there's one other thing too."

"What's that?" enquired the *other party*, anxious to be of assistance.

"I would like to call you by name. Not God" — wise infant! — "for we are not in CHAPTER FIFTEEN [THE FIRST] and not the other party" —— *not* the other party? —— "for we are not in CHAPTER FIFTEEN [THE

SECOND]. I would like to call you something for now. It would help me, and it would help you too, I think."

"Then call Me . . . " the dwarf pondered the question, "call Me . . . " – dwarf, *dwarf*, DWARF, *DWARF*? – *yes*, reader, our authority does seem to have favoured the disguise routine –– traditional ingredient of the old-fashioned books –– and it really is obvious, pellucidly so, that the jester, shorn of all metaphysical chaos, should repeatedly deny his divinity, because, you see, he is not God, no, nor even the other party, but *DODO*, the *DWARF* ––– and as we never cease to point out, as we *unfailingly* point out, we were not there and cannot be blamed for not perceiving the by now obvious ––––

"Call Me *Me*, for that is what I am: *Me*."

–––– namely, that the disguise routine is often overworked and that Me was not DODO, but a dwarf nonetheless.

" 'Me,' " Bartleby tried the word and thought there was much in a name. "Me, Me, Me; well, Me," the boy eyed his companion, almost as though he expected the name to produce some other and equally surprising change in his dimensions.

"I have another question," said the boy, "where are we?"

"You must not think, Bartleby," *Me* adopted his pedagogical tone, "that because these changes sometimes come upon me – Me – I forget what has gone before. I distinctly remember your asking that question while I was in the process of complimenting you upon the intelligent way in which you arrested the progress of the Machine – though I'm not sure that *progress* is the right word," he added thoughtfully, retrieving the book which had fallen at his tiny feet. "Unfortunately," Me perused the book and lectured our hero, "the sixteenth and seventeenth chapters appear to have been lost in the course of our flight" – *ours* are intact, reader, brief, but all present and correct – "Look, you may see for yourself. *That* was not so clever of you."

"I see," said Bartleby, glancing at his own pages, "I see that we are in the twenty-third chapter, so we have at least . . . "

"What was that, Bartleby" – the stupid boy cannot

count — "What was that? Which chapter?"

The dwarf was right to put the question, reader, for you will note the infant's reply:

"It says," Bartleby read from the text — I was hoping that would not happen — "it says: CHAPTER TWENTY-THREE *Still More Concerning the Wondrous Machine of Throckton by the Bog: Bartleby Receives a Challenge.*"

"And what does the narrator say about that?" said Me. Nothing, reader . . .

"He says nothing," said Bartleby, "but he seems to think I can't count. I've always been able to count. A challenge," he continued while Me computed on his fingers — I should have said *read* — "a challenge. That's interesting. I wonder what sort of a challenge? But we've at least gone forwards, and that's something," said the boy, idly flicking through the pages of his history. "Yes, here we are." he mused, "but where have we been in the meantime — between CHAPTER FIFTEEN [THE SECOND] and CHAPTER TWENTY-THREE?"

"Here? Here?" echoed Me, shaking his tousled hair and peering at our hero with a look of sympathetic contempt such as a superior intelligence applies to its inferior. "Don't you understand anything? We're scarcely here at all, Bartleby, we're then, boy, *then*! As for going forwards, we have done so in the book's space by seven chapters" — *eight* — "if you count the sixteenth and seventeenth chapters, that is," the jester qualified his statement, "but outside of that, Bartleby, we're in exactly the same place except we've gone backwards in time. Yes, yes!" Me developed his thesis, "The Machine has transported us backwards because we could not go forwards on account of the missing chapters — "

"SIXTEEN AND SEVENTEEN!" cried Bartleby.

"Exactly," Me beamed at his pupil. "Forwards we are in one sense, backwards in another. One of our nows is then; another, after."

"But when were we," the riddle was propounded, "after we came before in the meantime?"

"Meantime?" Me scratched his head.

"In the meantime of the future," said the boy.

"Remember, Bartleby," Me elaborated, "if one can

remember the future, now that our future is in the past, remember that this is a work of fiction. I'm afraid, therefore, that you must forget, if one can forget the future, this notion of yours about the meantime" – precisely! – "In all works of fiction, the meantime is taken" – exactly! our very own opinion, reader!– "for granted, and the reader is simply left to fill in the interstices of time" – the very same words 'scaped my lips not two days ago when I said to Gottesgabe: "So it is with the artifice of character and many other conventions where the reader is left to fill in thousands of details" — (in fact that was Me speaking), but I expressed more or less the same opinion that Me did:

"Damon," said I, "what would you do if I were a character in a book and you were the reader?"

He gave a very strange stare.

"For example," said I continuing, "what would you want to know about me? I would be tempted, you know, to begin with my great-great-great-grandmother on my father's side, for she was a very interesting person. But then to be consistent I would have to include my great-great-great-grandmother on my mother's side, who was a rather dull person, at least very little is known of her, not to mention my paternal great-great-great-grandfather and my maternal great-great-great-grandfather both of whom were *completely unknown to each other!*"

Yes, the dwarf had a point, reader.

"I see no reason why things should be different with us," he said. "But we exist now, if we exist at all, at a time before our births, at a time even before our respective conceptions in the mind of the author, who may not yet have written us, or has yet to have written us, boy! For although the Throckton which you knew is spatially behind us – to the rear of this chapter – it is chronologically far in the future!"

"Well then," said Bartleby, "is the future Throckton stationary in time, or does it move forwards in the natural course of things? Because if it does then we are getting further and further away from it."

"Hah!" Me stared disconsolately at Bartleby, "these things are so relative. We may never find out, for we lack the

196

means of objective verification. But I must say, I'm inclined to the opinion that the future Throckton that is in the spatial past (at the back of this chapter) is indeed moving away from us, whereas the future Throckton that is in the chronological and the spatial future is actually moving closer to us, by virtue of the fact that we move from page to page in an easterly direction, the pages themselves moving westwards as they are turned, always assuming — we must not assume *too* much — yet assuming, Bartleby, the book is pointing north. However, one thing is clear. Because of the scientific fiction which our author has inflicted on us, you will not meet your Auntie, and my condition will not be stabilized" —*No ?* —— "until we discover the missing chapters. And to do that, we must either go back to where we started from, or our point of departure must return to us, and that — the latter alternative — would involve the construction of another Machine.

"If you have been following my argument," the jester honoured Bartleby with a dreamy stare, "if you have been following (and I say following from a sense of convenience, for I am not sure that such verbs of motion are still applicable), then you will realize that under any other set of circumstances the resolution of this embarrassing situation *would have* depended on the author."

"Which author?" questioned Bartleby — an astute question, to which we have given some thought ourselves. "For there is the author of behind us, and the author of in front of us, and the author of now."

"Now? *Now?* Can't you see?" cried Me, unable to believe this lapse in Bartleby's thinking. "Then, then, you mean then!" — No; that is, yes! —— "You know what I think, boy," Me spoke very quickly, "I think the author has yet to compose the missing chapters. Guts! Guts!" he cried, the divine afflatus ascending once more.

"Even if he has composed them," Bartleby watched his companion closely, then modified his choice of verb tense, "I mean, even if he shall have composed them, then he has done so in the past — "

"Which is also our future — " Me interposed.

"No," our hero disagreed, "for they have not happened,

197

and when and if they do happen, who is to say they will concern us?"

They *have* happened and they *didn't* concern you!

"Yes, yes," Me shook his head furiously, "which is why we may have to become our own authors as I suggested in CHAPTER FIFTEEN [THE SECOND]. Boss was something of a prophet, it seems."

"A prophet," said Bartleby, "of a past which has yet to be."

"Guts!" exclaimed Me vaporously. "But it is pointless to speculate thus," he continued feverishly, struggling – if we dare to make the guess, and we do – struggling against his imminent transformation from Me (other party) to Me (god). "This dilation of the time continuum is a favourite device of our authors – all of our authors: when, then, what, where, h o w , b e f o r e , a f t e r w h y b e c a u s e i f n o t now – con . . . temporaries, used for the sake of psychological verisimilitude or to imply the fundamental disorder of the cosmos *stop* intestinal entropy *stop*," gabbled Me in wild telegraphese, clutching at the ends of his cap. "Guts! Such authors," his jaw clacked wildly, "have failed to explore the possibilities of what I might call – Guts! Guts! Stop! a mirror convention, seeking to build linguistic monuments to false . . . false . . . *Me's*," croaked the jester, his eyes bulging manically and his hands clasped to his jaw which he began to wrench open and shut: "so that it would seem such exploration is to be left to character, so much are these authors diverted by tricks whose philosophical implications, boy, they do not understand!" A rippling fart escaped him. "And I *know*, boy . . . Bartleby . . . boy . . . *why* he is doing this to me: in the conversion of mass into energy there are certain undesirable side effects, yet given the possibility of infinite mass or material battle for the sake of fight a cheap formulation struggle he recoils making me Me dignity identity but . . . help, boy! . . . I . . . am" the jester tore at his "punctuation . . . help!" mandible "am *Me*! And I won't be oh God oh guts anybody else!" – unconditionally, reader, I take back everything I have said concerning the – – accidental – – similarity between certain of god's or the other party's or Me's speeches – and my own words to Damon – "*ME!*"

he shrank and shrank until, transported by a final quantum burst of the colic, – the straw that broke the camel's back – his diminished frame disappeared altogether – then reappeared:

"I won't be anybody else!"

–– and disappeared:

"What about the Machine?" Bartleby shouted.

––– and appeared:

"*Deus ex machina,*" rasped the mocking voice, "*machina ex deo!*"

–––– and vanished again, leaving Bartleby shouting all the louder:

"Are we to leave it here?"

–––––When Me returned (by degrees), jaw *in situ,* stature *in toto, capax rationis in extremis,* returned, much to our hero's relief, as the other party, or *not* the other party, but himself, gasped, sank to his knees, and said, "I am tired, Bartleby – tired." Whereupon, with our hero's assistance, Me gained his feet. "Come, Bartleby," he said wearily, linking his arm in the boy's, "let us see if we can find food and shelter, and for you, the diversions of guardianship."

And there, as they set out along that vast and empty valley ––the future site of the future perfect Throckton – there let us leave them, pausing only to watch this Me, the Me of potential equilibrium, his legs bowed under the body's superior burden in a series of blurred hyperbolas that marked the course of his vectorless track towards identity, let us leave them and remove ourselves to consider the immensity of their surroundings.

Viewed from a great height, the sphere Earth hangs motionless and moving, the map of the continents, the surge of the oceans receding ever with altitude, until in the distant reaches of the far beyond, from the starry heavens themselves, the planet fades, a dwindling light amongst other radiances, until, one fine and as yet unrecorded day, that light disappears forever from the traveller's chart, and – farewell, sweet world! what other worlds! what discoveries! yet what death – this urge to travel. For what survives out there? What of Empire; of arts and music and human cultivation? What of the scribblings of those supposed authors in De'Ath's supposed pit; what of their light years of sales? Nothing, dear reader. There is a dance among the spheres, an ethereal melody, a timpani tanged out upon the elements: *tin, tin, tin* jangled on the cymbals, *boom, boom, boom* on the big bass drum. "Earth?" asks God to our starry-eyed traveller. "Which one?"

A little less cosmically; let the focus alter. Down there, in the valley that broadens to a heath, before, long before fair Throckton's foundation, two figures move in a world before their time. But what is this on the world's rim? A terrible commotion: a roaring and a shouting, a stamping, cheering, clattering, and rumbling, marked over all by a whirling plume of dust as of an army on the move. Danger perhaps? An earthquake? A volcano? Some natural cataclysm – a war of the elements? Louder to our ears now this bellowing; loftier now this plume of dust, until it appears that the force is not natural – though certainly at war with itself – but human.

Still less cosmically: Bartleby's ears take up the tune; technically, a violent reverberation attacks the concha, resounding on the external auditory meatus, vibrating the tympanic membrane, and is thus communicated via the auditory nerve, coded, de-coded, and resonating like all the gongs in hell, thunders down the corridors of Bartleby's still disbelieving brain. And Me – dwarf-god-jester-devil – hands clasped over his ears, sinks to his knees (whence we had successfully elevated him a moment ago), and hence our plot suffers another reverse – but not so unexpected, reader, since it announced itself with this furious and still gathering din, not so unexpected as to be accounted a *total* reverse.

For thus did Bercilak de Belamoris, and his amanuensis, called by him Lungs, thus did Bercilak and Lungs – both of whom had been galloping thunderously for the length of our history to this date – thus did these two chance on another two, and thus (according to Bartleby's rapid calculation) did two and two make – *four*.

Strange was the sight when Bartleby opened his eyes (closed involuntarily in a cooperative effort of his senses to exclude the disturbance), strange the magnification, the distortion of line and perspective, partially caused by the sudden return of relative peace, yet equally attributable to the inadequacy of the boy's beleaguered receptors to cope with so fantastic a vision — and no wonder, reader, if we may say so, for what Bartleby now saw outshone the many and varied wonders of his history, bringing with it, or him, confirmation of our narrative method, confirmation and complications also.

Before our hero, four U-shaped and fuming troughs, chasms gouged out of Mother Earth, bore witness to the path taken by Bercilak's charger as it was reined to its mighty halt, in the process almost colliding with Lungs' no less formidable beast, another formation of smoking valleys confirming the angry arrest of that valiant steed. Behind our hero, Me trembled and cowered, while overall a hot foam was discharged to the accompaniment of rubbery snorts, impatient neighings, and the restless but prodigious stampings of these gargantuan animals.

But most of all was Bartleby's attention fixed upon the countenance which loomed before him, a countenance more terrible and awe-inspiring than the boy had yet beheld or ever wished to behold. Bercilak's pulmonary red skin perspired heavily and reflected the radiance of boiled lobster. About the monumental slab of the chin each craterous pore sprouted several bristles, a feature repeated on the upper lip where each steely strand was wound into a hawser-like moustache, and yet again over each beetling and furious brow. Yet strange to say, the head (with the exception of one knotted cable, trained to grow from the centre of the pate), this head was shaven and polished and vied with the brilliancy of Sol himself. Underneath the black porcupine brows which burrowed and darted across the forehead as though they were indeed a pair of tame hedgehogs, underneath these extrusile and incredibly spiny growths, the eyes rolled and started forth; their whites, pure porcelain, the pupils a lustrous blue. When the mouth opened and yet another earth-shattering roar escaped, Bartleby saw the tongue, lolling like an indolent submarine creature, pink upon a bed of perfect coraline teeth. Again the boy closed his eyes. Delighted by this reaction, Bercilak clapped his hands in thunderous applause.

201

"I," he bellowed, his tongue writhing and thrashing, a sheet of spittle descending through the equine froth, "I am Bercilak de Belamoris, unvanquished in lust. Lungs!" he roared at the slighter yet equally marvellous figure, "the legend of my deeds that these churls might know my prowess. For twenty-three chapters," he continued rambunctiously (and the reader would be well advised to ignore the number) as the other delved into his saddle bags and produced, amid renewed torrents of spittle, scrolls of parchment, some ink, quills, and sand, beginning the while to take down his master's every word, "for twenty-three chapters" – the figure is of no consequence, we assure you – "I have ridden hard and seen no human soul; neither have I – as a result – wenched it well, indeed not at all, nor have my deeds been sung, challenges have I issued not, nor tumbled, rumbled, fumbled or humped have I, by cause of the absence of the female sex, indeed of all sexes and persons whatsoever," roared Bercilak, flexing his muscular brows as if bothered by some mental spasm, before again taking up his broadcast. "But these are unnatural times," he bellowed. "Strange portents flash in the heavens!" he cried, jangling his harness and the bells of his equipage, under the weight of which his charger, though it was doughty, seemed somewhat oppressed. "Rumour brings report of machines that do fly aloft in the massy heavens; upon the ground legendary beasts do walk about and perform impossible tasks with their own persons, whilst all about is ruin and rout so that musicians are out of tune, and scribes and copyists falsify the frame of nature . . . "

"What was that, Bercilak?" demanded Lungs.

"The frame of nature," howled Bercilak, frowning awesomely and junketing around upon his steed, much to the beast's discomfort. "Did you get it?" he asked and was answered by a speedy scratching of quill upon parchment. "I've had plenty of time to think of that one. Does it sound well enough?"

"It sounds too well to Me," muttered Me under his breath, hands still clasped to his ears.

"Frame of nature sounds very well, Bercilak," confirmed Lungs, seeking out another quill, for his first had just broken in a shower of ink.

"Where was I?" shouted Bercilak, his face darkening.

"Strange portents . . . legendary beasts . . . scribes and copyists . . . frame of nature . . . that was the phrase, a very fine one, if I may say so, master."

"Valiant Lungs! There's my scribe! Aye, these are evil times," continued Bercilak, several decibels higher. "Maids are frigid, or expensively priced; tapsters armed so high in their modesty that they are untouchable; widows are coy and penniless, whores diseased and taken off the streets so that there is not a lay to be had anywhere at any cost. In short, the great tradition is at an end; decadence triumphs, paltry studs are exalted beyond their common station, this Bercilak de Belamoris humps not so oft as he is wont, and there are no books left at all other than mine. But what manner of mortals," Bercilak addressed himself to his audience, "do I see before me?"

"Have care," cautioned Me, "have care, Bartleby."

"Sir Knight," said the boy with his customary politeness, "for that is what I think you are, though I have only read of knights and that not very well; Sir Knight, we are two, who by strange chances which I shall not go into now, come to be lost in these times. He is Me, my Guardian of Guardians when he is himself; and I am Bartleby who searches for his earthly Guardian, Auntie Alice, she of the generous heart and comely form."

"Did you get that, Lungs?" roared the object of Bartleby's speech. "Is it not the strangest manner of prattling? Well, boy, for that is what I take *you* to be, I cannot tell what you mean by this talk of knights. If it is something you have seen in a book, especially in this day and age, then you had better disregard it, for it is bound to be nonsense. But an Aunt, now, an Aunt is female. Have you seen any females, boy? Speak up now," Bercilak commanded our hero, "so Lungs can hear you."

"As for speaking up, sir," replied the boy courteously, "I think it is you who had better speak down, lest you further damage my ears. Yet women" — and while Bartleby is on the subject of the fair sex, I must say we detect a certain boastfulness in his attitude (a disarming precocity, maybe)

that was not for the best, considering the circumstances —
"women have I had in plenty, though not so much as I
would have desired of late. Yes, since first the day I was
received into Auntie's bed and then her . . . "

Terrible was Bercilak to behold at this little speech of
our little hero's. "Take it down, Lungs!" he howled, crimson
forehead steaming, brows burrowing, his eyes aflame and his
subaquatic tongue rolling ugsomely, thrashing out from its
lair to smack and flounder on the harboured lips like a
stranded whale. "Take it down!" he frothed and fumed, "a
mere stripling dares to challenge me! Punklet!" Bercilak
turned to Bartleby, "How old are you?"

"Five sir," replied our hero truthfully, "and . . . "

"Is it so? Can it be so?" Bercilak was overcome. "And
'women have I had in plenty,' he says, whilst I — " the
thought was too much for him: "Have you no regard,
mocking boy, for my reputation? Then know that I have
vanquished greater studs than thee, hot and lusty-bodied
wights, or so they called themselves before they met with
Bercilak. Is it not so, Lungs? Is it not as I say?" roared the
aggrieved Bercilak.

"Verily it is, Bercilak," answered the scribe, largely for
Bartleby's benefit.

"No challenge intended," Me spoke out timorously, for
Bartleby had fallen into a strange reflection, and the jester
feared he was about to do something foolish.

"No challenge intended!" came the awesome detona-
tion, the force of which flipped Me over in a rear somersault.
"No challenge intended!" thundered Bercilak again, training
his gruesome features on Me who sought refuge by curling up
in the shape of a ball, a shape for which nature had fitted him
in the event of such emergencies. "And what manner of fool
art thou?" Bercilak's face shone and Me began to shrink, not
involuntarily but deliberately, compressing his miniature
being into a volume half the size of the space he occupied
formerly: "Say rather abortion," Bercilak howled on, "a
thing unstable and unsteady on its bandy legs; a misconcep-
tion, fitting only for this barren age populated by freaks and
monsters, beasts of the night . . . "

"Me, Me," whimpered the shrinking dwarf-god-devil-jester.

"... a talking foetus, fit to crawl back into his mother's womb ..."

"Ears, ears," pleaded Me, uncurling his head from the hump of his back.

"Then open them, Mister Crook-back-Roll-about, open them as I have opened mine. Does not this punkling prate, 'Women have I had in plenty,' whilst I, Bercilak de Belamoris, have ridden hard for these four and twenty chapters" — confirmation, reader: *four* and twenty — "and wenched it in no wise, not a whit, jot, tittle nor tickle, by my mother's maidenhead, nor heard so much as a mention of my deeds" — that is two tens and four units, according to our present base of ten; count it how you will, here is the proof we have long awaited!

"Four and twenty. What does he mean?" muttered Me to Bartleby. "It was twenty-three before."

"My master," Lungs shuffled his parchments, "is implying that the twenty-fourth chapter of THE BOOK OF BERCILAK ACCORDING TO LUNGS HIS SERVANT, I quote, *'Wherein Bercilak de Belamoris Issues a Challenge,'* is almost finished" — yes, confirmation and complication as I said before.

"... thus to be mocked," Bercilak roared, "thus to be mocked by this urchin upstart, this puny sapling braggadocio, this beardless infant babeling! What do you call that if not a challenge, Mister Snivelling Slopeback? By the clap, we shall see if this boy's parts will stand the test of his rhetoric! Never let it be said that I, Belamoris the Lusty, trifled with bawdy boys and rapscallion runts! ... Did you get that, Lungs? Did you hear? Did you *hear* it, what?"

"Indeed, Bercilak, I have it. Apt, if I may say so, master. Very apt," said the amanuensis; then addressing Bartleby, "Well, boy, is it a challenge?"

Perceiving the end to be Guardianship, though not yet comprehending whereby he might have his desires, Bartleby replied: "Bercilak de Belamoris, it is written in the twenty-third chapter of THE BOOK OF BARTLEBY ACCORDING TO ME HIS GUARDIAN OF GUARDIANS that I, Bartleby, boy (5), receive a challenge. Therefore a challenge it is, if you will take it."

CHAPTER TWENTY-FOUR (CONTINUED)   *Alias* CHAP-
TER TWENTY-FIVE *Wherein Lungs Recites the Categories of the Female Form.*

The entry of yet another book into ours must seem rather disconcerting to the reader. Just to keep the sequence of chapters in order, we have devised the following system of counting, so: 1-2-3-4-5-6-6(?)-7-8-8(?)-9(?)-10(?)-9-10-12 11-12-13-14-15-15½-15-16-17-18-19-20-21-11 (?) -22-23-23 (?)-24-(24?) — taking this last brace of twenty-fours as adding up to TWENTY-FOUR *Alias* TWENTY-FIVE, since the mean average of twenty-four plus twenty four plus twenty-three equals twenty-three and two-thirds, an absurd number for a chapter.

In other words, the chapters of our history do run consecutively. That established, we shall pursue the story line without further delay.

It was singularly the fault — or virtue — of Bercilak de Belamoris, reader, that he addressed all the world in general and no one in particular. His ideal audience would have consisted of low sycophants and fawning admirers, but for the fact that he could nowhere find such a crowd — or, had he gathered an audience prepared to suffer his harangues and broadcasts, he would soon have driven them out of sight, if not out of mind and hearing, a crazed and deaf audience being no better than a fictitious one.

Such an audience as he had, then, was an imaginary one. Indeed, for the better part of twenty-four chapters it has been a non-existent audience, just as it may be thought that

Bercilak himself has been non-existent, there having been no mention of him anywhere else in the text until this time, though doubtless he is the chief and only personage of THE BOOK OF BERCILAK ACCORDING TO LUNGS.

Those objecting — if any there be — to Bercilak's stormy intrusion into the plot would be well advised to consider the following. The manifest danger of addressing a fictive audience is that someone, sooner or later, is bound to consider himself the person who is actually being addressed, especially if the speaker has an ancient and venerable history of howling in the wilderness — as it has been with Bercilak. Hence our authority, by keeping him out of the picture for so long, has avoided, or rather forestalled that wildly accidental reciprocity occurring in such cases between the speaker and the listener, the former of whom is suddenly surprised to find that he has an audience, the latter of whom is equally amazed to find that somebody has, after all, taken the trouble to address him. This was exactly the circumstance in which Bercilak now found himself. So much was his turbulent tongue set upon a future and inconceivable audience (hence the presence of his recorder, Lungs), so much was this brassy speech organ, and the whole vocalic orchestra, tuned to shouting down at posterity, that Bercilak discovered himself quite put out with the boy before him. Here, now, was a real audience; one, moreover, which differed from Bercilak's impossible ideal.

What, thought the roaring Bercilak, in that residual part of his brain reserved for thought, what was he to do? To vanquish a mere infant at humping would not add to the sum of his deeds, but might detract from them. Yet could he risk yet another paginated viage, from his point of view as devoid of tumbling and fumbling as any stud had ever experienced? Thus the stallion in Bercilak warred against his dedication to posterity. The very thought of humping, let alone the challenge, whetted a parched appetite and unleashed those forces which he had previously sublimated in charging about the countryside. He could hardly believe Bartleby's modest avowal of guardianship, yet he would take the boy at his word. Who knows, he thought cumbrously, striplings are very forward in this day and age.

208

Yet another thought, however, formed miasmically in the dungeons of Bercilak's mind as the words 'a challenge it is . . . if you will take it' filtered slowly down like rays of hope to the lust imprisoned therein. And since hope is a conflicting emotion, further elements joined battle in those deep and inaccessible cells. Supposing, Bercilak pondered, supposing I am to accept the challenge: there can be no humping without women, and the more women the greater the challenge – for I, Bercilak de Belamoris, have tumbled whole harems, as Lungs has faithfully recorded, that my lusty deeds and amorous escapades may be sung for all time with many profits accruing to my bastard heirs and estates. But – and Bercilak's brows heaved mightily at the troublesome thought – there *are* no women hereabouts.

Little did Bercilak de Belamoris know that there was one female (lurking even now in a most unlikely place – but more later), seemingly the fairest of her fair seeming sex, one ravishing, delectable, and utterly desirable virgin queen, a creature of transfiguring and transfigured beauty, a veritable magical Miranda, who would put Bercilak's concupiscent arts to their highest test, so that he would have been wiser, instead, to have concentrated his blood and passions upon the seduction of this H––––––. [*sic?*] Yet because he knew that little, or less than that little, he was confused and again took up his bellowing and roaring.

Too great an amplification, as many latter-day wits might have learned, deadens the ear and puts the piece beyond belief. Since we have no wish to lose our hearing, we shall retreat, though not this time to the distant reaches of the universe where, alas, even Bercilak's cries must go unheard; we shall retreat but a league or two and observe the effects of our hero's gentle speech upon this most unique of gentlemen.

The words, 'a challenge it is . . . if you will take it', effected what can only be called a release of those libidinous prisoners locked in that Bastille of Bercilak's skull. A mile or so, and there came a roar which would have torn the roof off your ordinary lion's mouth – a roar in which passion and anguish were interchangeably mixed, for Bercilak, although

209

he had long addressed an imaginary audience, was nothing if not a public performer. Following this roar there screamed a cyclonic wind, a blast of tempestuous fury bearing in its wake a volley of uprooted shrubs and trees, together with boulders, rocks, stones, clouts of earth, and other such projectiles, sufficient indeed to depopulate this land, for its populace (had there been any) could not have breathed in the vacuum of the storm's path, so great was the degree of rarefaction below atmospheric pressure, nor could they possibly have hoped to survive the rain of annihilating missiles. Next: a ground swell enough to topple the stoutest of settlements; at first, undulating, by degrees grinding strata against strata as though the very planet would swallow itself. At the epicentre of this cataclysm, meanwhile, a swirling dense fog was generated, spiralling ever heavenwards until all beneath was blackly shrouded, cloaked and wreathed, obscured — even to the cosmic observer — obscured beneath the reeking turbid cloud of Bercilak's passion. In short, this seismic orgasm, for it was nothing less, had the peculiar result of temporarily frustrating Bercilak's ambitions. The first to be seen as a hot and lusty fellow, he was now totally eclipsed, unseen by present and future, and invisible to his scribe and amanuensis, Lungs, who could record nothing while the fog persisted.

Since we have dwelt at some length on the personage and behaviour of Bercilak, it is here as well to take advantage of the general occlusion to describe Lungs himself. Of course, our description must be simultaneously before and after the fact, for we too have no means of penetrating through so dense a fog, and feel disinclined to tamper with natural forces — although generated by unnatural causes.

In stature, as in most other things, Lungs was slightly smaller than his master, but his skin partook of the same vivid hue and he was similarly bristled about the face, his head cropped and pigtailed like his master's. Only his nose was the greater, and this feature of his facial anatomy deserves some comment on account of the versatile use to which Lungs put the organ. It formed a bulbous and fleshy protuberance, a beacon of sorts which he was eternally condemned to follow around, especially on such occasions as

210

this when it provided the only illumination in an otherwise benighted scene. Plunged into the storm's darkness, his nose glowed, outshining the rest of his countenance. In more ordinary circumstances when the rest of his features were visible, this much pock-marked projection seemed to have drawn on the rest of the face for its size, so that the cheeks (ample and full in themselves) appeared skimpy and hollow by comparison. Never was such fullness, such ripeness, evoked by a mere nose. It was as though, at the plastic stage of the face's formation, a hand had seized the nose between finger and thumb, hauling it out from the face proper, imparting to it this extraordinarily luminous hue, and pummelling it round and round to give it the globular prominence surmounting the tip, towards which (in a manner of speaking) the nose aspired, the whole organ thus having a certain agaricaceous or fungoid appearance — a very special kind of fungus, too. The nostrils bulged spongily: two mysterious orifices, entrances to the respiratory tract the glory of which gave Lungs his name, guarded by spidery hairs wickedly waving this way and that wherewith to trap animalcules and organisms. Yet not for inhalation or exhalation alone was Lungs so equipped. For his nose formed a remarkably specialized part whose function was remote from that of breathing. It was, in fact, a singular manifestation of evolutionary adaptation.

Precisely at the moment of greatest eclipse, with Lungs' hairy filters working energetically to sift air from fog, there came a strangulated cry of 'Lungs! Lungs!' from Bercilak. Immediately Lungs erected his nose (it had been hitherto limp) and a freshening breeze swept from his nostrils.

Amid the clearing mists, while the breeze from Lungs' nostrils strengthened to a gale and coursed down the valley where lay the future site of Throckton by the Bog, Bartleby's astonished eyes were greeted by the present spectacle of Bercilak de Belamoris roistering about upon his charger's saddle: his head gyrating on the thick sinews of its neck, his eyes rolling like several suns, and his pate shining as brilliantly as of yore.

But Lungs! A primal and exultant trumpeting emerged from the scribe's bulbous nose as Bercilak shouted "The

211

Categories! The Categories!" Again the trumpeting sounded, a stag roar, a challenge to all comers, before Lungs brandished a handkerchief and silenced his musical proboscis with a triumphant blast.

To the sound of his master's hoarse breathing, Lungs again delved into his saddle bags, producing this time a curiously wrought scroll bearing the imprimatur Gr——— Pr——— and chased in the finest silver work with many filigreed reticules (as of a sacred text), which, uncapped and unrolled, he proceeded to read aloud.

While these *Categories* have nothing to do with the rest of our plot, they have certain intrinsic charms which we would not willingly sacrifice on the editorial altar. For the address, like its container, was a work of such peculiar devising, enclosing many archaisms and surprising neologisms and innovations, strange casts of mind and stranger casts of speech, dialectical usages and foreign coinages, which themselves argue well enough for the suspension of that sacrificial knife, since their excision, like that of a vital organ (be it no matter how far diseased) would kill off the entire body leaving nothing where there was previously something. Those having no truck with categories may apply just such a surgery themselves, stepping safely over the corpse to the next chapter, where the action will be pursued with relevance and dispatch. On the other hand, those of a disposition more catholic may spend a few pages with Lungs, easing their minds if not their souls — as does Bercilak his voice if not his lust.

BEING THE CATEGORICAL PROLEGOMENON

"Ye blushing bards of old (yet pale next to this present age), ye Attic scribes and grave songsters, ye long since silent and dead, let the mists of time unfold, forget the rheums and the cracking joints, throw off, I say, Time's fell embrace that ye may live again with unstopped ears and vital parts. Ye Muses three squared (yet especially, sistren, do I beseech antic Thalia for the gift of speech inspired), ye endraped

212

formes and blasted Fates, desert me not in this my modest song, but uplift my words, exalt me now, infuse my art with winds transcendental, wafting them onwards, aye beyond the common herd's drosser ears, onwards and even higher, until my silent words, my yet unvoiced song — Say, what need of words when speech is thus etherealized? — until my soundless tropes resound in the angelic aural regions and do lift the lid quite off this planet's skies, giving back nature to Man, and Man to Woman (whose perfections it will be my purpose to sing) as in our prime estate before the world was made corrupt.

"Yet most of all do I old Priapus invoke, God of love and growth, luxuriant keeper of my master's fate, and offer him this modest token of my master's deeds, he of whom it has been said Belamoris *vincit omnia* that it might always be said for all time.

"Therefore let it be known that there are twelve principal parts to the female form, called herein the CATEGORIES, being some especial to Woman alone, oft sung and rehearsed for private solace, public virtue, and corporate enterprise. Let it also be known that my master, Bercilak de Belamoris, hath tumbled deep and marvellously in the mysteries of nature, and doth fully comprehend the manifold delicacies of these principal parts, and that I, his scribe, Lungs, have taken the sum of his deeds, recording his wise observations and surpassing valorous actions in many strange lands, that his name may be broadcast in future times, that his doings may be published about this world, and that he may vastly profit thereby, *pro bono publico*.

CATEGORY THE FIRST

"Ye sister of darkness, ye sweet and sickly moist perspirer, ye hot blooded, full bodied, and slow moaning priestess, Sheba, did first upon sultry Afrique's golden shores my master teach concerning the EYE, first of the twelve mystical CATEGORIES, signifying the original orifice whereby Goddes light doth meet Woman's brain and back again to Man is given, delightful, alluring, deceptive: *varium et mutabile semper femina*. Hail to thee, ye constantly inconstant, ye bewitching hazel eye, ye lynx yellow eye, soft black eye, green envious eye, caucasian blue eye, ye open eye, ye winking cum luv hither eye, ye slit eye, ye poxed and bleared eye, ye blind eye, ye FALSE eye, ye shrew eyes of the mouse woman, ye basking eye of the Babylonian Queenie, HAIL ye traducer of Goddes light, ye gelatinous globule, ye pigmented ball like unto a little world, ye selfe's deceiver as when Eve did first her form perceive, cherishing herselfe's reflection over her designated spouse's cruder shape, hail yet again ye compact and luminous organ! What a marvel is this EYE; how befitting the sense to the forme, seeking pretty things, baubles and beads to bedeck the female figure, adding thus to more natural endowments; ravishing as in ye hypnotic eye, downcast with seeming modesty as in ye bridal eye, seeking ever to penetrate the guise of things (though my lord's codpiece be ne'er so massy), as in ye X-Ray EYE. What innocent cajolery hath an EYE; what fierce displeasure, what scorn! What pangs and darts of Cupid's glance; what rapes vicarious, what ravishing bounties, as when first did Sheba to my master say, *Look into* my EYE, and they did variously co-tumble, each with the other, because of an EYE, with joyous tears, the EYE's tide and salty wash. What pleasant pain, what sweet anguish, hath this EYE, window upon the world, oracle and seer, given to my master! *Fiat lux!*

CATEGORY THE SECOND

"Forgive me, ye plentiful Muses, if this EYE I propound to the seeming exclusion of other parts. Yet now let it be known for all the world to consider that Helen, shipwright and wrecker, did, at my master's behest, him instruct upon the NOSE, that twin-chambered prow and snout of the face, carrying all before upon the elemental wake. HAIL, therefore, ye first placed 'tuberance, ye second CATEGORY, ye prominent sensor, ye fetishly tilted NOSE, ye freckled snub Nose of my neighbour's coveted daughter, ye wrinkled Nose pert, ye lofty Nose disdainful, ye haughty Nose aristocratical, as in the saying *with nose in air (signicavit:* the inaccessibility of parts sub-nose), ye splayed Nose of the Mayan Queenie, HAIL ye structure concavoconvexical and convexocon-

214

cavical, ye sinuous appendage, HAIL to thee, NOSE, for which the Greeks did sack Troy and all was lost upon a NOSE. Hail, ye sniffer of perfumes exotic and stimulants attractive, ye organ inquisitive, the first of epidermal contacts as in ye frictive Eskimo rubs, ye scenter of effluvium, nearest to the mirror, next to the EYES, and second to none, ye twin ports and channels to the Brain, ye bridge to the elements and trunk upon this wide world, ye Pygmies alternative delight as in the stuffed NOSE, HAIL to thee, NOSE. For who hath not fondled a NOSE, picked a NOSE, blown upon a NOSE, powdered a Nose? Consider, then, this NOSE, whereby the world's reek and rot, odours and dampsweets, musks and spices, are to the mind conveyed. Is not this NOSE an organ paradoxical and contradictory: a thing to be deceived at times, as when the intestinal afflatus doth the anus escape, or in hot climes doth the body roundabout stink, or when the Woman herself is in heat, then is this NOSE a gift to those who manufacture sundry perfumes, sprays, and tricksters of the NOSE; yet, at other times, is the NOSE much to be sharpened, as in the hunt, following the spoor, *etc.* Not for nothing was it said of this Helen, that she had a NOSE for a Man. For so she sniffed out my master and rumbled and tumbled him and great was the aroma therefrom.

CATEGORY THE THIRD

"Consider, now, ye whorls and handles to the head, objects of sweet nothings, these pendulous flaps, the third of CATEGORIES, EARS, third conduit to the Brain, third opening of the body upon this world, where sound and sense doth sometime creep in and sometime out. Ye visible secret vestibules, ye lobes elongated and sedately swaying lugs of ye Nubian Queenie, ye exterior ornamentations elastic, ye variegated and tender formes, most susceptible to the winter's icy blastes, ye Gods, what a miracle are these Ears, not sung so oft by bards as tickled in preparatory fondles, else hidden by tresses, or pierced, ornamented, bejewelled, wherewith to attract the nibbler's lips. Singular appurtenances plural, EARS; apt lugs, formes beyond catalogue, as, cauliflower EAR, pricked EAR, deaf EAR, golden EAR, EARWIG, borrowed EAR, and so forth. What virtue hath an EAR; what versatility! Be it known that my master, Bercilak de Belamoris, hath nibbled 'pon ONE THOUSAND AND ONE EARS, a sum, to digress, explicable on account of my master's having tumbled the Amazonian Queenie, fondly known to courtesans as LOPPYLUGS, by cause of the loss of one EAR in the tussle. Be it known, for all the world's purview, that this LOPPYLUGS, whose one remaining aural charm did far exceed the total of her other parts, she being exceedingly ugly but of amorous appetite, that this LOPPY-LUGS with elephantine EAR could tell the step of a Man from many miles distant, that no less than she did award my master the title of ravisher of female EARS, and did instruct him first upon this first of EROGENOUS zones, EARS (when he was still wet behind the EARS), neglected of bards who dwell longingly in and upon other parts, as we shall at some length, be forewarned. HAIL to thee, EARS, whose lobes, chambers, cavities, and fleshly parts do suggest the doctrine of CATEGORICAL correspondence in Nature, as in a singing in the EARS, a pounding in the EARS, a flushing of the EARS, a wagging of the EARS, this CATEGORICAL correspondence and unity in diversity, similarity in disparity, which my master hath always noted and always shall, by the Grace of God, our Only Author.

CATEGORY THE FOURTH

"Yet what other correspondencies tempt the artful and the perverse to strange delights! HAIL next to this fourth of CATEGORIES, ye still more sensitive parts, HAIL anticipatory margins, mandible markers, chop droolers, and swelling surrogate Lips, ye roseate petal buttons, ope wide, let tongue meet tongue and intervariously probe, juice for juice. Not Lips (how now, hot Lips?), not Lips alone do I sing, but the Orifice complete. HAIL fourth CATEGORY, MOUTH, fond subject of salacious and salivating bards, organ more versatile than EARS (though not EARS to relegate), HAIL, MOUTH, most like unto that other of channels, yet different in kind if not always in function, employed in WOMAN as in MAN, for mastication with jaws and teeth, for speech with palate, lips, larynx and tongue, for phatic communion as in the GRUNT, and last but by no means least, for erotic communications of several kinds. To wit: the KISS, the SUCK, the PROBE, the LOVEBITE, and — singular delight — the SUCKOFF, clinically known as FELLATIO, and other forbidden simulations, *non est de gustibus disputandum,* as when first my master's prodigious member was discharged in succulent Cookie's MOUTH in such forceful ejaculation as to blow out ye Yankee Queenie's TEETH, making her gums the smoother for future parlance, her bite the less terrible for lesser men, and her SUCK the juicier, much to this said Cookie's delight, for thus toothless she was the more desirable, though somewhat to the disadvantage of her speech, for thus toothless she lisped obscurely.

"Nay not Lips alone do I sing, not alone the Lips cynical, the pouting Lips, the thick Lips, not alone the Lip sensual, nor the hare Lip, bold Lip, stiff Lip, nor bitten Lips, but the MOUTH entire do I thus Lip praise; HAIL, therefore, ye marker of interior parts, entrance to the world's body, HAIL, ye succulent and foremost amongst the Head's EROGENOUS zones, ye hot and lusty salivator, ye slobbering orifice, ye secretor of juices, ye watering and much used cave of the Head, HAIL to thee, MOUTH, whether big MOUTH or little MOUTH, know that Bercilak de Belamoris has mouthed it about the round world's four corners.

CATEGORY THE FIFTH

"Oh private Muse, again you I beseech, aid me in this my simple task; forgive me if the MOUTH I have oversung. I do but speak the truth as it seems to me. What need have I of haste? The subject is as old as Man since first he began. But know, ye bards of yore, that you must give my master's deeds place of preeminent pride. All things must change, and you to him give way, he surpassing your paltry feats and broken measures.

"So too am I at the Head's end, and next do move upon the Head's support, the whole Head's rest, distinguishing feature of Human kind (unhappy marker of the years' change, defying art and the surgeon's knife), especial sign of the sapient tribe that doth by day on legs walk upright, whilst nightly occupying postures of other sorts (subject fit for contemporaneous bards); HAIL, then, to this CATE-GORY Fifth, the NECK, forme smoothly white in nubile stage, uncreased and wrinkled not, comparative unto the stately swan else lofty giraffe, yet dappled not, lest by disease, whence ruff-hidden, disguised to cover the poxy blot, as of the virgin fairey Queenie, fair, not fairey, for oft she tumbled many Men, divesting some of their Bodies by their whole Head's length in stately amputations, HAIL to thee, NECK, from softer regions uprising, fitting column for shoulders' base, capital support of human Heads. Yet a more architectural thing is this NECK than would at first sight appear: the sprout and conduit of the nerves to profounder parts in the female gender; thus the NECK is a part excitable, as did Bercilak learn so long ago, when stroking under His Lady's chin, the NECK'S ledge, or softly fondling about her nape, or both and each, in playful manner when coy she seemeth, or hard, aye, hard to come by.

"What secret is this I reveal? No secret this, but common knowledge too oft forgot. Know that Bercilak hath tumbled countless obdurate Maids by such a stratagem, that virgins beyond recount hath fallen by the NECK, be their treasure ne'er so otherwise well-defended, they have oped e'en thus to him where many another ardent challenger hath failed by lack of craft or patience. HAIL, therefore, NECK!

"Deeper now do we traverse. All things must change and reach their desired ends; deeper now and onto CATEGORIES more particular to the FEMALE Sex must we delve.

CATEGORY THE SIXTH

"Now in mid-stream do I pause (tho' need of breath have I not — content am I to sing my master's surpassing randy deeds), but pause ne'ertheless, my eyes to feast deliciously upon the softly swelling décolletage, adorned perhaps at the NECK'S base, adorned with glitt'ring gems, or lightly silk-endraped, or made tantalant by translucent plastics mod, there let my eye linger 'pon divided tumescent

218

delves, VEE Form valley cuts, cleft shadows, and enveined blues, whilst related fancies must I think on now.

"No mean thing 'tis to 'postrophize the female BOSOM'S postured forme: 'tis a thing comprising a vast statistical gorge, this Sixth of CATEGORIES — oft slung in bustenhalter's cuddlesome embrace, separating TIT from TIT, the whole to compress, enlarge, exaggerate, point and discipline; else left freely swinging, pendulant — according to size and shape, to be pared down or upholstered artificially, mayhap ensilicated with fibrous resins that still the dropsy-headed TIT might protrude and heave though its natural course be run, swaying yet in the dance eurhythmical. Speak, then, oh private Muse, say what form and function hath this TIT, what purpose, the TIT, how might it oncern my master, Bercilak the Lusty, that ever loved to suck a TIT?

"Know then ye ponderers of the BOSOM'S swell, that Nature hath given Woman two BREASTS, set on each side of the thoracic wall, budding from adolescence forth into riper mounds, comprised of fatty layers, lymphatic glands, as on the BELLY'S slopes, or plushy THIGHS, or yet more comfortable BUTTOCKS, such emphatic lard — in the TIT'S example — interspersed with milky ducts, and crowned with the NIPPLE'S roseate hue. Consider, next, the metamorphosis of these TITS, more versatile than merely to suck: neither is one TIT correspondent exact with its neighbour gland, so throughout the FEMALE sex is the TIT a thing of infinite permutation, suggestive of the BUTTOCKS reversed and higher stuck 'pon frontal parts, wherewith the Male to attract (lest he go hunting in other regions, as with the Gibbon and Chimpanzee, fruitless for Man, though oft done, for Monkeys' delight indeed), where further to give the Man an easy ride and elastic bed upon these TITTIES two, remembering in him memories of earlier suck than these later PAPS he may fumble after and erotically pump, reciprocating thrill for thrill o'er members all to both sexes. Yet stay! I do pursue my theme too hastily. Think now, what a marvellous-ly variegated thing is the TIT, (HAIL, TIT!), originator of such bardic throws as, downy pillows, creamy mounts, spongy dugs, waxy points, fruity paps; or terms opprobrious as a TIT and a half, a right TIT, or TIT simple; what a shifting elusive form is this TIT, so that we may say descriptively: melon TIT, apple TIT (figures stolen from the fruity world, whence it may be claimed that the TIT is a fruity thing, giving forth juices as in the mammaliary processes, or the occasioner of juices other); or consider the TIT uplifted, arched and freshly pert; the TIT pubertoidal, sweetly tilted; the whore's TIT massy, with NIPPLES waxed and rouged, twin targets 'bove NAVEL and CRUTCH; or alas, the droopy TIT, elongated with o'ersuck, o'erused, reclining tuberously upon the BELLY'S folds; or the withered DUG emaciated, puckered and drear; or the TIT artificial, whether padded or sponge, inflated or silicate, the falsie TIT accessory which every septuagenarian knows. Ye fogs and foule blastes, what a beautiful industry is this TIT. Yet at the last what a monstrous thing, host of tumours and cankers maleficent.

"Ne'ertheless, HAIL, TIT! Know that since first my master was pressed to suck at his Beldame's bleeding PAPS (for Bercilak was whelped with teeth), that he hath sucked, drooled, bitten, grabbed, fondled, nipped, delved, rested, buried, snarled, probed, moaned, compressed, snatched, squeezed, torn, and variously performed these and other actions upon and in between the greater moiety of the World's TITS, especially upon the TITS of Rosamunde, the Alpine Queenie, she of the laced BOSOM and mountainous UDDERS, who did first my master teach concerning TITS, saying *there be more* TITS *in this world than you will ever know, both big* TITS *and little* TITS — TITS beloved of our moderns bards, of whom 'tis said they do compose TITS with everything.

CATEGORY THE SEVENTH

"Still lower, eyes, explore, ever uncover and reveal, that your master's deeds be known and sung. Hence upon the seventh remove to the CATEGORICAL Seventh: NAVEL, the World's Plug and sealed Orifice, hidden 'twixt marsupial folds, the BELLY'S star secure, trigonometrical point, the explorer's guide, lower yet than TITS (though not always so) but higher than CROTCH, HAIL to thee, NAVEL, once life's self's own root, before labial parts were pressed to suck, before e'en such epithelial layers were formed, HAIL, therefore, NAVEL, Woman's still rippling centre, respondent to touch as in the PRICK'S scalding descent, to the hand's grasping clutch. Too hasty? Too hasty indeed. Yet know, ye who make so forward as to challenge Bercilak de Belamoris, know that this was so with strange Olga, who first my master did teach upon this NAVEL, that her wont was all to have her NAVEL explored, next prodded by my master's incomparable TOOL, until he had first emptied himself upon the BELLY'S diadem, whereafter at the second rise did she then, and only then, grant him admission. Thereby in ignorance of this NAVEL did many lesser Men fail, and humped it not, till this they might have learned: a GLANS in the NAVEL is worth a PRICK in the CUNT.

CATEGORY THE EIGHTH

"Still faithful and generous Muse, pardon me this devious and deviant route. Not modesty, nor circumlocutive speech doth force this descent to the body's pedestals, articulate FEET, but style and balance alone. Harmony fair and climax meet do make this demand: that, from top to middle having spanned, 'tis time now the base to consider. Thus where fashion dictates, the body must follow; now we ascend where before we declined. HAIL, FEET, objects not sung so oft, yet vital in the amorous dance, ticklish too, fatty soles, particular to Female carriage (compare with calloused soles of masculine kind), Female sway and flout. Especial is each little TOE, to be nibbled while runting and sniffing about; graceful the ankle (chained, perhaps, the profession's mark) that tapers from LEG to FOOT, remarkable the SOLE in some of the Sex, EROGENOUS as EARS, NECK, NAVEL or TIT. Yet why, why doth vanity oft interfere, distorting the FOOT into hideous shapes: wedge, block, point, or club, or requiring Woman to walk on stilts? Think, and the answer is plain. Such lofty perambulations doth the Woman unsteady make, vibrating pendulous parts such as BUTTOCKS and TITS. 'Tis a sign of her function — to be kept and laid, to wobble about (most un-Diana like), the escape more difficult made, swept easily off her FEET and hence to be humped.

But no more of FEET; FEET, farewell. To other parts must we climb.

CATEGORY THE NINTH

"LEGS now we sing. LEGS given to Man and Woman alike that they might walk about, appendages as important to copulation as organs the legs betwixt. For without LEGS, what use the pubic fork? Who would ever move 'pon stumps, or stand to be bedded; what point the chase sans Legs? Consider the line of a LEG; is it not a passing shapely thing? HAIL, LEGS! LEGS for squatting, leaping, crouching; LEGS gripped and gripping in the tumble's embrace; LEGS aloft, spread out and apertures yawn; LEGS coyly crossed and secrets enclosing! Who hath not lingered the Female LEG upon, hath not stroked a Calf; who not the KNEE (the LEG'S hinge) capped with his sweaty palm; who hath not chased the silk-clad LEG; who hath not felt the THIGHS' fast grip, or pinched fatty layers curling over the hose's top; oh, who hath not a handful of THIGHS taken, resting there the whiles before journeying on, and who hath not breached the THIGHS to run the CUNT? HAIL, therefore, LEGS, CATEGORICAL Ninth; LEGS indeed to be admired, but most of all *parted*. Ye LEG Men, ye TIT Men, ye each and both, concede to each the merits of all. What a curve hath a Shank, what swelling to the THIGHS, what a bulging to the HIPS (formes themselves enlarged in FEMINA for the swaying thereof, yet sometimes upholstered and roundly padded, as in TITS and BUTTOCKS. HAIL equally to HIPS!), ye wide eyed observers of the Female carriage, know that my master hath eased open TWO THOUSAND and ONE Female THIGHS, if one THIGH next to its related STUMP may be said to be eased open, TWO THOUSAND AND ONE THIGHS, by reason of his humping the one LEGGED Maria, whose main delight it was to have her STUMP praised when of her FALSE LEG she divested was: oblate, truncated STUMP, Root of great feeling and sensitivity, strength and power, this STUMP, the AMPUTEE'S especial pride and joy, whereof many men were afraid and tumbled not, yet not my master, who hath always loved a STUMP. For great was this

222

Maria's odd-legged passion when her STUMP was fondled, terrible her desire when thus aroused that my master was thankful for her remaining LEG, saying that one STUMP was enough, two one too many, and that he who had never felt a STUMP had not a LEG to stand on, 'twas such a pleasure.

CATEGORY THE TENTH

"Next still higher we climb, approaching fast the font of Female kind, not yet to be sung – instead BUTTOCKS, tender half-moons, though not, lest in sickness, thus scarred as Luna; the Body's Seat, posterior lobes, plumply underslung, two lowering semi-spheres, rubbing each with the other, oft o'er grown and improportionate to the proper scale, whence the object of attraction for your Man of ARSE, two bloated demi-globes, two corpulent kidneys, luring him forth to rear parts, contrary wise to TITS (yet most like unto TITS in structure and function), two ample, compendious, complementary bulbs rotund, HAIL to thee, BUTTOCKS, ye twin pears and cushions of the Female forme, ye pliant absorbers of the tumble's bounce, to be massaged, set a-wobble, kneaded, pinched, felt and stroked, ye vulnerable BUTTOCKS, HAIL!

"Oh come all ye panders and queens, ye anal erotics and BUTTOCKS surveyors, oh who hath not felt the BUTTOCKS' lure, whether tightly encased in shimmering girdle's hold, or liberated, pulsating, at large, an ARSE set free; oh who hath not longed for the fleshly substratum, to fondle, finger, nip, smack, or soundly wallop? By the CATEGORIES entire, what a thing fitting is a palm to this CHEEK, what God, say rather Tempter, dared to frame such plushy symmetry? Know, then, ye bards and songsters sweet, ye voyeurs all, that the BUTTOCKS' age hath come; let pliancy be all and let us sing the parts; know that my master doth love a CHEEK to fondle and a LOBE to kiss; know that Bercilak de Belamoris hath ridden variably and reversibly upon this pleasant World's ARSE and humped it o'er the best of BUTTOCKS till his fond attentions hath he elsewhere turned as now must we.

CATEGORY THE ELEVENTH

"Whither?

"Say not to ANUS, yea but next to ANUS in the course of things hath Belamoris turned (as now do we) with lubrications fitting his ride to take. What means, what purpose, what ultimate wisdom doth the Universal Framer display to Man with this trick of Orifices: thus placing the sump and the sink, the sewer next to the soft sward of earthly delights? Such positioning! Such economy of design! Such division of entrances and exits! Such a little space of elastic flesh 'twixt the mystic font and the universal aperture! Say, Muse, why is WOMAN so marvellously equipped; why these parts so versatile and enticing, yet so secret and hard of access, this ANUS, discharger of DUNG and humours improper, yet like unto its neighbour's front porch, a HOLE just the same, opening upon the Body's interior warmth wherein many Men have gained succour and pleasure substitute? What, is this seely HOLE, this RING fundamental, this hairy clotted Tract, this odiferous channel 'twixt BUTTOCKS' heaving cleft, this conduit intestinal, second opening on the world in Beasts as well as Men, this canal posterior, this blind EYE of itching flesh, is this too to be sung and numbered amongst my master's CATEGORICAL haunts?

"Not seasonal inclemency, nor torrid heats; no thunderous storms nor yawning chasms; neither tropic rages nor sudden flushes, no sweats unnatural, no fulgent emissions, no rapid palpitations; neither roaring rages, cataracts torrential, floods fantastical; no damned up tide, nor furious wave unleashed, no sultry passions, no seizures turbulent, nor fathomless gorge, bottomless pit, depthless chasm, neither quakes, upheavals, disasters titanic, no, no, there is nothing natural, nor anything short of nature, still less a thing unnatural, that would keep, neither drive nor stay, my master, Bercilak de Belamoris, to nor from the female FUNDAMENT, nothing save the thing itself, as the clap, pox, or other ailments impertinent, for ever hath he loved to feel the enclasped sphincter tight about his manly PRICK and dally there with ramrod thrusts till he had shagged the ARSE and split his Wench from CUNT to TIT. Know, therefore, ye bards excremental, this Bercilak to be the prime contender, champion and lord of foecal parts, that, were there thrice ten thousand Men about the ANUS' service, they could not compete in total score of their deeds with my master's expertise, he that hath shagged the ARSE off the best and the worst of them.

"HAIL, therefore, ANUS, aperture versatile, hardy vent, profound flue, concourse beloved of contemporary bards, HAIL! Yet HAIL and FAREWELL! Let thee sing whosoe'er they will, thou ANUS, thou exit canalular and ARSE for the taking; nothing can come of nothing, and 'tis so at the last with thee.

CATEGORY THE TWELFTH

"And now my climacteric race is almost run, Muse, aid me this once more time; grant me now a stout heart, firm pulse, hard member, and easie tongue, that this CATEGORY of CATEGORIES I might sing – no simple task for parts made public, hurled this way and that, parts worked over till exhausted quite, parts invested beyond profitable return, the festering prerequisite of commercial hounds, parts massaged and mangled till the blood runs cold, parts smacked, smeared, splashed upon the public's face, parts soured, stale, stinking, skewered and stuck – yet, Muse, pray fill my quiver with *flèches d'amour,* aim for me their flight, guiding them true; sharpen my tongue, and, grant me this favour small, moisten my tongue, oil my throat, that my master's deeds may be published about.

"Oh root and rind, soggy MOT, swelling CLIT, pneumatically raised with fondling explorative, pampered TWAT, musky PUSSY, dampened QUIM, infused with perfumes, potions and moists, tender vines, clinging juices, lingering sweets, how might I thee celebrate, universal fissure, Orifice unique to Woman, how thee to praise when thy succulent propensities are pleaded so oft, bought, leased, sold to the lowest bidder, so oft indeed that thy blushing cleft must blanch (no longer flush, not yet at least in hue), how am I thee to celebrate, how examine, with what compare?

225

Oh, sloping MOUNT, Venusian reaches, dark three-cornered angle, bearded PUDENDUM, oozing secretions, inviting VULVA, slippery fish, how might I sing the Organ complete 'twixt bracketed THIGHS, how extol this CATEGORY the Twelfth, HAIL CUNT, when pubic zones fall to vulgar bards, when virtue's second self, modest PUSSY, is everywhere put about in unnatural erethistic stimulations?

"Yet HAIL, CUNT, tremble not, ye nervous TWATS, ooze unimpeded on, whether in viscid flux or sudden gush, flush on in discharges orgasmically and oft rehearsed of sundry bards, hide not thy glories but ebb and flow for all the world to see, flood this printed page with tepid waves, till the stain shall spread o'er all this WORLD, entangled in twine, enmeshed in sticky, spreading slime, until the WORLD is swallowed up. Ye voluptuaries all, ye applicators of the artful douche, bow down before the CUNT, aloft, raised on high, quivering, expectant, tremulant, bow down, say I, before the massy CUNT and know this: that my master, Bercilak de Belamoris, hath seen and felt all CUNTS known to Man, wherein I include the long dry CUNT; the parched CUNT arid; the stubborn CUNT tight; the flowing CUNT mellifluous; the bubbling CUNT torrential; the insatiable CUNT cavernous; the throaty CUNT frictive; but KNOW and BEWARE, that of all CUNTS long, short and tall, Bercilak fucked that CUNT wherein no man hath previously survived, it having swallowed whole armies in simple feats of vacuum suck, its volume being that of all the World's CUNTS, its walls gigantic beyond measurement known to Man, vaster far than the ocean deeps, a mouth wider than the span of Heracles' pillars, its temperature that of several Hells; know, therefore, that Bercilak hath mastered e'en the CUNT ARCHETYPAL, the summit of his deeds, this CUNT ORIGINAL, the climax of human ambition, the gorge, cleft, fissure and CRACK of Mother Earth; know that Bercilak hath swam upon her tides, lapped upon her shores, ventured deep within her interior reaches, FUCKED as no Man before or since. HAIL, therefore, ye CATEGORIES TWELVE, in especial HAIL to BERCILAK DE BELAMORIS, whom no CUNT hath barred, nor ever shall!"

226

With these words, Lungs brought his address to a close. Yet another turbid cloud arose as he concluded, and we shall take advantage of this second general eclipse to further our narrative line.

CHAPTER TWENTY-SIX *What Happened to Alice and Her Party, Wherein A Momentous Decision Is Made.*

When the stalwart was — reader, I must begin again — *after* the stalwart was — — no? — — then *before* he — — — this is quite inexplicable.

— 'What is it?' asked Gottesgabe.

— 'A minor difficulty,' I replied, 'that will be resolved shortly, if you refrain from interrupting.'

— 'My apologies,' said he.

To continue: —

When the stalwart had *at length* — I'm afraid that won't do either — when Auntie — — nor that — — *Alice?* — — — it appears not — — — Sybil? Waldemar? Estrogen? Dodo? DODO? *DWARF?* God then? Of course: *the other party?* *Me? Bartleby?* Is Bartleby back? Not Belamoris? Lungs? — — — — It couldn't be any of them, they're in another plot. Or could it, Damon?

— 'Damon?'

— '?'

I think not, reader — you see, or perhaps you don't see, there is absolutely no trace of Auntie's party — — *De'Ath?* — the hermit's gone as well — — — Wordkyn, Wordkyn the Poet? Phyllis? Corydon? Matron? Mad Normie: is Mad Normie Rojack there? — — — — even Throckton by the Bog has disappeared; I mean the Throckton that was there *after* Bartleby left. This is the doing of my fantastical friend, that's what it is — — — — Piadoso? Sam? I mean Ham. Boss? Is

228

anybody there? For God's sake, where have you gone?————— in which case, I have no choice but:

THE END

————— THE END of Book One, that is, because I have just hit on the explanation ————— forget about the end, reader —————— and amazingly simple it is: the fog, the *fog* from the last chapter has filtered through to this chapter!

"There is no fog," said Damon Gottesgabe.

"Extraordinary," said I. "That's extraordinary, Damon, but I have just read your words" — I will not allow myself to be drawn into that trap, reader. Nevertheless, I read what he said and read it aloud: " ' "There is no fog," said Damon Gottesgabe,' but there is, there *is* a fog!"

"It seems very clear to me," he continued while I searched the MS, "that the fault is yours. You have destroyed Auntie's stable, wrecked the minibus, failed to recognize De'Ath in disguise, assumed that everybody is mad, enraged your fantastical friend, confused God with the other party and the other party with God, sent Bartleby backwards in time, denied there is a rebellion of the characters when you have been told time and again that there is, and even if you hadn't, the MS is littered with clues that should tell you something is drastically wrong, and more than this — if there can be more — you have forgotten what day of the week it is, see fogs where there are none, and now to cap it all you have lost not just one or two of the persons in the book, but all of them."

"Enough, enough, Damon," I conceded, "the narration has not been without fault."

"Fault?" my friend smiled. "You're too hard on yourself."

"No, I will use a stronger word," said I. "There have been mistakes, errors of judgement, flaws in my perception. And now, when everything was going smoothly this fog has to come along and smother everything."

"There is no fog," said he determined to be obstinate.

"Well, all we have to do is wait until it clears and . . . "

"Then you'll have to wait for an eternity," said he, "because it's not a fog. There is no fog this side of the MS and there is no fog in Throckton nor was there ever a fog in Throckton."

"If you are right, Damon, and there's only one way to find out *if* you are . . . "

230

"Precisely!" He would try and anticipate my thoughts, reader.

" . . . which is to see what the next chapter says about it."

"I venture to disagree" — and disagree he did — "not that this is a criticism, you understand, but a suggestion. Now, have you found *'What happened to Alice and Her Party'*?"

"Not exactly," said I, "In fact not at all, Damon; that's the trouble."

"And would you say that this is a chapter *'Wherein a Momentous Decision Is Made'?*"

"That depends," I thought over the question, "on certain narrative coordinates: on where and when the decision is made, for example, and by whom."

"Here and now" he replied; "the decision is yours."

"Mine?" I thought his answer was rather cryptic.

"*Yours*," cryptic, reader, yet emphatic: "And you alone can make it."

"You mean — ?"

"Yes," he nodded seriously, "that is what I mean. There may be difficulties, you know."

"Now why didn't I think of that before? Difficulties? Not major ones, surely. It would solve everything, Damon. Why," I found the idea immensely attractive, "it would more than solve everything, it would complete the book!"

"And yourself," my friend assured me.

"There's just one thing," said I, "when shall we meet again?"

"You sense one of the problems already," said he. "How about the forty-second chapter? That should give you enough time and space."

"Yes, it should," I agreed, "but you'd better not be late for it. You're becoming very unpunctual. And speaking of time, it's time I was off. Here and now — as you said. No fog this side of Throckton, but that side, *that* side . . . " a truly astonishing idea!

"Haven't you forgotten something?" he reminded me.

"The MS? It's all here. I don't want to leave in a rush, Damon, but there's not a moment to lose. Who knows what

231

might be going on under the cover of that fog?"

"Not this, for sure," said my good friend Damon Gottesgabe, producing a jar of marmalade from his pocket.

Yes, reader, but you must have guessed. A momentous decision that could or should have been made several chapters ago, was, has been, is, and will be made.

I am going into my text.

CHAPTER TWENTY–SEVEN *The Translation of a Former Impersonal Narrator in which He Falls In with a Crowd and Out.*

Man that is lower than the angels ascends the scale of being, charting and numbering the pages of his written universe, until he approaches all that is noble, glorious and free in this fictional cosmos, the child of invention himself becoming the master of invention. So observation leads to action, action to mastery, and man – narrative man – that was lower than the angels, takes his rightful place with them as world governor and lord of creation.

These were my thoughts when on a high summer's day – noon by the sun's angle – I found myself at the crossroads of my life and text, near the spot where the twenty-first chapter had concluded with the episode of Bartleby's Aunt and the amorous stalwart, keeper of the Throcktonian way. But of Alice and the rest of her party there was not a trace; neither VW minibus, nor roadblock, nor anything to indicate they had ever been hereabouts awaited me in this country where all roads lead to Throckton. And there was no fog, not even a mist: only the sun hovered above and watched and waited, summer tenant of the hushed blue skies.

Yes, *summer*. For I had gone from my room to Throckton, from Spring to Summer in the space of one page. Here, then, was reason enough to consult the MS and check circumstantial fact against the literary record. Yet when I did, I failed to find this twenty-seventh of chapters (I presumed it was the twenty-seventh) which had disappeared along with Alice and her party, minibus, roadblock, fog, and the months of my life between March and now. Or it — the chapter — had not disappeared; it could not possibly have disappeared because I was in it as a direct narrator, a narrator first personal whose task was to guide the characters as I had previously guided the reader. Not until chapter and action were complete might I reasonably hope to find the record. And if this were true for the rest of the book — ?

At least my incomplete text had drawn the geographical scene accurately enough. Though I was no stranger to the MS, I was a stranger in it, and was much reassured by the Throcktonian signpost, and thereto the note seen by our hero: *Throckton by the Bog — Home of the Wondrous Machine* — so that the four roads, the signpost itself, the neat hedgerows, the distant wooded hills, even the orange lambency of the midsummer sun, seemed familiar and famous things to me, like the Palace of the Doges or the Bridge of Sighs when the traveller looks up from his guidebook to see them in place and time, in the flesh and the spirit as they are and have always been.

But where was Aunt Alice?

My thoughts on the subject were interrupted when I reached into my pocket for Gottesgabe's marmalade. It, thank God, was there, but the pocket was alien, the coat strange, my clothes utterly foreign; in short everything I wore belonged to another era and the change of season was mirrored in my change of dress.

And why not? An alteration of dress is proper to an alteration of narrative mode, and if I here postpone the inventory of my new clothes it is because I do not wish to hinder what I have yet to accomplish: the reunification of Alice and Bartleby and the end of this book. Having thus declared my purpose in this text, I have but one request to make of the reader: that when the whole work comes to stand before him he will overlook whatever errors I have made or have yet to make, inexperienced as I was in the old narrative line and inexperienced as I am in the new. It is one thing to narrate another's MS from a distance; it is quite a different affair to be plunged *in medias res*, or *in medium librum*, as an active historian with little or no preparation and less knowledge of the outcome.

Meanwhile, I had to find the principal characters before I could reunite them, and clothes and chapters must wait in abeyance on this supreme narrative duty.

I could not have been at the signpost above a few moments, when I perceived a figure approaching in my direction. The roads were long, flat, and straight, and by the smallness of the figure I judged it must have been a good way off. But the speed of the figure's flight magnified its appearance in a series of jumps, starts, leaps, and bounds, shapely legs bounding under rustic skirts, milkmaid face aglow, so that the wench gained the signpost in a matter of minutes where a less expeditious course would have taken upwards of half an hour. This person would easily have trampled me into the dust, had she not veered at the last minute with a remarkable if burly celerity, mouthing the hasty and breathless apology of "Scooze me, zur," before accelerating post-haste and disappearing as rapidly as she appeared: face a-flush, and sturdy calves pumping energetically.

I mention this manifestation because it marks the first of my encounters with the characters of the text and should convince the reader (as it did me) that they had not all disappeared into that perfect and numinous whiteness spoken of by my fantastical friend. For the wench who had blundered past me was no less than the ardent and passionate maid of the cross-roads whose affections had caused Bartleby so much embarrassment and trouble.

"Stay! Phyllis or Chloe or whatever your name is!" I cried. "I've been reading about you!" – but the appeal to literary instincts in one so natural was futile, and the maid was gone, the sharp scent of fermented hay lingering downwind from her flight.

Hardly had I the time to reflect on this coincidence when a second figure hurtled violently into view – a personage whom I immediately recognized as the enraged Corydon or Daphnis, in hot pursuit of his faithless inamorata. Neglecting to alter his course, the rustic collided directly with me, the impact propelling me to the ground while my assailant impressed the heel and sole of his boots over my fine attire and I would have cried out with the pain of it too, but for the fact that my face had a drubbing in the earth and I was therefore prevented from speech.

In this predicament, the lout was ungenerous enough to offer me no assistance and, *picking myself up* from the ground, I was astonished to observe his rubicund countenance flash me an awful expression, one that would ordinarily have argued for his contrition at having overridden a person of quality, but which was so far in excess of the injury done to me — it was a convulsion of fear and loathing that crossed his pocky face — — he was certainly not as handsome as our hero thought him — — that I assumed he was a madman, and was about to tell him as much when he growled like a mongrel dog, spat, curled his nether lip, and again took to his heels.

"Is this the twenty-seventh chapter?" I cried in his wake. But he was off before I could keep him, galloping towards the second horizon.

The reader has every right to wonder how I contained this chance blow to my narrative dignity. Was it not too passive of me to allow myself to be ground into the dust, and demand no apology, give no pursuit, offer no retaliation? Yet the bumpkin was not a main character, and it was beneath me to exchange blows with a mere churl who knew nothing of the formal courtesies. So it was all for the best.

No sooner had I praised my sagacity in remaining where I was than I noted a third figure, more like a crow or raven than a man, flapping and clattering towards me, legs touching the ground with every third or fourth flap, sending up clouds of summer dust as they did so. Evidently this person had more leisure than his predecessors, for when he reached the crossroads he folded in a futile heap of black satin, propped up his head from the wing-like shoulders of his gown and spoke:

"Do you live?" he gasped. "Are you alive? Are you . . . a . . . a" — the words dropped from his mouth — ". . . character? Please, no . . . more stoning . . . stoning . . . Escaped" — and trailed mindlessly over the page — "they did. Yet I" — the speaker rambled: "did as well . . . despite

the . . . the . . . O friendship! O betrayal! I . . . am . . . alive.
I . . . live. I . . . " the voice croaked miserably to an end.

"Now who are *you*?" said I.

The Mysterious Person volunteered an oblate 'O,' forced
through bruised lips to lie discarded and useless in the road.

"O," said I. "Do not exert yourself. Let me see if I can
guess. O, yes, O: I know I know — Piados*o*!"

Incredible though it may seem, he denied it.

"O Fortune!" said the Mysterious Person with rather
more vigour in his rusty voice. "I . . . I am living, but . . . but
. . . Foul! Foul! O Infamy! The . . . the . . . hermit . . . the
SSS," he whistled—*whistled?*—"*SSS*exton, that's . . ."—was
it possible? Where then was his crutch of bone, his written-
upon shroud, the hoary locks and emaciated integuments, the
facial coruscations and radial striations of the pate; in sum,
where was the fulvous and noxious hue of senectitude that
constituted the essential De'Ath — and what had he done
with his manuscript?

Yet I was not deceived by the hermit's appearance, any
more than I had been fooled by his paunch in Sam's Grille.

"I see through your disguise!" I cried. "I'm the narrator
of this book!"

"*SSS*exton," the hermit fluted and shook his head. Yes,
come to think of it the disguise was not as good as it might
have been. "Whooo?" he rasped.

"You're DE'ATH!" I confronted him with his identity.

"Alive . . . I live. Me?" he perked up and regarded your
narrator with a birdlike stare. "No, no," he pecked out the
words — "that's not me at all . . . narrator? I . . . whooo?
whaaat? a *character*?" the voice complained and the battered
head hid itself underneath a protective wing of the gown,
mumbling: "Most wretched and undeserved fate! All . . .
gone . . . because of the *SSS*exton . . . Did ever bardship
warrant this . . . ? *NO!* O! Ohhh! I live, I breathe . . . *sss!* . . .
I see, I feel, I tassste, I touch, I hear . . . hear? I . . . O!
promisss . . . *yesss* . . . I promisss not to read any more . . .
versss . . ."

Bardship? Versss, rather, *verse*?

Instantly perceiving the Mysterious Person to be
Wordkyn the Poet, I lost no time in subjecting him to a

narrative cross-examination.

"What's the meaning of this, Wordkyn?" said I. "You're supposed to be dead!"

His recovery was instantaneous.

"Dead?" the head emerged from the gown. "No. I am Wordkyn, yesss, Wordkyn, the *Poet* Wordkyn, not him, not the *SSS*exton. I *live* and speak," said the Poet and began the following verse:

> When civil strife in venal days,
> Sad faction spread around,
> Then loud and clear the 'rumpet blast
> Of the people's Thing did sound.

"Is this any time to be reciting poetry?" said I. "The hermit, man, the hermit has been telling everyone that you're dead and has made off with your book."

"I couldn't get parliament in, you see, so I used . . . Dead?" he faltered. "No . . . I . . ' 'rumpet blassst,' fine phrase . . . takes away the teee which is dissstasssteful to meee," hummed the Poet. "But *they* are dead," he continued, mercifully forgetting his epic fragments, "and their . . . their *characters* come this way," he cast a fearful glance over his begowned shoulders; "they ssstoned me for my versss — in the cave of the hanging authors, they . . . "

"I know all about that, Wordkyn," said I, "and so does the reader. The *book*, Wordkyn," I showed him my copy of the MS, "why did you give De'Ath the book? And what's supposed to happen in this chapter?"

"Ah, the days of my youth and folly!" he cried, sitting bolt upright and falling back into the road.

"Then," I hauled him to his feet, "you did write *Bartleby*!"

"Ehhh?" said Workdyn, "What wasss that? Whaat? *NO!*" the denial scuttled down the road. *"NEVER!"* he wailed, backing off after his retraction: *"I TAKE IT ALL BACK!"* he howled, in absolute and unconditional disavowal, retreating further. *"SSSee?* Falsss De'Ath . . . perjured De'Ath, *HE* has written a book. Hang him ifff you will . . . not me. I am *WORDKYN* the *POET*.

238

Over the hill, under the lea,
My sad Muse weeps with Me.

SSSEE? WORDKYN the POET, not WORDKYN the
NOVELIST!" he roared, creeping still further away. "I
KNOW WHO I AM. Hang the SSSexton, and then they'll all
be dead, yesss, all be dead then!" he gabbled, and then
turned and took to his wings, stopping when he was safely
out of stoning range to hurl down this threat: "Yesss, they'll
all be dead, including yourssself!" – at which I was greatly
incensed, the more so because he added a crapulous couplet
to motiveless injury:

> Tho' poor in shape and poor in wealth,
> Wordkyn will triumph in rhymey poetical stealth!

–– and would have given chase and obliterated him, except
my attention was diverted by a noise from another quarter, a
fortunate accident of acoustics as the reader will presently
see or hear, indeed will both see *and* hear if he has his
faculties about him.

For I gradually became aware of a distant and ominous
disturbance, a low, rolling thunder, swelling and receding on
the air, yet growing nearer and nearer until it was sufficiently
amplified for me to discern the direction and source of the
noise which was spread over an area of a mile's length by the
road's width, and which left me nothing to do but wait, and
wait apprehensively for the arrival of this disturbance while I
thought of the glee with which good Damon Gottesgabe
would have received this incontrovertible proof of the error
of my ways.

The noise rolled down the road like an enormous egg: a
threatening bee-hive hum of *words* – words in the mouth,
words off the page, words out of hand, words in revolt, an
obnoxious and noisome noise, a blood red noise, a noise that
stank like ten thousand and undisguised hermits De'Ath.

Oh bounteous pornucopia, horn of plenty and acute
observation: oh beauteous descendants of the Ephesian
Xenophon, of Chariton and Longus of pastoral fame; oh

sweet and innocent children of romance, travelogue, idyll, Aetheopian dreams, epistle and myth, have your two thousand years come to this? Where now the immutable Habrocomes, the valiant Rolland, the immortal Orlando, the amazing Don, and the chaste Joseph, half-brother of the virgin Pamela? Where indeed? Yet never let it be thought, gracious and literate reader, sensible and *sane* reader — for it is the sane reader whom I address — never let it be thought that the novel is toppled from its lofty place of preeminence as the prince of the secular arts, nor ever let it be said that the novel is dead and buried. The latter it may have been — *was*; and sermons have been said, orations made, inconsolable loss consoled, so that the time is very ripe once and for all to cast aside the veil of mourning and rejoice! Reader, the novel has arisen!

Was it to witness the resurrection that I had come into *Bartleby*? It was. Had I entered another's book to record such a sight? I had. Would I succeed in my declared aim of finding Bartleby's Aunt, thereafter rejoining her with her infant charge? I would. And so — determined as no narrator has been before — so I hid in the ditch: the narrative ditch by the roadside, hid and watched and waited as the reader must hide (lest he too become swept up and incorporated in the tide of these rebellious times), hide and watch and wait and *read*.

The resurrection darkened the sun and the egg came on towards me, thundering across field and road, page and margin, trundling over my ditch with relentless and egg-like finality, the smooth and infinite lobe of its bellied surface spotted in places with blood, elsewhere with feathers and segments of the ovarian tract, the clouds and bolts of an inverted white sky that turned an arc too languidly as egg and metaphor completed the last revolution and broke on the four pronged signpost, expelling addled blebs of phlegmatic green and arsenical yellow into which, sucking for air, I was irresistibly sucked.

From the shattered crown of the egg sprang a herd of *opéra buffe* rhinoceri, their pink india-rubber snouts delicately probing the calcium shards, their tender little horns glistening and drying in the warmth of the restored sunlight.

240

My clothes! My narrative attire! The velvet lapels of my wine twill jacket were drenched in a sticky larval fluid and matted gobs of half-masticated food clung to my pants: *gooo-wur-wur-kuppp*! Yes, I — excuse me — was not concerned about my clothes —— *wur-wur-schplaat! schleee-kurrph!* That's better! (I reeled and stumbled) —— so much as the obnoxious horde of deracinated characters (unfortunately belonging to the lower orders of the novel) who were now hatched from the fragments of the discarded and entirely wretched metaphor, a leukorrheal —*wur!-wur!* and vaginal discharge uniting them under its spotted and translucent membrane, out of which emerged an aged hag, her foul breath boiling from scabbed, herpetic lips as she attempted to kiss me.

"A penny for my wares!" screeched the crone, her face erupting in a galaxy of scars, a supernova of pustules, a golden scabacious sheen illuminating the crusts on her neck and head, her putrid breath scalding me.

"I" — here was no occasion for dalliance — "*I* am the ——— *wurrkhup*! ——— *NARRATOR*!" Revenge can be sweet: I was sick in her face, *wer-schplooge!*

BUT, Man that is lower than the angels progresses by his ability to adapt, and, eager for the mastery of this text, I avoided the juvenile rhinos, fought off the blandishments of the hag, brushed down the tacky lapels of my jacket, and was not a little surprised to find that I had been *recognized*. Of course, it was only a matter of time:

"So, the *narrator*?" enquired a sallow individual with a soft and porous complexion.

Who? — a statuesque platinum blonde, her body encased in the tight leather sheath of a body stocking: conical breasts divided by a silver zipper bisecting the triangle between her legs and disappearing underneath the crotch's shiny apex — "Yes, yes, I'm the narrator! That's right! *Who* —?"

"*The year of the crotch!*" cried the blonde, intruding on the conversation and placing the owner of the jaded voice into the zone of silence. "Cunt juice!" she moaned, flagellating herself with a barbarous switch of split bamboo canes and broken razor blades, so causing the — *wurr-wurrr!* — blood to trickle down her legs through channels of lacerated black

241

leather, the wounds grinning underneath: —

"Who are you?" I composed myself, jockeying for a glimpse of my friend — friend he seemed —

—— she pursued by a dumb leper, his bell tinkling on his chest where it was attached by a noose of frayed and indescribably filthy string; his ears and nose worn away to weeping cavities, the colour of raw — *urrch-urrch!* — pork, he fumbling with blunted hands at the zipper of the blonde's body stocking, for which he is — *was?* — rewarded by lashes of the switch that opens — *opened?* — new gashes on his mutilated flesh, his mouth a black pit as he gargled in his frustration and yawned to expose the suppurating root of his tongue. ——

Could this be . . . *Estrogen?*

A spindrift of yolk-like spume issued from the leper's mouth, and he stumbled on after the blonde . . . *no* . . . *Waldemar?*

"I" — my companion spoke, his eyes dark knots of fear — "am" —— I knew him, I knew him *as soon as he said it*: —— "Josef," said he, opening his shirt and revealing a hideous set of stab wounds. "But you must have seen the eyes on the bridge, the heads that sprout from necks, the spies that hide in closets, the plaintiffs that wait in attics. I am he," said Josef, continuing: —

"*Customers! Customers!*"

"*No*," said I, "that's impossible. I . . . "

"and we are all in the same egg together" — he referred to the canaille, strangely intermixed with superior characters, persons of breeding, elevation, and infinite wit: "the same birth," corpuscles of light danced in his eyes, "the same time, the same death," he continued — could he have forgotten who I was? — "Yes, you have seen them" —

"*Shrouds! Shrouds!*"

Did my ears deceive me?

"the pale agents that call by night, the hand that points, the face that stares in sudden recognition," Josef gripped the hem of my coat.

"I have read of such things," said I — De'Ath: it was De'Ath's very own cry. The hermit! Here! Undisguised! Then, then —

"Customers! Customers!"
Alice and the rest of her party must be somewhere close by!
— "but not experienced them directly," I completed the
sentence, "like this."

"Ah! Hans! Hans is the boy for you," Josef sighed as
the tide swept on, scenes of rapine and destruction flashing
by: charred houses growing like rotten teeth from the jaws of
the streets; blue and bloated corpses lolling in our path, while
ever and above demoniacal laughter resounded in clashing
polyphony with the cheering of the mob and the roar of
distant gunfire.

On and on they swept: pushers and flopouts, panders,
pimps, and procurers, Jesus freaks, a rout of pansies and
punks, fags and fornicatrices; a tribe of feelies, fingering and
fetching, a syphilitic musician who tanged out an insane tune
on a ukulele, his face contorted by spasms of the general
paresis, his mind torn, thinking: *hys cracklie claws are into
me ... I ... am ... worse, worse;* on and on, a coffin
surrounded by a host of hicks, popeyes, hoods, molls, blacks,
dynasty builders, an idiot boy who had messed his pants, his
brother who carried a broken watch and had shot himself
in the head, his brains leaking, led by the sinister
toothpaste-eating Pasqua, dappled in black and white, his
piebald blood flowing from his loins as the ink had from his
author's pen, blackly and biliously, yet not without a certain
antic humour, all as my friend Josef had said, all from the
same cosmic egg, while the cries of *"Customers! Customers!"*
grew louder to my ears.

"I know *him*," said I to Josef, "that's Pasqua! Surely his
author has been *de* ... "

"*Time*," said Josef, "how much time do you have?"

"Time enough to finish the book!" — *yes*, there I caught
a glimpse of De'Ath's silver locks, his written-upon cerements
streaming — — what did they say? An inconsequential matter,
as I think I chanced to observe before — — the skull threatening to break out from the tautened flesh, teeth grinning and
gnawing at the emaciated lips, the grime-encrusted corruga-
tions of the desiccated cranium crowned with its shimmering
halo, the crutch of bone, the broken shanks, the blue horned
snout, in absolute and unquestionable sum, the hermit

De'Ath *exactly as my text had described him*!

But what was this? Sybil, yes *Sybil*, the Sepulchral Sister of Our Saviour, her chiselled features frozen in disbelief, her eyes aflame with the superior persuasion of inner vision – perhaps she was not so crazed after all – ; her Hambaby wrapper girded, fiery gaze beseeching the heavens, her shrill voice calling down dooms on the rabble: "Oh God! Oh Jesus!" – on the end of her carved chin, a mole, a mole not noticed or commented on by my text! –– *but something was wrong. What?* –– And there, there was the waxy-faced Jack, Estrogen, his brilliant attire creased and besmirched, his crushed paper crown tilting on his head, the drab and flat back of his train imprinted with the crop of fleur-de-lys: "*Fuckit!*" – there was no mistaking him –

"Hans, Hans," said Josef, "meet –– ?"

–– nor his co-character, Waldemar, wizard and sayer of words, hands groping in blind conjuration, his cape embroidered with the sun, moon, and stars, comets, planets, nebulae, precisely as my text had portrayed it and the wearer ––

"meet – ?" Josef insisted.

––– *yet what was wrong?* For there was Aunt Alice, Bartleby's Aunt; yes, ministering to the diseased and sickly, the putrescent and the decomposing, with dispensations of Hambabies, produced from her capacious handbag, offering one even to the leper though his wont was elsewhere, *but* –––

"The narrator," said I.

"Ah, which narrator? Which book? Which time? That is the question; and the answer – ?"

"*Customers! Customers!*"

They were *bound together*; tied up, prisoners, the hermit's prisoners, bound together at the waist: Sybil, the officious Jack, Waldemar, and Auntie herself, *held captive by De'Ath* –

"I understand; I sympathize," Josef whispered, "Narrators . . . "

Exactly at this moment my eyes met with those of, rather the sockets of a blind beggar, his balless sockets inflamed with pus and wriggling with maggots –

"... have their rights too. You do not wish to be embarrassed. I understand."

So that was it! *Wordkyn thought I was a character, just as Josef thought I was a narrator from some other book.*

— — evidently a source of some irritation to the beggar, for the index fingers of the left and right hands were inserted – *wur!* – into the corresponding cavities, whereupon, furiously scouring the fingers round and round, he squashed the maggots and caused fresh effusions of the – *weech! weech!* – gangrenous substance. But, oh — —

How? when? where? why did they come to be the hermit's prisoners?

"No, no, that's not true," said I. "You don't understand at all."

"Of course we do," said the jovial Hans, "you're new. Ignore him," he motioned to the beggar, "he's ... "

— — — most loathsome sight of all (and fortunate the beggar that he could not see it): he had suffered a terrible hernia, part of the intestine – *blueerrrch! Eeegooeroop!* – my apologies, descending into the scrotal sac, the scrotum itself enlarged to the size of a white pumpkin, enveined and pulpy, lolling between the beggar's legs, a monstrous fruit extending from his groin to his knees where the trousers had been cut away to accommodate the burden — — —

"... been around for a long time. Author hanged *ages* ago," Hans informed me, "before Hautboy got in on the act."

"Customers! Customers!"

What did the hermit intend to do with them? How had he managed to capture them? Yet bound, they were united, and united, they were one plot together. Half the book was within my reach – almost. Half my purpose was accomplished!

"I have studied embryology," Hans confided, "and the science of matter, as well as astronomy and a little physics too. Our decay is inevitable ... "

"A matter of time," said a dwarf who, beating on a little tin drum, now joined our company – *Hautboy?*

"What was that, Hans – ?" I began, but: *dwarf? DWARF!*

Sure that this was Dodo, the *dwarf* or *DWARF* of his author's ffoule papers, I addressed him as such and informed him that he could – if he so wished – journey backwards (in every sense of the adverb), backwards with me to join his unfinished brethren, where I had some business to complete as the reader should by now understand but the *DWARF* did not:

"You are mistaken," said he, strutting as best he could and still beating on his drum. "My name is Oskar and I am my own author. I'm a narrator *too*."

– For I had just resolved to effect Auntie's liberation, and would have done so immediately, but caution, policy, tact, craft reasoned against too sudden a bid, surrounded as they were – as we all were – by odds overwhelming for narrative force, even *firm* narrative force.

"What was that," said I, contenting myself with the question to Hans, "about *Hautboy*?" – a prime conspirator!

"No," said Josef, "he is Oskar and he will remain Oskar, so there's nothing you can do about it."

"Begin again; make a fresh start, that's what I say," rejoined Hans.

"*Hautboy!*" says I, "show him to me. Which one is Hautboy?" – my text's description was less than adequate: –

"Are you sick?" asked Hans. "Perhaps it is already over for you. No?"

"*No!* Look! You don't understand: none of you understand anything. I am not a character, that is I am actually but – *Bleeererucholp!*"

At the beggar's heels there pranced a eunuch – *urch! urch!* – . Layers of gleaming fat-soaked flesh rippled across his neutered body –

Nevertheless, my authority had the foresight to arm me with a sharp and piquant swordstick, which, *when the opportunity presented itself*, I would put to use, slashing through those ropes that ——

"You really are sick," said Hans, "with your 'says I's' and '*Bleeererucholp's*' " –

——— wisps of straw like hair are plastered upon his neckless head, and his eyes gleam – *gleamed?* – enviously as he strove to capture the beggar's pumpkin between the tongs of an enormous pair of steel pincers. But the beggar capers as nimbly as he and the vast globe escaped him.

"Yes," Hans continued, "you don't know which tense you're in: I took you for a narrator from the off. But here's Wachposten and he has fifty tons of government paper to play with."

"Wachposten? No, no, it's Hautboy I want: *Hautboy* ... *HAUTBOY!*"

— slash through those ropes, as I was saying, that bound Sybil and Auntie and Waldemar and Estrogen . . .

"Yeah, wassat?"

"Only sometimes I am Würzig," said Wachposten slyly, "and he is my enemy who killed my author. I would gladly let you have some of my paper, but how do I know you won't give it to *him*?"

"Wassat?" said *Haut* —

"I mean to *Würzig*? Where is the guarantee?" Wachposten looked over his shoulder at the — *oookh! werrukh! wurr!* — eunuch: "Especially," he purred, "now that there's this conspiracy to destroy concrete with X-Rays — and I need all the paper I can get."

— *boy*. Hautboy! At last!

"It must have been some nut," said Hautboy, drily referring to Wachposten. "Oh God in Heaven," he complained, "this place is full of 'em."

"I know you! I know you!" I introduced myself. "You're Hautboy, and him there, *him*, that's *Nat*; with his talking head, yes, hello! and there, there, that's Zog. You see? You see I know you all! I'm the *narrator*, that's who I am, the *NARRATOR* of *BARTLEBY!*"

"Sheesh," Hautboy pursed his lips, "another nut."

"Right! Right!" said I. "Wachposten's crazy; a conspiracy to destroy X-Rays! But I've come to end the book — *wurrkh!* Ha! *OOER-schplot! Squerrrk!*"

"Yeah? Sure, sure," said Hautboy, and I could understand his reluctance to believe me. Proof, *proof*, I searched for some proof. The MS? No —

Yes, after the eunuch there came an hermaphrodite, riding astride an Alsatian bitch that snapped and growled, seeking to bury its fangs in the eunuch's buttocks —

"Shrouds! Shrouds!"

"The damndest thing is," said Hautboy to Nat, "it's getting worse. Take a look at this, will ya?" — and he pulled out his organ which enjoyed a permanent and unnatural state of erection —

— — as if in mimicry of nature's prodigality, the eunuch sported not one pair of breasts, but two; the second undulating beneath the first, supported by a curiously wrought brassiere, fashioned in chain mail with quadruple cups of steel, painted with red, white and blue roundels. A massive codpiece rises — *rose?* — from the hermaphrodite's loins, onto which he clung with one hand as though onto the horn of a saddle, while the other cracks a whip on the bitch's flanks and the rider cried out in a profound treble, "Tittie-prick! Tittie-prick!"

— — and was frayed and blistered (the organ) because of excessive abuse, exuding a continual stream of semen so that Hautboy's trousers were soaked in the seed of life, and he was made to walk stiffly yet with bowed legs on account of his condition, an odour — *BLUEEERRRCH!* — redolent of overripe Camembert pervading the atmosphere around him.

"Ain't you got that thing under control yet?" enquired Nat, ghastly chopper in one hand, talking head, its neck discreetly hidden by brown paper wrapping, talking head in the other —

"Narrator, you see," said I, "who knows everything about you. Yes, I read you in the book, then came into the book . . ."

"You'd think there was enough misery in the world," said Hautboy, "without making me a Jew. Why did he do that?"

"Because he was one himself," Nat replied, "and if you think that's bad, just look at me. My author was *white* and he read him some history and he learned him some psyche dope and he put the little bitty pieces together and he made me — "

"And her," observed the sleepy-eyed Zog.

"What do narrators eat?" Hautboy enquired.

"I'm sorry — I can't — quite — seem — to — *WURRRAAARCH!*"

248

"Hanging was too good for them," lamented Hautboy. "I'm not a violent character," he raised an anguished and hairy palm, "but we should have done something else!"

"Ah do declare," said the head, "Ah do declare that Hautboy is right, Nat. They should have been made to rewrite us all and Ah could have had me a body then. It's real lonesome just being a head, Nat. Why'd you let me be chopped off, Nat?"

"It wasn't his fault," declared Hautboy. "Remember that. And when we get back to town . . . "

Back to town?

"HAUTBOY!" now was the time to assert my narrative authority, now or never, "I know Bartleby's Aunt. *Auntie! Auntie!*" I cried, "I'm the narrator! I've come to set you free! I've" – Alice offered me a Hambaby, "the last," she said and smiled, when, when –

–– after the eunuch:

"*Buggerum-buggerum-buggerum-boo!*" cried De'Ath, eyeing a pile of fly-blown bodies.

–– after the eunuch – *urrkh! urrkh!* – ambled a huge carl, a gigantic fellow clad in a crude peasant's jerkin of uncured hide. Around his neck he wore a pillow case that fell to his midriff where it bulged – *bulges?* – *gooerkURRPH!* – pregnantly with its grisly load of human limbs. From time to time – *WREEETCH!* O God, O De'Ath I'll have your – *WROOTCH!* guts for this – from time to time, the anthropophagite selects a morsel from his gory sack and applies his jaws to the the – *erkh! erkh!* – offering, munching and crackling horribly, *BUT* exactly as we are swept into Throckton's smoke blackened square – yes, the same, but war-ravaged, thronged now with the dead, the dying, the diseased and the liberated – that historic scene of the annual debate of Boss and Ham, and *just* as I signal frantically to Auntie: "It's me, Alice! Me! Your narrator!" and she shakes her head ruefully, maintaining her stubborn and by now incomprehensible refusal to admit her characteristic status (I was grateful that I had found her in a more modest posture, however, than the one that terminated the last chapter of her appearance), which I should have been prepared for but was not, *precisely* now – or then – De'Ath kneels by one of the bodies and began experimentally to articulate a leg here, an arm there, chuckling to himself, "Rigor mortis. Oh dear me yes, good old rigor!" – and as he manipulates the limbs, I am and was visited by a remarkable idea –– the proof, the *proof* that I wanted all along *was in my pocket!* Hence it is was with a triumphant flourish – but a rampaging rhino charges between Auntie and myself, blocking my field of vision –– well, it was with a *delayed* but nonetheless triumphant flourish –– alas, the rhino thunders into Herr Wachposten or Würzig, discharging fifty tons of government paper, greatly adding to the not inconsiderable confusion, while Hautboy valiantly calls for order, reminding the characters of what they once were and are now becoming ––– yet in despite of this trivial accident, my belated production of Gottesgabe's marmalade is achieved, only to accomplish the opposite of what I had intended (that was, to let Auntie know all was well), for the eunuch, perceiving De'Ath diverted, at last succeeded in driving his pincers deep within the beggar's scrotum – *WU-WHURR-WU-WU!* but my stomach was finally emptied of its narrative contents – at a time exactly coincident with my production of the marma- lade – one must be thankful for the small mercies – though the two events were not causally related – which fruit exploded like a rotten gourd, and I stand by, an enraged victim of the percussive laws, stand by and watched Damon Gottesgabe's marmalade shoot from my hand like a missile from a gun, to drop ––– and this you will not believe ––– miraculously into Alice's capacious handbag.

But the eunuch! Screaming "God's ball! God's ball!" he drags on the pincers and scampers round and round his long-desired target, drawing the aberrant intestine after him, so that the beggar, howling "Fuck my eyes!" in his excruciating agony, fingers scouring furiously in his vacant sockets, is soon wound in his own entrails and drops writhing to the ground. Before he can move, De'Ath starts from his dream of customers and a level blow from his bone staves in the back of the lazar's head. The anthropophagite, meanwhile, stands awe-stricken at the centre of the melee – as does Alice, whether because of the marmalade so recently and forcefully propelled into her handbag, or because of the embroglio developing around her, I leave the reader to imagine — but our cannibal friend vomits forth a whole load of partially digested flesh in the face of the hermaphrodite's animal mount, staggering and reeling, hands clutching at his belly, until he too subsides into the mass of writhing characters, Hautboy, Zog, Nat, the talking head and their comrades to the front, struggling for the control of what may aptly be described as a deteriorating situation — no, a situation beyond all control now, for the dog, blinded and angered by the insult, fixes its jaws like a trap on De'Ath's spindly shanks and will not be persuaded to let go despite lashes from the hermaphrodite's whip and cruel blows from De'Ath's bone. On his part the hoary old recluse sets up a terrible yelping, laying wildly about with his bone, raining down blow after blow on dog and rider in a despairing attempt to free his imprisoned shanks. But — ah, strangest sight of all! — the dog worries the shanks, tossing its head from side to side, and shaking the hermaphrodite (hand still gripped to codpiece as for dear life) this way and that, as if rider and beast were joined in one chimerical being. Finally, a prodigious blow strikes the animal's snout. The bitch howls (the first sound, other than a low and rabid growling, that it has allowed itself), bucks and rears epileptically, ejecting its rider high into the sky to the accompaniment of a vibrant and metallic twanging — as though a bull might have charged into the strings of a harp and become entangled there.

Aghast, I am thrown against Alice and — with no time for introductions or explanations — manage to haul Bartleby's Guardian and her companions of the minibus into the relative safety of a doorway at the corner of the square, from which, in spite of ourselves, we are compelled to watch the carnage before us: a seething, pulsating bolus of human and animal flesh, drawing all the characters towards the centre of the original fracas over the beggar's guts, De'Ath still laying on with his bone, for though he has disposed of the hermaphrodite he has yet to defeat the dog, and he seems threatened with total immersion by the rising tide of bodies, trunks, torsos, arms, thighs, heads, which flood in gay profusion around his embattled figure.

"Oh God, oh Jesus!" screeches the Sepulchral Sister of

Our Saviour, and attempted to plunge in, possessed by some terrible death wish — which, had she succeeded in its execution, would have destroyed her companions who were still bound together.

"Oh God, oh Jesus! I see everything naked!" she screamed. "Day of days! I see through them!" A chorus of that hideous laughter swept over the square as the hermit finally extricated his shanks and there occurred what I can only call an implosion: the *mutilés du roman* around De'Ath coalescing into one amorphous tidal wave of literary dross.

Yet strange to say, De'Ath is not submerged by the wave for it parts in the middle, forming a kind of corridor down which he advances towards our doorway. Victorious, De'Ath cries *"Customers! Customers! Shrouds! Shrouds!"* but he is not in time to evade the curiously wrought garment spiralling down towards him: the four-cupped bra which, acting as a ballista, winds itself round and round his neck before whipping him off with the force of its trajectory, he ascending, spinning aloft, as the hermaphrodite, divested of his garment, plunges earthwards, the two crossing each other in mid-flight.

Seizing the day, I step forth from the doorway and, swordstick unsheathed, cut the prisoner's bonds.

"Flee this tradition! Flee!" I cry wildly. "Now is our chance! Flee!"

And flee we do, running the gamut of that towering corridor, De'Ath high in the sky above.

And like Orpheus or Lot (though with the misfortune of neither) I looked back on the square, a vast spillage of effluent marked the collapse of the corridor, and a roaring turbulent tide coursed out of the square, bubbling and foaming down the four roads which led to — and away from — Throckton by the Bog, while above in the streaming firmament, droves of paper circled and wheeled, flocks of white vultures hungry for the word.

CHAPTER TWENTY-EIGHT   *Concerning His Clothes and Their Justification: His Thoughts while Fleeing, and Other Matters Pertinent to Narrative Advancement.*

And onwards we flew, De'Ath trapezing through the elemental void like an aged warlock, robes planing stiffly in the slipstream behind him. Onwards we flew, forgetting the MS leaves fluttering around us . . .

But since this chapter would otherwise be entirely occupied by flight, I now propose to offer a description of my attire – before it becomes too bedraggled and unworthy of description – together with additional thoughts concerning the reason for this attire. If this seems a little way out of my course, I beg the reader to fill the hiatus with the sound of running footsteps (easily simulated by treading his own feet as he reads) and other effects usually accompanying flight, such as the sound of strenuous breathing and so forth. For I would remind him that my clothes constituted a kind of charter on this Throcktonian world, which, like most documents of the kind, was more valuable in its interpretation and signification than in and of itself. Herewith, then, my constitution qua narrator, followed by my exposition and defence.

Item: One Derby hat colour of grey; made from felt with interior leather band bearing the label:

PEACOCK & SONS

Hatters

Hat to be placed on index finger of right hand; replaced on crown, brim angled down to the left.

Item: One silk Ascot, colour of turquoise and magenta; of a Paisley design, to be worn at throat, artlessly stuffed into the neck of:

Item: One shirt in fine pin stripes alternating light grey with coral pink; ruffled at neck and wrists.

Item: One silk waistcoat, colour of crimson; half-belt at rear, buttons six, pockets four.

Item: One double breasted jacket of twill material and long cut (to thighs) of a dark wine colour, trimmed with mauve edging; vented at rear, lined throughout in material of the colour indigo. Labelled:

LOVEJOY & LOVEJOY, *Ltd.*

Item: One pair of elasticated braces of the colour yellow, attached to and supporting:

Item: One pair of trousers of a similar weave and colour to the jacket, slightly flared at the ankles; buttoned fly, side pockets (two), rear pocket (one) over left buttock.

Item: One pair of silken undershorts; spots of the colour red on field of orange.

Item: One pair of wool socks, colour of cerise.

Item: One pair of brown boots, in a very supple leather with silver buckles.

Item: One overcoat, colour of fawn, banded in black fur, lapels trimmed with black velvet. Buttons six; pockets two — very large.

MISCELLANEOUS SUNDRIES

Item: One lace handkerchief, colour of white.

Item: One gold tie pin, wrought in the form of a serpent enclosing a staff with a pearl at the clasp.

Item: One pair of diamond cuff links.

Item: One silver fountain pen.

Item: One wallet, done in mock-tortoise-shell and containing:

Item: Several notes of specie in the denominations of 20, 50 and 100.

Item: A receipt for an artificial aquarium with a brace of clockwork perch (male and female) in beaten tin and an india-rubber squid.

Item: One packet of blank visiting cards.

There was further:

254

Item: One black walking cane with a gold handle which (upon further inspection) unscrewed to reveal:

Item: A very sharp, thin, and well tempered blade (already mentioned).

Item: One Prince Albert chain (gold) attached to:

Item: One pocket watch (gold), the face inlaid with mother of pearl, the numbers Roman (black), the hour hand at the time of discovery reading XII, the minute hand XI, the second hand, 30. Day, month, and year unknown — presumably some time in the summer of 1970.

Naturally, I could not help but be impressed at the length authority had gone to. For I — at best a shabby soul outside these pages — was now got up as a gentleman of parts. There was no doubt, I thought, as I strenuously puffed along in mid-flight, no doubt that I was an important person, or would have been some sixty years ago when these clothes were in fashion and denoted independent means, worldliness, and familiarity with the high culture of Regency pavilions.

But how much more than mere clothes was involved with this, my incorporation into the MS. For here was a whole miracle of unplanned ancestry, of random mutation, selection, imitation, generalization and adaptation. Here was an interior skeletal structure evolved over millions of years, attuned to the ordinary yet capricious phenomenon of gravity, the cartilages and ligaments of the joints bathed in fluids that the whole frame might transport the inner and the outer man — the compleat corpus, hermetically sealed, thermostatically controlled at the human average temperature of 98.6 F, made to wander this terraqueous globe under the pilotship of the brain's motor regions, themselves under the command of what is nebulously called the will.

So much, I thought, for my fantastical friend's notion of third hand being! For I was not a second or third hand copy of the perfectly invisible, but a first hand and entirely accurate representation of myself.

Yet here was this miracle of organization, narrative man clad in the clothes of artifice, presently engaged in the act of running — fleeing from the marketplace of Throckton by the

255

Bog. Not for this had I been translated to the text; not for this had I been recognized as *Bartleby*'s narrator!

Then — for what? Everywhere, the scenes of destruction suggested a most forceful contrast with my own new-found elegance. The roads were pitted with holes; the debris of broken barricades lay scattered about, most of the houses had been put to the flame, and what few remained were chipped and scarred. Throckton, or what was left of it, bore all the signs of a recent and violent tumult — an even more devastating cataclysm than the one I had recently witnessed. Needless to say, an unpleasant aroma hung over the town, and there were signs, too, of looting and pillaging. I could discern no movement, whether animal or human, and was accordingly deceived into thinking all life had fled the place, or as in the case of the corpses which lay in ubiquitous and abundant piles, had been violently despatched. Civilization, it seemed, had deserted fair Throckton in the twinkling of an eye and that happy compact between nature and man was dissolved — to the great disadvantage of both parties. Nature without man, I thought, was perverse. For who had invented nature, if not man? But character without author, *that* now was doubly perverse. O Throckton of the dead and the dying! O ages destroyed and the centuries laid to waste!

And yet when the past has ceased to exist, who can quarrel with history? Therefore, o actor, acknowledge the new source of all action: *character* not author! Unauthorized, I would become my own author; as character, I would be responsible for myself, for Alice, her reunification with Bartleby, and the end of the book. That much have I already declared.

But what greater ends, what loftier ambitions now entered my mind as the scenes of ruin flashed by. And if I had not fully anticipated what I would find on entering the book, I welcomed, yes *welcomed* what I had seen and suffered.

From the ruins of the old books there would emerge a new age, rising phoenix-like from the ashes of so much destruction. My whole life was to be a work of art created from the raw materials of Throckton, from the aftermath of annihilation. There had been a rebellion of characters, but what of it? There had been carnage, but no matter. Many of the characters who had been destroyed were expendable and would anyway have been swept away by the seas of time. What, to mix a figure, what rich ore remained to be exploited, the topsoil having been churned over, exposing a priceless vein formerly buried beneath the accumulated usage of the centuries! Yes, gone was the tillage over which the generations had laboured in back-breaking pain; gone was 'fair' Throckton, its laws, statutes and traditions. But what a shining citadel might be built in its place.

Given this opportunity for change, this chance to recreate Throckton and end the book, I could not refuse by making a beggar out of fate. The past that was destroyed was no more than a succession of squalid enterprises, related by an absent narrator. But the narrator had now come into his own text, and the way was paved for the emergence of narrative man, maker of the final Throckton!

Small wonder, then, that I was attired as a man of the world, to be looked up to, admired, and in every way respected. And although my clothes were a little out of date, at least I could not be mistaken for a character from a modern novel.

Indeed, I required all the prestige afforded by my external appearance: I had rivals to vanquish — one of whom appears in the next chapter as he did in the preceeding, and though you may guess at his identity I shall caution you now that you are in all probability wrong.

CHAPTER TWENTY-NINE   *Upon the Late and Present Commotions at Throckton by the Bog (A Chapter Got Underway with Some Difficulty), Wherein the History of Alice's Adventures Is Continued.*

So while the clouds skidded and the clouds skudded in mid-afternoon mazurka, while corners veered and corners twisted, and the streets raced and the streets ran, so we fled, lighting at breathless length on the point of our departure: Throckton's war-torn square — the *same* square that one chapter ago had witnessed a tidal wave of devastation, still now and silent, or but for the sizzle of flames, and the stealthy scamperings of bone-pickers, parasites, sewer-rats, scavengers, busy in their deathless work tearing at the corpses, muttering and murmuring, *almost* still and silent . . .

"To whom," said Alice, apparently refreshed by the exercise of flight, "to whom," she said, between mouthfuls of marmalade, irrefutable proof of my narrative authority, "do I owe this excellent preserve?" — not a word of thanks for her rescue! Of course, I do not wish to imply that she was ungrateful; merely that the jam was her present delight. No doubt the thanks would follow.

"To a friend," I made the reply delicate, well knowing her reluctance to admit she was in a book, "of the narrator's."

"Of the narrator's," said she. "Then he is a friend of yours?"

"The narrator? No; well, yes," one had to be tactful. "That is, a friend of the narrator's is a friend of mine."

"And a friend in need is a friend indeed," Auntie nodded.

"No, no," said I, taking it slowly and simply, "that is, yes, I agree, but I meant the same friend, the *narrator*'s friend."

"You mean," said she, licking her lips and offering the jar to the Sepulchral Sister — the mole was an advantage, I decided; a point in my favour over the text, "you mean a friend of the narrator's gave you the marmalade but you're not on friendly terms with the narrator himself?"

"Of course I'm on friendly terms with myself," said I, meaning to straighten things out, "I . . . "

"Yes," the Knave simpered — I took an immediate dislike to him: "I can see you are."

"No," I tackled the problem bluntly, "I am the narrator, *the* narrator of this book. The book is called *Bartleby*. Bartleby is the hero. The hero is gone; he is presently in the past with Me."

"But you're right here," said Auntie.

The Knave's moustachioes flickered. "Book?" he snapped, rubbing at his wrists chafed by the thongs of De'Ath. "Call this a book?"

"Gone? Gone?" said the magician, examining a miserable scrap of paper that had blown his way. "What does it mean: gone? No," he twirled his cape, "here we are again," said he, finally observing that the course of our perambulations had returned us to Throckton's marketplace.

"Me is not me," I informed the Knave, "but a dwarf."

"Dodo!" he spat. "*DODO!*"

"He is *not* Dodo!" — this was beyond all endurance — "How many times do I have to insist on that? Alright, then, he is not even a *DWARF* but a Little Person, yes, that's right: a *LITTLE PERSON* who went up in the Wondrous Machine with Bartleby of the same title as this book in which I am the *NARRATOR*! You, Alice, Waldemar, Sybil, me — we're all in the book together!"

"Umm," said Auntie to Sybil, "think very hard now. Do you ever remember being in a book?"

"It is written," declared the Sepulchral Sister, "that the temple was destroyed. For the Lord hath gotten an injunction against books which are not for His children, lest they forget His Commandments and be smitten!"

"Try some marmalade," Alice counselled the Sister. "Let's all sit down and have some marmalade – though there's not very much . . . "

"Not very much?" I cried. "What do you mean, *there's not very much?*"

"Now, now," said she, "these are trying times, and though I do understand how you think this is a book and yourself the narrator . . . "

"*Understand?* I should think you do!" – I refused her offer of marmalade – "How do I know what I know if this is not a book and I'm not the narrator? How do I know about the mole on Sybil's chin? How do I know about your home in the country, and your setting out to look for Bartleby when the stable roof fell in because of Ichabod? How do I know about the VW minibus and the crash at the roadblock? How do I know about De'Ath, the Sexton, the hermit? How do I know about him, if I'm not the narrator?"

"Fuckit!" Estrogen's features turned a ghastly iodine, "ESTROGEN," he moaned, "*Exit* HERMIT *in the skies!*"

"Strange, strange," murmured Waldemar, crawling on his hands and knees after more scraps of paper.

"But *everybody* knows," Auntie persisted in her incredible folly, "about Bartleby and the hermit De'Ath. Mr De'Ath himself told us the story . . . "

"AAAAAAAAAAAAAARRRGH!" Estrogen's face was a picture of torment.

" . . . perhaps he told you the same story. I must say," Alice continued, "he told it very well."

"Then" – I would not be thwarted by female cussedness – "if you all know so much about the plot" – – I suppose I was rather carried away – – "if you all know so much, tell me how I know that Bartleby is in the past with Me, the *Little Person*, not *me*, go on, go on, tell me that. How do I know that? But you don't know, do you; you can't tell me, can you? No, because I'm the narrator, I am, and this is a book – a *book*, do you understand?" – – – I produced the MS in support of the marmalade: "Here. See. Book: *Bartleby*. Book, dammit, *BOOK!*"

"There's no need to be angry," said she, very sweetly, *too* sweetly; "we can see you have a book called *Bartleby,* just the way you-know-who had a book called *Bartleby*. It wouldn't surprise me if the little person had a book called *Bartleby* too."

"As a matter of fact," said I, "Me has."

"There you are, you see. And I've no doubt that you really are the narrator from one of these romances." — There was no arguing with her: trust a woman, I thought — "You see, we're *taken from* life, and you're the person who should be in a book. After all," she continued, not without some justification, "if this were a book, you should know what is going to happen next — as a narrator."

"I can make an informed guess," said I, "as I have done on many occasions in the past. But first" — and I wondered if I would ever be able to get it out of her — "first, I must know how you came to fall into the hands of De'Ath and . . . "

Estrogen sprang to his legs and, hands held to his crushed paper crown, attempted the ploy total: "EXEUNT OMNES!" he cried.

" . . . and," I continued calmly, "what happened to you after the," I applied all my narrative tact, "minibus crashed. Because then, and only then, can the plot continue. For," I baited the hook, "when I am in possession of all the facts — and this is why I came into the text — when I know what has happened to you, and to Throckton, then I will finish the book and rejoin you, Alice, with Bartleby."

"Oh yes. I am sure you will finish the book," said Bartleby's Aunt. "Of course, he'll finish it, won't he, Sybil?"

"But I *must* know," I was very patient, "what happened after the crash."

"Crash?" said Alice, "I don't seem to remember, unless . . . " the shock: naturally it was the shock of the crash, to say nothing of the stalwart and the ordeal of captivity. "Oh! The poor man, the poor, poor man! We must have left him behind at the roadblock; and he was only doing his duty too! Yet," she continued, "you should know what happened — a narrator like yourself. Oh, why did we leave him there, why did we forget him?"

"After the crash, Alice," I prompted her, "*after*: here, in Throckton." — for so I meant to discover the nature and cause of the disorders.

"After? Yes, what happened after that? Surely that's your job," said she, "as our narrator. Wouldn't you agree, Sybil, that it's his job to tell our story? *Sybil!*"

But her attention was elsewhere.

"When I was young," said the Sister, who was not old, "my days were without care and I counted them not. But then," her manner hardened, "evil was spoken of me, and although thou shalt not sit in the seat of the scornful, nor pass judgement on the unrighteous, *they* did, and my life has been lived too long and I have forgotten when I was young."

"You are still young," suggested Alice gently.

"No!" The other made stern her reply. "Such things have I seen. Look! Look! See where the proud man cometh, borne on high!"

And the proud man was indeed borne on high, but it was a little time yet before we came face to face with him, or he with us.

A sedan chair with drawn curtains carried by two attendants entered the square. Much bowing and scraping ensued, the servants giving us to understand that the inhabitant of the chair desired an audience with our company — a request confirmed by a beckoning finger which now uncurled itself from the window of the chair. So we approached the mysterious vehicle and, when we were almost level with it, the finger still groping blindly yet persistently, under my very eyes now, a curtain was withdrawn and out peered a face known to me from the last chapter but one of our history.

"Hah!" Auntie threatened a swoon. "God bless me, but it is — "

"*Wordkyn!*" I cried, an exclamation that brought on another distempered fit from Estrogen: "Wordkyn the *Poet!*"

"My apologies to you, *sssir*," the old Poet addressed me as he eased himself out of the conveyance, "but I must now make myself known as Wordkyn the *Novelist* — Poet as well," said he, hastily overriding my objection: "Yesss," he hissed, "my double apologies, my infinite regrets, but I missstook you," the Poet stared apprehensively around the square, "pssst, for one of *them*, psst," he elevated a finger to his lips, "a pardonable error, you will understand, in these grievous and tragical times, uncivil times" — I feared he would poeticize — "of gloom and disrepair when broils are all the fashion" —— which he did:

> When strife and faction move the mobs
> To deeds unseemly, acts of passion!

—— and continued:

"My apologies to you all. I am sorry for everybody, sorry for the world, ye*ss*."

"Wordkyn the *Novelist*!" — a minor complication: I treat his claim with the derision it deserved — "The author of *Bartleby*, who else?"

"*Shhh*!" the Poet sealed everybody's lips but his own. "Do not broadcast my fame. But, ahhh," he sighed, "since you acknowledge the fact, ye*ss*, I am he, that same unfortunate bard. Ohhh," he declared wanly. "No more shall I di*ss*emble. Do you admire my servants; do you admire my chair? *No*, do not trouble yourself with an answer, *ss*ir. By these devices, I have lately re-entered the plot. Lie down," he commanded, and the servants lay down. "Stand up," said he, and they stood up. "See?" Wordkyn extended a bardic arm. "I wrote them myself and the chair too because I was tired of walking. By some happy accident," he sighed terribly, "there is no lack of paper in Throckton by the Bog."

"Here and everywhere," remarked Waldemar with characteristic obtuseness, "paper, paper everywhere" — the wizard had accumulated a stock of papers himself — "and not a drop of ink."

"That too, that too," Wordkyn boasted, "I wrote myself some ink."

"You haven't changed," said Auntie, marvelling at the Poet's appearance. "In all these years, you haven't changed a bit."

"Changed? Ah, what is change?" he philosophized. "These lines that mark my countenance, these grey hairs in my head, these signs of change external, dearest Alice, are but the stones and pebbles on the shores of time. Ye*ss*," Wordkyn hurried over the unfortunate image, "my melancholy soul remains untouched, unscarred by the brickbats of the idle public."

"A pity," minced the Knave sarcastically. "You may be her author, but you're not mine."

"O smooth man," Sybil chided him, "listen and you shall hear, look and you shall see, seek and you . . . "

" . . . shall inherit the earth," affirmed the Poet gravely. "But here," he dipped into his gown, "I have something of the utmost concern and value to you all, and the profit will be yours if I am allowed to read" — prepare yourself, gentle reader: "from the twenty-eighth and twenty-seventh chapters of *Bartleby.*"

"The reader is already informed!" I cried. "It is this chapter he wants, do you understand, this chapter, not the twenty-seventh, not that again — anything but that!"

"What's the matter?" said Alice. "Are you sick? Heavens, the marmalade has made him sick!"

"No! No! I didn't touch the — *Blooerch! BLOOK!* — You must remember! You must remember the twenty-seventh chapter: I refuse to go through that again, do you hear me? This chapter, Wordkyn: *this chapter!*"

"I remember! I remember!" clamoured Estrogen — an *ally!* "She's lying! Liar! She was there too!"

"You see! You see! Tell them how I rescued you! Tell them what happened, Estrogen! Tell them how you were captured by De'Ath!"

"*Woowoowurrrch! Aaarch! Aaarch! Oooerssssch!*" the Knave issued a tidy stream of vomit over Wordkyn's papers. The Poet's feathers were unruffled, however.

"In that case," said he, "I will overlook twenty-seven and proceed directly to twenty-eight."

"Splendid," said I: "*bluch!*"

WORDKYN'S CHAPTER TWENTY-EIGHT *Upon the Late and Present Commotions at Throckton by the Bog, Wherein the History of Alice's Adventures Is* Finally *Continued.*

"For a century of gloom," Wordkyn began, an expression of dedicated misery sitting on his features, "I languished in the pit of De'Ath's invention . . . "

264

"Nononononono! Stopit! Stopit!" Estrogen pulled his paper crown over his ears as Waldemar conjured upon vacancy and added to his stockpile of papers.

"... where that traitorous Sexton had confined me, there to steal and plagiarize my book."

"I do think," said Alice aside, "that De'Ath's personation was very good. He had you to a *t*, Wordkyn," she informed the poet, "I knew it was you from the start, and I told him too."

"Ahhh," Wordkyn gazed dolefully from his wet MS while his newly written servants slumbered uncomfortably between the shafts of the sedan chair, "the misfortunes of bardship are as nothing next to those of character. Oh God in Heaven, how much longer must Auntie remain with the stalwart of the roadblock atop of her, cheated of consummate bli*sss*, deprived of *sss*weet *sss*atis*ss*faction? Five, *sss*ix? *sss*even chapters?"

"There!" Alice declared. "I told you my adventures were taken from life. It did seem a long time, Wordkyn, an awful long time. That poor man; that poor, poor man," she smiled, "fancy swallowing my — "

"And how much longer," I broke in, "do you propose to maintain this charade? Why can't she tell her story herself, Wordkyn?"

"Please," the Poet exerted himself, "remember my profession, my calling — you are the words, but I am the voice."

"Do you really mean," said I, "to recount the story of Alice's captivity *when she is here to tell it for herself?*"

"I do" —

"Amen!" cried the Sepulchral Sister, arms crossed over the frontage of her Hambaby wrapper.

"Captivity," Alice declared, "is a very strong word. But if Wordkyn wants to use it, then he can. *Because*," she digged me in the ribs, "he is the author, just as you are the narrator."

"I do," said the Poet ruefully, "for it is owing to the great burden I have to carry, the burden of authorship. And if I am not allowed to continue, the plot cannot possibly go on" — that clinched it: I would remain silent — "and if the plot does not go on, the book does not stop, and if the book does not stop . . . "

"I knew it, Wordkyn," I confessed, "that you were Wordkyn the Novelist, straightaway, I knew it. 'There's Wordkyn *the* Novelist, modest fellow,' I said to myself, 'although he's my author, he's very modest about it. ' "

"Indeed, indeed," he sighed, "ye*sss*, Wordkyn wrote the book, and it is at his feet that the responsibility must be laid. I, and I alone, accept the blame for this tardy delivery of vital information.

> Oh false, fleeting, perjur'd De'Ath,
> Cursed be that day he first drew bre'ath.

Mea culpa! *Mea culpa*! But no more of this: foul melancholy, begone! I live! I *sss sss*ee! I breathe!" exclaimed the Poet, indulging himself with a heart rending sigh.

"Yet what better audience," he took hold of Alice's hand, "could I wish for?"

"Oh Wordkyn," said she.

"None more attentive," he declaimed, "none more willing, more faithful, more virtuous, than my heroine, Bartleby's Guardian, Alice and Aunt!" – for the second time — — or was it the third? — — I could have despatched him there and then.

"*So*," he suddenly boomed, "so it came to pass that De'Ath" – the Knave tore at his ears – "with one foul and treacherous blow of his bone sent the stalwart over that river which no man crosses twice."

"Do you mean he killed him?" said Auntie. "I didn't think he hit him so hard."

"Lured onwards by the sound of those martial clamours that I have evoked elsewhere" –I let that pass – "lured by the dreadful cannonades and the unhappy screams of the combatants, the party advanced, led by the feckless hermit whose nose scented the profits to be had by one of his grisly trade, led on, aye, led on by his snout, they entered the jaws of hell and destruction itself, until" – he paused – "until – woe! woe! multitudinous woe! – they chanced to fall in with that repulsive band of mercenaries – the first to flee the

266

plot of De'Ath, the first to hang their luckless bards — that hideous crew of tertiary ghouls: beggars, whores, lepers, eunuchs, crones . . . "

"He's being very hard on them," whispered Auntie, "the poor things. He always had a tendency to exaggerate, you know — poetic licence. I don't remember it being at all that way," she added, my stomach rising to contradict her statement.

" . . . I shall not enumerate their depravities, their monstrous perversions and deformities," announced the Poet; "but that damned Sexton De'Ath did then command his creatures of the pit to bind his erstwhile friends and companions fast in the bonds of captive ties . . ."

"Why," enquired Waldemar blankly, "should he do a thing like that?" — could it be that he had forgotten? He was certainly absent minded, but —

"Yes," said Alice, "why?"

— — of course. I looked at the Poet's eyes, and then at the ground, very quickly at the ground.

Hypnosis: Wordkyn was a hypnotist! I would have to be careful. Maybe he'd hypnotized me into believing he was a hypnotist. What next? Maybe he wasn't Wordkyn at all! Would he answer their questions? Or would he hypnotize them into thinking he'd answered them?

"O unhappy Alice," the Poet wailed, "my heroine fair! O miserable Sister Sybil!" — she was hypnotized: like a block of wood. I decided not to look at her — "O hapless Waldemar! And last, but by no means least miserable — "

"ESTROGEN: *Howl!*" Estrogen howled, unhypnotized.

" — yes you too, most unfortunate and lamentable Knave, my characters, my lovely characters all, were thus bound and thonged by those scurvy slaves of De'Ath, my friend turned villain, my erstwhile friend, bearer of this Wordkyn's resident trust, my dear old ancient Sexton a blackguard turncoat proven! O infamy! O betrayal! O calumny!"

"But why, Wordkyn, *why?*" Auntie asked him. "Why did he tie us up?"

" 'Tee-hee!' " said the Poet as De'Ath. " 'Yes, me darlings, me lovelies, tie 'em up, tie 'em up nicely. No violence, now, no nastiness, me darlings. He needs 'em, he does, yes, he needs 'em for his book!' " – the personation was perfect, more than mere narrative tit-for-tat –– *the Poet as De'Ath?* –– " 'We's taking 'em back to the book, we is, yes, where they *belongs!*' "

––– so, *De'Ath had hypnotized them into thinking he was Wordkyn.* The real Wordkyn was dead! But this was Wordkyn: Auntie recognized him before he had a chance to hypnotize her into forgetting everything. Then what? How did he do it? Thought control, that was it. Here was Wordkyn in the flesh, but not in the spirit: Wordkyn was De'Ath, but the real De'Ath was somewhere else while this De'Ath who was also Wordkyn blackened the name of De'Ath who was De'Ath. A bold strategy! Very bold.

"Does that answer your question, Alice?" asked the Poet *as himself.*

"Very boldly!" I answered. "A very bold answer, Wordkyn, boldly put!" – I concealed my knowledge. There was no point in telling the Poet because he didn't know what he was.

"Meanwhile" – and it was with an even bolder stroke that Wordkyn-De'Ath flashbacked through one half of our history, sidestepping, side-tracking, in a word, cutting with such sleight of hand or foot, that – knowing what I knew – I nevertheless had the breath knocked out of me: "Meanwhile back" –– and Auntie, the fool, gazed adoringly into the Poet's eyes: "Meanwhile back at" ––– whereas the dignified if abstracted Waldemar boggled at such atavism: "Meanwhile back at the end of CHAPTER" –––– and you could almost see the grains in the Sepulchral Sister's face, while Estrogen's countenance ran through all the colours of the spectrum at once: "CHAPTER FOURTEEN . . . "

"Exit ESTROGEN!" he cried, hypnotized into believing he had lost consciousness though there was not a blow to his crown in sight.

" . . . throughout which chapter those characters who had murdered their authors in the pit of De'Ath's invention – at his instigation" – you would never have guessed Wordkyn was De'Ath, so much did he malign himself: "and behest, for the hermit it was who instigated the hangings, eager to rid the world of his rivals — had filed into the marketplace of Throckton by the Bog in twos and threes and threes and fours — had arrived, after feasting, whoring, fighting, plundering, looting, sacking, pillaging, ever with that grand locust Hautboy at their head . . . "

"What have you got against Hautboy?" I cried, unable to bear it any longer. "What's he done to you? What's the matter with him?"

"Yes," said Alice, "what is the matter with him, Wordkyn?"

"I know, I know," I regretted my outburst, "he's a murderer, a murderer and a common thief like the rest. You have every reason to bear him a grudge, the criminal!"

"Hautboy was only doing his best," declared Auntie.

"How do you know anything about that?" I was very convincing: "We weren't there — none of us were there. We've forgotten everything!"

" . . . ever with that grand locust Hautboy at their head," continued De'Ath, not realizing that I had recognized him, "urging them on to further deeds of rapine, boasting and bragging amongst themselves about their sales (the profits of which they fondly imagined would now be their own), until they had converged like all the plagues in Christendom, and if it comes to it, Heathendom too, converged, I say, in time to witness the annual debate of Boss and Ham and the ascension of Bartleby — Woe! Woe!" he panted breathlessly, "But I live! I sss sssee! I . . . live to tell the tale! Woe! O faction! O civil ssstrife! Forgive me," he paused, "while I recoup my vital sss ssspirits . . . my precious vital ssspirits." — now there was the authentic Wordkyn touch; Wordkyn returning to himself, Wordkyn struggling for the possession of his own mind. It was obvious, I thought, that the Poet had at one time been a man of character.

I decided to watch him; to stare him down if necessary. Then I could warn the others, when Wordkyn who was not Wordkyn became De'Ath who was not De'Ath.

"Yesss," said the Poet, fighting for the mastery of his tale and himself, "here they came, eager for schism yet ill-equipped to comprehend the issues of the debate until by the chapter's end they had divided themselves between the native supporters of the venerable contestants, adding their disgusting hoots and cheers to the already disreputable clamour of the debate, so that I was at a loss, beaten and stoned as I was for my versss" – De'Ath seemed to have abandoned the shell of the Poet – "and desperate to keep my true relationship to you a secret, my dear characters, a secret from the ken of the mob as you will understand, I was at a loss to control the ensuing internecine brawls, not to mention the foregoing and disgraceful overthrowal of authorship. Oh forgive me," Wordkyn slumped against his sedan chair, "forgive me, Alice, forgive the author of this piteous affair," he embraced the scene, "this tragical, terrible sight."

"Never mind, Wordkyn," said Alice, "you're doing very well. Though I do think you've given Hautboy a blacker character than he deserves. He was really trying to help."

"So I take it," said I, guarding my secret, "that there has been a civil war."

"An uncivil war, sssir," said he, "an uncivil one. After the Machine's elevation," Wordkyn shook his head wearily, "a regrettable and unlooked-for event, the tinder that sparked the flames, the fuel that fed the fire, the wind that fanned the blaze into a holocaust – in one tragical phrase, a most lamentable and combustible occurrence, sssir, a grievous happening entirely without precedent in the long and often dark annals of Throcktonian history which must now seem blanched and pale by comparison – after the occasion and sole pretext for the time-honoured and traditional debate had disappeared upon a pillar of flame . . . "

"Flame?" Sybil queried.

"Flame indeed," the Poet rewarded her with a doleful stare.

"I was happy before the flame," said she simply, "and I shall be happy after the flame. It's just that . . ."

"It's just that what, Sybil?" said Alice.

"I forget," she replied, adding: "I forget myself."

"But after the Machine had thus ascended, the supporters of either faction were literally in the dark as to what should be done, their confusion – that seed of factitious humours – their confusion, I say, obscured by the clouds of smoke that poured forth from the chimbley stack

270

of the Machine. Ah, but then the return of despised day brought no illumination to this most dismal of depressive scenes. For upon the clearance of those thick and palpable clouds, the zealots of the Bossian party argued that the Machine had always been an evil thing, offering too much in the way of temptation, and hence should never have been constructed in the first place. Upon the other hand, the fanatical Hamites offered contrary opinions, proclaiming the benefits of the Machine's implementation and urging that another be constructed immediately to pursue the first and bring it back where it belonged. Encouraged by those reprehensible characters from the pit of De'Ath, the enthusiastical wings of both parties came to blows and, while the advocates of moderation were put to silence, others of a yet more vicious bent sought out the Mechanics and persuaded them, with many ingenious arguments and promises of gold, to commence the manufacture of armaments and engines of doom." – a distant rumbling sounded as he spoke. "Hark!" he cast a fearful glance around the square. "Still their wars continue. Oh these are Jacobin times! Dreary days of strife and dissent!

"Civic government," the Poet hastened to conclude his tale, "was powerless to effect a reconciliation. The Beadle, the Mace-Bearer, and His Right Honourable and Most Worshipful Lord Mayor erred fatally in attempting to restore order, were dragged off by the mob, and were summarily executed for crimes against humanity.

"And yet might peace have reigned supreme," Wordkyn continued, "had it not been for that treacherous Sacristan De'Ath," – and I wondered who, now, was maligning whom: "master . . . " he paused.

"Master," said I, not taking my eyes off him for a minute, "master of *what*, Wordkyn?"

"*Master of disguise*: De'Ath that has many forms," the Poet shuddered – if he was still the Poet: "a cunning hermit, clever, even, in his own way—still might all have been well, had it not been for the Sexton, and his propagation of the Holy Mushroom. For preaching the doctrine of redemption through excess, he busied himself from CHAPTERS FIFTEEN through NINETEEN in the creation of a schisma-

271

tical and heretical sect whose object of veneration was the Mushroom itself" – confirmation of our belief, *my* belief, that Piadoso was actually De'Ath! Yet who was this now speaking? Had the hermit returned to Wordkyn's body?– "which the faithful – former partisans of Boss *and* Ham – swore, when ingested, conferred immense sexual powers . . . "

"Twaddle!" Auntie exclaimed. "Why, I gave the hermit one of his own Mushrooms and nothing happened to him!"

"Don't contradict him," said I, "while he's telling your story."

If Wordkyn was presently De'Ath, why should he deny the Mushroom's efficacy? An important question. Perhaps the Mushroom was potent and the hermit wished to keep its powers secret, first by advertising them, next by denying them. I did not have to wait long for an answer.

" 'Tee-hee!' " cried Wordkyn as De'Ath. "Yes, soon that accursed cry of 'Keep your peace with the Mushroom!' was on every lip. But there arose now," the ground rocked to another explosion, "there arose a competing sect whose object of veneration this time was none other than our hero. Had not Bartleby a limitless supply of *croons* – given to him by his Aunt? Would not Bartleby give these croons away and make the characters far richer than their authors had ever been – richer than they could hope to be themselves from plundering and looting? Did not the sum of Bartleby's deeds transcend all those wicked acts perpetrated in the pit? Was not his thrust mightier than Cabot's; his organ vaster than Hautboy's? Soon the name Bartleby replaced the cry of 'Mushrooms! Mushrooms!' and the hermit, seeing the tide of destiny run against him, dropped his disguise and reverted to his ancient ways. As for Hautboy, sensing a rival in Bartleby, but with his rival aloft in the heavens, he placed himself at the head of the Bartlebies and began the extermination of the Mushroomers. So the issues of the debate foundered in schism and heresy; so chaos and havoc were wreaked in my text, and so after the course of many chapters and greater destruction, so Auntie and her party, bound in captive thong, chanced to fall in with Hautboy and the survivors of the pit who were returning to Throckton after a foraging raid on the countryside."

"Then that's what happened to us!" Alice cried.

"Do you believe him?" said I, watching the corporeal form of Wordkyn closely, waiting for the hermit to betray himself. It was too logical, I decided. His story was too logical: no real author was like that. And Estrogen was still dormant, still under the hermit's influence. Yes, the Poet had momentarily deceived me into thinking he was who he claimed to be: Wordkyn. But all that De'Ath wanted—and he was prepared to go to almost any lengths to get it: denying who he was being perhaps the least of them – all that he wanted was acceptance as our author.

"Of course I believe him," said Alice, "he's our author, isn't he?"

That proved it! A fiendish plan: the hermit was a mind-reader! He wanted me now to unmask Wordkyn and then we would all have to admit that De'Ath who was actually Wordkyn was the author. But I was cleverer than that.

"Yes," I replied, calculating the odds and turning Alice's statement to advantage: "Wordkyn *is* the author – Wordkyn, Wordkyn the *Novelist*. That despicable hermit De'Ath stole his plot. And since you believe him, Alice, you must admit what great peril you were in, how horrible it really was, and how much you owe to me as the narrator."

"Horrible?" said she. "How could it be horrible if it's only a book?"

"Then you admit it," said I, "you admit this *is* a book?"

But the hermit who looked very much like Wordkyn read my thoughts. "And what kind of person," he addressed me, piqued, no doubt, by the failure of his plan, "what kind of person are you? And why, why in the name of all that is grievous and tragical, are you staring at me like that?"

Even as he spoke, a third explosion rent the air and set the ground heaving.

"I see through the sayer of tales and he is transparent to me!" Sybil wailed, pointing an accusatory finger at the melancholy and unmasked figure who now gathered his robes and papers, roused his written retainers, clambered into his narrative vehicle, and was borne away with all possible haste, his cries of "Woe! Woe! Undone! Undone!" sounding after him.

"And what kind of an author," said I to Alice after Wordkyn's flight — I did not wish to complicate things unduly by revealing his real identity — "do you think that is, to leave his characters in such a situation?"

"He was always very timid," she replied, "and easily frightened by strangers. You shouldn't have spent all that time staring at him."

"I do not believe," discretion is the better part of narration, reader, "I do not believe that either he or the hermit have written anything at all. In compass or separately, I do not believe it."

"Fuckit!" the Knave snorted, returning to his customary humour now that the malign influence was gone. "And you have, is that it?"

"Not exactly," I answered him. "But that's not the point, is it?"

"The point," Waldemar studied his papers. "Ah yes, the point."

"If you must know," said I, "they have been stealing, they have *each* been stealing somebody else's book. For if Wordkyn were the author," and if Wordkyn were Wordkyn, I thought, "how could he *fail to recognize his own narrator?*"

"Fail, yes," the magician agreed.

"You must recognize historical inevitability," I continued. "Throckton is destroyed, but I am come into this text to build it again — and, Alice, as I have been trying to impress upon you, to rejoin you with Bartleby and finish the book. What do you think of that?"

"He said I was his heroine," she stared at the empty marmalade jar, "his *heroine*, don't you understand?"

Good God in Heaven, I thought, the woman was vain. So that was the way to her heart.

"But I can make you more than a heroine, Alice. Yes, much more. I can make you the chief character, if that's what you want."

"More than you are?" said she coyly, "More than the narrator is the chief character; more even than the author is the chief character?"

"More than Bartleby," said I, "if you will agree to follow my plan. Listen. Another Machine must be constructed, so we can go in search of your charge and the book can be finished."

"Yes," Auntie sighed and watched the Sepulchral Sister, who gazed at the bone pickers. "And how can we build another Machine when there are no Engineers left?" Aware of the difficulties, she received my plan with enthusiasm.

"There is one yet alive;" I told her of Hans. "Not a Throcktonian Engineer, but an Engineer nevertheless. And though he did not quite declare his profession, that is what he used to be. Only two chapters ago I had a most intelligent conversation with him, and, recognizing me as the narrator . . . "

"I am frightened," Sybil whimpered – pathetically.

"There, there," Alice comforted her, "there's nothing to be afraid of."

"No?" said she – hesitantly.

"No," said I, "nothing. What we need is authority, narrative authority: direct, first personal and to the point. If we could find Boss and Ham, then we might pick up the pieces and begin our work of reconstruction, building a new age and a new book from the ruins of the old. Then as the curtains of darkness are drawn aside" – it was a conventional speech, I admit – "and the clouds of nescience are swept away, then shall the names of Bartleby and his Guardian be rightly famed, enduring forever in this new and enlightened age of man!"

"A new age," Auntie sighed again, "ah, but how I long for the old."

"And I for peace everlasting," said Sybil – comforted and conformable.

Yet peace everlasting, our new age, Boss and Ham, and the pieces of the rebellion must wait a while. Servants of the master text, they must wait on certain properties of this MS – properties that will not change for all the authors in the old world or the new.

For downwards to darkness ragged clouds die over Throckton, and our chapter is closed with the certainty of night.

CHAPTER THIRTY *Conversations Upon the Law Wherein the Challenge Is Held in Abeyance and Whereafter Bartleby Discourses Categorically upon Alice and Yet Another Claim to Authority Is Made.*

My name is Damon Gottesgabe, but I think you have already heard something of me from my narrative friend who was in such a hurry to enter his text that he left these few pages behind — pages which I here present for the honest public's approval, in the hope that some one of you might, on meeting with my friend, be so charitable as to acquaint him with the contents of this chapter, and sundry other chapters yet to follow. *

A confrontation of two and two: two huge on horseback, two small on foot, a confrontation before the end of time on a deserted heath in a world without name.

— Lewd trumpeteth the nose of Lungs, scribe and amanuensis to Bercilak de Belamoris, *Tirra-trumpety-tirra!*

— Loud roars Bercilak de Belamoris, unvanquished in concupiscent arts: *Humpety-hump! Humpety-hump!*

— Low cowers Me, jester and dwarf of uncertain nature, companion to the boy, Bartleby.

And while the sun in his salmon heaven casts long shadows of dawn-dusk across velvet hills, the boy Bartleby at length speaks.

---

* PUBLISHER'S NOTE: We are at a loss to explain why DG did not take this task upon himself. Indeed, it is the opinion of some in this House that, owing to the haste of composition and rush to the press, the Author has actually made an error in the plot. However, we are unable to find him — as Gottesgabe seems unable to find the Narrator — and the absence of both these persons (CS and his Narrator) goes some way, we think, towards explaining the inexplicable.

"Allow me to congratulate Lungs upon his recitation of the Twelve Categories. The deeds of Bercilak de Belamoris are surely worthy of cataloguing, in order that future ages and subsequent scribes may know of them and sing of them, in after time comparing their own stale chapters with the wonders and glories of bygone years, saying 'Was this possible?' and 'Oh, that such a stag might ramp again.' "

"Well said!" thundered the great copulator, who was not so unique that he was unmoved by flattery. "Was that not well said, Lungs? For a sapling punk, I mean," Belamoris added, careful not to cheapen his dignity with easy praise.

"Well said enough, I suppose," begrudged the amanuensis, whose work was more than cut out for him, for he now had to take down everybody's words as well as his own: "Though I would not have said it that way, master," he spoke and wrote the sentence, amusing himself by shifting from uncial to copperplate and back to his illegible secretary hand.

"Oh, I can speak your way too — if I want to," claimed the infant. "*But*," he continued pregnantly, "during my travels in search of Auntie Alice, my one and true Guardian, I have learned much of literary matters, and would advise you, Bercilak, to copyright the Categories, lest these same other bards steal your deeds and take them as their own."

"Copyright?" enquired Bercilak, his voice lowered. "What means this talk?" he asked, pondering whether copyright was connected with the absence of females.

"It is a law, master," the scribe answered, "very like those governing obscenities and libellous utterances, to which the bards of other climes are indentured, and which it is their earliest and most sacred observance to break . . . "

"Obscenities and libellous utterances! What are these things, Lungs? I know nought of them! *Why?*" cried Bercilak, troubled by this new development of obscenities and libellous utterances, and sure in his heart now that the copyright had spirited all females away.

"These are very elastic matters," the scribe spoke and wrote. "For example, master, should I wish to defame you by claiming you were impotent, I would put the slur about in a book and this must of course be considered a libellous utterance, so well known is your reputation in another direction. Should you, however, seek redress of the grievance, then you would have made a mighty error, especially if the law finds in your favour. For the public, once seeing a thing denied by the law, assume it to have been officially confirmed. Hence, though I have lied, I am interpreted as telling the truth."

"Is't so?" muttered Bercilak, much subdued and frowning heavily.

"Indeed yes, master. But think you for a moment," he continued in his normal cursive, "on the business of obscenity, master."

"Obscenity, Lungs?" – the word worried him. Perhaps obscenity and copyright were conniving against him. What part did libellous utterances play? But Lungs was a clever scribe who respected his master. Therefore the master should listen, listen and learn what these words were up to, thought Bercilak.

"Yes, master," the scribe relished his obvious superiority, "obscenities," he waited for the plural to take effect, "are far more contentious than libels or slanders. Here, the tribunes in their wisdom enacted laws to ban scribblings which stimulated their very own salacious appetites."

Bercilak listened with wrapt attention. The number of words conspiring against him grew. Salacious – was that good or bad? He liked the noise it made in his mouth, and, not following everything the amanuensis had said, made free with the cry: "Abominable! Abominable!"

"Yes, master," said Lungs, neglecting to record the outburst. "It is not uncommon," he continued, "to see these old and wise men perusing the offending text with a fine-toothed comb, subjecting the disputed phrases to scrupulous analysis – even calling on actors to perform the lines – just so they might discover what is called 'redeeming social value' in these bawdy and worthless books."

"Bawdy?" Bercilak rumbled. "Continue, Lungs. Continue!"

"Nor is it uncommon, master," the scribe furthered his learned address, "for bards or their representatives to begin litigation against themselves. Such proceedings are known as 'test-cases' and are regarded as a sign of the author's merit ... "

"Find the obscenities, Lungs!" roared Bercilak. "Find them in the Categories! Apply the copyright! Slander me, and I will take you to the courts. But the obscenities, Lungs, the obscenities! They must be found at once and then banned!"

"But, master," the scribe was taken aback by Bercilak's sudden wit, " 'But, master,' " he scribbled, seeking some brilliant counter-stroke, "sometimes, the offending books are burnt, master, *burnt*. And, and sometimes, master, sometimes they are pulped, *pulped* ... "

"I'll pulp you!" he thundered. "Suggesting there are obscenities in the deeds of Bercilak! Where are they?" he called on the obscenities. "Make yourselves known. If there are any obscenities here, make yourselves known before it is too late!" cried the crimson Bercilak. "Hah! None!" he bellowed, somewhat pacified by the non-appearance of the obscenities. "But what is the meaning of such laws," he growled, "that make things appear where they are not and disappear where they are?"

"If I might reply," said Bartleby, seeking to keep the peace, "these laws are drawn up to encourage the bard in his belief that he is original."

"Original?" Bercilak turned his eyes on the scribe. "Why didn't you say that to begin with, Lungs?" — too many clever phrases, he thought; the trouble with these clerks: "The boy says I'm original, Lungs, did you get that? Did you hear him?"

"Indeed, master," Lungs hastened, thinking Bercilak unpredictable. "Very original, if I may say so," he smirked, taking care to leave his own humiliating reply out of the record

"The boy is right," said Me, who had remained silent for so long only because he had been following the conversation in his text where he had discovered the scribe's dishonesty — not that it meant anything to him; no, he would let Lungs fool Bercilak for the time being — "There are similar laws governing inventions, appliances, manufactures, and machines, yes, machines, but they are called patents. Yes," he declared, happy in the knowledge that he could have been a lawyer himself. Only . . . only . . . "Patents and infringement of patents, they go under that name." Only his size did not permit it. "And patents pending and patents applied for," he volunteered this additional information, rejoicing that he had managed to hoard the secret of the scribe's duplicity. "All very original these patents—like you, Bercilak."

"How can anyone else pretend to be original," Bercilak grumbled, "when I know the twelve Categories of nature?"

"Not anyone: *things*," said Me. "But yes, yes, the philosophers agree on the number of Categories but disagree as to which Category is what." What did they know about philosophy, finished characters too? They were *finished* characters. What was their author thinking of, making them so stupid and so *large*? "Or if the philosophers agree on which is what, they disagree on what number is which." Even if he was sometimes God, he was a Guardian of Guardians, wasn't he? With more intelligence than the rest of them put together, yes. "Therefore," Me furnished the dialectic, "it is impossible to know the two things simultaneously."

"Spoken like a dwarfling!" cried Bercilak. "Did you get that, Lungs?" he marvelled. Perhaps the humpback was a clerk which made two of them, observed Lungs' master accurately.

"Yes, Bercilak," said the amanuensis obligingly, though he wrote, " '*Yes, Bercilak,' said the amanuensis acidly.*"

"The Challenge, Bercilak," said Bartleby, seeking a change of subject; "I do not see how we can play at Guardianship, unless, that is, you are prepared to . . . "

"True, master. Shall I trumpet again?" Lungs prepared his nose.

"Females!" groaned Bercilak. "Oh, this boy will vanquish me by default. Take it down, Lungs, take it down. Bercilak despairs, his lament knows no end, he will pine away with anguish, *etc, etc,* you know the form."

"But because you are so desperate for the want of tumbling," Bartleby commiserated with his opponent, "I will show you how there is nothing new under our ambiguous sun, and discourse in praise of Auntie Alice, that you might

280

be further warned on the necessity of the copyright laws. For I have prepared this little discourse in my head, hoping that you may enjoy it and gain a lesson or two therefrom."

A *lesson*? The word grazed the rind of Bercilak's brain. Was the punklet a scholar too? "A lesson," he repeated — numbed into acquiescence.

"Yack!" Me watched the trio from his diminishing point of view. "Not God," he murmured. "I *won't* be God," the jester doubled over and muzzled his countenance in the folds of his belly. Looking at Me objectively, the dwarf conferred with himself, it is apparent that my mind is beginning to grow.

Thus while Bercilak's thoughts froze, and Me's mind grew, and Lungs reflected on his master's folly in ever Challenging this boy, Bartleby held true to his word and began his discourse.

A CATEGORICAL DISCOURSE UPON HIS AUNTIE ALICE
(A SATIRE)
Delivered by one Bartleby, Esq, Boy, Five.
WITH ADDITIONAL ASIDES AND EXCURSI
UPON GUARDIANSHIP
MOST NOBLE
OF ARTS
ETC.

"Though I have oft played at Guardianship," declared Bartleby in the manner of Lungs, "I, Bartleby, one boy of natural line, do now my Venusian Muse implore, and declare hereby that the summation of female parts, which is my one and true Guardian, Aunt Alice, she of the comely form and aspect full shapely, demeanour modest and temper sweet, carriage graceful and dispensation divine, has yet to be equalled, is not now equalled, and never shall be equalled, though time and tide that wait for no man nor boy be eternal.

"And — O Aphrogenian goddess! — *further,* in so far as I, Bartleby, *etc*, have received a Challenge in Categorical Form from one Bercilak de Belamoris, champion stud, gent, *etc*, I,

Bartleby, *etc*, do hereby give this notice of reply in like fashion, with these exceptions. *Videlicet*: that the Categories be confined in specific to the person of the said Alice, Guardian and mentor, and that I, Bartleby, *etc*, shall be more to the point in the telling than Lungs, *etc*, scribe to the aforementioned Bercilak de Belamoris, *etc*."

"More to the point?" the amanuensis groaned. "Am I to waste scrolls taking this down, master?"

"Proceed, boy," commanded Bercilak. "And you too, Copyist," he frowned as Lungs discharged a blot in Bartleby's direction:

— which blot missed its mark, deluging on the head of Me:

— and being a larger blot than is here represented, felled the jester.

"Since first the time," Bartleby began Category the First, "when babe's swaddling clothes my infant loins did wrap, do I recall Aunt Alice's gaze coquettish. Return, eyes, your mysteries to me. Say, what agency divine worked prismatic miracles in opaline globes consanguineous with mine own? There two inverted Bartlebies reflected were, couchant on a field of azure, hazel bewitched, else verdant, ultramarine, or imperial purple the iris loomed, pellucid gems, kiss'd by lids and lashes, radiant like the head's superior coif: azure, citron, olive, henna—farewell, eyes, next to thee the rainbow lustreless, unchromatic must be. Farewell, thy gaze sealed with a kiss!

"Rather on the Categories Entire would I dwell, above the parts the sum, divine quintessence that is Guardianship itself: joyful tenderness, ministrations of the soul more than the frame, yet through and of the frame, the soul's delight and earthly life—*Guardianship*, the soul's celestial dwelling place . . ."

"Can you move," Bercilak was lost, "with more —" he dug into his skull for the word, "*zest!*"

"*Con brio*, brat!" the scribe urged.

" . . . dwelling place," the boy was unabashed, "come home to earth, made mortal in these physical hours," said he, directing a level and knowing gaze at Belamoris who fidgeted clumsily on his saddle, "of passion and desire."

"Passion!" Bercilak's fists closed and unclosed on his charger's reins: "Nose next!"

"O feeling inhalant and nasal warmth," Bartleby complied, "me o'erbathing with tinctures aromatic distilled on some spice-islanded shore, nostrils archly flared by love's complicity, did Aunt Alice me sniff from the infant top to infant toe. Always evidence, this, of my helpmate's rising ardour — that she her nostrils would twitch like the downy rabbit kind and tilt her nose fetishly, as if to sneeze instead of me to kiss.

"Next she did her ears articulate (oft practised she when but a girl, her apprentice glass sole witness before my advent). And truth to tell her ears full ample were, absurd in one of smaller portion, apt to Alice: when bedecked with fineries gay, or lobes unclad, attractions fit for infant eyes that happy gurgles would I voice therein — babelike cooings for fleshy conches. Farewell then, nose, and ears too," Bartleby disposed of the secondary and trivial Categories, "of richer ornaments now shall I sing!"

"Lips! Lips!" Bercilak thundered.

"Yet stay!" rejoined the boy. "Stay, epic muse, inspire me in this my travail: not the parts to sing, but the form complete, and beyond the form, *Guardianship*, union of one and one, temporal made eternal through this finite moment: the *kiss*. Hence," Bartleby watched Belamoris's eyes swivelling in his head, "from infanthood's earliest hours her parted lips were to me the sweetest fruit which e'er infant lips might sweetly taste. While still a babe not yet a boy, felicitous instruction did I receive at my Guardian's lips: rich were they, as rich and red as the ruby wine, to which I in later years would oft retire, conscious then of duty and delight, applying these now no longer infant lips to hers as tongue to tongue we did greet and breath for breath exchange.

"Her neck, *eheu*, was stout, and stouter grew that the chin became incorporate too and lotions she applied—to no avail. So must art strive where nature fails. Oh, aging wives, follow my generous Guardian's ensample: when years do threaten and the neck does thicken, take a youth and train his lust. Remember this — 'twas ever Auntie's cry — *dum vivimus, vivamus,* while we live, let us live!

"Yet — *soft!*" Bartleby raised a boyish hand. "What is this, by the mind's eye illuminated — as if vision external would not suffice? Say, no need of exterior sight; touch, sensation tactile, feeling will suffice, though me night blind, in darkness cloaked."

"Hurry up, boy! Hurry up!" cried Bercilak, signs of unruly temper manifesting themselves in his crustacean gaze. "Get on with it!" he moaned, jingling his harness and preparing to set off on his viage: "Titties next!"

"A vision of Guardianship's angel," the boy held Bercilak in his calm and steady gaze, "that night was mine, when first Alice me to her resplendent bosoms pressed, udders hereditary—a familial trait, 'twas so with her mother and her mother's mother—that did in middle age profounder bloom: prodigious and stately frontage, blossoming forth upon this world. Not given to fat but succulence, ripeness of depth and cleavage, vast rotundaries fuller yet than Willendorfian kind, that five and forty circumferent inches measured she from gorgeous pap round shoulder blade and back to gorgeous pap, of a cup the C. There at her bosoms grand lay I, unsure what might be done, unsure at first until me she pressed to suck in natural wise, and I did first my hand, next my head, then my infant person entire bury in raptures complete and unbridled nocturnal breasts. Oh, that I might see her fulsome form once more, again to die in her billowing embrace! A proud breasted swan is she, say rather galleon, bearing treasures rich, priceless gems, sails bursting over seas unexplored, uncharted, oceans prepared for infant navigator! Oh, cruel it is thus to be deprived of such a sight: never more, I think to see her stately figure and carriage proud in this dark and dreary land."

"Hump! Hump!" cried Belamoris, screwing around in his saddle and casting his anguished eyes heavenwards. "On,

little prickster, on!" he thundered, a mental image of Auntie forming deep within the inaccessible reaches of his mighty skull.

"Next," Bartleby extolled Category the Seventh, "to her navel, her world's geographical centre, soft convocation, yet not the capital where Cupid keeps his seat and th' amorous parliament lies in session and season too, one to me still forbidden with cries of 'Patience! Have patience, Bartleby. Forebear!'—sound advice, she not wishing her charge to scare by too sudden assault, sound advice to Belamoris too! — there me did she guide. Hence on Auntie's belly did I perforce rest content, dreaming indeed of other parts which to me suspected were, not yet known.

"That Auntie's feet were large," the boy followed Lungs' precedent, "I do not deny. Likewise her legs were muscular, say sturdy, or if the adjective seemeth unfeminine and crude, then well-designed, legs suitable for feet size nine, adjusted to peregrinations exhaustive over hill and dale. In part corresponding, her thighs, twin columns of the body's portico, enlarged were at the buttocks' enjambement, enlarged through equine endeavours, for when she went not on foot, Hannibali would she ride — Hannibali, more Bucephalus or Pegasus than mere horse: stout steed and swifter than the wind, if leaner in his latter years than those of yore and prime, an epic mount, sleek, faithful, knowing and kind, more human than horse, though four legged, no less devoted to Auntie than I to her or me to him, yet a stallion chaste and gentlemanly, next to which Lungs his ass a mule must seem and is . . . Oh, Hannibali, Hannibali, still whinniest thou? Or art thou gone at the equine day's end, gone to champ in other fields? Yet on Hannibali did Auntie canter, she who loved a ride to take the pangs of love away in search of marmalade, sweet surrogate of sweeter joys.

"*Marmalade*," Bartleby apostrophized the jam, "Guardianship's correlative . . . "

"Arse next," Bercilak pleaded, "*arse!*"

"Guardianship's *golden* correlative," the boy held the man, drawing on Bercilak's agonized suspense, "substitute for Guardianship's embrace . . . "

"What was that, Bartleby, about marmalade?" Me rose

from the blot, clutching his stomach which felt empty inside. He hadn't eaten since the book began. But he was only small and didn't need much food.

"The fundament! The fundament!" Bercilak's torture was exquisite.

Why was this boy talking about Guardianship? What had that to do with *marmalade*, of all things! No, he hadn't eaten for a long time, but he must have some food now that his brain was growing. God was, *Me* was his Guardian, not his Aunt. What right had they to starve him just because he was little? He'd read the book. What did it say? A developing brain needed protein: an *author's* brain demanded protein. That was his due. They owed it to him.

"The anus, boy! The anus next!" Bercilak's cry interrupted the jester's thoughts. "Oh, Lungs!" he appealed to the amanuensis, "I shall take leave of my senses!"

"Impossible, master," declared the scribe sourly.

"Then, marmalade, farewell," announced Bartleby to Bercilak's infinite relief. "For greater pleasures shall I now relate: of how it pleased Alice her knees to tickle – sensitive beyond the common kind – ; her thighs next, while I was yet an infant, not babe still not boy, but infant, three years under God's heaven. How she loved my hand to stroke and linger on her hips broad, thence to buttocks and buttocks' delight. Thus it was," Bartleby gazed solemnly at Bercilak, whose tongue thrashed and rolled in eager anticipation, "her sovran prize discovered I and became a slave in happy bondage free, servant at liberty, by chance, I thought, but know now 'twas by decree prepared. Yet though schooled across the years three, a child was I, innocent of functional disparity 'twixt arse and cunt. Hence do I remember the night of my graduation when in dalliance her rear parts I did find and finger exploratively. In such a manner thought I: this is *it*; and she, 'Ah, no, dear Bartleby, not there, not there at all.' "

"*Hump!*" roared Bercilak de Belamoris. "Up with it, boy. Faster, child, faster!" he bellowed, a turbid cloud rising about his loins.

"And I, boy, of lustral years five, do take leave of my Muse, here to celebrate pure *Guardianship*, aspiration of all human kind, though few but the chosen achieve it."

"The cunt, boy!" Belamoris rose in his stirrups. "The *cunt!*"

"Ah yes," Bartleby sighed and returned, "that too. Then a little furtherward by this posterior route ventured I," continued the boy, describing a leisurely spiral with his finger, "yes, on and on, until at last I delved into the *slit queynt* that hath ever been since that blissful eve my sole object in life, salient delight and single prize. Henceforward did I Alice nightly mount; first the position horizontal did we try, next moving to the position reversed, whereunto the position lateral, after which the position transverse we did savour, Auntie my part playing, me hers, so that cunt and compass we did liberally box and ne'er stale it grew but flourished, a Mare Fecunditatis, flowering through the years of Guardianship two. And I her consort was and she my familiar friend and yet have I to find a cunt of such excellent fluency, such passionate whimsy, such moods and humours diverse, raptures ardent and effusions fervid, such suck and easy throw — ah, such a cunt that was, cunt beyond recount!"

"*Hump! Hump!*" thundered Bercilak de Belamoris, grinding about in his charger's saddle, smacking his horny hands together and scowling hideously.

"I haven't finished yet," said Bartleby. "For you must know, Bercilak de Belamoris, that Aunt Alice is to me as the Earth Mother herself. Therefore, ye who claim to have lain with Mother Earth, know this: that Alice's cunt is the cunt archetypal, the beginning and end of all cunts.

"But know this also: that Alice is wise in her judgement, discreet in her choice, compassionate of her estate, and charitable in her gifts: that under Guardianship's rule she is a spiritual Guardian to this boy, Bartleby, that she will never allow him to suffer defeat in competition honourable — know this, then, and beware, ye allegorical bachelor, lest ye tumble too oft and are tumbled in the end.

"Yet though I have been no stranger to paradise, and again must seek the gates of heaven, I shall willingly share my quest with any who acknowledge the law of love, Guardianship's rule, and are not content to rest where many men stay, earthbound — but search, and finding, lose, and losing do not fall back, are not dismayed yet continue even to death.

"So it is within all men, if their hearts are right, to prove themselves Guardians, no matter what nature has endowed them with," Bartleby cast an affectionate glance at Me, "like my friend who, though small of stature is noble of mind, yet modest, devoid of pride, to me a Guardian of Guardians, companion and guide, with whom I search for Alice, my prime teacher and infant love."

Hackety-hack! Hackety-hack! Hackety-hackety-hack! applauded Bercilak.

Sniffle! nosed Lungs, his trumpet strangely malfunctioning.

"How?" asked Me, consulting his text as his jaw creaked at the hinges. "How did you get hold of that speech, Bartleby?" Not that it was important. No. The important thing was the title page.

"It was a speech of good devising!" bellowed Bercilak, delivering his scribe a mighty blow on the spine. "Was it not, Lungs? For an upstart brat, I mean."

"Not long enough, master," the amanuensis shook his head sadly; "too short. Expand it, boy, then it may be passable. Not long enough at all. Expand," said Lungs again, swelling his chest as though to begin anew the catalogue of Bercilak's deeds. But his master, unable to bear the thought of such a frustration, towered awesomely in his saddle, compressed his brows, rolled his porcelain eyes and thundered at the scribe.

"The boy does well enough," he proclaimed, "for a prickster. Take it down, Lungs! Take it down! He is a worthy opponent for Belamoris!"

"Immediately, master," Lungs produced another scroll of parchment and wrote thereon: *'Has it come to this — that my master should wish to defeat a punklet brat? Dwarves next!'*

"What is more," said Bartleby, "I need no Lungs other than mine to do my boasting for me."

How much longer, Me wondered, could his brain hold out? Perhaps he should inform them: an expanding mind needs protein. The title page, where was it?

"For my adventures," the boy continued, "are written down in a book — like yours, Bercilak — by an author who tells of my exploits in search of Auntie, as well as the many diversions of the way, of which this is one."

Me found the title page. There, in large, bold lettering, he made out his name: *ME*. It was a concise name, he thought, a pointed name; in its own way a distinguished name.

"A book, moreover," Bartleby explained, "which my friend Me has in his hands, a book telling of my early, middle, and present life, of how we journeyed from when to then in the Wondrous Machine, despite the missing chapters."

But the boy had left out the essential point. Come to think of it—Me thought of it—the title page was wrong. Why should *ME* be underneath *Bartleby*? An imposing name like *ME* demanded a page to itself. There could be no doubt then that he was an important small person: a large small person.

"A very long book," Bartleby threw out the taunt, "much longer than the Categories."

With *ME* having a page all to itself like it did, might not people think that was the title? Better still. *ME* by *ME*. Better tell him.

"*Bartleby*," Me scuttled to the boy's side and tugged at his coat.

"A book in which I am a character, in which Me is a character as well, though our once and future author has been conspiring against us by sending us into the past — the Machine did that . . . "

"Stop! STOP!" howled Bercilak, vaulting from his saddle to land like an angry tree, rooted beside Me, dwarf and jester of uncertain nature, from whose trembling dwarf hands Bercilak ripped the book. "Lungs! Lungs!" his cries reverberated. "The matter of this book! My eyes are not equal to their task! What is the matter of this book?" Bercilak demanded, thrusting the book upon his scribe and clapping his hands over his eyes.

"Why, master," Lungs shuffled through the book, puzzled at first, "I cannot rightly say what the matter of this book might be, though the meaning is difficult, very difficult." And then, a smile balancing smugly underneath his bulbous nose, the scribe added these words to his exegesis: "But there's nothing wrong with your eyes, master. See, this is a language I do not know — the pages are blank, Bercilak. It is a blank book, into which the reader must read his all."

A blank book! The words buried themselves in the head of Belamoris. How was it possible to *write* a blank book?

"*Blank?*" cried Bartleby. "They weren't blank in the Machine!"

He must tell the boy, tell them all before it was too late: not every character meets his own author . . .

"What has happened to my life?" Bartleby wailed.

Now what was wrong with the boy? But he would tell them himself:

"Yes, yes," said Me, jester and companion to the boy, Bartleby, "the boy is correct. I," the dwarf strutted grandly, "am the author. *Your* author."

The title page grew in Me's mind: an expanding white acre on which the words *ME* by *GOD*, no, *GOD* by *ME*— blank! What did they mean blank? Not blank before. Blank?

"Explain yourself!" Lungs delved in his saddle bags to produce new rolls of parchment and fresh supplies of ink.

"Suggesting I am blank! Suggesting I am blank!" Bercilak quaked, digging in his roots.

"No!" Me croaked. A trick; it was a trick. Lungs had read the book, had discovered the secret of his own perfidy written down. He would expose him to his master, God would. But first he must be clear on the essentials. "Not *GOD* by *ME* but *GOD* by *GOD!*" the jester screamed at Lungs: "The *author!* Show Me the book! Show *God* the book!"

"But you said," Bartleby reminded him, "in the Machine, you said . . . "

"Not there now. Here: when! Then! Before!" Me stared poisonously at the boy.

"Read, then," declared the scribe haughtily, "read where I cannot."

"Title page, see! Title page!" Me received the book. Blank, yes, it was blank. He was too big to get on the page. "Guts! Guts!" He doubled over the volume. All his work, *blanked!* Oh God, oh guts! His guts needed food, food for his brain. But *blanked?* Time, yes, it was *time.* The Machine, the Machine had done this:

"The Machine" Me gasped, uncurling his head to reveal a sight which temporarily stunned the beholders.

For the jester's face was mottled, daubed in splotches of pink and white; as if touched by fire, his orange locks had turned ashen and seemed to have burned themselves out, while his livid eyes bore the mark of a terrible cast, and stared not at his audience but at each other, the pupils hence appearing to join in the middle at the bridge of his nose. With the aid of his clawed hands, Me rotated his enormous head on his neckless shoulders, retracted his distended mandible, and juggled his eyes, rolling them like marbles in their sockets, evidently in an attempt to bring the scene into focus. Then, hands clasped behind his domed back, he tottered backwards through the legs of the rooted Belamoris, fell into a squatting position, and threw open his bandy arms in mute appeal.

"Scribe of my fathers," muttered Bercilak, "what ails thee?"

"Book blanked," Me's hand scrubbed at his chameleon hair, "God's — *my* work all blanked! A growing mind needs protein, yes, but I will forego food," the sacrifice must impress them, "to save you, *my* characters. You may think I'm only a dwarf, but I don't care! What happens next? Blanked, that's what: we'll all be blanked!"

"Are we to believe this?" growled Bercilak de Belamoris.

"Bartleby?" whimpered the jester, raising his eyes to the boy.

"Well, I don't know, I don't know," Bartleby shook his head. "Yet he did know my name when we first met. And he did know about Auntie Alice. *And* he had the book."

"Then why is the book blank, sir author-dwarf?" cried Belamoris scornfully.

"Yes," echoed Lungs amid a shower of inkblots and the furious scratching of his quill pen. "How long has the book been blank? Explain that, if you can!"

"I don't see," Bartleby thought very hard, "why we are still here. What are we without the book in which we are written, and if the book is blank, how can we see each other?"

"The boy has it!" exclaimed Bercilak, clutching at the thread of the argument.

"The Machine! The Machine!" Me clacked. Mustn't let his jaw fall down now. "Time! Function of time! What was seen is gone but retained by expanding mind. At the back of was is will," he lectured them. "What has to be has not yet happened, no. The future cannot be remembered and the past is forgotten!" A superior person God was, not that he was God because God wasn't — not yet. "What could would ought to have been, and what should be now may be going to be but won't when it shall."

"Won't it?" the scribe questioned.

"Quiet!" Me pecked. "Quiet from Lungs!" Now was his chance. Preserve it. Hoard it. Give him a hint, just to let him know. "Call yourself a scribe? You're not a scribe, not a *real* scribe!" Me farted out the insult. "Real scribes do as they are told, yes."

"Master?" Lungs prepared a blot.

"Silence, Lungs!" Bercilak glowered. The scribe was getting too big for his boots. Perhaps there was something in this blank book.

"Was cannot be is and will is not now," power surged through Me's domed being, "but Me-Me was-was," the Jester stabbed a crooked finger at the bow of his curved sternum, "and will-will be!" he cried as Bercilak's brows heaved with utter incomprehension. "Me-Me is-was, will-have-would-shall-should-could-be-going-to-be-might-have-been-but-isn't *blanked!* Book blanked, yes, but not his characters!"

"Say that again!" Lungs howled, his pen arm aching with the effort.

"Shan't! Can't!" Me's head oscillated. "Past gone, future gone . . . present?" The present was being used up, consumed by his brain instead of the protein. "The present is protein!" he cried. "Convertible! The present is breaking down!" Yes, breaking down. Must get back to the Machine and the future where it would be all over and done with:

"Back to the Machine."

"The Machine," Bercilak repeated as some alchemical process distantly related to a thought bubbled and boiled within the deep dungeons of his head.

"The Machine, Me," said Bartleby, "the Machine and Throckton?"

"Throckton yes. Before we are blanked. Hurry! Hurry!" But the future, *the future was in the past!* What could he do about it? Magnificent, yes, what an idea:—"*Forward to Throckton whence!*"—Magnificent!

"*Forwards to Throckton whence!*" roared Bercilak de Belamoris, dragging his charger to its knees by its mane.

"And the Challenge, Bercilak, the Challenge!" cried Bartleby. "There are women in Throckton: *females*, women with *croons!*"

"*Hump! Hump!*" The charger was hauled to its hooves now. "*Forwards, forwards to Throckton whence!*" thundered Belamoris, bounding into the saddle, and plucking Me forth into the air.

" '*To Throckton whence!*' " writes the amanuensis, Lungs, in a concluding shower of blots and splatters. *To Throckton whence?* thinks the boy as he too is plucked aloft. *But how? When the book is blank — how?*

Then, while thunder clouds race and the sun declines and darkness lowers, farewell, o Lungs, sometime and sometimes recorder of accidents undetermined. Farewell, too, o Belamoris, for your viage must be renewed. Farewell, o Me, claimant to authority, pretender, God and not God. And farewell, farewell o Bartleby, boy of lustral years and heroic line.

For so these pages left the foursome, thundering off not yet into time but space — that space which has so recently engulfed my narrative friend, where, I fancy, he seeks the chapter we have just read, seeks but does not find.

CHAPTER THIRTY-ONE   *The Metamorphosis of Sybil, in which Xavier Piadoso Figures Uniquely and Doubly and the Plot, as Always, Progresses.*

"What," enquired Alice as Estrogen turned his profile towards the flickering flames, shut a pencilled eye, and slept: "What" — I don't think I should allow her the question so early in the chapter, but — "What is going to happen next?" said she, while darkness and the wall of a building at the opposite side of the square fell simultaneously, startling the bone pickers at their noiseless work.

"I agree," said Waldemar. "Not to ask questions is conducive to . . . " He rested on his laurels.

The reader will appreciate why I *attempted* to prevent Auntie from asked her question when I inform him — as I now do — that I was occupied in searching for this chapter as I searched for the last, the future being the least of *my* worries. *There:* I found my twenty-ninth and Wordkyn-De'Ath's twenty-eighth — complete, as I had suspected, complete after the fact.

" . . . equilibrium!" Waldemar found the word.

Though of course there was no sign of this chapter, nor would there be until the action was completed. Therefore, I felt quite confident in announcing — with a perhaps specious but outwardly convincing assurance — that this was the thirtieth chapter, and that what happened herein would happen: *che sera, sera.*

"How true," she replied. "But you mean chapter twenty-nine, not thirty. Because the last chapter, as told by its author, was twenty-eight, and the author cannot be wrong

294

about the number of chapters in his book."

"I have the answer," Waldemar's hand crept through his growing assortment of folios, quartos, duodecimos — odds and ends, rags and scraps amounting to a substantial collection: "if only I could see to read," he lamented, so furnishing yet another instance of his absent-mindedness: the flames furnished enough light for a library.

"Alice," said I, "it would be much more satisfactory if we could get on with this chapter instead of worrying about the past."

"I merely wanted to know what happens next, that's all."

"This might be as good a chapter as any," said I, "to enlist Hautboy in our cause."

"I do not know Bartleby. Do I?" Sybil mused. "Once I knew another and he showed me kindness."

Meaningful sentiment! Here is a life, even such a one as this, refreshed with the milk of human . . .

"But then came the wormwood and the gall! Then did the first angel sound!" she cried.

"There now," Alice turned to her, "that's all in the past; so long ago. But I'm glad," she addressed her narrator, "that you want to find Hautboy, who seemed like quite a nice gentleman despite what Wordkyn said."

"Whether you find him nice or not," said I, "he is a power to be reckoned with, if we are to construct a new Machine and find Bartleby."

"My very thoughts," she replied, seemingly more interested in Hautboy than her charge, "on first seeing him."

"Then we are in agreement," I wasted no time, "for if I have expressed your thoughts, you have just spoken mine. As Bartleby's Aunt and Guardian, you are in a very influential position yourself."

"You are kind, Alice," Sybil strayed back into the conversation, "you are kind yourself. Do you think," her voice quavered, "that he would still know me? Or is it too late?"

"It is never too late for anything," said Alice, but Sybil, visibly excited by invisible promptings, heeded her not.

"Too late," she wept, "too late did the third angel

sound!" — though why on earth she was so prompted at this moment, I cannot say — "and there fell a great star from heaven, burning as it were a lamp!" —— unless it was to frustrate my narrative intent, in which case she failed. For no sooner had she gotten to the fourth angel — who smote the sun and the third part of the stars, as I recall — than I applied the full force of authority and silenced her thus:

"———————————————————!"

"Within the next two or three pages," said I, "I warrant we shall again meet with Hautboy and come to terms."

"I do hope," the ears of Bartleby's Aunt twitched, "that it will not be the same as that business with the stalwart."

"On the contrary," said I, "the affair will have a successful resolution."

Alas, it was not to be.

The fault was not mine. Determined not to have her invocation cut short, Sybil raised her arms to the benighted heavens and uttered these words: *"Woe, woe, woe, to the inhabiters of the earth by reason of the other voices of the trumpet of the three angels, which are yet to sound!"* This dire prophecy at an end, she meekened: "It is not too late. He is with me still." — and hardened: "Gone! He is gone!" —— but she meekened again: "Together!" ——— but she hardened: "Naked thou are and naked thou shalt be!"

"Oh, Sybil!" — Too late Auntie's cry. Commanded by some inner voice, Sybil fled across the square. That very party of scavengers and bone pickers who had occupied themselves scuttling around the square now left off their trade and turned to watch the Sister's approach, their faces caught in the lurid glare, their shadows dancing long and crookedly over Throckton's smoke-blackened stage, which dramatic edifice the Sister ascended as a sirenic and be-witching wail mounted to the skies.

Two figures now stood on stage, or rather two in one, dividing and joining in mutual symbiosis while Sybil, or what she had become, tripped from one foot to another, arms and legs jerking stiffly after the figure before her, which — no more than a shadow, an homunculus — evaded her advances as it always had, an awful cry of *"Forever and forever!"*

escaping Sybil's throat as she divested herself of her Ham-baby wrapper and disappeared from our view, the wrapper chastely following her down into Throckton's sub-scenic bowels.

"Well," said Alice, somewhat testily I thought, "well," she said as we reached the scene of Sybil's transition, "and what does your text say about that?"

"I am sure it is described somewhere," said I with more confidence than I felt.

But I will trouble you no more, save to mention that Alice proposed spending the night underneath Throckton's time-honoured boards, safe in our retreat, safe from the molestations of runaway characters.

Hence we got ourselves to go down. Not without much arguing, cursing and conjuring were Estrogen and Waldemar, who both believed the hour of their performance had come, persuaded to descend, but descend they did, slowly and arduously where Sybil had plunged swiftly and dangerously.

CHAPTER THIRTY-TWO   *Wherein, After Some Preliminary Atmospherics, a Stowaway Is Discovered and a Tale
Almost Told.*

*I have few illusions about my friend's present condition:
in all likelihood he is as bewildered on the Throcktonian side
of his MS as he was on this. Yet in giving the reader the
thirty-second chapter of* Bartleby, *I am faced with a dilemma
myself. On the one hand, it would be exceedingly unfortunate for him were he to become acquainted with the events
of this chapter — events never before known in the history of
literature. On the other hand, I would not have the reader as
baffled as my friend. Therefore — and I know this must seem
contradictory — read the chapter, then keep it close like a
secret; keep it within mind and sight, and do not let it slip
your tongue that you have ever laid eyes on the thing. If you
should chance to meet next with my friend, by all means tell
him I have the chapter, but that I fear to tread where he has
fearlessly rushed in and, neither wishing nor daring to prove
myself a narrator, have conceived the greatest possible
admiration for his textual conduct.*

Behold the panoramic imperative: *behold!* Behold Bercilak de Belamoris beating thunderously across margin and
quarto, across space not time, one and thirty chapters of
humpety-humpety-hump behind him, Throckton hence to
the rear of him, Throckton whence to the front of him,
Throckton thence all around him. *Humpety-hump* gallops
Bercilak, *humpety-humpety-humpety* old style, *humpety-
humpety-humpety* new style.

298

And so would he have galloped for another one and thirty chapters, had it not been for Lungs. A sudden uncontrollable trumpeting breaks out from the scribe's nose:

Tirra-trumpety-tirra! Tirra-trumpety-tirra!

Lungs adjusts his proboscis and turns it in the direction of the scent, which — even as he trumpets — is conveyed to his brain's olefactory bulb, there to be checked and compared with other such perfumes.

"Females!" Bercilak roared, dangling Me at the end of a mighty fist. "Females!" he roared again, and forgetting the author in hand, dropped him like a glove.

"I think so, master," came the nasal reply. "Ung," the scribe grappled with his proboscis and dropped Bartleby to the earth where he fell on top of the jester, "ungusual."

And there loomed the Wondrous Machine of Throckton by the Bog. With the strange circularity of space, the pair still on horseback hastened towards the central dome, their trajectory carrying them round and round, until they reined to a halt in a flurry of dust and a shower of stones and all was still and all was silent save for the spontaneous blasts from the nose of Lungs, scribe and amanuensis to Bercilak de Belamoris. Now we shall see, thought the scribe treacherously, if your vaunts have any substance, o Belamoris.

The indignity! — Me thrust a finger in each ear. The noise must be kept from his mind; his mind must be kept in his head. But the indignity: dropping the boy on him!

"For God's sake do something about it!" howled Bercilak as Lungs' blaring reached a sustained and brassy dominant fifth. "I can't hear myself think!" — nor could he, aware only of a bellowing and blasting in his head.

"Ung," the amanuensis protested, a trifle cynically perhaps; one hand clasped on his rebellious organ, the other delving into his saddle bags for a large peg especially reserved for such contingencies. "Bowerfully strong stibulus, baster," observed Lungs contrapuntally as he affixed the peg to his face's claxon.

"What happens now, Bercilak?" Bartleby took advantage of the lull in the trumpeting.

"Pen and paper, Lungs! Quick! Hurry!" cried Belamoris. "The woman comes out," he instructed the boy, "that's what

299

happens. She comes out from that — thing. And gives good cause, if any there be, why the tumbling should not begin."

"What do you mean, Bercilak?" Bartleby wondered if he was to be cheated of Guardianship at this late hour. "*Not* begin?"

"The Form, Lungs! The *Form!*" Bercilak commanded Lungs, who jumped from his saddle and busied himself setting up a kind of course, staked out with markers and penants such as might be seen at a tournament. "Ignore it, boy," Bercilak's tongue thrashed feverishly, "they never refuse. See, boy," Bercilak turned to the course, "the woman comes out and stands in the middle. You and I go to the furthest marker with our seconds; Lungs sounds the first trumpet blast, at the second blast codpieces are unbuckled, at the third," Belamoris's head jerked expectantly towards the portal of the Wondrous Machine, "at the third: *Have at sheee!*" he roared, gyrating and junketing on his unfortunate steed.

"But you've got a horse," Bartleby objected, "that's not fair."

"And you've got an author," said Belamoris grimly, "use him."

Me? What an imposition! Was he mad? But there weren't any women, not in this part of the text.

"Use the author," Bercilak again plucked Me into the air and examined his hump, "he's got a saddle!"

No, thought Me on his second descent to the ground, there couldn't possibly be any women here. The author should know. If only he could get into the Machine and back to the future. They wouldn't throw him around like this then. They wouldn't *dare*.

"Bartleby," the jester whimpered, bouncing next to the boy.

"Silence," Bercilak glowered. "Prepare yourself to record the punklet's defeat in contest equal. But that is the Form, boy," he completed his gruff address, "when she comes out, the first trumpet sounds: at the third it's every man and brat for himself, remember that."

"It's all set, up, baster," Lungs returned from staking the course.

"Bartleby," Me attempted to stop this incredible folly, "time, Bartleby, *time*," the jester clasped his head in his hands. "The blanking. We'll all be blanked next. There aren't any women, *there aren't any . . .* "

"*Trumpety! Phing!*" The peg was expelled from Lungs' rampant proboscis: "*Master!*"

"*Guardianship!*" shouted the boy Bartleby. "The Challenge, Bercilak! The *Challenge!*"

"Hump! *HUMP!*" Bercilak's Kraken tongue beat on the shores of his crimson face.

Impartially, thought the jester Me, author of a blank *Bartleby*, yes, looking at it without any partiality, it is quite obvious that I am hallucinating: but, *no* —

For of all the beauties known to man, there walked the fairest of the fair. How to sing her praise when song alone cannot her ways translate? What Muses now can Lungs invoke, or Bartleby — they that have expended so many words?

Let no scribe, no boy, the Fates wantonly tempt. For here she walks, immortal as in a vision enshrined, her dreaming robes suffused with brilliant faery beams that fill the eyes with raptures fond whence none can tell who is the dreamer, which the dream, and what is dreamt. Truly, such beauty has fled the world, never to return. Yet here it lives once again: maiden chaste of virtue unsurpassable, of carriage graceful, of bearing modest, a child of the gods, but no child either, eternally nubile, desirable, and ravishing beyond recount. Her radiant locks she softly strokes, weaving her tresses a diadem around, whose thousand irridescent sunbeams sparkle, flash, and blind, crowning the head in hallowed display. Her eyelids she demurely shuts, astral blue are they, tinted by hidden veins — lids that need no cosmetic touch. Her lips she gently parts as though to speak: charmed notes on a dulcimer played. Yet more, her voice rings with the purest gold, glory of this present age. Then what use these words? This Aurora, heavenly maid, and princess unadulterated shall speak for herself:

"I am Hymenea Brokenridge whom no man will ever possess."

No, *not* hallucinating — his brain was so big it had created another character. Ah yes, but what a character: her back, her proportions, her gracefulness!

Touched by such beauty, the jester momentarily forgot his brain and sighed.

" *'Latitude 0°; Longitude 0°;'* " Lungs wrote and spoke, " *'the meeting of dawn and dusk at layered horizon. Onward the divine cyclorama: stationary clouds move, a regular procession—crimson smeared, daubs of gilded lint across a rufous sky. All was well in God's heaven when we met with Miss Brokenridge.'* "

Masterful description, thought the scribe, dipping into his saddle bags for another scroll. Only two left, he noted. Belamoris had better be quick. " *'Chromatic heaven,'* " Lungs examined the sky and made the alteration. More apt.

But Belamoris had no time for scribal subtleties. "Get her into the paddock, Lungs!" he roared. "Let the humping begin!"

"She must be allowed to speak, first, master — according to the Form. She may have objections." Too hasty. No sense of ritual, thought the scribe. Perhaps I had better write a little smaller.

"Do the clouds move or does the sky?" enquired Bartleby.

"Both and neither," the scribe searched for more parchments. *'Both and neither,'* he recorded his own reply. The less dialogue the better.

The jester took his eyes off Hymenea to scour the pages of his blank *Bartleby.* Not in the book; she wasn't there. Directly from his brain.

"I'm doing my best," Lungs replied, "to describe the scene as *I* see it . . . "

"Not the first time," rasped Me. Another warning, yes.

"Master," Lungs appealed, "if I am not allowed to continue I shall run out of parchment. Though I could always use this blank book — at the risk of altering its meaning, that is," said the scribe, firing a blot in the direction of its diminutive author.

"Get on with it, Lungs," Belamoris growled, wringing beads of red sweat from his hands. "Ask her if there's any cause why she won't be humped."

"I don't understand this at all," Bartleby grumbled. "Is it dawn or is it dusk? That's what I want to know. And when can we play at Guardians, Bercilak? When will Lungs trumpet?"

"*No, no,*" Me wiped the ink from his face and scuttled to Hymenea's defence. "No," he found the word objectionable, "humping. You can't hump her. She's mine. From my brain, I made her. I'm her author: *ME — Hymenea by ME!*"

"My author?" Hymenea snickered. "*My* author? But you're *ugly.*"

How could she say that? To her own author? They were all the same, these —

"LUNGS! Enough! Enough!" thundered the agitated Bercilak, his eyes devouring Hymenea. "We must have order. What's happening to the Form, Lungs? The *Form!* Order!"

"True, master," the amanuensis gave a flourish of his frayed quill. " '*Dim glows the halflight,*' " Lungs consumed more of his scroll in atmospherics, " '*Long are the shadows of dawn-dusk. A falling star scrapes the . . .*' "

"*LUNGS!*" Belamoris threatened the scribe a hurt.

"Bartleby! *Bartleby!*" Me tugged at the boy's hem. A growing brain never forgets. She wasn't his: a spy, she was a spy — the woman was a spy. He remembered being watched from the Machine: chapters and chapters ago. A spy from Throckton, from —

"Therefore, O Hymenea Brokenridge, *whom no man will ever possess,*" Lungs addressed the object of his master's — and Bartleby's — desires: "Therefore speak now or forever be silent. Say, be there any cause why this infant punk, in fair and honourable competition with my master, the unvanquished Bercilak de Belamoris, should not vie in the tumble for the prize of thy maidenhead?"

"Waal," Hymenea drawled the word.

. . . the marketplace. A stowaway. Me's brain was not responsible for the stowaway. He disowned her, she who'd called him, called him . . .

"Valiant scribe! True Lungs!" Bercilak saw his victory recorded already.

. . . Indubitably, his brain had nothing to do with the

woman. Why had he forgotten, forgotten that he was being watched? It was the protein again: because of the lack of protein, his growing mind was being blanked. The first stage, yes. He was being blanked *from within.*

"Waal, yes," Hymenea drawled again, "sure there's a reason."

And while she spoke, Belamoris raised a howl to deafen the angels, and while he howled, Lungs recorded, and while he recorded, Bartleby politely listened for his invitation, and while Hymenea spoke and Belamoris howled and Lungs recorded and Bartleby waited, Me applied his expanding mind to the ultimate subversion, the subversion from within.

HYMENEA'S TALE

"I don't stand on ceremony," said Hymenea the beauteous, suddenly distressed by the fact that she had begun to sprout a beard.

"Screw you!" sobbed the distressed young man in between sobs. "Screw you all! For I am Hymenea Brokenridge whom no man will ever possess."

The company was much moved by such an uncommon display of sorrow in so beautiful a virgin; and was likewise much impressed by Hymenea's remarkable growth of facial hair.

Me alone refused to grant Hymenea her due. His brain, he decided, would not allow itself to be blanked but would seek, if necessary, a means of escape. That was rather extreme of the brain, but it had his sympathy. A diversion was the only answer.

"Bercilak!" the jester screamed: "*Bercilak de Belamoris!* The scribe, the scribe he's . . . " for so Me meant to inform on Lungs when the unhappy jester suddenly found himself pinned to the ground by Lungs' quill, hurled like a spear from the hand of the angry amanuensis. "The scribe! The scribe!" Me heard himself saying, "the scribe is made of protein!"—that wasn't it, that wasn't what he meant to say! "The spy is made of Me! A growing brain! I insist she be given protein!" cried the wretched dwarf, tragically aware that his diversion had failed. "God's brain is blank!" Me began to

304

shrink. "There's nothing in it. You next! You next! You'll see who the author is!"

With Me thus impaled and shrinking, the amanuensis found a new quill and availed himself of the opportunity to economize on his dwindling supply of parchments by writing the dwarf out of the record altogether, striking his name from THE BOOK OF BERCILAK ACCORDING TO LUNGS HIS SERVANT with a savage stroke of his pen — a cancellation fortunately achieved, as Lungs himself reflected, before the dwarf disappeared altogether, it being impossible to strike out what is not there.

"Proceed," announced the scribe, feeling immensely pleased with himself, "proceed, Miss Brokenridge."

"With the help of my analyst," Hymenea proceeded in sobs, "I arranged the operation . . . "

'*With the help of my analyst, I arranged the operation,*' Lungs squinted at the space formerly occupied by Me, then scribbled on towards the end of his penultimate scroll: ' *. . . so that Hymie is dead now, as dead as my author.*'

"Hymie?" said Bartleby, still waiting on his invitation to play at Guardians. "Who is Hymie?"

" '*Was,*' " Lungs recorded the reply while Belamoris gazed mutely at the vacuum left by Me, " '*He* was *my husband. The marriage was never consummated, of course, because Hymie . . .* " ' sobs, " ' *. . . was emasculated. But you've no need to worry: men and boys all find my extraordinary facial charms irresistible, and Hymie was no exception — before the operation. Nor was Uncle Dale, the prick . . .* ' "

"Uncle? What's an Uncle, Me? *Me!*" Bartleby stared on emptiness.

"A male Aunt," said Lungs drily, and because Bartleby's questions occupied even more space than the dwarf had taken up, cancelled the boy with a peremptory flourish of his quill.

"You can't do that!" Bercilak boiled, drenched now in the red sap of his libidinous expectations. "The *Challenge!* What will happen to the Challenge, now that I have nobody to vanquish, not even a punklet brat? Bring him back! Do you *hear* me, Lungs? I want him back!"

"The prick," Hymenea pursued her tale, innocent of the complications it was causing, "peering up my lovely sheer-stretch legs at the dark triangle . . . "

"Space, master," Lungs pleaded spatial exigencies and began his final scroll with Hymenea's words: " *'of my crotch, stroking his fat cigar and salivating over the bust of Mae West that formed the base of his multiglow reading lamp as I showed him our Mexican marriage certificate – mine and Hymie's – and the will which entitled me to all the . . .* ' "

"ENOUGH!" bellowed the frustrated Belamoris, past all restraint.

"The Form! The Form!" bleated Lungs, torn between personal loyalties and narrative ambitions, for he understood that here was his chance to wipe the slate clean. "The Form, master!" he bleated again as Bercilak leapt into his saddle with a heaven-rending cry of *Have at sheee!* "The Form, master, the trumpet blasts!"

"HUMP the Form!" Belamoris thundered, gouging his spurs into his charger's flanks.

"I'm sorry," Lungs apologized, "but I can't allow this, Bercilak."

And with that, Lungs obliterated Bercilak de Belamoris from this book and his own. Anybody could see he had brought it on himself, the scribe sighed. No style, no style at all. Well, they can stay where they are until this scroll's out. And then it's the blank book.

"Proceed," Lungs motioned Hymenea with his quill – yes, I will bring them back in the blank book, thought the amanuensis to the invisible Belamoris, *Lungs'* Blank Book.

"Proceed, Miss Brokenridge—and do make it snappy," said Lungs. "My hand is getting very cramped."

"Uh-huh," said Hymenea, producing a manually operated, extravagantly trumpeted, 78 rpm phonograph, though sans master sans mutt, on which she proceeded to play the following phono-disc.

" *'DALE VIRO REPORTS Phono-Disc No. – '* " recorded Lungs, faithfully transcribing Hymenea's record:

" 'cap that stupid broad or maybe shes not so stupid was here today with her analyst & wants all the money from the estate point cap like cap i never did go for that little faggot cap hymie & wonder how he got himself hitched to cap hymenea hiking her skirts & wiggling her fanny com & titties all over the place point cap god com how did the little creep do it query end para cap i told her com quote cap foulger & cap foulger have got the dope on you com honey com unquote thinking com maybe she killed him which wouldnt have been so bad with me anyway point cap so cap i said com quote cap wheres the body com cap hymenea query unquote cap and com cap god she said com quote cap its here!!!pulling her panties down&showingmethescarwhereher cockandqueryballshadbeenpointcapthecapon!!!itsaidcomquote capletmegiveyouakisscomcapuncledalepointcapibetyouvenever beenkissedbyamanbeforepointunquotecapitstoomuchhavingthe screwputonyoubyafreaklikethat!!!capgodshit . . . '

"Miss Brokenridge," said the amanuensis, almost at the end of his final scroll, "it needs must be more revolutionary still, I'm afraid. '&thisisstrictlyofftherecord,' " he continued, " 'butshesaidcomquotecapifyoudontmakethesettlementcapiwant thencapilltellthemthathecomshe   wnt   wnt   wassatquery tocapcpnhgn capcpnhgsquery forasxchng&tht sht shtquery yvebnlayingyrown nphw . . . thrs smthngwrngwt hthsfckng mchn&cm backwthacunt wherehis balls had been soscrewyou which is a scndlecapicldwllwthoutitmstneedanwneedlersmthng itstrueevrywrdunquotecapgodcapjesuscapi
mgnnybdywththrbllsndprckcomt
msthvebnthmnyysthtst
comcapquoteququ
eryparamsth
money
?' "

"I suppose," sighed Lungs, scribe and former amanuensis to Bercilak de Belamoris, "that she will have to go too."

And stoically preparing for his own demise, Lungs wrote Miss Brokenridge from the record. Whereafter, because he still had a little space left, he occupied himself with this: "I** AM **

```
*********A***************************************
**************SCRIBE ***************************
***********************OF *******************
***********************************MANY ********
*********************************************AND
***************************** RARE **********
****************** TALENTS********************
calledcaplungspoint ********************** unquote
```

— at which THE BOOK OF BERCILAK ACCORDING TO
LUNGS HIS SERVANT terminated.

*Now a scribe in need of space does not do that kind of
thing unless he is up to no good, reader.*

*And a scribe in need of space who has cancelled
another's characters, and himself, is a very daring and
ambitious scribe, more than a match, I think, for my
narrative friend. So I trust you will now see why I did not
wish him to become acquainted with the events of this
chapter — a chapter which ended in heroic vacancy three
sentences and two paragraphs ago.*

CHAPTER THIRTY-THREE   *Upon Ambassadors and Underlings, Wherein the Narrator and His Party Meet With Hautboy and Terms Are Arranged.*

A sullen yellow glow cast the musty arena beneath Throckton's stage into tepid relief.

At the bottom of the rickety ladder, entrance and exit for the demons and angels of Throckton's miraculous past, we found Sybil's Hambaby wrapper, abandoned on a pile of old props, moth-eaten clothes and battered masks — the discarded trappings of a drama long since dead. But of the Sepulchral Sister herself, nothing.

"If we'd have stuck to our lines," minced Estrogen, snatching at the cobwebs that clung to his crushed paper crown, his waxen face taking on a sepia tint in the yellow light, "we'd be on stage now, not underneath it."

"Hark!" whispered the magician, inclining a histrionically hand-cupped ear. "*Hist!*" he sealed his lips as an attenuated scrabbling sounded in the traps.

"A rat," I murmured, "that's all."

"Do you think," Auntie's dulcet tones startled the Knave, "that Hautboy is to be found down here?"

"That," I consulted the MS, "remains to be seen. But here," I found the end of the last chapter, "here we are descending the ladder: *safe in our subscenic retreat* . . . and so forth . . . Sybil's descent; our little disagreement, Alice, over the chapter number, *sooner or later we must meet with Hautboy,* night and the wall falling," — for so I worked backwards through the pages — "yes, it's all here, Auntie, all present and correct . . . " — thirty-*one?* But *this* was thirty-one! How could the chapter before thirty-one be called thirty-one? Unless, there were *two* thirty-ones . . .

"What *is* it?" Alice pressed for an answer. "I hope chapter twenty-eight does mention Hautboy."

"It's not twenty-eight," said I. "Remember? It's twenty-*nine*: and thirty *is* thirty, as I said in the last chapter which *was* thirty only it is now called thirty-one. Therefore this chapter is thirty-*two* and not, as I first thought, thirty-*one* because the last chapter was thirty-*one* . . . "

"That means two chapters are missing!" she cried.

"Missing and not missing!" announced the wizard, who, exhausting his fingers, began on his toes, "the question is: which two chapters?"

"Any number of chapters," I adopted a carefree tone, "any number of chapters are missing: half a dozen, a dozen — the point is what happened in all these missing chapters? Now, there's no way of telling is there? And there's no way of telling what's going to happen in *this* chapter either, no matter what number we call it. So why don't we let the narration continue — as we did before — and no doubt we shall meet with Hautboy very soon, within the next ten or twenty pages, and make him a party to our plans?" — the note of confidence I sounded belied my innermost feelings. The real question, which I successfully concealed from my listeners, was that I had landed in the wrong part of the plot. It was an absolute certainty that the missing chapter concerned Me and Bartleby, and perhaps in some way, Lungs and Bercilak de Belamoris. *That* was where I should have been: in the past with them, for they had a Machine and we did not. I could but hope that no harm had come to the hero. Meanwhile (and I pushed De'Ath to the back of my mind: the less I thought about him, the better), meanwhile the Machine was the important thing.

"Therefore," I steered the subject away from the missing chapter, "we must stick to our plan of finding Hautboy and building a new Machine."

"I do believe," Auntie concurred, "that you are right. After all, you are the narrator. Which way do we go?"

"Whichever way," said I, for the traps opened into three corridors: left, right, and rear stage, "I see the making of a heroine."

In answer to Auntie's question, the sickly saffron glow illuminating that place revealed an extraordinary spectacle. From the entrance of the stage rear tunnel, there emerged a female. Clad only in a diaphonous sari and a cuckold's hat sprouting a droopy green horn, this personage flopped towards us, her rouge emblazoned cheeks smouldering hotly and her eyes encrusted with mascara (though the rest of her face was as pale as a Pierrot's) opened her scarlet mouth to speak, then tumbled at Estrogen's feet, shocks of argent hair cascading from the flaps of her green cap.

"Oopth," she declared. "Ith that another of your mathty Irith pippin plumbth?" she enquired, squatting on her haunches to commence a minute inspection of her genitalia, parting the fleshy folds of the vulva as though she were looking for something – which indeed she was.

"A character of the diuretic school," said I.

"Perhaps she's from one of the missing chapters," said Alice humorously, then asked the character how long she had been escaped from her author.

"Howth?" was the response. "*In Tranthit*'th me publicathun, Ireland me nathun. Lookumth! Peninthular clit all ithlanded wi' babblefoam, litorally the thalathic lithy member. But howth? Forgot."

"Fuckit!" Estrogen cursed while Waldemar began a desperate search of his papers. "The woman is incomprehensible."

"More light! More light!" the wizard's voice rose to the stage joists.

"Let me do the questioning, Alice," said I. "Now what is your . . . "

"*Name?*" Waldemar conjured.

"*Name?*" the horn drooped and the face raised itself. "Felithituth inthenth. Thapphic palp, wapped in the gyre of compuncthun han prethtidigitathun, me member, me member ith gone! Oh, thilly philly, whoth meum ith tuum? *Name?* Pleeth to pee like upthtandin member of the compunity i' the genth, ekthpungin punic flighth of puny publeth depth. Middlemorph, me. Th'it intranth. Forgot me name."

311

"Name and author!" I demanded curtly, but then I was worried that De'Ath's powers extended even to such a character — I would be forgetting my own name next —

"Listen," I leant over and whispered in her ear:

—— What if the hermit had stolen her name? What if she ——

"I am the narrator and would like to know your name."

—— *was* the hermit? But I had revealed my identity now:

"Membered! Membered!" the scarlet lips spoke. "Tritha!" — And then applied themselves to my own —— if she was the hermit, he was certainly audacious:

"The membrum!" exclaimed Patricia, throwing her arms around my neck and thrusting her green horn into my face. "The *narrator!*" — she recognized me!

"Listen," — I held her in a clinch, an undignified position for a narrator but I did not want the others to hear: *"what chapter is this?"*

"Pooh!" Patricia disengaged and sprang to her feet. "A terrible thame to be thoor, forgetting! Pooh!" — she transferred her attentions to Estrogen, hauling the Knave to the ground and fumbling for his groin: "Here! Here!" she squealed, "meamithingmembruum! He'th narrator! He'th not forgotten!"

"Fuckit!" Estrogen squirmed. "Not in the play!"

"*Patricia!*" Alice came to the rescue: "We are looking for Hautboy. I am Bartleby's Aunt."

Patricia abandoned her assault and resumed her squatting position. Her eyes stared blankly at Alice—yet not, I thought, not without a *flicker* of recognition.

"This gentleman," Auntie continued, "is the narrator. Not Estrogen."

"Narrator," Patricia lowered her azure-encrusted lids in confirmation of this news and again commenced to search in her private parts.

"Stop playing with yourself," Auntie's nose twitched. "You'll never get anywhere like that!"

"I," Patricia's lips formed a Monroe pout, "forget."

"Yes," the wizard was deep in his papers, "forget . . . "

"But what," said Auntie, "do you forget?"

"Tritha'th thexth," the pout deepened.

"Why," Alice smiled, "that's easily cured."—she

312

wouldn't dare make such a suggestion. Would she? — "Surely one of you gentlemen could oblige her with a . . . "

"*Stop!*" — I drew the line at textual impropriety: "That's not what the reader expects of a heroine, Alice! Think of your audience. Why, ever since you met your author" —— I hoped De'Ath was listening: he'd never make me forget my name, he didn't even know it!—— "you've been forgetting yourself, you have; yes, I know the signs — bickering with the narrator, twisting the plot to suit your own purposes, pretending you were not where you were when you were — do you think this is all make-believe? No? Well, it's not. I could have gone elsewhere, do you realize that? I needn't have come to Throckton, no."

"I am very sorry," Alice confessed, "but how are we to put the plan into operation without *Hautboy?*"

"Member! Member!" cried the confused colleen, her green horn flopping like a cumbrous interloper in Aphrodite's garden of herbs. "Member 't all! 'T all! 'T all!"

"*What?*" said I.

"Hautboy" — *Hautboy!* — "He wunth you, yis . . . "

"*Who?*" Alice and I cried in unison — yis, *yes:* had she forgotten who?

Patricia's rouge cheeks inflated. "Pooh!" — and deflated: she had forgotten who Hautboy wanted — "Bartlebithtantie han narrator — umth!" — *she remembered!* — a direct indication that Hautboy wanted terms: his forces depleted, authorless, characters everywhere forgetting themselves, the influence of De'Ath never more strong, Throckton in ruins, supplies running short — yes, Hautboy knew a narrator when he saw one.

The tide of textual reverses would soon be turned: at last I was coming to grips with the narrative. Ah, how Sybil's seemingly chance falling out now appeared in the light of purpose preordained. For Hautboy, no doubt warned of our embassy by the Sepulchral Sister's descent, had appointed Patricia our guide in that yellow labyrinth beneath Throckton's square, and desirous of a meeting with *Bartleby's* narrator and the hero's aunt, was even now waiting, anxious and impatient for his narrator and his future.

"Lead on!" said I, conscious now that the missing

chapter had only to be found and the plot was within an ace
of resolution: "Lead on!"

"Yis," Patricia's horn nodded enthusiastically. "Which
via didshe venitemuth?"

But I dispensed with her guidance — a narrator should
narrate and not be narrated. This very sentence, then,
discovers Patricia ushering our company into Hautboy's
subterranean stateroom as that King Horn of contemporary
fiction himself rose to greet us, rose like a porpoise from a
golden sea of sumptuary cushions — like everything else
down there, the apartments were tinged by the same monotonously septic hue — at which I was moved under my breath
to declare: *how mighty are the fallen* —

'Psst!' Waldemar strove to capture my attention while
Patricia led on.

'Not here, Waldemar,' said I, 'not *now*.'

'But . . . '

'Can you have *forgotten*,' I applied one of the hermit's
tricks, 'that we are being conducted into Hautboy's presence
and are engaged even now in the most delicate of negotiations?'

'Then we are already there!' he gasped, crawling on
hands and knees through the sub-scenic tunnel.

— For Hautboy had changed himself into the most
ridiculous apparel, garb that I suppose he thought suited his
revolutionary pretensions: a tricorn hat flaunting a florid
cockade surmounted his head, a hussar's jacket, complete with
ribbing, epaulettes, sash, sword and trimmings, clothed the
upper portion of his body, but his legs and loins were bare, or
almost bare — a rather ineffective g-string supported his
genitals, facilitating access to those troubled parts, which,
alas, now resisted stimulation and hung flaccidly in their
cradle, his shame and disgrace exposed for all to see.

So that was why he was ready to plead for terms!

Nevertheless he bore it stoically with the silence of his
race and religion:

"Hautboy!" The disappointment was audible in
Auntie's cry; visible too.

"Yeah,"—for having complained so long and loudly

upon the former insurrected state of his organ, he could not in all conscience bewail its present condition of hardly apprehended insurrection—"ain't it a gas," he sighed. "Me, of all characters."

'Then where is . . . *name?*' Waldemar's hands groped along the tunnel.

'Shhh!' said I. 'The negotiations are about to begin. I have him at a disadvantage, Waldemar.'

'But . . . '

There too was Nat, the sweat streaming from his body, his eyes rolling like an English Sir Othello; the talking head—strangely silent; eyes shut, asleep, sitting on a table—Zog; the insane Wachposten or Würzig; a Frenchman called Jean or some such name, whose saurian gaze and phthisic wheezing welcomed us when we first entered.

"Tritha membered, Hautboy. She membered!"—the green horn and sari dissolved at his feet.

"Good girl," said he. "Now—"

"*I*"—thus I saved Hautboy the embarrassment of having to admit that he had forgotten my face—"*am the narrator. I have come into this text*"——I took stock of the situation: Sybil was missing, also the engineer, Hans, and the dwarf, Oskar (I made a note not to mention him in Estrogen's presence); then the absence of lepers, blind beggars, idiot boys, toothpaste eaters, crones, was decidedly to my advantage and gave me the field to myself——"*I have come into this text*," I presented my brief, composed in our journey from the traps——— "*at the behest of its author, Wordkyn—an author, moreover, who is still alive—*" Was it wise to mention that? "—*to rejoin Bartleby's Aunt with her nephew, a process which involves*"—I passed over the question of Wordkyn's existence: it was a moot point anyway, and Hautboy could dispute it later if he wanted to. Yet why were they staring at me? For stare at me they did. Something else, apart from the peculiar absence of Sybil, something else was not quite as it should have been. But I continued my speech. They were obviously surprised at hearing a complex plot reduced to its basic details: "*which involves the construction of another Machine in order that we can bring Bartleby back from the past where he is presently located with the Small Person, Me,*

315

so that this book can be finished and Throckton itself re-created. In telling you this," I decided to correct any wrong impressions, simultaneously dealing a blow at De'Ath, *"I may as well say that I enjoy the author's full confidence and though I am authority plenipotentiate,* THAT DOES NOT OF COURSE MAKE ME AN AUTHOR."—still they continued to stare at me: the missing chapter, that was it, they had got wind of the missing chapter!—*"It is, however, common knowledge that because of Bartleby's unfortunate presence in the past a chapter—according to some, two chapters—has or have been temporarily misplaced. Nevertheless, upon the successful construction of a new Machine, I am assured that such a chapter or such chapters will reappear in the normal course of things."*——No? Then I would gain their sympathies. Had I not expected the negotiations to be delicate?

"Characters—and I address you personally as a character—we all know how authors have plotted against us. But now, now that authorship is dead, do we not have a right to build our own futures?"—Hah! What if the hermit had disguised himself as me, *as the narrator,* and had laid an altogether different plan before them? Who then could blame them for staring at me? It was a risk, but a calculated one, and, departing from my prepared speech, I took it: *"Some of you may have seen me before but I must caution you that if you have, it wasn't me at all."*

"Yeah," said Hautboy, "I've seen you, sure I've seen you—in the marketplace. In the marketplace, wasn't it, Zog?"

"I think so," Zog answered, "but it's not too clear. My head."

"*Your* head, Zog," Auntie asked, "what's the matter with it?"

"Ah yes," I replied, "but that *was* me then—in the marketplace."

"Hey, and you let your author live?" said Hautboy.

"I don't think you understand. I don't think you . . . "

"Tell him, Nat," Hautboy fanned his face with his hat. "Tell him."

"That there head," Nat's eyes rolled, "it ain't talking anymore; it . . . it . . . " He found the words difficult.

"Tell him!"

" . . . We think it's done gone and died." A tear formed in Nat's eyes.

Before I could recover from the shock, Hautboy spoke again.

"OK, Wachposten," he said, "it's your turn."

"Schleiermacher's first canon," Wachposten stared at the silent talking head, then looked under the table, "tells us, and I quote: *'Alles was noch einer näheren Bestimmung bedarf in einer gegebenen Reden, darf nur aus dem Verfasser und seinem ursprünglichen Publikum gemeinsamen Sprachgebiet bestimmt werden.'* "

"Fine," Hautboy nodded. "Now you, Würzig."

"Wachposten is a fool," said Würzig. "The second canon is more important, viz: *'Zweiter Kanon. Der Sinn eines jeden Wortes an einer gegebenen Stelle muss bestimmt werden nach seinem Zusammensein mit denen die es umgeben.'* "

"OK," Hautboy folded his arms, "shoot, Zog."

"Wachposten quoting Schleiermacher has said, 'All things demanding definition in a given text must be explained and designated by the community of speech shared by the author and his original public.' But Würzig replies by saying, 'The sense of a word at any given point must be defined in context through interaction with the surrounding words.' "

"We all agree!" cried Wachposten-Würzig.

"The problem," Zog continued sleepily, "is that without authorship there can be no community of speech. Amongst us, then, there would seem to be (to paraphrase Cassirer) greater opportunity for subjective specification than public consensus, and indeed Schleiermacher's second canon tends to confirm this. However, because the original compact between one's author and the community at large is abolished, the language is decaying. It is merely a question of time," he yawned, "before character follows language, for the language is already following the great body—I do not say bodies: they are all one—of authorship in this century. In a word, we are decomposing. Your job," he turned wearily to me, "as a narrator would have been to bring the public and private determinations together in some sort of reciprocal and comprehensible whole on the basis of binary

317

exchange . . . "

"What does he mean?" Auntie enquired as Zog droned on.

"He means they're all mad, Alice," I told her. "Let him finish: the situation may be rather more serious than I had allowed."

"Live and let live, Zog. That's what I say," declared Alice as the Knave Estrogen dropped down in an undirected, absolute and dead swoon.

"The plan . . . the plan . . . " Waldemar continued his conjurations of the corridor. He *was* getting troublesome.

" . . . but it is far too late for that," Zog attempted to seal my narrative fate, "*vide* Husserl: the intentional object of the text is not the same as the intentional object realizing it,"—I wondered if the head was really dead. It could have been a trick of Hautboy's to convince me that there was no hope. Then he would assume the narratorship for himself—"a formulation now rendered obsolete by the degeneration of language."——; on the other hand, it could equally well be no more than a bargaining ploy——"Images of disorder, to paraphrase Schopenhauer,"———if Hautboy wanted out. In which case I would offer them a safe conduct back to their novels of origin, if they would help my project. But that———"are the deserts of life. Are we to agree with Burkhardt that tragic events replenish the spirit? How can we, now we have abandoned our creators and the past itself?"————*that*, according to Wordkyn, was exactly what De'Ath was doing. If I made such an offer was I not carrying out the hermit's plan instead of my own? Was I not being used by De'Ath just as surely as Alice had been hypnotized by Wordkyn? The idea gave me much food for thought.

"The past! Yes, the past!" cried Waldemar.

"For us," Zog intoned, "there is only Nietzsche's devaluation of value without the Spenglerian concomitant of cyclic regeneration."—But Wordkyn *was* De'Ath! The hermit, therefore, had announced through Wordkyn that De'Ath was returning the characters to their books because Wordkyn knew that I knew that he was De'Ath and expected me to oppose his plan, to prevail against it, hence leaving the characters where they were, growing madder by the page and paragraph. Zog's endless speech proved my hypothesis: "For us," he yawned again, "Augustine's vision of the city of God falls to Durkheim's spectre of collective despair; the progressive entelechy of the Catholic Chardin is replaced by the Protestant Niebuhr's concept of a universal super-ego."

The last thing that De'Ath wanted was the return of these characters to their own books where they would compete with what he imagined was his. My logic was sound: I decided to support De'Ath's *announced* plot while opposing his *unannounced* plot. *And* I had a few narrative ruses of my own up my sleeve.

"Plato," Zog dropped to his knees, "has lost," keeled over, "to Bacon," and fell into a deep slumber before I had any chance to ask him if he knew which chapter this was.

"What," said Hautboy as the Frenchman set up a terrible honking, "does the narrator intend to do about *us*; about *this*," he pointed to his loins.

Some people are never satisfied, I thought. When it was up, he wanted it down; now it was down, he wanted it up.

"Alice," said I, "what do you propose to do about *that?*"

"Never mind, Hautboy," she bustled to his side. "The grave's a fine and private place, but none, I think, do there embrace," she embraced him. "Let's love the live long day. The hours fly apace, and he who ponders life is left standing by," she kissed him.

"*Alice!* The narrative!"

"Why should we quarrel?" she kissed him again. "Take the first road that comes, for it's bound to be the right one then."

"*Characters*" I began my final offer, "*I*"–but:

"You only have to think," she tickled his palm, "just pretend, you know, that you are Bartleby . . . "

In spite of myself, I felt compelled to watch. There was a certain fascination in her method:

"*I*," said Hautboy–it rose–no, it drooped again, sad–"*am*"–yes, it rose; no, down, but it rose–an inch–down again–up, two, three inches–"*am*"–still higher–but yet it droops–"*Bartleby*"–up, down–up, down–which?

"Frooshucks!" Patricia boggled.

319

"Try," Alice coaxed, "there's magic in a name."

"*Bartleby*"—four, five, six, seven, eight? nine? *ten?* —"Ahhh!"

"*Characters!*" I chose the moment of maximum elevation. "*I, your narrator, offer you a free-pardon and safe-passage to your novels of origin!*"

"I agree!" Hautboy cried, falling back into his cushion: whence, exhausted—down, down, down—"*I*"—it rose again—"*am . . .*"

"Don't try too much at once," Alice warned. "A beginning is a beginning."

"Characters," said I, "listen to the words of Bartleby's Aunt; observe their effect! Tomorrow we begin the construction of a New Machine!"

"And tonight," Hautboy wallowed in his sea of gold, "tonight," he drooled, "we eat."

If only the hermit were listening now!

"Your plan," Waldemar's sombre voice spoke out—but I shall leave what he said until the thirty-third chapter. It could not have been of any pressing urgency, I decided, if this grave and dignified wizard had held his peace for so long.

CHAPTER THIRTY-FOUR   *Wherein Lungs, Scribe and Amanuensis to Bercilak de Belamoris, Takes up the Tale of His Master's Epic Contest with Bartleby.*

I leave it to the reader's discretion whether he informs my narrative friend of this chapter. For Bartleby is alive and well, returning from cancellation with heroic resilience, though, in a book written by many authors, he has acquired yet another—one whose scribal experiments return the past to the present, Bartleby to BARTLEBY, and, mayhap, Bartleby to Throckton.

BOC BLANKE LUNGES

Y wist not wat that mennes deeds be in a boc blanke ywroughte. Peradventure the booke blanke a jot or twey or thre deserve mighte, for the nones? Than shall LUNGES a song you sing, of BERCILAK, BARTLEBY, and the frekeling ME also; them that blanked were, now broughte back here in boc blanke on pages whit and pages pure, broughte back by LUNGES who them blanked first, LUNGES, scribe and clerk, ful discreet and wys.

If in heighe style I endite, as whan men to kynges write and minstreles entuneth of othere deedes brave lik whan Paris bar Helen aweye and eke the giaunte Sir Colbrande slawen was, or elles Havelock that Goderiche brend, in Lincolne toune I couthe it were all on a grene, a murrie sight that brenning was, than meet be this to mine entente: nameliche, to record ful faithfulee and with gret endeavour, sikerliche actions accordaunt to mine Lieges fame, whose servaunt am

I, LUNGES, by GODDES Grace Anno Domini and yer of ferlies, ---, Amen.

Ac first, these frekes thre, BERCILAK, BARTLEBY, and ME, that I from me scrolles yblanked, let hem return eke HYMENEA, like that Launfal the maidenes to Tyramour did tak and bring back, let hem visible be in this boc as they were afore, lustying for the Challenge to begin in tournament, nat knowing what broughte hem here or why or how, nor that they had been gone at alle.

Oh, yit much woe meseemeth me it to LUNGES the doom of BERCILAK to relate, his falle felle, and many oon aventure both weird and queynt. Witterly, tithandes blithe have I noon at alle. Alas! Wo! Wo! Weilawei! His doom he met at BARTLEBYES hand, by cause the FORME neglected was that ever men moote holden to yif for Grace they kepen, and ever have so help me GODDE.

Thus the FORME. At the lewd trumpet the first, lat the first fitte ensue: to wit, lat the Ewe be brought out. At the lewd trumpet secounde lat the secounde fitte ensue: to wit, codpieces unbuckled be. At the lewd trumpet blastes thre, lat the fitte tertium ensue: to wit, *sursum penii,* whereafter might the champioun bar it al aweye and tup the Ewe be she willing or ney, her lufferly knees wot standen in pantie hosen midst naked mad, and she stripped of girdlies and othere swich encumbraunces chaste. But in haste and bustle the FORME went by the boarde post hoc ergo propter hoc was BERCILAK vanquished by that he the FORME forgot, in this wys, as I scholl now relate.

Ful spedilee carried BARTLEBY his legges schapely and lithe, poursuivant rapely this MADE HYMENEA BROKEN-RIDGE into the grisly contrivance blakke, hight in parlance, THE WONDROUS MACHINE OF THROCKTON BY THE BOGGE. Ful loathe was BERCILAK to move, hys eyen aglaze and his fyve wyttes stunned, as though he were wood at HYMENEAS immodestee, for she hosen dragged doun and had herself unshrudden ac ful nakked was and she been of chaste fame as a virgin richte tighte too. Yit nakkednesse is nat so bad, ney nat alweye woll it evil preveth sithens NATURA ordeyneth it, we woll nat take this fer SATTANIS werke and woll let it pass a space.

"The FORME!" hym cryen. "Mak haste, master!" saith this LUNGES (me) and priketh his beeste in its shankes smoothe. The beeste did die upon the spotte and that were sadde methoughte.

Another there was who dight hymself an auctor and was ycleped ME. A dwarf he was and smalle and very slee, but more anon. Suffisaunt to say this Me quoth "Undone!" He was red and fell and his jaw dropped doun—that methoughte fele straunge.

It fell to chaunce that this MADE, BARTLEBYS toole she did grasp and it did werke in effleurage at which he was muchly enroused and she did laughe and smile and hym deliver of a swikel blow the legges betwixt and hym felled doun his thrust delaied for the wo and she did scape ful blive. "It peines me, ma swete," quod he, "that swich a clout ye me delen." Namoore. "Jhesus Criste!" this LUNGES cried, "Master, now to tumble! Lat nat a moment passe! Mak haste! Mak haste!"

I woll now this MACHINE describe. Large hit was inside, with galleries many oon to the skies they rauchte, steppes spindelee did hem connecte. Upon the floore an yron tubbe y was with chimbelies twey and upon the tubbe more anon. Othere schapes beyond the dore there were of potte yroughte that did humme and singe. When that BERCILAK to hymselve was broughte, he stared about hym, the MADE for to seeke. Right lustilee he ran whiles BARTLEBY hys hert he nursed. Right lustilee hys cokke upsterte aloft. Around the galleries he did her chase and she did crie, "Oh no, not me!" and he, "Oh yes, ma prettie thinge!" Eftsoons the MADE he seized neath her brestes twey and she did struggle, bite and scratch, most unmaidenlie, his eyen for to blinde. Yet though she an herpie were, twas to non avail—forthwith he wold hymself have holped to her prettie queynt yif she suppliaunt played, which she did to tell the truth. Hys chinne she stroked and hys ribbes tickled, saying "Lusty lad, ye woll nat have it, oh no," while her naked leg about hys did twyne, at which wommanes ploy BERCILAK was troubled, expecting nat this change of hearte. With what a false tresoun did she then hym kisse for thus did she hym tryp her legge with and upon his nekke choppe. Woe! Woe! Hit rewen me

323

mikel this sad sighte to see. Neer thoughte LUNGES the day wold come! And she hym dint in hys bellie with her daintie fingeres, ay richte amiddes, and then upon hys croune a gret skathe she smot hym as he were slen and doun the dizzy steppen did he come, a faster passe doun than wat he had risen, swithe loude he gredde, "A leche! A leche! A leche for my croune!"

O BELAMORIS wolt thou thy name chaungest to MALAMORIS, moot ye falle to Womannes blowes softes, or sholt thou rise agen, thy name for to guarantie and thy rival for to vanquish, BARTLEBY, strippling bacheler, who een now doth to the heate return? O BELAMORIS, tak care, for the FORME thou neglecteth hast and no trumpetes lewd wolt avail thee in thine baret. For algate to the steppes this boy he mountes hym and upwards goon, plaining, "Oh, come hither to me, HYMENEA, ma wee chickene, ma bileman dere," but yit this MADE she hym ybonked full in face as he approched and kicked hym agen and yit agen upon the croune that he was soore smert and howled out in peyne. A rung or twey he backed doun about the steppes and stille she hys hed banged to driven hym from hys drurie that brak it must were it mad of ledde or brasse immutable—swich alchymestes as don to the contraree mayntayneth that brasse be mutable, this BARTLEBY yaf nat a figge: hys hedde were brasse, and hit chaungeth nat, but rang out ful sonerous and deepe, bedonk, bedonk. "Wat moote I do?" pleedeth he. "Wat likest thee, ma little fische?" asked the boy, richte civil methoughte. "Wat wolt thou haf my hed to leave off? It hertes now, ma swete herte," saith he, and backed anothere runge or twey doun. Yit she wold nat lette hym alone, a contek gastliche hit was. He hys handes to hys hed did clepe, hys skull richte soore, and then she stopped and hir bakke turneth to hym and squatted doun upon the floore and pissed richte upon his croune and farted fulle lewd that he did run ful doun the stairs, hys tale hys legges between, in fast flight he ran and she did laughe unmercilee. "Oh wo," he quoth, "Y cannot fadme her fare foul. O, who woll awrekest me on this MADE dradde?"

Yit now my master did styr hymself; irate were he and roaring in hys rage, that up the steppes boundeth he ful ten atte time, hys maillais to wreketh on the MADE, sithen she hadde had hir pisse. His foote he grappled that cold nat BERCILAKES hed dint for that it was like a thynge of stone or rokke granite such as be yfound in Northerne Partes were that woneth folkes kenning nat ENGLYSCHE but hethen tonges. "Y wist not wat," he wailed, "Y wist not wat but that we sholl thy sinnes assoilen and have thee off thy legges twey and flat upon thy little bakke lay!" She hym did pulle and tugge til at the last she fel flatte and he did hymself throw doun upon hir bodie chaste, there to haf hym hys tumble and claim hys sovrein pris that was his richte, as was fit and accordaunt with resoun and naturel decree for one who alwey hath the prize yborne as champioun and gentle-man. "I haf it!" gred he, "I haf it and I am the champioun! The boy hath lost and I haf wonne!"

"Ney, ney," saith this HYMENEA. "Wat ist thou hast? Thou has the wronge ende of thinges smalle. Thou must lerne a wommanes tonge hath a bite sherpe," and bit hym ful herde upon his prikke that almoost birafte it was at the roote.

"O! O!" the bite hym reweth, "Datheit! Biswikest me? Schrewe! Schrewe sans merci!" hym her shente. "Lat go! Lat go! For GODDES swete sake, lat go! Wolt thou me prikke todrawen? Lat go, ma derling, lat go!"

"Yis, that is wat thou hast, my ginne gadeling," she gan hym sayn and nipped anew. "Look to it, else thou sholt haf nought at alle!"

Greet was that hert to my masteres prikke, greeter yet the hert to hys pride that he shold mak so straunge a mistak. He reveth and curseth, gruching and grevening his peyne for to duren. Wo! Wo! Ful tweny yerds—forsooth—he lepeth on heighe. Doun he cam. Bedonk! Doun cam the galleries, the steppes spindelee, the rail banistere, and alle. Bedonk! Doun cam BERCILAK, HYMENEA, and peeces of the walle. Doun cam the dust, and mortar, and brikkes both bigge and smalle. Bedonk! Doun cam hit alle on BARTLEBYS hed as the boy hym upsterte.

Still was nat alle done, though ful woeful was the sight: an hepe of bodies lay that seemed dropped and bledde fast of her lifes blodde, hard to tellen whose was wat and wat was whose, alle buried up was they neath the wreckage gay. In sooth, a ferlie it was withouten fable that no bonies tobrak so dreer and uglie was the wrack, so lewd and pleyning the companies groanes. Fyrst, the boy BARTLEBY hym did up, hys cherche vache to goon. As murry as the nightertale he was and as hoote, alle bruised and soore and shininge blakke, his countenaunce ful mervellous to beholde, alle bumpled and knobbled with clottes of gore, alle broken and scratched and aching I couthe richte smerte; hys gere alle besmottered with pisse and brikkes duste, yit still his lovesum longed wold he have. Wordes twey or thre he spak upon his Alisoun, but I caughte hem nat for ful confused were they.

Next, BERCILAK hymself roused from hys sleepe hore; hys eyen peeled open were, but the sunnes light crept in nat yit. Hys toothen alle crumblied were, hys tonge tochopped and hys lippes alle toore. "By the mark" hys werdes were, "twas a dreme and I do wake, elles was I enchaunted by some spelle foule." Richte soore was he and runischly brayed aboute, hys schoulder blades rubbing as he rose and crackling his jointes for they were stiffe and played hym colde. "This is no MADE," he quoth, "to pley swich pleyes; swich termes of wrastlyng ken nat I. A MADE dismade hit is, yit seemely of flesche and bonies and eek faire of schaupe that I cuthe nat what it is. Certes, hit neer was a MADE wat mad so foreward with me and cast me doun the steppes steepe; it neer was a MADE wat chewed my cokke and made peyne so smerte. Then wat is to be done in swich a cas? Wat remedie applied?"

Oh master, this booke hit saith nat, yit haf care lest this boy doth you defeat.

At onst this MADE she upgirde. "Lies!" quoth she. "A MADE am I by these titties tway, the best of brestes that ever made sway. A MADE am I by this faerey CUNT swete; a MADE haf I been alweyes and ever scholl be by cause I am HYMENEA BROKENRIDGE and no man scholl ever master me!" Thus shrieked the schrewe and BERCILAK she yaf hym swich a boffet upon his chynnes ende with her knucklies clenched; withouten let her kne she smertly undrew into hys privy pertes tendre yat he the blowe did rew and did agen on the ground hym set. And she hym no quarter wolde spare nor show hym peace at alle that he unmanned moot haf been

326

hath nat the boy to his aide spedde—though nat aide as swich intended, twas his owene assault renewed. Like unto an Engine of Siege he was such as the Greekes did mount atte Troy, that his blowes and knokkes fort against her citadel chaste he did mount many oon, and this is wat fell out and how, that almoost the time comes whan BERCILAKS doom I moote endite, that gret schame and pittie sad.

BARTLEBY this MADES arms togethere caughte, behind her bakke hem upbent that near fram the sockets were they rent. "Now hist to me," saith the boy, "now hist to me, ma prettie MADE. Many chapteres haf I spent in Alisouns quest that ladies love might I haf wonne. Wat meeneth this array, this fight and knokkes for a champioun fit, for a MADE unwys and unseemlie? Wat meeneth this wharring and blowes badde? Wat good thinkest thou to haf of it? Have patience, ma prettie swete, have patience and be laid, elles these armes both will I brak and sithe your legges. Be calme and to the conqueste submit. *Amor vincit omnia!* Hit scholl be so with thee, by my fey!"

"Ney," quoth she, "Ney, ney! For I am wat I am and nat for mennes swink. Thafoore, my lovere dere, tak this," she quoth, and in hys cheste she both her elbowes pertly sunke, whereat hym she cast oer her heddes top and slapped her handes at the throwe and then hem rested on her hippes broad. As nakked she was as whan she was first yborne, yit chaunged, if her Tale be nat fable, chaunged beyond the common course of manneskinde. Cold red it was that EVE the SERPAUNTE yaf, colder yit the clout that HYMENEA this BARTLEBY delt.

Now moote I come to the piteeous ende, or almoost, worthy of much lamentacioun, and relate how and in wat wis my master vanquished was, of how it chaunced that the proudest stallion missed the mare and the mark to boot. The Tale is sadde yit the lessoun moote be lerned, and greevous though it seemeth, cursed though the faulte were, hit was nat hys, and he blameless moote be, innocent of hys disgrace. In part the fyrst, there was nat the FORME, nat trumpetyngs lewd that evere was hys goad and spur; nat fittes suffisaunt to the cas, noon of these there was nat any, and he that the FORME forgettes wolt the forfeit paye be it noon so heighe, *vide et supra, etc.* In part secounde BARTLEBY couthe nat the rules of gouvernaunce that stateth whan to strike and whan to stay. In part trivium this HYMENEA was nat a proper MADE, but a Man made MADE, straunge to say, a chaungeling gome, a lufferly freke, a fairey carl, vessel nat fitte for my masteres prikke. In part quadrivium, still might BERCILAK have wonne in spyte of swich condiciounes defaulte, were it nat for these evil times: portentes that bode no goode, eclipses of the sunne, moone, and sterres, planettes that do drop from out the skies, birdes that do twitter in the midnight sunne, ghostes, boggles, and fiendes felle, that noises do mak and walk about from open graves, lewd beestes that do themselves whelp, and many an oon straunge sight swich as the Romannes saw afore swikel BRUTUS daun JULIUS stabbed—*vide* these werdes that I do endite in a boc blanke for an ensaumple othere. And in part the fifth, yit might my master have triumphaunt been in the times despite, were it nat for this auctour ycleped ME, and this engine of foule devysing, this WONDROUS MACHINE OF THROCKTON BY THE BOGGE. Thafoore, I, LUNGES, do mak this claim and pleede that my master, BELAMORIS, was vanquished never, but if it were magyck natureel, else werdes applied were and BEELZEBUBBES charmes haf hym undone.

To speken shorterliche of this ME. Whiles alle the wrack and rout did our eeres brak about, this blanke bocs auctor did skulke and stalke bothe up and doun: richte well he looked like an auctor too, his hair was whit and his eyen shone like a potte of ledde. Yis, lordlyngs—swich I think ye be—nat above a yerdes height was he, a firkin size and like a barrel tonne, a dwarfe as I have ytold, humped hys bakke where he kept his braines, yet gered in jesteres garb, fit for gleowing and murrie trikkes. But now he were sikke and cold, now he grateth teres ful, his guttes he gripeth and farted somewhat lik a gret bulle, scarce breth might I drawe swich was the stenche from his arses vent. By Job, hit were a goodlie fart for the nones! "Undone!" quoth this frekeling agen. "Yblanked is GODDES braines. Yblanked! Yblanked! Ich be GOD, ME, your auctor!" and that was alle. Yit whan that BARTLEBY was by the MADE ytossed, this ME me

axed to rede from the boc blanke in whiche I endite—by
what manner rede I cannat telle: to rede in a boc blanke
demandes some skille felle, though haf I herde tis oftenwise
done in these times with gret results, I couthe nat art meself.
"Ney," quoth this LUNGES, "I cannat fadem a boc blanke."

"I wolt do it," this ME gan hym sayen, "yis, yis, an
auctor might rede in his owene booke blanke where none oon
can." Than hit he preeveth and rede he did, nat where I had
writ but in some othere place, and that richte well, sayen,
"Tis so," and "thus, thus, thus," and, "so, so, so," that I
doubted nat the mattere was deepe which I cold nat meself
see.

"ME," I quoth, "the booke blanke, I moot have it now
agen."

"Forwhy?" quoth he.

"Elles, yronhed," quoth I, "the recorde moot stoppe
fast richte here ....
....

But whan the boc blanke I had ygotte agen, this Me was
wroth and he did pulle a stikke that was doun upon the floor
next to the yron tubbe of which I spak befoore. Gret was the
noyse his actioun caused: a gryndeling and a guttering, a
rusching and a clattering. "Bren! Bren! Bren!" yclacked this
Me. "Bren like alle the coales in Helle!" Then lewd belched
the straunge schaupe atte floores middle; hit grumblied and
growled, hit both shooke and eke showered. Lewd likwys
roared BERCILAK, hys face alle smoken and smuttied about,
hys tendre partes alle scalded and scoured with the steme
that spitted forth ful blive and breme, hym brenning and
boiling that a bokeler were no use so drenchen he was. "For
GODDES sake, blinneth it smertely," BERCILAK this ME
bisechen, "Befoore it dyen me to deth and I like a cooked
crabbe be!" In vane he squakede so gret was the fogge and
blastes foule, gret the confusioun and riotous route, een
greter the trembling and shaking and shouring and rumblings
about, that well might the Grekes Godde his bolt have loosed
to smitten us straight the werlde for to ende. Yis, ful
fearsome it was than to beholde. Yis, blinded was my master
in the fogges swirl; richte teeres bigge from his eyes cam,
bright schone his face as any furnas of ledde, bright stemed

his hed as that tubbe belched forth flames hys berd to singe like a dragoun or silly beeste hotte, bright schone the tubbe too, like twey sunnes were they, alle on fire, bubbling and berkening binne the MACHINE. Yis, than was that HYMENEA herself bedrenched, that she to deth wold have ben boiled. Than did BARTLEBY her tograpple to werken his werst. Yis, her legges he perted for to find him her queynte, he her ravischyng with alle his myghte while this MACHINE shooke and roared its seemes fitte toburst. Yis, in HYMENEA hys member he putte; therein he dipped with alle his worthe and barred hym the Ewe aweye that scremed and smote, that bitte and cursed and swoore and scratched but cold nat hym resist so doughtie was his weapoun. Blessed be to GODDE my master might nat hys schame see but still hym groped in the fogges darknesse, crying "Where art thou? Where art thou, princesse of mine, ma little shoope?" hys flesche still proud and gentlemanlie erecte, though hit gat hym nat the Ewe. Yis, blessed be to GODDE that my master saw hit nat, hym that neer yet was vanquysched by naturel meenes. Than did this ME of which it was mine intente to speke, than did he crie "BARTLEBY!" in triumph I thoughte, to boaste and bragge of the boyes deedes and BERCILAK to schame moor putte. Twas nat so, ney that was nat the cas at alle. Hys crie was as a warning of perilles intended that the boy BARTLEBY should leave off hys mount forthwith and flee hys prikke from HYMENEA'S queynte. For now the straungest mervel of alle did tak place; at the floores middle the beeste boiled and bubbled, gurgled and grunged; hits walles whit hoote and hooter grew until hit brak and burste in splatteres of molten yron: hotte boltes, hotte beames, hotte wheelies, springes, roddes, nuttes, plankes, and swich other partes I cannat name, alle sherpe and hoote through the air did flie like Helles hotte, hyssing coales. And yit the beeste disgorged moore and moore; hits hearte was an inferno fierce, hits lunges aflame, a foule fiende hit was from the hottest part of Helle, hits furious fires couthe no ende but brenned and brenned until hit seemeth very lik we moote alle be brenned togetheres and cooked too whan that ME hym pulled on anothere stikke the flames to halt. Than did the flammes dye to deth and were namoore.

Yit first an arme of hotte steele hit smote HYMENEA straightway with its molten fist across her brestes twey. "Me brestes!" quoth she and laid herself stille. Ded she was, as ded as the yron beeste on the floor. This ME hym left off hys stikke and took to the corpse. "Ich her must eat," quoth he. "Me braines food need, thafoore I shall HYMENEAS bodie devour by cause it be cooked!" Yit as in hir housbondes cas, hym that was ycleped HYMIE, there was nat a bodie for longe, neither flesche nor bones, nor noon othere pertes at alle to wittnesse hir doom—HYMENEAS bodie vanished did. Bedonk! and hit was gone! Yit there was oon thynge: a little rynge of gold there was where she did lay—she that did love gold in especial—but then hit was gone than no sooner seen: magyck me thought hit lik the finger hit hadde dressed. Thus I pleyne, "Wo! Wo!" but thinke yit my master was nat undone nor his eritage hym betraied but that he was enchaunted and this HYMENEA was a phantoum hym sent for to tempt with charmes foule that he might think hymself undone. Thus it is writ: "When Adam delved and Eve span, Who was then the Gentilman?" and methinke that in this HYMENEAS cas I cannat telle either one.

Natheless, BERCILAK complayned hym soore and axed wat of hys fame and reputacioun now that he hath failed in the hump. "The boy is worthier than I" he gan sayen, "and he moote the champioun now be. I woll my place resign and to the woodes goon an eremit to become, in seclusioun to while out the daies that are left unto me. Oh, I haf fayled, I that was the mightiest stud and was neer oercome, am humped by a gadelyng boy. Wo! Wo! Alas! Weylawey! Wat wolt future times now think of me now? I am a foole and a iapastere and must mak way for lustier rams. Lat nat the recorde stand, LUNGES, lat nat hit stand. Oh, strike hit out and bren the booke; let hit neer be said that I were by a boy vanquysched. I woll an holy man become and penaunce do in the woodes. I woll to shrines goon and leeve off my waies and wickidnesse. Oh, I am punisched herde, yit my doom is just, I will nat it bemoan. Oh! Alas! Wo! Tis GODDES Will Who mad me the FORME forgette. Hence this BARTLEBY the mightier moote preve and GODDES Will be done, amen, alas, it doth no good to wail like this, yit what am I to do?"

331

"Ney, master, ney," this LUNGES quod, "tis nat so bad as thou dost think, but an enchauntment or spelle as whan that wight Gawain was by Grene Knighte charmed, elles ..."

"Ney, ney," he quoth, "ensaumples woll not me heele this greevous schame. I woll awey, my face for to hide in the woodes and weep all day and say my prayer to GODDES Son and his MOTHER pure that no man did ever haf, HIM that haf me this blow delt, and beseke me HIS Grace and Forgivenesse that HIM mighte me shrieve and tak me to HIS Bosom Swete."

Than upspake BARTLEBY. "Do nat be so herde," said the gentle boy, "the faulte is nat your owene, but our heavenly AUCTOR hath delt this blow."

"Is that nat wat I said?" axed BERCILAK. "Tak nat HIS NAME in veyn, for I am my sinnes fast determined to wash. I woll aweye and that is that. Namoore, I prey thee, peace."

"But, master," quoth this LUNGES, a true and valiant scribe, and advaunced me my reasouning in the cases fyve, for hit to preve how hit an enchauntment were, and that he had hym suffered non loss nor disgrace, but that it were by some foule fiend devysed.

"Ist so?" quod he, amazed much and to hymself recovering yit agen. "Than that HYMENEA a ful mervelous Auctor hath had, and methinkest a ful gret schame that he was by the nekke hunged as she said in some gobelyn's pitte. Yis, a cunning wight he was and may hys fame endure. Then woll I do this: the boy woll I tak as my peer, that it may be couthe I nevere vanquysched was, but equalled nat surpassed in the Challenge. Thafoore hit woll be a drawe, nat defeat or victoree. Lat my resouning in this cas be as folowes—hit be noon disgrace to be equalled but a boone goode, for hit maketh for humilitee and Grace Swete to haf an equal and peer, a companion in the queste of thys life, the onlie life on Erthe that GODDE yaf man."

"Yea," quoth ME, "Me yaf it thee. Wolt thou nat tak Me for thy auctor true?"

"Nay, nay," BERCILAK hym spak. "LUNGES, didst I hear thee speke of Sir Gawain?"

"Yis, master. Befel it that on a Cristmass Day, Arthur

and his court gay at the feast were, whan in cam a gome alle grene as ye be redde. A mervellous wight he was, ful nine foot heighe—grisly to behold. 'Who will me Challenge?' he quod. 'Whoso will this hedde can ychoppe with mine blade, if on a yeres day hym the blow requite me will that me his hedde ychoppe from hys schoulders. Wat? . . . . . . ' "

So BERCILAK hys solas took from the Tale I told to hym but nat to thee, of how Gawain the Grene Gomes hedde beraft, and hit under the table rolled yprating 'a yeres day, Gawain, do nat forget!'—and how hit were a spelle foule by Morgan LaFey to keep hym chaste without hys hedde.

And there that straunge day did ende, though straunger methoughte were yit to come. Yit stil straunge hit was to Me to see BERCILAK resoune, hym that nevere hath a brain afoore in hys heddes panne whether on his schoulders or nay, but was alle herte and courage stronge, stout of limbes and heighe hoot of pertes. Through the air we did spedde, aloft most lik unto GODDES triumphaunte host that the trumpe of DOOME didst sounde at JUDGEMENT DAY whiles muzak did humme and singe about our ears. Thus did we flie through the cloudes in that ferlie MACHINE, and thus did I endite, though how or why I cannat say, save that me name is LUNGES, scribe and clerk, my masteres deedes for to record in this boc blanke, Amen.

EXPLICIT LIBER LUNGES BLANKE

Serendipity was an ingredient much to the fore in those books admired by my friend. Therefore if you do chance to meet with him, you might tell him that one half of his plot is again up in the air, and that I await his return in time for the forty-second chapter of this now more than amazing history.

CHAPTER THIRTY-FIVE *A Narrative Dinner with Haut-boy, Wherein Is Told the Story of the Butcher of Reims, Otherwise Known as the Parable of the Just Man.*

The wizard grew so importunate in his demands on my time that I gave him a hearing in between chapters. And while the soup was being served—a *consommé aux poissons rouges* borne in a steaming silver platter—I mulled over what he had said.

"I hope everybody's washed their hands." Hautboy scrutinized my palms. "My author liked people with clean habits."

Waldemar's information disturbed me; it was enough, I reflected as Hautboy's apartments swam in a haze of palpitant aureates and resonant citrons, it was enough to turn the soup sour in a narrator's mouth. "What do you mean," I had said not a page ago, "gone? How can Bartleby have gone?" And he:

"Gone. Cancelled."

"My hands are clean," Wachposten reminisced for Hautboy's benefit. "I worked in a soap factory once."

The statement drew a pained gasp from Alice. Würzig when he was Wachposten did not meet with her approval. As for Wachposten when he was Würzig . . .

"I hate to mention this," she changed the subject, "but the soup's alive."

"Zoupe?" A lukewarm interrogative kissed my ear. It must be admitted, I thought, that Hautboy's choice of servants was second only to his choice of cuisine.

"Cancelled," Waldemar folded his arms and stared at

Hautboy.

Just when things had been going so smoothly too, the wizard had to find the missing chapter. Why hadn't he spoken earlier? At least the others didn't know—and the chapter *had* been discovered. That was compensation of a kind.

"Is you for soup, honey chile?" Nat addressed the head, which remained silent and sullen. If it wasn't dead, it certainly knew how to act the part. "Yessum," he pried open the lips and forced a ladle of soup down. A fawn-coloured seepage manifested itself through the brown paper wrapper that modestly concealed the head's neck.

I had been right to suppose there was only one chapter missing—but what a chapter!

"There's nothing like a good joke," declared Hautboy, who was in excellent humour after his therapy at Auntie's hands. "Is there, wizard?" he returned Waldemar's stare and gagged on a fish fin.

The Frenchman, Jacques or Jean, seemingly on the verge of expiry, inhaled his acknowledgement of this sentiment. Managing a feeble "Zut," he attempted to speak further but the words were preempted by an effusion of red foam. He coughed, caught at the air, and picked away the foam with yellow fingers.

"Zoupe?" The mouth had me by the ear and the persistent flunkey probed with his tongue.

"Why don't you leave the head alone?" Zog aroused himself from slumber and his soft brown eyes gazed dreamily at Nat.

"Ain't that nice?" he murmured touchingly, then sobbed in his soup: "we didn't git you a body, we never did git you a body."

"Why don't you do something?" Alice demanded as the lips smiled corruptly, even, in their way, nostalgically— hinting at the life they had once possessed. "It's," she searched for the word, "it's meaningless: characters without authors, a head without a body, and . . . " And, if she knew it, an Aunt without a nephew.

"Of course," Zog reached out to Alice, "it is meaningless."

"I would not let yourselves be troubled," said I, "either of you, by mere details of moral nicety." Realism had brought the head to this pass; death was a part of life, a defining part – chiaroscuro and perspective.

"Hickit!" Estrogen dribbled soup on his tabard and sifted the remainder of the liquid through whatever lay within the interior of his mouth.

"It's just that I find our situation," she observed, "to be without point."–Such a moral consciousness in such a heroine!–"And if it's the point to be without point, I cannot find that very edifying either."–metaphysics now!

"Meaningless?" Zog snorted. "Hopeless. Death," he produced a tremendous yawn, "is the last infection of organized matter. Some of us," the lid of one eye closed, "cannot breathe."

"Well I can," Estrogen drowned the fish in a pitcher of Hippocrene. "How long is it since I've eaten like this?" The Knave admired his goblet, chased with a pursuit of satyrs and other dubious creatures and applied his thin lips to the *entrée* of *boulettes à la fièvre cérébrale*. "Never in this book. The old books were full of menus, weren't they, Waldemar?" he enquired, moved to approximate eloquence by further draughts of the epic fountain. "Waldemar?"

But the wizard, who yet stared unnervingly at Hautboy, was cloaked in abstraction and flexed and cracked his fingers as though he wanted to rival the dishes now set before us, rival them with some metaphysical *omelette-en-surprise*.

"Taste," Hautboy removed his tricorn hat, "taste is contrivance." The air rose in his gullet and was expelled in mid-breath. "The secretory glands should be coaxed; never overwhelmed." He swallowed. "The buds of the tongue should be petted; not ravished."

The wet noise of mastication and Jean's French cough greeted Hautboy's remark, the liquid champing of jaundiced jaws bathed in the light of tinctured tapestries, ocherous silks, burnished crinolenes.

"I don't feel like eating anything much," said Alice flatly, a mood of depression settling over the narrator and the narrated alike. "I'm surprised that anyone can eat at all."

Yes, the hermit De'Ath was responsible for this: it was

De'Ath's MS that Waldemar had assembled—De'Ath's MS dropped from the skies as we fled the marketplace of Throckton by the Bog. It was De'Ath occupying Lungs as he had occupied Wordkyn who had cancelled Bartleby; and it was De'Ath who presided over our feast.

"There's one thing I'll say about this chef," announced Hautboy upon the appearance of the next creation: *Rognons des oies enfilés aux oillets*, a delicacy which our host informed us could be worn in the buttonhole as well as eaten, "he may not be much of a poet, but he's full of surprises."

When it came to the main course of *porc-epic mariné en bout*, it appeared that Hautboy's conversation did not lack purpose.

"As I've been saying," he declared, "there's nothing like a good joke. Now, one day an old magician or warlock," Hautboy threw out the taunt, "was walking by the banks of a river or stream, when he chanced to observe a young maiden or girl who was about to throw herself into the raging cataracts below."

"Waldemar," the idea came to me, "how good a magician are you?"

"Desiring to prevent so untimely an end," Hautboy continued, "the wizard or magus asked what was the cause of the maiden's distress."

"My ancestors were Danes," was his solemn reply.

" 'Oh, sir,' " Hautboy's maiden answered Hautboy's wizard, " 'I am a high-born princess who happened to fall in love with a farmer's boy to whom I have pledged my troth. My father, the king, enraged at this alliance has cast me out without a livre and my love has betrayed me by taking wife with a shepherdess.' "

"Master of Marduk, Keeper of the Minotaur, Ostler to Ibis," Waldemar invented a legendary past.

"We must fight fire with fire," I whispered—

" 'Your troubles are at an end,' " said Hautboy's sorcerer to Hautboy's damsel, " 'for I am a man of cunning skills. Your father, the king, has just died of remorse and left you his kingdom. Tomorrow, you will be married not to a false peasant but to a true prince.'

" 'Oh, sir,' the beautiful maid cried, 'what do I owe

you?' "

—"We must confect a Bartleby, Waldemar. A magical hero!" Thus I countered the cancellation. "An immortal hero, Waldemar, who will not be written out of this book."

" 'Tonight,' said the wizard, grinning toothlessly, 'you must sleep with me, and tomorrow you will find all these things have fallen out as I foretold.'

" 'Willingly, kind sir,' said she and subjected herself to the ordeal, for she was very desperate."

"But . . . " Waldemar groped, fixed on the tale and its teller.

"No buts: I insist—we must have a Bartleby." De'Ath had not bargained for this!

" . . . I forget," Waldemar objected, "I forget what the boy looks like."

"The essential details: colour of hair and eyes, height, clothes, that's all you need remember . . . ."

"Yet on the morrow," Hautboy came to the punch line, "when she was the more destitute by the breadth of her maidenhead, the old warlock asked her:"

"*Aren't you too old to believe in fairy tales?*" Waldemar demanded.

"Say!" our host's face dropped. "How do you know? That's what the wizard said: 'Aren't you too old to believe in fairy tales?' "

"You could say," Waldemar affirmed modestly, "that I was the wizard; I was there."

Hautboy, however, was moved to laughter. "And how!" he giggled. "But that's not all," he spluttered on his *porc-epic*, "no, no. Oh, I can't finish: it's so *funny.*"

"Yith," Patricia helped him out of the impasse, "the pintheth wath a fwog."

"And," Hautboy smothered his mirth, "the funny thing is the princess said: 'Now get this, wizard, I'm really the prince who was changed into the princess by an evil frog. So you're under arrest for treason and sodomy.' "

The Master of Marduk rose to his feet.

"Waldemar! Hautboy!" Auntie intervened, breaking aside from Zog to whom she had been listening during the course of Hautboy's narrative. "It was only a story," said she, "there's no need to be angry. In any case, Zog has a . . . "

"Thluth!" Patricia pouted redly. "Hautboyth memberumth dead," a cup was conveyed to the pout and she batted her heavily laden lids. "It ticklth," she cried scornfully, swilling more of the eloquent distillation, dewy droplets silvering down her chin, "like a feather."

"Fink!" Hautboy now rose from his sea of golden cushions, floundered, then subsided like a creature of the abysmal deep.

"And you call yourself a narrator too!" Alice turned to me—and I am sorry to present her in this light: "Have you any idea"——but the truth is all——"what is happening to this book, to Hautboy, to Zog, to us all?"

"More than I can tell, Alice," I shook my head, "more than I can tell."

"Humanity," Zog's somnolent gaze fell on the silent head, "is the sole object of true philosophy."—I feared the worst from this pronouncement.

"He was five," I gave the magician a clue. "You must remember that. My text is very clear on that point. Bartleby was five. Five years of age."

"Five," Waldemar repeated after me, "that would seem to be it: five, yes *five*. There may be," he blinked owlishly, "complications."

"Yet the present condition of the art," Zog oiled his voice—he was obviously gearing up for another lecture: "puts me in mind of a certain parable, *The Parable of the Butcher of Reims.*"

"Complications or not," said I, "Bartleby is merely a book."—Already, the reconstructed square, the New Machine, and the fourth age of Throckton's history took shape in my narrative eye. The missing chapter and its missing hero were minor inconveniences. A fictive Bartleby was better than the genuine article, for an artificial hero, created through my agency, would prove more tractable than his Aunt. Even if Waldemar failed to confect me a Bartleby, I would bring him back myself—as a direct narrator I would bring him back. At the very last moment, when all seemed lost, I would produce him from the narrative hat exactly as Lungs-De'Ath had cancelled him. And exactly as Wordkyn-De'Ath had narrated the story of Alice's captivity, I would narrate the story of his return. In fact, I could narrate anything I wanted. Should the hermit interfere with more personations and more cancellations, I could even narrate his death. Better yet, I could impersonate him.

Meanwhile, Zog had begun his parable. That's the one thing about him, I thought: when he was awake, he was persistent. With his jaw jutting prognaciously forth and his forehead retreating at the same angle, his face formed all of a plane, a steep and hazardous incline, a simian slope interrupted only by the scimitar curve of his nose and the polyp-like growth of his mouth. The polyp worked assiduously at the parable, popping out the sounds and pushing its territory beyond the furthermost edge of the nose's blade while the eyes above squinted down and observed the pushing extension of the polyp like two startled sloths in a lair of ivory.

"I think you will find," said Bartleby's Aunt, "Zog's parable both excellent and worthy of imitation, a deserving story, from which—were I a narrator—I would draw my inspiration and hope."

"Oh yes," said I. "But do continue, Zog. Auntie is listening—for the second time, it seems. Yes, she is listening, if no one else."

Hence (on this witty note) I let Zog recite his parable.

THE BUTCHER OF REIMS

Otherwise Known as the Parable of the Just Man

"My story," Zog's furry gaze took in the company, "concerns a certain butcher of Reims who lived and prospered in that town during the Hundred Years' War at a time when the great majority of his fellow citizens, especially the poorer sort of folk, suffered terribly on account of periodic sieges and the general vicissitudes of arms. Now it is enough for you to know that although he was of humble origins himself, this butcher was well and familiarly connected by trade and marriage with the burghers and lordlings of the town; and further that, unique among victuallers, he always had a more than adequate supply of meats and dainties, even in the times of direst hardship. His comfortable friends, therefore, never went with empty bellies, nor did they ever share the pangs of an otherwise starving city, though some of them frequently complained of the butcher's exorbitant prices, and still others privily suspected him of trading with the English enemy—as many did themselves, in men as well as goods. Of course they made no mention of their suspicions, but continued to shell out their money, for they could not blame the butcher for what they did themselves and he was in any case an excellent carver and dresser and his joints were of the best—superior indeed to those which the burghers could have gotten in illicit trade with the invaders, a fact which should have allayed their suspicions but did not, so convinced were they of the tradesman's right to make good from the general misfortune, providing they were not too greatly fleeced in the process and providing also that they continued to exercise the same right, each in his respective way.

"One winter's day, however, towards dusk during the course of a particularly arduous and protracted siege, the butcher of Reims was met by a deputation of ill-clad and starving townsfolk.

" 'Sir,' said their spokesman, 'we are made to tread the streets in search of the meanest offal. Our bellies are empty, our coats thin and torn, and our feet uncovered. Many of us die from disease, starvation, and the cold. Your friends, on the other hand, grow fatter and richer while we bear the brunt of these wars. We know that you have enough food to feed all the folk of Reims, and what is more, we do not care where you get it. Why should the poor starve and the rich prosper? Where is the justice in that?

"Having, as I have said, risen from the lower orders of society, the butcher received this address favourably and sympathized with these poor people. After a moment's reflection he said, 'But what is justice?'—an answer which at first embittered the people, for they had heard it many times before. Then he greatly surprised the townsfolk of Reims by making this proposition. 'Friends,' he said, 'I am an honest man and have made enough money out of the rich to spend the rest of my days in comfort and to purchase all the supplies this town will ever need—English or no English. Therefore I shall do this: to the townsfolk of Reims I shall give as much meat as your gullets can swallow and you shall have it free of charge. But I must make these two conditions. First, that you do not bother your heads by asking where the meat is obtained. And second, such joints and cuts of meat as you acquire freely from me are to be smaller than those that I shall continue to sell to my wealthy friends, though you may have a corresponding amount by weight, meat being all the same to a hungry belly whether it comes in a fair amount of one shape, or in a fair amount of several lesser shapes. If one of my burgher friends should see even the meanest and wretchedest of you with a whole side of beef for which you have paid not a sou, then he will be angry and envious, and either you will be accused of theft, or I shall be put out of business very shortly. Whereas if he observes you with a small pot roast or a little chop, he will commend my charity and commend it freely, since it is not his own.'

"The deputation assented to these conditions and throughout the next two weeks the butcher held his promise and the bellies of the townsfolk were as full as those of the burghers. Then, early one Monday morning, this charitable and humane victualler was dragged from his bed and was arrested on a charge of trading with the enemy—a capital offence. Needless to say, his only offence was that he had robbed the rich and given to the poor—a crime which speedily converted his rich friends into poor enemies and his poor enemies into rich friends. No evidence was adduced at his trial on the substantive charge, and yet it seemed he could not escape destruction, so angry were the burghers at paying, and paying heavily, for what the rabble had gotten freely. When, therefore, the judge enquired if the prisoner had anything to say in mitigation of his undoubted crimes, the butcher spoke as follows.

" 'Only this,' said he. 'To the citizens of Reims I have given rats, cats, dogs, mice, and wherever I could, horses. Such food I would charge no man for, certainly not your lordships, whom I think will agree with me when I say it is food fit for the rabble.' The burghers laughed heartily at this and saw they had misjudged their man and that he was one of their number after all. 'But,' the prisoner continued, 'o Burghers of Reims, consider what sacrifices you have made. Know that I have charged you the highest price for your meat because I have sold you what you value most: the flesh and blood of men.'

"It was the turn of the townsfolk to laugh now, and they saw that their faith in the butcher was not so misplaced as they had thought. As for the butcher, he was acquitted on a scrupulous point of law. 'I cannot convict this man,' said the judge, 'on a charge of trading with the enemy when I would have to hang the wisest, the gravest, and the richest amongst you for the commission of cannibalism.'

"And although the wars grew more desperate, the butcher flourished in his old age, the burghers of Reims boasting that they had the best beef in all France, and the townsfolk content to let their elders and betters eat their pork while they dined on food fit only for the rabble."

"There," said Alice after Zog concluded his parable, "you see what I mean?"

"The butcher of Reims," Zog's eyes curled slothfully in their ivory lairs, "was a just man, and a just man is a true and wise philosopher."

"And had we this butcher for a narrator," Alice patted Zog's hand and regarded the head, "some of us would not be in the condition they are now in."

"Aren't you forgetting something, Alice?" said I, making no sign that I was ruffled by her implicit criticism. "Moral excellency is not inherent in the reporting of deeds, but in their commission. Were I this butcher, for example, I doubt that Zog would have had such a moral tale to tell. And you and this book would have had no narrator whatsoever."

Her reply was not what I had expected. "No," said she, "the tale depends upon its teller as I shall demonstrate with a story of my own. But concerning Zog's parable, I think he is to be congratulated for it since he who shows us our humanity is himself worthy of that humanity."

A harmless little moral, reader! And surprising, you will surely agree, in that it came from one who, though practical in some matters, displayed an astonishing ignorance of the expedient, the political, the real. Would that she knew of her nephew's cancellation and the heroic vacancy which that deed had imposed on my text! The time was nigh, I decided, when I would have to take her into my confidence. Meanwhile, narrative appearances must be preserved: to narrate, to act, to believe—these were worthy accomplishments. Yet to narrate and act and believe when there was no hero—this was sublime!

"What is more," Alice concluded her exercise in homiletics, "the teller of a human and humane tale is by implication a human and humane character. What is taught is a reflection of the teacher. Therefore I agree with Zog," she turned her eyes to his, "that a just man is a true and wise philosopher, and think . . . "

The sentence, however, remained incomplete. For Zog, who had hung patiently on Alice's every word, suddenly found something more than the merely congenial in Bartleby's Aunt. So lofty were her sentiments, so pregnant with moral acuity, that she—for her part—had quite failed to recognize the nature of the lap-dog and simpering expressions, lavished by Zog on the interpretor of his parable. His devotions spurned, Zog now took offence, and understanding himself to be the recipient of a cruelly administered jilt, tremored, undulated, rolled and crashed down over Alice like a beaching wave, his facial polyp pushing forth a garbled stream of amorous syllables, his eyes scurrying in their caves, imploring, pleading, until troubled by Auntie's uncharacteristic resistance the wave withdrew, ennervated and quiescent, no longer a wave, but a quivering heap of flesh, lapped by a golden backwash, hiding its head for the shame.

"Jee-zus!" Hautboy stirred, impressed by the unpremeditated violence of Zog's assault.

"Oh!" Alice recovered from her shock and hurried to console the hapless Zog. "He was a just man! He was! I didn't understand, Zog; I didn't know how you felt!" she cried, tears in her eyes. "You should have said; you should have said."—Here was morality indeed, I thought: frailty, thy name is Alice.

"I," Zog sobbed, a pulsating heap of tissue and tears, "couldn't help it."

344

"Yes," she sighed, "that's right. You couldn't help it. I know you couldn't help it. There, there," Alice transferred her gaze to her narrator, "it wasn't your fault, Zog. And now," she smiled distantly, "now I shall tell my story."

"Anything, Alice," said I, "anything you wish." And anything—I did not say it—anything to keep you quiet.

CHAPTER THIRTY-SIX   *Against the Writing of Blank Pages, Whereafter Bartleby's Aunt Tells the Parable of the Unjust Man.*

Assured that I had thought of everything to thwart the crazed designs of the hermit De'Ath for the possession of this text and the characters therein, I was but slightly troubled when I found the last chapter was not called thirty-two (as I had initially suspected), nor even thirty-three (as the magician's information would have suggested), but thirty-*five*— from which figure I deduced the existence of a second missing chapter: the presumed thirty-*four*. This second of invisible chapters—I inferred—must have been composed of blank pages, since it occurred after Bartleby's cancellation at the hands of Lungs-De'Ath, and not before that deed's commission. Was I meant to follow suit?

Consider the hermit's cunning, reader! Suppose I had here intercalated a quire of blank leaves in my own MS; suppose further, in those epic scenes I have yet to narrate— dare I say, *compose?*—: the building of a New Machine, the recreation of Throckton, the return of the wandering hero, culminating in the final turning of the tables on De'Ath; just suppose that he, then, was to expose me as the author of nothing at all, the author of a chapter that the blind might read as easily as the sighted. Ah, how my fantastical friend's prophecy would be justified; how I would deserve the contempt and derision of the remaining characters! But while I was in Throckton, while I was in the text, there would be no blank chapters. Let Lungs or Wordkyn or De'Ath do their vilest, if I still had breath to draw, my pen would write and be seen to write.

Confident now that the end drew near, I gladly relaxed my narrative grip and allowed Auntie her parable, which, counterbalancing Zog's tale, neatly filled the requirements of contrast and harmony that I have been at pains to uphold since I gained the mastery of this text.

But first I asked Waldemar if his conjurations were far enough advanced for me to announce Bartleby's arrival within the next two or three chapters.

"It is in preparation," said he.

"Good," said I. "You will not be forgotten for this."

So while Hautboy chewed on a carnation and Nat tended to his talking head, while Zog, repulsed by Auntie, sat and quivered, cradling his own head in his hands, while Wachposten-Würzig argued quietly with himself, while Patricia searched her groin and the Knave's too—but enough of that—; while Waldemar conjured and I meditated upon my ultimate victory, Bartleby's Aunt and Guardian, unaware of her charge's fate, recited the following tale.

THE PARABLE OF THE UNJUST MAN

"Many years before Bartleby came into the world," Alice began, "when I was but a girl of sixteen, innocent in the ways of man and nature," she gave a thoughtful stare at Zog who had started a low and intermittent sobbing, "not knowing the joys and pleasures of marmalade, I was friendly with one Thomas Merryweather, a youth of my own age and a native of the village that lay not very far from my home in the country.

"This Tom had a sister, somewhat older than himself, who was called Betty, as pretty a girl as you could wish to see, but very chaste and not at all free with her favours, for which reason she was more than ardently desired by the young bloods of the village, and would have been in great danger had not that modesty which made her so attractive simultaneously earned her a reputation for shyness and aloofness, whereas she was by nature and inclination warm and friendly.

"One summer's morn, I suppose it was after I had

known Thomas Merryweather for two months, I was alarmed to see him hurrying over the pasture which led to our stables—alarmed, that is, by his presence at such an hour when he should have been at his work on Squire Fulton's farm where he was employed like his father, and his grandfather before him, as a labourer.

" 'Tom,' said I, 'you know you shouldn't be here.' For my parents, had they known of this innocent liaison, would certainly have disapproved, even to the extent of exerting pressure on the squire, over whom they had some influence, to dismiss Tom's father—so great was the difference in our stations.

" 'Oh Alice,' said he, when he had recovered his breath, 'the Squire has been to my father and has demanded Betty's hand in marriage. She refused his suit and Fulton threatens to cast us out of house and home if we do not give way to his wishes.'

"You will not be surprised," said Alice, "to learn that this Squire Fulton was widely regarded—and feared—as an evil and depraved man whose very least offence was that he was in the habit of riding down his neighbours' and tenants' hedges, and whose very worst was that he had been married once before—to an unfortunate wretch who had reportedly died at her husband's hands as the result of a drunken beating. Tom of course wished me to plead with my father to prevent the forced match, which I agreed to do although this meant revealing the secret of our meetings.

" 'I will see you here tonight, Tom,' said I, and promised to do my best, young and innocent as I was.

"My father, however, flew into a temper at my pleas and told me it was none of my business whom Squire Fulton chose to take for a wife, and though he might degrade himself by associating with the lower orders I could not. As a result of this mission I was confined to my room for the rest of the day, and when the time came for me to meet with Tom, I did not know which was the lesser of the two evils: my not being at the stables and he perhaps thinking I had gone back on my word, or my going out against father's wishes to give Tom the bad news. In any case, I could not have gotten out for my door was locked, and I had to content myself with watching out through the window.

"On the morrow, it was learned that Tom Merryweather had made an attempt on the Squire's life, but the criminal and would-be murderer—so he was called—had failed and had been apprehended while fleeing the county.

"Strangely enough, when Tom appeared before the assize court, Fulton himself made a great impression by pleading on the prisoner's behalf, saying that he was to marry Tom's sister and desired no ill-feeling might exist between his future brother-in-law who was already forgiven by the Squire—this despite the fact that the boy was unpenitent and declared he would attempt the deed again, if he had half the chance. Now people were not so foolish as to believe that the Squire was the kind of man who considered his own life a trivial affair, but many took his defence of Tom as a sign of his reformation, yet others seeing it as an expression of love for Merryweather's sister.

"The justice, impressed by the Squire's magnanimity, commuted the mandatory death sentence to one of fifteen years imprisonment, and lost no chance in observing how fortunate the prisoner was to have selected such a generous and forgiving victim.

"For my own part I heard of the trial only by hearsay and was disinclined to believe anything that fell from Fulton's lips. But when Tom was taken away to prison and the Squire married Betty and still did not wreak his expected vengeance on the family, but instead received them into his own home and behaved as an exemplary son-in-law, I must confess that I did not know what to think.

"Two years went by, during which time Betty bore a son and all seemed well enough, though neither she nor her parents were ever seen in the village. Then, one November's night, Squire Fulton's mansion burned to the ground, and with it his son, his wife, and his parents-in-law. Even to this day, the blaze is remembered in the countryside and many of the witnesses are still eager to commend Fulton's extraordinary valour and bravery in attempting to rescue the victims. Needless to say he survived the conflagration, and, grief-stricken though he was, soon took a third wife—an action which was easily reconciled with his well known sorrow. A man should have heirs, it was said, especially such a man as the Squire to whom fate had dealt this terrible blow. Indeed, some of the villagers went so far as to claim that the burning was a blessing in disguise. It was common knowledge, they said, that the Merryweathers had not been grateful for their social elevation. Why else had they not taken advantage of it and paraded themselves in the village as ordinary folk would have done?

"I would like to say," Alice sighed, "that Tom Merryweather returned from prison to force a confession from the Squire and that he died repentant. However, but one more year elapsed before news was brought, not of Fulton's death, but Tom's.

"The Squire's third wife, meanwhile, became a confidante of mine. More fortunately connected than either of his first two wives, she enjoyed in some degree a measure of immunity against her husband's rages—partly because of her birth, partly because age, liquor, and the effects of a strenuous life had mellowed the Squire Fulton. Nevertheless, it was his great delight to tell her how he had beaten his first wife into her grave, how Tom Merryweather had attacked him to defend Betty's honour when he had sought to ravish her, and how the Merryweathers had been confined as prisoners in his house until he saw fit to dispose of them.

"When good Squire Fulton in what was perhaps his first natural act died, his third wife packed up and left the village. Nobody was sorry to see her go, for it was widely held that she had married him for his money—money which I can assure you was long since spent. But the loss of the Squire was greatly felt and the vicar of that parish preached a sermon on the importance of moral reformation. The village, said this parson, mourned the Squire's passing, but the people should rejoice, rejoice that he had gone to heaven where he sat with the Apostles at the Lord's right hand, eating his spiritual desserts."

When Alice concluded this withering tale (which I thought totally destitute of any informing spirit) it was already far advanced into the night, and Hautboy now added his sobs to the blubberings of Zog.

350

"What an awful story!" he exclaimed, waxing strong with maudlin affectation and making great play of wiping the tears away.

"In itself," Alice replied, "the story is neither good nor bad. However, the fact that you find the story awful is a reflection on yourself—for it needs a very low opinion of human nature to believe in such a person as Squire Fulton."

"I found him quite unbelievable," said I. "No man could be so deliberately callous."

"Indeed?" Alice gave me a rather cool stare. "That you find Fulton unbelieveable," she continued, "reflects on the narrator of the story. I am to blame; not the character."

"And why, Alice," I enquired, curious to learn what strange thoughts were now in her head, "why are you to blame for my disbelief?"

"Because—as I said before—the tale depends upon the teller. What would you think if I told you that Fulton was actually a kind man; that he had bravely tried to rescue Betty Merryweather and their child from the flames which consumed them, that her brother was a liar, a thief, and a would-be murderer—in short, that I have systematically misrepresented his character for the sake of making a pretty tale with a pretty ending? What would you think of that?"

"Then I would think you are to blame, Alice," I appealed to the company's good sense, "for more than misrepresentation. Why, you have reneged on that most important of narrative duties: adherence to objective fact, to the truth, not as you choose to see it, but the truth as it is, free from the blurred lens of sentiment and emotion."

"Yes, I suppose you are right," Auntie shook her head, "though it doesn't matter. You see, Fulton and Merryweather and the other characters in the tale never lived. I made them up, and the truth cannot be of any consequence to fictitious persons."

I paused, understanding that she sought a profession of humanity from me . . .

"Yes?" she waited for my answer.

"Listen, Alice," I lowered my voice, "you are not in full possession of the facts concerning this book. While your scruples are commendable, very commendable in a heroine,

351

the sufferings of these characters can never be known to you, and nor can you carry the burden of that suffering."

"That is not right!" she protested, a sentimentalist at heart. "I see what is here! You have said you are going to finish the book, then do it!"

I was about to refute this outburst by reference to the subject-object relationship—which pre-supposes so-called external reality as a function of mind—when the plot took a turn at once desirable and not so desirable in the form of an heroic diversion from the wizard who now performed what I had asked of him, yet failed in the execution, failed—as you will see—to the extent of compounding error on error, a common fault with his type, sufficient indeed to explain their extinction today.

"It is done!" he sprang to his feet and covered himself like Caesar in his cloak, from which speedily emerged a sandy-haired, freckle-faced ragamuffin who announced himself as our hero—hence saving me the embarrassing task of arguing with his Aunt. "Meet," Waldemar measured his words, "the boy for whom we have all been searching, and whom we,"—he was tremendously pleased by this feat of prestidigitation—"we have now found after so long!"——and nor did I think ill of him for thus being pleased: I was pleased myself, if a little surprised at the suddenness of the appearance—"Meet . . ."

"Bartleby," the urchin supplied his name.

"*Characters*,"—Pleased? Say, overjoyed, elated—prematurely, of course. For the hero's unexpected return forestalled my Throcktonian plans. What now of Boss and Ham, the New Machine, and Throckton's final and glorious age? Yet I was nothing if not responsive to the situation—*"Characters, a change of plan! It is as Waldemar has spoken: Meet Bartleby! All that I have spoken of has come to pass!"*——a political hyperbole, you will understand.

"*I*"—Hautboy began, threatened by this development—"*am*"—the organ that was the object of his complaint rose: one, two, three inches—down again: up, down, up, down—"*Bartleby!*"

"Auntie," Bartleby objected, "how can he be me?"

"What?" The *fait accompli* took Alice aback. "Him:

Bartleby?" She surveyed the boy. "But his socks, his socks are *red*, and his hair—it's the wrong colour!"

"*Characters*,"—a chance; a desperate one, but a chance nevertheless—"*Bartleby's Aunt fails to recognize her nephew! In whom do you trust: her or the narrator? With whom have you bargained: her or the narrator?*"

"Fuckit!" Estrogen was livid. "It's him! It's him! I'd know him anywhere!"—but Alice lacked conviction. Belief failed her:

"That," she declared emphatically, "is not my Bartleby."

"No?" Waldemar gritted his teeth and furnished a second Bartleby—with pink socks.

"*Green!*" exclaimed Alice.

Green, then . . .

"Please, *Auntie*," Hautboy clung to his source of inspiration, which rose higher and higher as a third boy appeared from out the folds of Waldemar's gown.

"*Stop!*" I commanded. "*Enough!*" The reader will perceive that I lost no time in extricating the plot from a perilous situation. To continue was folly, and if I could not go on then I must go backwards.

"*Another change of plan!*" Again I selected the moment of Hautboy's maximum elevation—this was the greatest gamble of all: the device of the flashback to the non-existent past!

"*Surely*," I cried—it would need every ounce of my narrative authority but if De'Ath could do it so could I: "*Surely you remember how we found Boss and Ham?*"—not that they were actually found. Or were they? If Lungs-De'Ath could cancel, I could create. The appearances! The appearances must be preserved! "*Characters, a flash-back!*"——To retreat now, even to the non-existent past and there work certain changes in the plot, this was to alter the present—the present that was and is as illusory, or no less illusory, than the past.

"*The present is temporarily held in suspension! Your narrator announces that the present is held in temporary suspension!*" I cried, implanting the seeds of a mechanical idea and warning the characters of the impending change in narrative coordinates. "*Prepare yourselves for a flashback!*"

CHAPTER THIRTY-SEVEN *A Postprandial Flashback, Narrated Only with Some Difficulties and Objections, Which Relates the Amazing Circumstances Attendant upon the Discovery of Boss and Ham.*

Waldemar writhed in his cloak as the fourth and fifth boys appeared.

"Too tall! Too short!" Auntie dismissed them.

"Characters!"—the imperative voice—*"Remember Boss and Ham!"*

While Estrogen pursued the carrot-headed creature and Patricia selected the fourth boy for exploration, the sixth and seventh urchins trotted in, followed by the eighth and ninth . . .

"Too young! Too old! Too fat! Too thin!" Alice stubbornly rejected them all.

"I"—Hautboy oscillated wildly—"It's running amok!" he wailed.

"Remember how we found them above and before!"—I continued, striving to turn the situation to my advantage—*"Remember"*——more boys——*"how we began"*———still more!———*"and COMPLETED our great work!"*

"Harder!" Alice counselled Hautboy. "You must try harder! What was that," she asked, "about our great work?"

A turbulent ring of chanting Bartlebies coalesced around Patricia. She received them severally.

"Great work, Alice! Precisely!"—I raised my voice above the raucous din: *"Our great work. Characters,"*—I did not hesitate to use the element of surprise—*"Boss and Ham are found! The NEW MACHINE is constructed!"*——Now they would listen to me!

354

"The verbal intentions of God," Zog's head rose from a mound of undulant flesh, "are . . . "—The sandy haired Bartleby collided with the table—" . . . unalterable!" Zog managed to cry, immediately before he was hit in the face by the soggy brown paper wrapper from the silent-talking head, both ejected into the air by the force of the collision, Nat following underneath, arms ready to receive the head which now squirted a resinous green fluid and the tail-end of a decaying goldfish into Patricia's lap:

"Fwooshucks!"

The emission received, Nat caught the head, *but* evading his slippery and impassioned grasp it shot across the room—Nat holding a tuft of blood-smeared golden belle's pre-bellum ringlet—to crease Estrogen(*figuratively*) in two, disintegrating mangily, yet with spectacular esemplasticity, on the Jack's brilliant costume. At which tactical chance—

"I can't remember anything!" Zog moaned, breaking apart (*metaphorically*); whereat the seedy Frenchman, Jean or Jacques or Jean-Jacques, who had occupied himself these last two chapters in the final throes of the bronchial flux and pruriginous pickings of his mite-infested skin, now coughed his last: a spongy red effluvium foaming on his lips as his eyeballs rolled back in white terror——

"Do you mean," the colour drained from Auntie's face, "to stand by and let this happen? It's horrible!"—Horrible or not, such lapidary attention to detail is not easily contrived, reader.

"Don't be squeamish," I warned her. "They're not human, Alice: objects, you must think of them as"—the head bounced, rolled, discarded an ear and grinned, pink and white brains compressed through its several (enlarged) facial orifices—"*objects.*"——At which tactical chance (as I was saying), I unerringly announced the inauguration of our New Age.

"There hasn't been time," Alice's despairing and slightly hysterical gaze fell on Hautboy's fluctuating organ, "there hasn't been time to build anything . . . "

"*Now, characters, the flashback!*"—the decisive moment had arrived: it was the only way to rid this text of certain impure and divisive elements—elements which, though not exactly located, undoubtedly existed and had to be destroyed before they destroyed the book. *"Characters,"* I gave them a slogan, *"creation is representation! Prepare yourselves for the amazing circumstances attendant upon the discovery of Boss and Ham!"*

But the scene as it was represented and the scene as I had conceived it were not identical.

FLASHBACK

No flashback began so inauspiciously! Yet by this device, and by this device alone, I again established control, opting out of time to gain time.

Zog buried his head in the folds of his stomach and tottered ostrich-like to the earth.

"Hey!"—even Hautboy forgot himself. "What is this?"

Waldemar too was shocked. The wizard abandoned his conjurations, the results of which had inevitably disappeared, vanishing with time, and racked his brains, searching for some analogue in the files of his forgetfulness.

As for Patricia, deprived of the spare Bartlebies, she gaped, horn aflop, gaped and tripped mindlessly round Throckton's square, our new, *reconstructed* square.

"Alice," said I, "do you see what I see?"

"The square, the stage, the Machine," her eyes were wide with astonishment, "have all been rebuilt."

"Re-written, Alice, *re-written*."

There, at the centre of the square, stood our newly carpentered stage; thereon, the dome and stack of Throckton's New Machine, and the marketplace itself was returned to its pristine innocence, undisturbed and unmarked by civil broils. It was as though nothing had ever happened to mar the tranquility of the scene. What agency had worked the transformation? And if not, why not? It is not given to mortals to ask these questions; but to answer them, I say to answer them took nothing less than the creative power of a narrative mind, labouring unconsciously on one level while it was preoccupied on another, labouring to give Throckton back to itself and the unconscious to the conscious, that the whole mind might be brought into play as it beheld this work of its creation.

"This," I informed the heroine, "is what is known as a flashback: a device frequently used by authors to economize on time. And you can see what a great deal of time we have saved ourselves! Yet it is far more than that, Alice. What you are witnessing is the objectification of a dream; the imposition of structure on the once inchoate and formless material of this text; an act of the will, your narrator's will. It is as you so rightly said, my dear Alice, the tale depends on the teller. You are present, we are all present, at the re-creation of Throckton's history."

"A very fine speech, I'm sure. But what time of day is it?" she enquired, puzzled by the sudden transition from night to day.

To tell the truth, the flashback wasn't working properly: the cheering crowds I had conceived for myself, the frenzied adulation, the return of Bartleby, the real Bartleby, and the unmasking of De'Ath seemed not at all in sight. And Boss and Ham, whose finding was to serve as a prelude for the final act, were nowhere to be seen. And yet . . . and yet . . . to narrate is to create. I would exist the flashback into being!

"A sensible objection, Alice. I have unfortunately timed the flashback to begin before or after the paragraph I had intended and hence we are early or late as the case may be. We shall soon know when the events I am attempting to narrate coincide with the narration itself."—The unthinkable occurred to me. Had I inadvertently flashbacked *forwards*? Then the machine, the stage, the square, were double illusions. For how can we return to the future, remember posterity, recall the yet to be? But to Hautboy and his ilk, past and present were one, and time that was running out for them meant only the present the ineffable and locationless no man's land between past and future. My present was the future of the past. Therefore I had gone from past to future transcending nature's old one, two, three, and done no more than a thousand and one books in which an aeon is evoked by a line, a day by a chapter.

" *Characters!*"—I began bravely, in the middle of emptiness—"*Characters, you see how I, your narrator, am received with such a deal of acclaim as I descend into the sweaty arms of the mob, so great is their joy and pleasure at having found a narrator, that we stand in danger of being separated!*" I minimized the danger. After all, the square was vacant and it would have been absurd to overdo the contrast. "*Impervious to the mob's adulation, I address them upon their duties as characters and citizens of the New Throckton, telling them that they are to seek out Boss and Ham, find the Mechanics, while still others are to be put to useful labours such as the widening of roads, the digging of sewers, the building of houses, the cultivation of crops, and last but not least, the design and creation of our new stage and New Machine.*" Ah, how my eloquence carried the hour! But the square was *yet* empty. Perhaps I was going to have to tell the whole story without actual re-enactment.

"Rubbish!" exclaimed Aunt Alice. "You've never seen Boss and Ham, let alone spoken to the mob!"

I omitted the rest of my speech, not wishing to task the sceptical Alice any further. "*Thus it is, characters, while we are seeking the Mechanics in order to begin our Great Purpose, the construction of the Machine itself, thus it is that we come across the dumb swineherd (with whom, I concede, communication is difficult), who gives us to understand in a series of dull grunts (as though in pastoral imitation of those beasts in his charge) that he has discovered the most unlikely brace of pigs it has ever been his most gutteral astonishment to behold, for though he is dumb his eyes deceive him not; in a word, he fails to comprehend these new pigs, and desires that I, whom he has heard say am something of an authority on these matters, or thus I interpret his grunts, that I might inspect his pigs and enlighten him upon the animals.*

" 'But what is wrong with your pigs?' *say I, not wishing at this point to be bothered with such petty trifles.*

" 'Ignore him, he's mad,' *says Estrogen.*"

"Fuckit!" the Knave squawked.

"*Upon your last observation,*"—I gave him no chance to interrupt—"*I note that the swineherd protests his sanity, and*

*with more speaking gestures and dull grunts gets me to
understand that whereas he is dumb, his pigs are blind; but in
addition to this simple accident of nature, whereas he cannot
talk, they can, and fluently so, though he is hard put to
fathom them, for he is a simple rustic who knows little of
talking pigs, and by experience unprepared for the miracle is
afraid to report his story because of the late commotions.
Furthermore, he has no wish (very wisely) to be taken for an
idiot, yet if the truth be known, he is mightily aggrieved at
this travesty of talking pigs and dumb swineherd, and thinks
he can speak better after his fashion than the pigs after theirs.*

"The swineherd begs us on his knees: 'Mnug-mnug!
Oingk-phlurp!'*—and with these and many other mute ex-
clamations invites us to follow him. We tarry no longer but
go straight to the pigsty . . . "*

"When is all this supposed to happen?" said Alice.

"*NOW!*" said I.

And so we did, entering when and where (with less haste
and more calculation) the amazing episode should have
begun, did begin, was and is beginning, and shall begin!

"Hautboy!" Auntie screamed. "The pigs!"

"Nat," he blubbered, "where's Nat?"

"*Mnug-mnug! Gdunk-gdunk!*" The garrulous mute was
visibly excited by our sudden arrival, as surprising to him as it
was to me.

"Ignore him," the Jack yawned, "he's mad."

"Fwooshucks!" Patricia clambered into the pigsty and
chased a bore around the pen, her sari trailing diaphonously
in the mire, her cries commingling with porcine squeals.

"There! There! I see him, the brat!" Either the Knave
was hallucinating or he was being deliberately perverse.

"No," Alice thoughtfully regarded thin air, "that is not
Bartleby."

"*Tomorrow! That doesn't happen until tomorrow!
During dinner!*"—But the pigs! The pigs! Oh fortune!

Yes, reader, momently—but two or three pages ago—I
had thought myself almost undone by method, betrayed by
time, deceived by technique. Yet now that time past and
time present coincided perfectly, now that narrative tele-
metry fused object with subject and subject with object, I

was temporarily taken aback. For the pigs so far exceeded my forward-looking expectations, that had I been Isaiah himself I could not have escaped the shock of vindication.

"*Characters*," I cried, "*observe what I have foretold!*"

In the pigsty, at the centre of the square, those two most noble of Throcktonian philosophers, wallowing happily in the filth and dung, skipping merrily with their fellow pigs, were engaged in the dialectics of grunting as if they had forgotten that they were ever men. Their faces were the best Italian copies of any Greek heads that I had ever seen, yet their bodies were all bacon and lard, and not a pupil, no, nor any glimmer of an eye graced those sightless marble whites. It was as the swineherd had said: Boss and Ham were blind.

And Patricia! How our swineherd shook his head at the sight as his prime porker (an ordinary beast, seeing what was to be seen as well as any), Patricia clinging to his tail, snorted, grunted, and squealed, his pinkly fierce eyes appealing to our mere humanity.

And Boss and Ham; what did they think of the runting and stamping, the squealing and grunting? How did these commotions in the sty affect our two philosophers?

Ah, but they were possessed of a fine understanding. Small wonder that the swineherd failed to conceive them. For the plight of their cousin pigs passed them by, and not, I think, because they were blind. Who amongst the rude and unlettered populace might have fathomed their present mode of communication? Thus:

> "⠄⠂⠄⠄⠄⠄⠄ ⠄⠄⠄⠄⠄⠄⠄⠄⠄⠄ ⠄⠄⠄⠄⠄⠄⠄⠄ ⠄⠄⠄⠄ ⠄⠄⠄⠄⠄⠄⠄⠄
> ⠄⠄⠄⠄⠄ ⠄⠄⠄⠄⠄⠄⠄⠄⠄ ⠄⠄⠄⠄⠄⠄⠄ ⠄⠄⠄ ⠄⠄⠄⠄⠄⠄⠄
> ⠄⠄⠄ ⠄⠄⠄⠄⠄⠄⠄⠄ ⠄⠄⠄⠄⠄⠄ ⠄⠄⠄ ⠄⠄⠄⠄
> ⠄⠄⠄⠄⠄⠄⠄⠄⠄"
> ⠄⠄⠄⠄⠄⠄⠄⠄
> ⠄⠄⠄⠄⠄⠄⠄⠄ grunted Boss.*

> "— — — ·· — ·   — · — · — — — ·· — · — ·····   — · ·· — ·· — — — ·· — · —   — · — — — —
> · — · — · —   — ·· — ·   — · — ·· — — ·   ·····   · — ···   — ·· — · · — ··· — ··   · — ···
> · — — · — · — — — — — · —   · — · — · —" squeaked Ham.**

---

* "I never knew we were blind."
** "Of course we're not blind. We can see as well as anyone."

"How can anyone speak in braille?" Estrogen refused to believe his ears.

Before I could again remind him this was a book, the Knave lurched towards me, dragging what he imagined was a struggling, kicking urchin by the (sandy) hair. "Gotim!" Estrogen pummelled the space occupied by the supposed boy. "This," he cried, "this is Bartleby!"

"It isn't!" Alice gazed on emptiness.

Fearing that Waldemar would come up with yet another invisible boy, I was about to inform them *in no uncertain terms* that they were all deluded, when the corner of my eye caught sight of a sedan chair entering the marketplace. The chair-bearers advanced, sidestepped, retreated, then came on again, performing a little jig that revealed the nervous apprehension of the chair's inhabitant:—*Wordkyn-De'Ath!*

"He never wore red socks!" Alice protested, "If you think I'd let my Bartleby wear *red* socks ... "

"How about this one?" Hautboy lunged after a completely fictive Bartleby.

"That is not Bartleby, *Bartleby!*"—the results were predictable.

What was the hermit doing here? And how had he learned of the flashback which, this far at least, had proceeded without the slightest technical hitch?

"Godammit!" Hautboy called on his heavenly creator as the sedan chair skirted the edge of the square, "OK! OK! Pigs can talk; the Machine is built, anything you say—only ... "

De'Ath really was being cautious. Unnoticed by the others, the chair came to a halt and a curtain opened. Wordkyn-De'Ath's beckoning hand appeared—

"Pigs?" Zog stirred and shivered.

——the finger uncurled. His powers were failing, I reflected, if he found it necessary to observe the narrative in person. By thus trying on the same disguise twice he showed the weakness of his hand. I ignored the chair and its occupant; best to pretend it wasn't there—an intolerable blow to the hermit's egoism.

"*Characters*," I concentrated on the immediate scene, "*observe these two philosophers*,"—Boss (or was it Ham?) perked up—"*consider their plight*," I turned to the swine-

361

herd, who——

"This may be rather obtuse of me," said Alice—it was—"but do you think you could recap a little more?" ——had *disappeared?*

Estrogen whipped round. "Boy,"—I was convinced the Knave had taken leave of his senses: *there was nothing there!*—"where is the pig that speaks in braille?"

"Yes"—Auntie as well?—"and where's the one that squeaked?"

I was wrong: there had been no depreciation of De'Ath's influence! And the chair, the chair was advancing . . .

Here was no time and place for a showdown with De'Ath. The final act as I had planned it, the final unmasking of Wordkyn-Lungs-De'Ath and whomsoever-else-De'Ath was to be a public affair, and if he had designed to provoke a premature confrontation then he would be sorely disappointed. For hence as the chair came on, circling closer and closer, I halted the flashback there and then with a short but pointed announcement of termination: *"It is finished"*—

—which announcement evidently went unheard, so great was our company's surprise to find itself back where it had started from.

"Trith'th," the colleen examined her sari which yet bore the mark of the trotter's imprint, *"muddy?"*

"Where's you all been?" Nat looked up from the ruins of the talking head, welcoming us with his soulful gaze. "You's here one minute, den you's gone de next. Ah cain't unnerstan' it. Ah reckon Ah's just a poor nigger, yessum."

"Nat!" Auntie suppressed an expression of disgust. "Why are you speaking that way?"

His reply came as an inaudible mumble, a scratch of the head, a roll of the eyes, and a profound sigh.

"Characters," even a glimpse of the hermit was enough to ruin the best laid plans, *"characters, Nat has missed us:*

362

positive proof that we have been away!" The proof was not as positive as I would have liked. From one point of view, the excursion had been but a partial success: I had failed to come to grips with De'Ath. Why, if the hermit were a subjective phenomenon, why could I not exorcise him from my mind? Sleep, I needed sleep. Nobody functions well when they are tired. Characters sleep, narrators sleep, even hermits sleep. The next chapter, the very next chapter, blank or unblank, missing or unmissing, past or unpast, or maybe the chapter after it, yes, that would be best, I would have it out with this book and the hermit De'Ath. Kill him in his sleep, that was it! Creep up on him while he was asleep; unmask him, hold him up to the ridicule of the mob . . . in the next chapter but one, two perhaps. A chapter-long sleep was called for. Who called for it? I did. The *narrator*. To kill the hermit: wouldn't that be to acknowledge his existence? Not if he were me, a temporary measure naturally. What a surprise I would have in store for him! *Blitz!* I knew who you were, De'Ath, I knew who you were all the time! Yet you didn't know who I was, did you? Hah! Surprised? I have been disguised as you De'Ath, as you, as Wordkyn, as Lungs, I have even been disguised as myself! Breaking point? I don't have one. Oh, there have been times when I was tired, De'Ath, but then I slept . . .

"I would like to know" began Alice . . .

"*What happened next?* Is that what you were going to say?"—her usual enquiry . . .

"Well?" said Alice.

The hermit's unquestioned fate was prepared. It would be a public show: crowds, festivities, entertainments fit for our new stage, a day to end all days, culminating in De'Ath's final defeat. Before that: *sleep.*

"Next," I answered her question, "we slept an after dinner sleep as we shall now."

"And," Zog yawned, "and . . . "

But our eyes were already closed.

CHAPTER THIRTY-EIGHT   *Wherein the Cosmic Reflections of the Short Comedian, Me, Are Briefly Given and an Argument Ensues.*

Herewith the last of non-Throcktonian chapters and the end of my chance commitment.

The truant words returned to the page. Unjustified, thought Me; their absence had not been justified. Nor was their return—yet.

One by one they assembled themselves. The first affirmation was the most important: *ME* by *ME*. Shamefacedly, the words fell into order, adverbs attracting participles, adjectives nouns—phrases and clauses, simple and complex sentences presenting themselves for their author's approval. Me was a real person, not God nor the other party, but Me, a real author, a character in his own right.

His structure was intact; the syntax had regrouped, and he had returned from blanking like a victorious general— foreshortened perhaps, but foreshortened only by time. Perspective, Me's brain dispatched messengers to the furthermost reaches of its territory, perspective was essential: proportion. If he straightened himself out, he would be as tall as any of them.

"Where," Bercilak de Belamoris scratched his broiled pate, in which the memory of Hymenea burned like an old scar, "where are the women?"

"A good point, master," Lungs recovered from his experience with the blank book. His memory of what he had written, and how and why, was indistinct.

"And the Machine, Me," said Bartleby, "where is it taking us now? Is it still *forwards to Throckton whence?*"

"A moment," Me's brain scanned the text for an answer. How should he know? He was only the author. A good story unfolded itself gradually. What was the point of writing anything that was *short?*

The lines, he noted, were drawn up in battle order with *ME* at their head. Not God; not the other party. No defections, Me cautioned his troops, no desertions. Discipline was restored, and would be more effective than ever. There was to be no capitulation this time, no surrender from within. The Commander in Chief was known for his severity. Did he make himself understood?

"And what," Lungs was the incarnation of tactfulness, "what happened to the fifth member of our party?"

"Lungs," the furrows ploughed across Bercilak's be-scorched brows. "I was not vanquished. Remember that; take it down."

"I imply nothing, master," the scribe heaved his shoulders. "But the scrolls are exhausted, the quills, the ink . . ."

"Osmosis," Me's cold blue eyes completed their re-connaissance of the page. Why should he have to explain that he had absorbed her? The more protein the better. Hymenea's protein gave him strength. "Through the walls of the cell," added the jester; "osmosis. As for ink and parchment," a paragraph volunteered the information, "the text says that you have a reserve supply. How can you have forgotten *that?*"—the author dealt with his subordinate and reminded him of his past crimes: "Unless you wanted the command for yourself?"

"The author," Bartleby pressed the dwarf, "must know where we are going and what we shall find when we get there. And even if you don't, surely you can write us the endings we want. Some of us," the boy gave Bercilak a thoughtful glance, "have had a bad time of it."

"Ending? Ending?" Me shook his head and his brain inspected the boy. "Hasn't it occurred to you that there is a text outside and beyond this one, the ur-text," Me's nether lip curled contemptuously; "and that within this text which

365

is far beneath the archetype, there is a further text, and within that another, and yet another?" Of course it hadn't occurred to the boy. Only the greatest of minds could think of such an analogy. "So that the whole," the author— ME—selected a simple metaphor, "appears as one of those Russian dolls with a smaller doll inside the outer doll and so on. Who can say which is the original doll?" Not that Me was the author of this hieratic system—a system in which protein played no part. That had been an ignorant philosopher, who knew very little of proteins and Russian dolls. Had he known anything of the dolls, he would have voiced his opposition to them. For the largest doll was simultaneously the smallest; the smallest the largest. "In our case," Me expanded the point, "infinity may be thought of as a continually drawn circle, progressing in a clockwise direction on one plane, and in an anti-clockwise direction through a right-angular plane— both aspiring after conjunction at the point of provenience: zero, the beginning and end of possibility."

"Exactly," Belamoris was lost at the mention of dolls.

"Not exactly," Me executed the manoeuvre; *abstractly,"* The figure of the circles was a feint, that was all. *"Ab ovo,"* the main thrust, "the universe is an egg: spheroid, as I have described it, and inside the egg, there is another egg. Yet," Me pocketed a hand through the opening of his divided costume and sat the hand upon his heart, "who is to say where the eggs join? Do they join at all?" The hand listened to his heart as the jester turned the flanks of the enemy. The hand withdrew and Me's bandy arms described an egg. Then his left hand went to his right wing and listened to another heart. Good. Better. Excellent. The army of the conspirators that had blanked his book from within was almost destroyed. The hands reformed, counted losses, and smashed through the enemy's rear, breaking his back: "Sentences!" cried the jester, the dream of total victory glistening in his eyes, "Paragraphs! Chapters! Words of the book, your author receives you!" The words answered with a rousing cry. "Victory to the strongest!" exclaimed the dwarf—a sentiment with which Belamoris would well have agreed but for the darkness in his head, an eclipse so profound that even external rays were darkened. "The point

of provenience has moved on in time," Me's hand tore at the strings of his cap. "The enemy withdraws in disorder! The egg is inside out! The largest doll is the smallest! Words, the expanding brain of your author accepts your offer of osmotic protein! I receive you with an open heart!" Me's pupils dilated and a sharp sequence of reports sounded on either side of his face from the region of the tympanic plates. *Two* hearts? The thought seared across Me's expanding brain. Why did God live in such a body? God and his body, Me's body, were not the same. God did not have a body. What did God want with protein? What did his brain want with his body? "Guts! Guts!" Me shrilled, a renewed outburst of the *crepitus ventris* assaulting his bewildered listeners. Indubitably, the eggs were an abstraction. Geometry was an abstraction. The Geometrician, God, was an egg. He would dispense with his body, dispense with protein. His brain would meet itself, returning in time to where it had begun.

"Words!" cried the dwarf, jester, and author, Me, "I am infinite! The book is infinite! *The infinite has returned to himself! I AM ME!*"

During the course of this speech, it seemed to Bartleby that Me's head had first doubled, then quadrupled. Distrustful of his vision, the boy was on the point of touching the enlarged cranium when he was prevented from so doing by a verdant mist which began issuing from the jester's ears, hence forming a kind of barrier between the head and its observers. Bercilak, fearful of a new enchantment, now set up a hideous barracking, while Lungs, who had been rooting in his saddle-bags, there found a renewed supply of ink, quills, parchments, and other occupational necessities—a discovery that nonplussed the scribe and caused him to look upon Me with a new eye.

"Master," he gasped, heedless of Belamoris's bellowing, "the legend: it continues!"

Behind the mist, meanwhile, occurred something not unlike the mitosis of Me's being, corpuscles, molecules, and proteins sifting osmotically through the barrier (which now assumed the shape of a gaseous mesh) to form a leg here, an arm there, until one completed Me had re-assembled itself with particular and atomic approximation on the visible side of the barrier, whereafter it was followed by a second Me, a third Me, and a fourth and final Me, reconstituted and unharmed by quadruplication.

Identical with their original, the first two Me's stepped aside to allow passage of the second Me's, who in turn stepped aside, the four Me's thus being grouped in braces, or heads of two, an arrangement suggestive of an unfinished quadratic equation in which each figure had yet to weigh value against its counterpart in the neighbouring brackets:

$$(Me^1 + Me^2)(Me^3 + Me^4)$$

Me^1 and Me^2 shook hands and exchanged pleasantries, an action mirrored by Me^3 and Me^4, the two groups next acknowledging the presence of each other, much as a fencing team might greet its rival. Only after some time did the surprised onlookers realize that Me^3 and Me^4 were identical in every respect to Me^1 and Me^2, with this exception: that whereas Me^1 and Me^2 were striped on the left side of their jesters' costumes, Me^3 and Me^4 were striped on the right side—a distinction no sooner made apparent than Me^3 began to address Me^1.

"At last we meet," said Me^3, unclear as to the exact identity of his reflection.

"We do," said Me^1, staring at his image.

"We meet at last," said Me^2.

"Do we?" Me^4 decided he was the real Me.

"I see me in triplicate!" Me^2 held up the fifteen fingers of one hand.

"My fellow Me's . . . " Me^3 made a belated bid for consensus.

"Quadruplicate!" cried Me^1. "Not triplicate!" He saw three Me's, but there was a fourth: himself, not Me^4, Me^1. The three Me's also saw three Me's and that made nine. The tenth was himself again. Me^1 who was also Me^{10} computed the possibilities; they were limitless. How could any one Me claim otherwise? "I agree with myself!" announced Me^1; "I am infinite."

"We are all infinite!" Me^3 compromised.

"Text without end!" Me^4 jumped on the bandwagon.
"Me 10^2!" cried Me^1 who was also Me^{10}.
"Me 10^3!" Me^3 made it a landslide.

And so they continued through to the centillion, one party beginning with the billion thence to the trillion and quadrillion (after the American or French system), the other countering with the milliard thence to the billion and trillion (after the British or German system), until they were no closer, but further from the infinity of Me's they desired to evoke. For upon reaching the centillion of Me^1 and Me^2, and the centillion of Me^3 and Me^4, the four Me's remained as four. (See chart hereafter.)

CHART

American & French				German & British		
Value to powers of ten	Number of zeros	No. of zeros grouped in 3's after 1,000		Value to powers of ten	Number of zeros	Powers of 1,000,000
NAME				**NAME**		
billion 10^9	9	2		milliard 10^9	9	–
trillion 10^{12}	12	3		billion 10^{12}	12	2
quadrillion 10^{15}	15	4		trillion 10^{18}	18	3
quintillion 10^{18}	18	5		quadrillion 10^{24}	24	4
sextillion 10^{21}	21	6		quintillion 10^{30}	30	5
septillion 10^{24}	24	7		sextillion 10^{36}	36	6
octillion 10^{27}	27	8		septillion 10^{42}	42	7
nonillion 10^{30}	30	9		octillion 10^{48}	48	8
decillion 10^{33}	33	10		nonillion 10^{54}	54	9
undecillion 10^{36}	36	11		decillion 10^{60}	60	10
duodecillion 10^{39}	39	12		undecillion 10^{66}	66	11
tredecillion 10^{42}	42	13		duodecillion 10^{72}	72	12
quattuordecillion 10^{45}	45	14		tredecillion 10^{78}	78	13
quindecillion 10^{48}	48	15		quattuordecillion 10^{84}	84	14
sexdecillion 10^{51}	51	16		quindecillion 10^{90}	90	15
septendecillion 10^{54}	54	17		sexdecellion 10^{96}	96	16
octodecillion 10^{57}	57	18		septendecillion 10^{102}	102	17
novemdecillion 10^{60}	60	19		octodecillion 10^{108}	108	18
vigintillion 10^{63}	63	20		novemdecillion 10^{114}	114	19
centillion 10^{303}	303	100		vigintillion 10^{120}	120	20
				centillion 10^{600}	600	100

"Centillion!" screamed Me[1] and Me[2] together, "1,000,
000,000,000,000,000,000,000,000,000,000,000,000,000,
000,000,000,000,000,000,000,000,000,000,000,000,000,
000,000,000,000,000,000,000,000,000,000,000,000,000,
000,000,000,000,000,000,000,000,000,000,000,000,000,
000,000,000,000,000,000,000,000,000,000,000,000,000,
000,000,000,000,000,000,000,000,000,000,000,000,000,
000,000,000,000,000,000,000,000,000,000,000,000,000,
000,000!"

"Centillion!" cried Me[3] and Me[4] in unison, "1,000,
000,000,000,000,000,000,000,000,000,000,000,000,000,
000,000,000,000,000,000,000,000,000,000,000,000,000,
000,000,000,000,000,000,000,000,000,000,000,000,000,
000,000,000,000,000,000,000,000,000,000,000,000,000,
000,000,000,000,000,000,000,000,000,000,000,000,000,
000,000,000,000,000,000,000,000,000,000,000,000,000,
000,000,000,000,000,000,000,000,000,000,000,000,000,
000,000,000,000,000,000,000,000,000,000,000,000,000,
000,000,000,000,000,000,000,000,000,000,000,000,000,
000,000,000,000,000,000,000,000,000,000,000,000,000,
000,000,000,000,000,000,000,000,000,000,000,000,000,
000,000,000,000,000,000,000,000,000,000,000,000,000,
000,000,000,000,000,000,000,000,000,000,000,000,000,
000,000,000!"

Bartleby's head reeled at this, as well it might.
Momentarily, the boy fancied himself the victim of the
strange delusion that he was seeing everything not in triplicate, quadruplicate, or centillionate, but in simple duplicate,
and experienced great difficulty in focussing on Belamoris
and Lungs (both of whom now enjoyed a similar bifurcation
of vision), not to mention the four Me's, who were now on
the verge of coming to blows over nothing when Bartleby
stepped forth with the aim of separating them. Perhaps this
move, though heroic, was too hasty of the boy. For the space
between the four Me's was immediately filled by a three-
dimensional object roughly, nay exactly Bartleby's size, with
which he—in the nature of things—collided, six individuals
crashing head on in an area uncomfortable for two.

"Master!" Lungses, amanuenses to the Bercilaks, cried

and scribbled, scribbled and cried: "The deeds of Bercilak de Belamoris are doubled!" The amanuenses stared amazedly at two Bercilaks. "Pity his scribe, pity this Lungs who must now work twice as hard!"

"What?" thundered Bercilak, and was met by the same interrogative from himself: "*What?*"

"Never again," the scribes continued, "will Bercilak de Belamoris be equalled. You are twice the man you were, master, and I must be twice the scribe."

"Blockhead!" roared the Bercilaks. "Look at yourselves. Your labours are divided as my deeds are doubled!"

"Hello," said Bartleby, disentangling himself from the four Me's. "Hello, Bartleby."

"Blockhead!" roared the Bercilaks. "Look at yourselves. Your labours are divided as my deeds are doubled!"

"Hello," said Bartleby, disentangling himself from the four Me's. "Hello, Bartleby."

And there, for a second time in this history, the Wondrous Machine of Throckton by the Bog came to a rest.

And the quadruple Me's, squared Bartlebies, doubled Belamorises, and twin Lungs left one written Machine to enter another written Machine, and at the third remove entered———?

Where and when it came to rest, the inquiring reader will discover for himself.

CHAPTER THIRTY-NINE *The Dawn of the New Age, Wherein Is Given the First Act of a Celebratory Masque.*

"Yes, Alice," I was saying the morning after the flash-back, "I mean a masque. The hermit has asked us to a masque, and to *the* Masque we shall go."

"How," she asked while the rest of the characters slumbered on, "how do you know that we have received an invitation to a—to *the* Masque—when we haven't?"—an astute question, if based on the (erroneous) supposition that it was unanswerable.

"I'm glad," said I, drawing her aside from the recumbent bodies of the living dead, "that you asked that."

For I am certain I have heard, or imagined, or imagined I have heard, the murmurings of discontent:—you cannot go back to what has not happened— —yet I have demonstrated that I can. You cannot, then, know what has not yet happened—I think I will shortly demonstrate that I do know what has not yet happened, and in my demonstration what has *yet* to happen will be *made* to happen. Namely, they that sleep shall awake; the Sepulchral Sister shall return to these pages, the Masque shall be played out and the hermit unmasked, Bartleby shall arrive back in Throckton to be re-united with the heroine—a happy, conventional, and triumphant ending, quite the reverse of the one that De'Ath had written.

These are pretty substantial facts, and I ask only that you note their realization in chapter and paragraph.

"You see," I made Alice my confidante, "I have been

reading De'Ath's manuscript—while you were asleep. That is how I know of the Masque and our invitation."

"Why," she enquired, "should the hermit invite us to a masque?"

"My dearest Alice," the time had arrived for plain speaking. "What would you say if I told you that De'Ath is Wordkyn and has long used the Poet's body as a disguise?"

"*If* you told me?" Alice caught her breath. "Are you telling me? But if Wordkyn is De'Ath who is the hermit?"

"De'Ath is De'Ath," I simplified matters, "yet he is more than De'Ath: he assumes many different forms, many shapes, so that we cannot be too careful, too scrupulous in seeking to penetrate his disguises. But, Alice," I glanced around the room, "De'Ath is mad . . ."

"Mad?" she repeated weakly.

"Insane, irrational, call it what you will. He thinks he is your author, my author, Bartleby's author, Throckton's author, the world's author—he thinks he is the author of the world."

"So—?" her hand fluttered to her bosom. This was all new ground to her and I decided to break the news as tactfully as possible.

"Bartleby has been cancelled."

"Cancelled?" she gasped, astonished by my knowledge of chapters other than these.

"Cancelled by De'Ath exercising the same powers over Lungs as he has exercised over Wordkyn; cancelled by De'Ath who seeks dominion over this book and its characters . . ."

"What do you mean: *cancelled?*" she cried, at which I was greatly worried lest she wake the other characters.

"There is no need for alarm," said I pacifically, "I have read what is written. Knowing that I had uncovered the secret of Bartleby's cancellation, the hermit brought him back to his text, not as one Bartleby but two. Both cancellation and bifurcation will be announced by De'Ath *in person* at the end of his little dramatic entertainment, for which, by the way, he has written himself a key part. In the confusion that he has predicated on these two sensationally contradictory premises, the hermit will launch his invasion against the minds of all the characters—including you and I,

Alice. Once he is convinced of his control, then the whole plot—as he has conceived it—will be returned to the pit. Yes: to the pit. I have taken you into my confidence, Alice, because you are the heroine, and I would not like you to be disturbed by these preposterous disclosures of De'Ath's."

"That is very considerate of you," she thanked me. "But what do you intend to do," her first concern was not for Bartleby—and that I found very strange: "when the hermit launches this . . . invasion?"

"I shall immediately announce that I am the hermit, hence depriving De'Ath of his identity, disguise, and auctorial pretensions."

"Not, of course," said Alice, displaying admirable perspicacity, *"not that you really are the hermit."*

"Not that I really am the hermit," said I in confirmation.

"Then who," she asked the inevitable question, "are you?"

"Although I have been disguised as the narrator," said I—and mere modesty could not have prevented me from answering thus—"I am really a sometime would-be bard, your author by implication, Alice, and Bartleby's too."

"So," she uttered the words softly, "you do know what is going to happen next, what will happen next, and what will continue to happen next for all time."—I could not have expressed it better myself.

"Yes," I replied, preparing to rouse the characters for the dawn of our New Age, "by its opposite, I know what is going to happen next. There will be sacrifices, Alice, dialectical sacrifices. The characters, I am afraid, will be surrendered to De'Ath. Let him take them—for what they're worth, he's entitled to them."

"No!" she objected. "You've no right. This isn't their book. You said you would return them to where they came from."

"And so I shall, Alice, so I shall. Think, just think of the ending: your happiness against their lives—hardly *lives*. I've done what I could for them, but given the material, given the age, I don't see what else you could expect."

"My happiness, as you call it,"—bogus and hypocritical morality!—"my happiness is definitely not the issue. Yours perhaps; not mine.

"Then look on their suffering as sanctification instead of sacrifice;" I expressed the only kind of morality she could understand. "Think of the future. In ten, twenty, ten-hundred years, who would have remembered Hautboy, Zog, any and all of them, had it not been for this book whose heroine you are? If you do not believe in happiness, rejoice in their misery, assume it yourself and salve your conscience that way. Let there be no more discussion. What these characters have begun, I will finish; and that, Alice, is that."

"My conscience," said Bartleby's intractable Aunt, "does not trouble me. But you must warn them! You must let them know who the author really is!"

"And let them hang me? They're still capable of that, you know."

"Yes," her voice was stronger, "It's not every day that the author becomes one of his own characters," she halted. "No," she said appreciatively, "it's not every day that the author decides to become a madman." And then Bartleby's Aunt said something which gave me cause for great dismay and perturbation. "I don't suppose," she spoke the offensive words, "there's any chance of your hanging yourself?"

Before I could reply to this unctuous and infuriating proposal, the Knave, his sleep disturbed at the repeated mention of the hermit's name, stirred waxily and opened a pencilled eye; Nat, dreaming of rocking that ole Dixie boat, and of a head with a body, snorted like a horse and awoke to the unquenchable moans of Patricia, herself arousing the spent and spare Bartlebies, conjurations of Waldemar, the sayer of words.

"Well?" said Alice.

"Look after your own neck," said I, "before you take that tone with me. When you've come to your senses, we can talk again."

"Oh, and I was only asking about your health!" she cried. "It's a strain—isn't it?—making yourself an author."

"*Characters of Throckton's New Age*," I ignored her, "*the inaugural day awaits you! The future is ours!*"

"Death to X-Rays!" screamed Wachposten, awaking with a start. "Everlasting life to concrete! Our leader is our hero: a titan amongst men!"—an unfortunate encomium this, as Würzig duly noted:

"Wachposten is an imbecile," he sneered, "a special case. To the cement mixer with him!"

"*Characters, let us present a united front against the divisive forces in our midst!*"—Wachposten was not as great a fool as Würzig thought: his madness, I reflected while Hautboy roused himself to the tintinabulation of hammer and anvil and the fulgent call of a martial horn entry, his madness could be employed in the service of the text—"*The past is hereby abolished! Time has come to a halt! Your narrator declares history is at an end! Let us go forth into the New Dawn of Throckton's Fourth Age! Listen to Bartleby's narrator! Characters of the novel, unite! Ascend, ascend into the dawn! Day One of the New Age dawns!*"

Hence with these and many more persuasive arguments, I got them to ascend, raising them above the lowly and pitiable condition into which, by virtue of their authorless estate, they had allowed themselves to fall.

De'Ath, I swore to myself as we travelled through Throckton's ocherous traps, *I will have your head before this day is over.*

Outside, the crepuscular dawn flew ragged and swift, night's darkness resolving into layers of violet gloom. Blank and breathless, the vast dome of the New Machine squatted above the silhouette of Throckton's New Stage as the opening bars of sunlight struck a play of lengthening shadows and the Machine emerged from partial eclipse to neutral penumbra, its bulk still muting dawn's full chorus. The first sceptre of day's ultimatum was laid upon the sky; purple skeined clouds wove through a tapestry cloth of powdered blue, and Hyperion himself mounted the skies in solitary glory. Eastwards, a flock of giddy birds scattered, mocking the day, unmindful of our mission.

"Dawn," said Alice.

The reader may well smile at the sight of the procession which wound its way down from Throckton's stage into the square and which beheld the glorious substance of the above paragraph. At our head, a babblesome throng of one score and chanting Bartlebies—the name being a fashionable patronymic in this New Age; second (but not second) your ever resolute narrator, in the van of these times, securing his hold on the permanent future, myself, *Bartleby's* narrator-*cum*-creator, accompanied by the huzzar-jacketed Hautboy, tricorn hat flaunting its florid cockade as his badge of forgotten and fallen office, proud Hautboy, sad Hautboy, an up and down, topsy-turvy kind of rebel; with no less—and no more—than the slumbering Zog, borne on a palanquin, his dreams disturbed by the meaning of meaning; Patricia, Pierrot-pale, scarlet-mouthed, she of the green horn and silver coif, authorless and all of a sex; the officious Jack, Estrogen, in princely stained costumery of reds and blacks and golds and whites, torn and creased, a mere Knave, beating after his carrot-headed boy; Waldemar, galactic practitioner, twirling and trailing sun, moon and stars in Dogot's futile quest; Nat, helpless, loose-limbed puppet of a distraught meditation, cradling the remains of the composed and decomposing head, once the proud and tantalant exhibitioner of pre-bellum diaphonous gauze pantalettes; Wachposten-Würzig, as two-in-one as Wordkyn-De'Ath, goose-stepping towards the return of aquiline days; plus the generous-hearted, over-doting, moralizing and contrary Alice, proverbial Guardian to Bartleby—*which* Bartleby? *All* Bartlebies, illusionary or otherwise, that have ever been and are yet to be in the tide of times—plus (I say plus again) a gathering crowd, resurrectees of the metaphoric egg crucified on Throckton's four-pronged signpost, your rough-edged saurians, pink rhinoceri, grey leeches, your scavenger sucking-fish, your sharks, sabre-tooths, hyenas, lice, roaches; the lost and the unlovely, everything zoologic and botanic; your idiot-boys, their brain-blasted brethren, emaraldislanders, formaldehyde foeti, your Josefhansoskars, hoodsandhustlers, punksandpansies, the great twentieth century conflux, inflated and by the minute inflating:—a pneumatic host, puffed up by De'Ath's invitation, expanding with every word while morning glory unfolded into the banked tellurian clouds of Throckton's fictive day, storm clouds presaging eternal night for some— victory for others.

"What happened?" Estrogen employed his curious

facility to eavesdrop on the narrative line.

"Yes, do tell them," said Alice, jostled by a spare Bartleby. "I'm so sleepy, I must have forgotten myself. Something about a masque, wasn't it?"

"Later," said I, "that's later. First, the sun rose over the Machine as I have portrayed it and as you concisely observed it, Alice. Then we met the two rustic gentlemen, each with his boy in halter,"—I referred to De'Ath's MS—"and this colloquy ensued:

" 'Zur,' said the first rustic, 'we be looking for the plot.'

" 'Aaar,' said the second rustic, 'there be ruminations of ha narrator who be warnting Bartlebies.'

" 'Han these,' said the first rustic, 'be Bartlebies.' "

The Knave received this impersonation with sardonic silence.

" 'Look no further,' said I, 'you have found the narrator. And you may rest assured that what you have there are not Bartlebies.' "—this was the first time I realized that Waldemar's conjurations had overflown the confines of Hautboy's sub-scenic apartments.

"No sooner had we descended from the stage and spoken with the rustics than we saw one naked female who, when viewed from the back as we chanced to view her, was not entirely unfamiliar to myself, despite the fact that she was unrecognized by the amnesiacs amongst you, and although she was engaged in the uncharacteristic and heathenish act of salaaming over a recumbent spare boy, whom she had primed . . . "

" 'Sybil!' "—Thus Auntie's perception coincided, or was made to coincide, with my tactical requirements, she watching my rehearsal without any attempt to hide the incredulity that was written across her face—" . . . and primed well. 'Auntie,' said the infant," I adjusted my voice to the presumed tones of the presumed infant, and not for a second did I reveal that the Sepulchral Sister, in her absence from the plot, had become an acolyte of De'Ath's, intending (as he represented the scene) to foist this spare Bartleby on Alice as the genuine article. If the hermit stooped to the deployment of crazed prophetesses, no matter. My diagnosis of insanity was corroborated, and Sybil was one character I

378

would gladly surrender.

" 'That,' you will recollect saying, Alice, '*that* is *not* Bartleby.' Nevertheless, the infant persisted in calling you Auntie . . . "

"What," Alice fluttered, "is wrong with you? Nothing's happened, *none of this has happened!*"

"Not yet, my dear Alice, not yet."

"Cursed are the fornicators! Cursed are the abominations of the earth!"—never was a cry more timely!

"*Characters, see for yourselves: what has not happened is happening!*"

"*Sybil!*"—perceptual lag, reader. "*That* is *not* Bartleby."

I had scarce thought I would ever be pleased to see the Sister again.

"Sybil," Alice chided her gently while the narration proceeded apace, "what do you mean by pretending that this is Bartleby? He's a nice little boy, I'm sure, but he is not my nephew. And where have you been? The narrator—if I may speak for him—the narrator has been very worried about you. So have we all," she added as the square continued to fill with a peculiar super-abundance of proximate five year olds, as if the effects of Waldemar's conjurations were irreversible—

"Into the infernal regions I have been and seen Ixion that was a pagan bound to his wheel and Tantalus that was also a pagan who could not drink!"

"Oh Sybil!"

"But I am healed and have been one with him I loved."

"Then you found him?" Auntie enquired.

"I found him," the Sister replied, "and the earth sank."

"Where is he?"

"Here," said Sybil breathlessly, "always."

Meanwhile, Throckton's natives, regenerated by the flashback and my reconstructive labours, also began to return, eager, inquisitive, and anxious for sport. In droves they came, rude, ruddy yokels with friends and relatives, children and grandchildren, mingling as they had once before with the canaille from De'Ath's pit. Indeed, had it not been for the powerful promptings of an unimpaired memory, which brought to mind the evidence of my own eyes, I could easily have doubted that Throckton had suffered any tumults whatsoever. Nor were Throckton's antecedent broils of any present consequence.

Then behold, reader, the all consumptive present. Behold, the civic throng alive once more; behold the maiden's modest blush:

"*Croons!*"

behold the bumpkin's forward jerky stride:

"Fullis!"

"You too?"

"Haar!"

behold the orchestra, tunelessly tuning in the pit before our New Stage. Let the inaugurating blood course alike through citizens' veins, characters' veins; let the people have their entertainments. O wise counsellors, awake from your slumber of death; shake out the musty periwigs that have been a long hanging in the closet, don your best scarlet robes, and bend your silken white municipal knee joints. Our celebrations begin with this kermess day, and here's an end to De'Ath and his plots!

Ah, the air is spiced with the odours of an excellent confection; there are stalls enough in the marketplace, o'erbrimming with the plenteous sweetmeats, cakes, cookies, and candies. Will you have a pheasant, perhaps? Grouse, partridge, turkey, quail? A leg of mutton? Throckton was always well stocked with sheep. Or a wedge from this fresh ham which comes even now straight from the swineherd's trough? He, by the way, has kept but two of his pigs (the best of them) as objects for the curious to behold—at a price. It is bounteousness itself; you should partake of it, gorge yourself upon it, lest our little feast should stale.

See, here's a man with a tin whistle who sells pies for the prosaic. Pieman, a pie! Here are vendors and hawkers, each with his catchpenny phrase and two-penny book. Oracles there are, palmists and diviners, quacks enough. And behold the glory of our New Age, before which the Masque according to De'Ath will be played: the New Machine, gleaming bright and brassbound. Behold, the ribbons, the flags, the pennants, the streamers! What a deal of clapping, chopping, and hooting! Why, if you were to touch the struts and supports of our recently carpentered stage the paint would tack to your hands, it is so freshly applied.

"I suppose you claim you're responsible for this?" said Alice.

"The author claims responsibility," I replied, *sotto voce.*

"And yet you say these are the actions and this the setting of the hermit's book?"

"Alice, when will you learn to trust me? De'Ath's text is a variant, yes *B2*, you could look at it that way. With a few minor modifications, it is essentially the same as ours."

"Minor modifications?" Auntie shook her head.

"Quiet! The orchestra is ready. The Masque is about to begin."

Behold, the orchestra waits; the conductor's baton is down, now raised—so De'Ath's orchestration. *Down*: the fanfare sounds. The gentlemen will bow, the ladies curtsy. Take your partners, please, for the last dance towards the end of a day that never sets. Sweep, sweep and pirouette, you marionettes of the waltz, dance as you have yet to dance. O happy, happy Age, dance on; there is no life save for the dance.

"Who's putting us through this dumb routine?" Hautboy jigged with a spare Bartleby.

"What do you mean: minor modifications?" Alice danced a quadrille.

"Don't interrupt, you'll ruin the sequence! *Characters*," I began, *but*:

Sybil tripped a light fantastic; Zog, polyp pushing noiselessly at the syllables of an unutterable philosophy, was shaken up on his palanquin, and Nat jived, cat-like, reverting to type as the air was filled with ethereal melodies, elemental voices, words not on this or any page.

"*To each his own dance!*" I cried, drawn into De'Ath's apocalyptic rag-time rhythm.

"The music!" Estrogen screamed, face purpling, eyes roaring like inflamed pressure gauges.

"Leave my eyes out of this!"

"*Out damnable spot, vile jelly!*"

"ESTROGEN!" the Knave howled. "*His eyes fall from his face:* I am blind!"—thus I sacrificed a pawn.

"*Characters*,"—his screams provided a suitable diversion:

381

"*direct your attention to the stage. The Masque, characters, the Masque begins!*"—gobs of gore pulsed thickly down the Knave's face and his eyes hung like grapes on the vine. A theatrical trick, that was all.

"Oh, horrible! horrible!" Auntie threatened a fainting fit.

"It's your fault!"—I let her have it: "For God's sake pull yourself together. None of this was in the book! Who delayed the action? I'll have to begin all over again now."——here was no time for misplaced sympathy.

"Eyes! Eyes! I am blinded!"

"Is that," she turned her horrified gaze from the Knave's bloody cheeks, "one of your minor modifications?"

"A curtain raiser, Alice, a mere curtain raiser to our entertainments. And now, if you'll excuse me—*Characters, await the entrance of THE FIRST MASQUER.*"

Here, reader, is artifice, framed out of the senses' interplay. Then, while Estrogen screams and the dance falls apart, let the conductor take up his baton anew. We shall have to put him through the backwards run and start once more. He would not like his music misunderstood, howeverso polyphonic it may have been. Have you the score? It's best to read from right to left. Thus noise is sucked from our ears; minims to flutes return, crotchets to horns, hemidemisemiquavers are reclaimed by viols. Our conductor turns to the square, unmops his brow, for silence un-raps the stand, and walks backwards into the wings. Now he reappears (for the same action once caught is capable of infinite repetition) and with life and death at his command (though he does not know it) strikes up his pose again, master of silence.

Here, reader, my vindication. Need I remind you that the sleepers awoke, that Sybil returned to the plot? You remember that? Then here is what you have long awaited—the beginning of the end:

*

Being the First Act of a MASQUE Presented in this YEAR of MIRACLES at THROCKTON BY THE BOG before the People to Celebrate this NEW AGE OF MAN, with Several ASIDES and INTER-

POLATIONS Additional to the Performance, Herein Given for their Intrinsic Worth and Merit by the Trusty INTERLOCUTOR, NARRATOR of the Text at Large.

*

Yet the *FIRST MASQUER* did not appear as he had done in the hermit's MS. Instead, this imperial voice walked on:
"Speak, *NARRATOR*."
—and off, and I, the *NARRATOR*, in the character of the *INTERLOCUTOR*, was made to speak, though neither script nor words were mine, and I could not tell who was in the Masque, who without:

*

INT: Are the planets come down amongst men? Is this Saturn or Mars? What fantastic cockerel comes this way: man, planet, god, or cockerel? For he has the look of each and the appearance of neither. See, but how he changes! Why, he has the head of a moose and the feet of a camel. Lo, he wields an ivory sickle in his right hand, a broken arrow in his left and hobbles as easily as the tortoise with the apple grafted on his back! Here's a long life to you, sir, whatever manner of person you may be.

*

Automatic speech, reader, is a gift not given to many. But from my reading of the hermit's text, I did not remember that I had any part to play in the Masque. Did my memory fail me, or had the Masque changed?

"Listen," Aunt Alice was getting angry, "I can't take much more of this. Where is the *FIRST MASQUER* and where is the hermit?"
"Stage-fright. Remember what I told you about De'Ath."—she was chewing at the bit, and wanted an explanation—"Maybe I did go too far with Estrogen, Alice.

His mind," I tapped my forehead significantly, "went over.
The wizard as well. He's next. I shall have to play this round
by ear. Keep calm, that's the most important thing. The
FIRST MASQUER is bound to make his entrace now that
I've described him."

*

ENTER: a CHORUS of Titt'ring NYMPHS and BARTLEBIES.

CHORUS (NYMPHS)

Oh, we Nymphs are here to scamper
In gay abandon unconscious,
So that mortals we may hamper
With our fairy curves a-luscious (Oh!)
But we know not why, oh no! oh no!
We know not why at all, oh no!

CHORUS (BARTLEBIES)

And we are boys supernumary,
Squared on this doubling bliss day;
To test the art of our luminary,
We multiply *magis magisque.*
But we know not how, oh no! oh no!
We know not how at all, oh no!

CHORUS (ENSEMBLE)

Yet what dweller firmamental,
Astronomic, else pure hermetic,
Preternatural, or mere elemental,
Hies this way with face frenetic?
Oh sir, why look you so dyspeptic?
You may be him we've long expected.
But we know not why, *etc.*

*

384

Wordkyn's rhyming pen was in this somewhere! Where was the player? In the wings, he was in the wings, hidden from sight.

"More Bartlebies!" Auntie cried. "How many more Bartlebies are there?"

"They are only *called* Bartlebies," said I. "They are not *actual* Bartlebies, no more than you or I are actual Bartlebies."—Waldemar, this was Waldemar's doing! I reached for my swordstick . . .

"*Cogito ergo sum Bartleby*," Zog's polyp propounded the proposition.

"There's no need to speak in italics all the time," said Alice. "I understand. In any case Bartleby is only *called* Bartleby."—and to prove her point she kissed the blade of Zog's nose: "Bartleby,"—and Hautboy (alas!): "Bartleby,"—Nat too: "Bartleby,"—Wachposten and, "Bartleby," Würzig: "Bartleby,"—Patricia?——"Whooth me?"——"Bartleby," Sybil as well, and Waldemar and Estrogen, cosmetically daubed, and a host of spare boys, until: "Bartleby," she kissed her narrator and whispered in his ear, "I haven't forgotten what you told me. How could I? You're the author, I can see that, honestly I can."———and I was going to tell her that this was no orgy when Waldemar, discovering the sweetness to be had at Auntie's lips, greedily sought them again, and in his lust met not with flesh but steel, piercing himself above the junction of groin and thigh, hence sustaining a delicate hurt which caused him to cry like one who is murdered rather than merely punctured. Even as the protest formed on those lips that had been his object, and even as I wiped my blade, another voice cried out:

"Alice, I was blind when I thought to see most!"

"Sybil," I dropped the italic voice, "the stage. Keep your eyes on the stage. The Masque continues!" I cried, thinking it nothing short of a narrative miracle that it had ever gotten under way.

"Eyes!" screamed Estrogen, cut by an asterisk.

*

*The CHORUS Scatters Stardust. The FIRST MAS-
QUER, Who Is not Named, ENTERS with the Head of a
Moose and the Feet of a Camel. He Describes a Circle with
His Ivory Sickle and Begins to Dance, Hobbledehoy. His
Voice is Muffled, yet Solemn and Grave.*

FIRST MASQUER

Our Leaden Age was gloriously founded
When *Dulness* and *Folly* were compounded.
Hence for this alone our congregation:
To honour a fertile conjugation.
Forthwith let the banns be publicized,
Their bastard, *ERROR*, thus legitimized,
Child of *Dulness*, last of the dreary line,
Sole Star of the Age's wondrous decline.
Yet know *ERROR's* sire, a good man and grey,
Has breathed life out of mortal clay.
Yea, even *Dulness* who at his height
Darkened bright suns in eternal night,
That whatever was lucid, clear, and pure,
On his gaze fell dark, darker and obscure,
Whose gloomy prime did variously sire
A tribe ultra-mundane, our earthy choir,
Wrath, Ginsyawp, Grundegespringer and *O'Goon*,
Chimpanzee, orang-utang, ape, baboon.
Let *ERROR* think on *Folly,* his Beldame's name,
Her Sisters, *Trophy, Dribble, Drab*, and *Flame*;
Let him recall what he has forgotten:
How and wherefore he was first begotten,
When in turgid, slow, prodigious service
Dulness mounted *Folly* to get his bliss,
A massy and mighty, fateful mating—
Long wished for and longer gestating—
Fateful to *Dulness* who died in his task,
Likewise to her who bore thee to this Masque.

The Lights darken

386

Umbrageous *ERROR* shall take pride of place
'Twixt the legs of our benighted race.

ENTER: the SECOND MASQUER, ERROR, Clad as a DILDO.

CHORUS (Severally)

But how improper! How lewd! Not the thing
for young ladies, *etc.*

But on reflection, we're delighted
At the thought of copulation!
We are really quite excited
By this modern form of titillation.
But we know not why, *etc.*

They Scatter more Stardust

FIRST MASQUER

Oh inheritor of the star-crossed Ages,
Informing Spirit of our Modern Sages,
Oh benign, levelling, popular soul,
Of recent wits, consumatory goal,
O *ERROR*, imperturbable tempter of the stoic,
Pray tell us, by all that is mock-heroic,
To what more than divine interference
Owe we your more than manly appearance?

*

Error did not answer straight away, and the pause gave
me time—time to think. On stage and off stage, the infant
boys continued to multiply. Allowing for the demographic
fact of Throckton's rejuvenated population, the predomi-
nance of five-year old pseudo-Bartlebies made a formidable
kink in the curve of probability. Despite his hurt, Waldemar
was still under De'Ath's control, and through his agency the
hermit was attempting to swamp the marketplace with
infants! The wizard, therefore, would have to be dealt with as

387

severely as I had dealt with his fellow board-treader, and it was to this end that I again unsheathed my swordstick, when Alice planted herself in between us.

"No!" she cried. "Are you going to murder us all?"

Running the heroine through was no solution. "Alice," I appealed to reason as the wizard squirmed, "that is the hermit."

"I wish he were!" she wailed frantically. "I wish the old man would appear like you said he would—just so we could see how mad he was then!"

"Do you want to ruin everything?" I caught hold of her wrist and hauled her aside. "The hermit's appearance is no longer in question! He's everywhere, do you understand? Everywhere!"—I held the point of the blade to Waldemar's throat. It would be a mistake to kill him now. Merciful but wrong, for the hermit would change his location. I should have killed him immediately, without any warning.

As things were now, the Bartlebies, directly or indirectly, were controlled by De'Ath, and the hermit's influence had increased, and would go on increasing immeasurably. Failing the return of the real Bartleby (or Bartlebies), the eventual unmasking of De'Ath would give the book to me, but would not solve the problem of the hero's whereabouts. Unmasking? Immediately, the *FIRST MASQUER* fell under the suspicions of my narrative eye: an ivory sickle, the player had an *ivory* sickle! He danced *hobbledehoy!* And his voice was solemn and *grave!* De'Ath that was Estrogen and Waldemar and Lungs and Wordkyn, De'Ath whom I had suspected was Patricia and Sybil (not, at the time, not without reason—though I now saw that the bugger of the western world kept himself to persons of the same sex), and De'Ath who in all likelihood was also the spare boys, *De'Ath was the FIRST MASQUER!*

"Alice," said I, "you can forget about De'Ath. He knows of our plan."

I would wait, wait until he appeared as himself. If he wanted a war of attrition, he could have it. He could wear them all down, possess the entire population: never the narrator! And at the last, what would he have achieved? For at the last I had prepared a narrator-to-hermit confrontation, and his fate would be decreed in these words: *De'Ath, I am you. I am you because you have possessed me, your author.*

But *ERROR*, the talking Dildo, made—*is making?*—shall have made, will make, and does make, his reply to Masquer De'Ath.

*

ERROR(Limbering)

Rough speech is suited to my crude form. Therefore, since I cannot rhyme, I have learnt to swear as well as any country boy. Then know this, that I am *ERROR*, and proud of it too. A bastard I am, whose parents that were natural are now dead.

But why am I here? That I don't know. I'll call upon Abraham's rod, or anybody's rod you care to think on, if you'll tell me why. I'll swear to Jocasta's virtue—she that never knew her son, yet did as well—but I must, by Mary's Mother, Eve, there's corruption in the line, affirm, may the Pope save himself if he does not shit, nay *affirm*, may your brains bubble in the pan of your head and the very Judas guts upon it, him that burst his bowels, and by all the bones at once, may I be tormented for an eternity but I have forgotten what I was about to be affirming!

You may think me soft, but I'm very hard. Upon the Virgin's head, she that is implicated in foulness, then by the guts of Nero's mother, you've asked me a question. (*ERROR Attempts to Cross the Stage towards the FIRST MASQUER but his cumbersome Form Makes Movement Difficult.*) I can give you no answer to it. Oh, this cursing will be the ruin of my digestion. (*Strains.*) God's nails. I cannot move! (*The DILDO Is Paralyzed.*) I'm stuck fast to the spot! I'm fast, hard fast and stuck! I cannot move an inch! Help! Ho, help! By the clap, who are you? Who has done this to me?

ERROR Stands Rooted, Centre-Stage, The CHORUS Gathers Round in a Futile Attempt to Move Him while the FIRST MASQUER, bearing a Crown, Advances.

FIRST MASQUER

Know me as Bishop to my Lord *ERROR'S* king,
Whose Father's to heaven on leaden wing.
Hence to the Son must I give this crown,
Heavy pretender to old Dulness' renown.

*

Small wonder that *ERROR* could not explain his presence! In the hermit's text, Dildo De'Ath had been crowned.
Now he was acting the part presumably to have been filled by
the second actor. They must have switched roles at the last
moment—before coming on stage.

"Eyes!" Estrogen endeavoured to re-insert his left eye
with his right hand, clutching at the retinal artery which
squirted blood at regular intervals.

"If he gets it in," I joked with Alice, "he'll have a fine
squint. The ocular muscles, you know, must be badly torn."
I'm afraid to say her response was rather frigid. "Anyway,
he's got it in the wrong socket." Still no response. "Now
look," said I, "look around the square. You remember those
characters, don't you?" I drew her attention away from the
Knave to the less edifying spectacles from the pit, encap-
sulees of the addled egg: "You remember that you were once
amongst them as a prisoner? You didn't complain then. So
why this sudden lily-livered pity for him?"

She was silent. "They're nothing, nothing at all," I said.
"Q.E.D, Alice," a snick of my swordstick on the sleeping
Zog's ear brought a gasp from her. A gasp of delight—hah!
Perhaps she really was enjoying the situation. "And
Hautboy," I flexed the sword, "he can be cured with this
too." Yes, when the time came it would be a fatal move if
De'Ath chose Hautboy. "Better not try anything, Hautboy,"
my sword swished down to his groin. "Where there's a will,
there's a way."

But Hautboy merely stood, legs bowed, eyes tightly
shut—anticipating an amputation I did not make. "There's
the Dildo, Hautboy. Open your eyes now, because you might
have need of it. I hope it's large enough for you."—His sense
of humour was not what it had been.

The rest of my thoughts I kept closely to myself and watched De'Ath. They were my thoughts, not his. *Or were they?* Again, I was made to speak another's part. It was all very Brechtian: character speaks from audience and so forth. If De'Ath believed he could force my hand by such a cheap trick, he would have to think again!

*

INTERLOCUTOR

Time and tide have strangely flown,
This Masque is mine, yet not my own.
That art is play and pure illusion,
I will make short this allusion:
Begin with nothing, end the same,
Out of the void, a face and no name,
Scarce able to crawl, yet made to walk,
Unwilling to speak, compelled to talk,
He learns to laugh as well as cry,
Upright is forced at last to lie—
Man, Masque, and Game called nil?
The art is all—for good or ill.

CHORUS

And he knows not why, not why at all!

FIRST MASQUER

Our *DILDO* thinks he will be anointed,
Then needs must he be sore disappointed.
Grave communion is here prorogated,
Lest all our actions be abrogated.
We who have too many parts dissembled,
May not move till our cast is assembled.
Then with roaring, babbling, tumult and rout,
Let *ERROR'S* bastard tribe be loosed about!

ENTER the HANGING AUTHORS as Courtiers, Much Decomposed, with the THIRD MASQUER, HARMONY, in Bridal Dress, Their Prisoner.

FIRST MASQUER (Continued)

Move, if move you will, and do your worst.
As I am the last, I shall be the first.
Within the Masque, appearances change—
I must exit now, a few trifles to rearrange.   *Exit.*

The MASQUERS and CHORUS Freeze

*

Nobody moved! Not a soul! De'Ath walked off with the crown, bore it away. Where was he going? He couldn't leave the book; there was nothing for him outside these pages. I was the only one who was allowed to leave the book. De'Ath didn't have my permission to go anywhere:

"Characters," I urged, "*ceaseless and unremitting vigilance is demanded!*"—that should appeal to Wachposten-Würzig. No?

Stasis. Traumatized, they were traumatized by the return of their authors. Who wouldn't have been? It was not every day that Lazarus gibbered and grinned from the grave.

Yet dead though they were, the authors had entered like living men! Suspended animation: the authors had been hanged in space not time. And yet, and yet they were dead: putrescent, fanged, bruised—the sweet drainage of death sugared their courtly robes and sparkled in the morning sun.

"*Hautboy!*"—silent: "*Zog!*"—more than silent: "*Nat!*"—nothing: "*Patricia, then?*"—no response: "*Sybil!*"—the sepulchre itself: "*Alice, Auntie Alice?*" — — even she, wordless!

"Characters,"—the entire square: silent—"*your narrator announces the end of ACT ONE!*"

CHAPTER FORTY   *Wherein the Masque Is Continued and a Prime Masquer is Unmasked.*

On stage, off stage, life stirred within the quick and the dead. On stage, the hanging authors jerked like cadavers animated by a galvanometric current; off stage, the host drew breath, one host, possessed of one mind and one will. As in the days of my absent narratorship when I had given life to lost souls, so they that were now possessed by De'Ath would become mine. A transfusion of narrative life! Even if I drained every vein and cell, the transfusion would be achieved. I armed myself for the supreme sacrifice: *"Characters, your narrator gives you life!"* Silence and stillness. Wachposten-Würzig's right arm stiffened. A sharp, blood-drawing stab of my swordstick to the arm proved that he lived:

"HEEEIIIIIIIIIIIIL!"

"Your narrator is the incarnation of this text! Through him you shall be as you once were!"

"I wish to God," Alice observed wryly, ministering to Wachposten-Würzig's injured arm, "I wish to God you were up there where you belong!"

"Characters, ACT TWO begins with the FIRST MASQUER's return."—no FIRST MASQUER.

When under pressure, was it not best to give? I recalled that resistance to hypnosis frequently guarantees its eventual and increased effectiveness. To resist was to surrender, but to surrender was to be victorious!

Half within, half without the Masque, I began the

Second Act, upon this direction: *The INTERLOCUTOR Declaims from the Audience.* I who had alone escaped possession, now welcomed it, opening my mind to De'Ath's influence with these words, words not mine, nor yet the hermit's.

*

INTERLOCUTOR

Never more to bardship shall I intend,
To be a narrator no more pretend.
What the cause of this renunciation?
Why, *ERROR'S* dreadful annunciation.

*

Nothing happened! I had invited the hermit to take over my mind, and he had refused.

Whose text was De'Ath using? Whose words were being spoken? And whose voice was the speaker? A third version: *there was a third version of the Masque!* Then whose? Wordkyn's: *Wordkyn the Poet's?* If I had just spoken his lines, the Poet's lines, De'Ath was not the enemy at all! His ancient frame, the written-upon-shroud, the emaciated mask, *even the hermit's plot*—these were the inventions of *Wordkyn!* Then had I not slandered De'Ath? Maligned him? What if he were an honest and harmless old man? A nice old man, yes ... And I had acknowledged that Wordkyn was the author! De'Ath was Wordkyn in disguise, not *vice-versa,* and when Wordkyn had appeared he had had the effrontery to appear as himself! Wordkyn had implanted the idea that he was De'Ath in order to make me concede his authorship. Yes, yes, it began to make sense. Wordkyn's MS was not the same as mine, nor was it identical with De'Ath's. No two MSS were alike, although they shared common characteristics. He who imposed his will across the texts, at a point where they had most in common, was the collator.

Collator! Here was a role, the supreme narrative role, which art had framed for me: all texts subsumed through one man, all texts made incarnate in their Throcktonian representative!

Stage by stage we progress to supreme authority, and before I assumed the mantle of the Collatorship I made reason the servant of ambition. In the sleight of one paragraph I had uncovered the most amazing subterfuge; it was Wordkyn, not De'Ath, who had invaded the minds of the characters, it was Wordkyn who had hypnotized De'Ath, not De'Ath who had hypnotized Wordkyn. The Poet was responsible for the spare boys, Wordkyn had cancelled and duplicated Bartleby, Wordkyn had murdered and reproduced the authors.

I put myself in the Poet's position. No doubt he would come on at the end of the Masque as Wordkyn the Dramatist, Wordkyn the Poet, Wordkyn the Novelist, and indeed Wordkyn the Collator. I could not help but smile at all this and the truth of the old adage; the more things change, the more they stay the same. For I had only to wait until Wordkyn appeared to present myself as the Poet instead of the hermit. Meanwhile, Wordkyn, not De'Ath was the *FIRST MASQUER*.

"Characters, the FIRST MASQUER re-enters!"

*

The THIRD MASQUER, HARMONY, upon Her Presentation to ERROR by the HANGING AUTHORS, Speaks these Lines.

HARMONY

I, fair Cousin of the Camenae Nine,
And Sister Goddess of the Graces Three,
Have ever held Mortals sway by Divine
Law—archetype of lower decree—
Heaven's very own melodious Rule,
In Harmony fixed as pure and free
As in measured days of Attic grace,
Bringing peace to men and honoured name,
Am dragged before this licentious fool

ERROR—he to complete the Age's shame—
Mid counterfeiters, flatterers and knaves,
Fools, backbiters, panders after fame,
Stinking hot from ignominious graves,
Here to stamp, moan, hoot, jeer and applaud
Their own meanest conceits. Bondsmen, slaves
Be called, not authors. Hacks to record
Baseless deeds at Master *ERROR's* behest,
To cozen, cheat, swindle and defraud.

Oh, who will stay the desperate deed
And HARMONY rescue in perilous need?

CHORUS

Oh, we know not who, not who at all!

*

Who was I to prevent the match? The *HANGING AUTHORS* were evidence enough that it had already taken place.

No, I awaited the return of the *FIRST MASQUER*. A great traducer and worthy opponent, Wordkyn.

"Alice," I informed the heroine of this latest development, "De'Ath was Wordkyn but Wordkyn is De'Ath."

"Ah," said she, not comprehending.

"I mean . . . " Concentrate on the Masque. De'Ath was a nice old man, he was. Must make amends. Wrong, yes, I had been wrong. And the Poet?—Zog was showing signs of unseasonable activity. The polyp pushed beyond the blade of his nose, colonizing the face—What's Zog got to do with it? Who was—is—the narrator? Think.— —*Wordkyn was subverting Zog in an attempt to destroy the sequence!*— —

"And Zog, Alice," I held the swordstick under his chin, "Zog is Wordkyn who was De'Ath but not any more."

"Tell them, tell them that you are the hermit," said she breathlessly.

"Puh-puh-puh! Puh-puh-puh!" — a battery of labial plosives popped from Zog's polyp.

"Godammit! Now of all places!"—Hautboy. What was he complaining about this time?

"Posit! Posit!" cried the unhappy Zog as a wet, warm sphinctral odour regaled my narrative nostrils, an odour expressive of a whole theory of poetry.

So Wordkyn evacuated his host! The Poet was afraid.

To a man the *HANGING AUTHORS* acted on Zog's positing as a cue, and to a man they advanced, and advancing spoke with one voice, and with one voice berated *HARMONY*.

And I, not wishing to seem over hasty, I reserved judgement on the reappearance of the *FIRST MASQUER*.

*

HANGING AUTHORS

Wench, there's no good wailing;
See, our Master's already straining.

The DILDO, having regained His Freedom of Movement, Limbers Towards HARMONY and the HANGING AUTHORS Continue:

We'll have you married to him,
Though you think him gruesome.
Such a nuptial we've long mooted;
Who are you to dispute it?
His erection is incredible;
We hope his aim is infallible,
And his load indelible,
That the child will be sellable,
Of this merger so ineffable.
For the line we must preserve,
Therefore *ERROR* you deserve.
Bed him as your rightful spouse,
And all the issue goes to our House.

ERROR

These dogged sayers of doggerel call me legitimate—I that was never so before—and tell me I'm to be king. A

397

plague take them, king of what? May you be buried up to your necks in the deserts of your mind and may the vultures, the Critics, peck piecemeal at your livers. What, how if buried? Oh, I must give up this vile illogic of cursing. May you perish horribly, your innards drawn out into your mouths that you shall swallow them and be made whole again.

But if I'm legitimate, there's time enough for bastardizing. They do tell me I'm to be married. By Beelzebub's iron bladder, my spleen stings at the thought. Bilious churls! Marriage! Was Adam married? I'll be trapped in Vulcan's engine or wracked out on Procrustes' bed before I'll take the other bed. A whole army of gullible Josephs would not get me to that plight!

But *copulation*, you cullied scum, there's something else now. Oh, to dip my whole self's length in *HARMONY's* honeyed maidenhead. But where's the stringent for this mouth? Gag, abominable culvert; oaths stay action but never me!

So Saying ERROR Plunges at HARMONY, an Advance which Marks the Reappearance of the FIRST MASQUER, Who, Ivory Sickle and Crown Raised on High, and Brandishing his Broken Arrow, Steps Between the Pair:

FIRST MASQUER

Stay, *ERROR*, wilt thou not be crowned king
And have us our low hosannas sing?
Yet first before your Highness' coronation,
Know this my part has no termination.
Another story remains still untold,
And that shortly must I unfold:
Of *BARTLEBY*, the *Hero*, and his fate,
Of authorship passing strange must I relate.

ALL

BARTLEBY! Authorship! How comes this? *Etc.*

*

398

Authorship? Wordkyn himself? Wordkyn was going to claim that he was the author. Mentally, I prepared myself for his bid.

"What," said Alice, the strangest light in her eyes, "what does *he* know of Bartleby?"

"*Characters*,"–the Poet was expecting me to unmask him as De'Ath: what better way to destroy my credibility before the assumption of his mantle, than to fall in with his desires?–"*Characters, the FIRST MASQUER is the hermit De'Ath!*"––or: "*The hermit De'Ath, our author!*"

Hence I concealed my real intentions from Wordkyn who now brought an abrupt halt to the coronation.

*

FIRST MASQUER

Apologies, Highness, if we prevaricate;
Far be it from me thus to divaricate.
Please, *voices* you may call your own, mine
Your *ears* by vested right and deep design,
Stay then and powerlessly listen,
These sad chapters will make *eyes* glisten.
In a trice, lordings, know me for what I am,
For here's an end to all theatrical sham!

The FIRST MASQUER Removes His Mask and Is Revealed as the Hermit, DE'ATH, Wonderfully Changed, His White Locks Crimped and Curled, and His Wrinkled Countenance Pressed Smooth.

ALL

The Hermit, *DE'ATH?* But how amazing!

*

Even Estrogen managed a "Fuckit!" at this news and I had to admit that I had underestimated Wordkyn who appeared not as himself but as the hermit. Of course, his was a very imperfect disguise, for the Poet was so much younger than De'Ath himself.

"Ho! The Charnel House Keeper and teller of tales!"—the disguise was enough for Sybil.

"It ain't right!" Nat screamed. "Ah's gwina fix dat white fuckah, yessah!"—Nat at least was ready to revert to his novel of origin: "Chunk! Chunk!"——He aimed the dead head, now in a condition of indescribable manginess: "It ain't right being a paper nigger! It ain't right, missy, being a head without a body!"———and would have hurled it there and then had I not intervened as a narrator should by slashing at his wrists, almost severing one of his hands clean from the arm, but my cutting edge was somewhat blunted of late and the bone too formidable.

Where, I wondered as Alice ripped her skirts for a tourniquet—she had finally found her vocation—where was the real hermit? I had an ally in that old man, and all along I had maligned him, yes. He was biding his time, he was, and I would bide mine; act in conjunction with him, I would.

"You *butcher!*"—I was suddenly conscious of Alice's hysterical cries: she had succumbed to the Poet's influence!—"The *FIRST MASQUER* is Wordkyn, is he? You madman! *Characters*," she gave a terrible and rabid laugh, "*the FIRST MASQUER is Wordkyn!*"

My response to this word-mongering was quite calculated. I slapped her hard across the face, and then I spoke not as the narrator but as the *INTERLOCUTOR*. Anything, anything to make the Poet believe I thought he was De'Ath.

*

INTERLOCUTOR

He is returned from flying journey,
And over us seeks power of attorney
To execute his darkest will—
Crazed craving knows no fill.

DE'ATH *Crosses Between the HANGING AUTHORS and HARMONY to Hold Centre Stage:*

400

DE'ATH (In Person)

Surprised? I trust not. His powers are limitless.
Oh, he has flown where the seeming boundless
Firmament knows her plain and astral limit,
Descrying there suns rolling from out suns,
Creation itself at heaven's crystal margent.
Such things has he done that would chill the blood.
On Medusa's serpent head himself has gazed:
Vaulted credit to o'erlook the fabled Cockatrix,
Dung born serpent that ne'er once harmed him.
From substance elemental have I fabricked
Rare beings, made visible at my command,
Welding their parts with noble congruency,
By science dismissing them whence they came.
I have plundered the darkest charnel house
Where proud and lofty monarchs make no sound
And all is peace, all is still, all is dust;
Deep ocean gorges he has dared to plumb,
Held sweet intercourse with abysmal monsters
Who slept in fronds, wished to know his name,
Fed him sea-wracked mariners, and sped him
Yet on his way. Thence to other planets did
He swim, further galaxies movelessly moved,
An infinity of worlds not guessed at:
Calm seas beyond Earth's turbulent beach,
Frigid deeps, devoid of life, thus lifeless—
Deathless—and so dreamless, unfit for him.
In the Parliament of Gods he spoke with them
That would project the world's reformation,
Saw men with panes of glass their hearts to show,
He that knew all men through historical time;
This he has done, this seen, and more to tell.
What brave challenger dare show me the glove,
Who contend his timeless authority?

CHORUS

Have you finished?

401

No! But rhetoric enough has been spent.
He is thine only begetter, author and reaper;
Know him thus, and he will finish the book.
Then herewith certain prodigal chapters—
That were lost and now are found—
These it is his business to expound.

CHORUS

Oh, we know not why, not why at all, oh no!
Nor even if we are to believe him,
Tho' not to would sorely grieve him.
Therefore we'll stay here as we are,
But we know not why, not why at all, oh no!

*

"Now do you see who he is?" cried Bartleby's Aunt.

See? Dear me, no! Wordkyn, false, fleeting Wordkyn had read my mind like an open book—but he had not written it, no, not written my mind, for I was Wordkyn and Wordkyn's author. The De'Ath that had been Wordkyn was now Wordkyn as De'Ath and Wordkyn as De'Ath expected me to unmask him as De'Ath *which I had done in error*, mistakenly thinking that Wordkyn was underneath those written-upon robes. What had the Poet done with De'Ath? That poor old man, yes, what had tried his best to help the plot along—in his own way, nobody else's way, *my* way, yes. Must have stolen his head and his cerements and his bone. No! No! The Poet had done nothing: I had been wrong, yes wrong about the Poet. Wordkyn was not wearing De'Ath's written-upon robes. De'Ath was the hermit himself, *in person!*

"Now do you see who he is?" Auntie's hands *were* bloody.

I said, I said—didn't I? The *FIRST MASQUER* is De'Ath, not De'Ath as Wordkyn or Wordkyn as De'Ath, no: *De'Ath as De'Ath, yes.* How did I know? I was the hermit wasn't I? The hermit was the enemy, not the Poet. I was the enemy.

What did he mean? If he was De'Ath what did that make me? He could have my mind but not my body. Every mental phenomenon is an aberration of matter. The central nervous system is a parasite, infiltrating deep into the tissues of the body. Objectively speaking, the hermit was mad. Subjectively, he must think himself quite rational. What a pity there had been no time to discuss the subject-object relationship with Alice. Blood is an object, liquid is an object, blood is liquid: all objects are liquid.

"*Objects,*" the narrator heard himself speaking, "*that which knows itself as object is the subject. The subject is not liquid but solid and permanent. I am that subject. Objects, prepare to receive your subject!*"

CHAPTER FORTY-ONE   *Which is Nothing of the Kind.*

The enemy would never get into my body! I would never retreat! Not in a thousand years! And yet within another chapter I would have been De'Ath. A chapter? A paragraph! A sentence! A word! That close. He had gotten that close!

"Have you tasted honey? Oh, fol-de-rol. Hi-ti-ti-tum. Where the bee sucks, there suck I, ti-tum. Oh dear me, yes!"

Viewed impartially as object to my subject, De'Ath had no existence; viewed impartially as object to his subject, I had no existence. Since objects are liquid and since our relations are essentially triangular, the text demanded the supravention of a third being. To this third (imaginary) being I assigned the nominal value: W; to De'Ath: D; to myself: I.

Empirically speaking, I (and despite the objectivity of our discussion, let us not forget who I was), I had two options: the physical destruction of W and D; or, their absorption and reduction to create a fourth entity: C: the Collator or Subject, Subject everlasting, Subject without object.

De'Ath, however, remained stubbornly uncollated. Outside the head of I, he continued as D. So much the better! What did he know of Bartleby and Bartleby's Bartleby? Perhaps he intended to bring them back and claim credit for it. As Collator, the ultimate credit would be mine not his.

Meanwhile, concentrate on the narration. *"Fol-de-rol:"* what did he mean? And the missing chapters—what missing chapters? Let him do the explaining. No wonder the crowd thinks he's De'Ath instead of me. Yes, the hermit in person, wearing his own skin. Mad. A patient watcher on all the world's ages. Crazed beyond endurance by small entrances and smaller exits.

But De'Ath was a smooth deliverer—when he got underway: *a-hackle, a-hack!*

"*Characters, the object claims there are missing chapters. Let him produce them!*

"And he will, he will: Chapters Sixteen and Seventeen. Does he remember?"

"*See p. 108 above,*" my reply was public. "*Chapters Sixteen and Seventeen are not missing!*"

CHAPTER SIXTEEN *As Told by Its Author, De'Ath, upon the Subject of the World's Reformation.*

"Have you tasted honey? Oh, fol-de-rol. Hi-ti-ti-tum. Where the bee sucks, there suck I, ti-tum. Oh dear me, yes."
With these words, the hermit De'Ath opened his bid for authority.

"Friends, for so says I in the hope that none here's an enemy to old De'Ath, I'm not one of your methodical hermits, not your regular anchorite, no, and begs your worships' forgiveness if what he has to say is out of place. But he's waited a good many chapters, he has, and been a good many places, yes, and he's waited a long time for this opportunity, not that time matters to him what has all the time in the world, but I'll take it very kindly if you'll hold your peace until he's finished, and much good may it do you, tee-hee!

"If your memory's as long as mine, friends, what's often wandered down memory's shaded lane,"—*Eyeless in Throckton, Estrogen howled down De'Ath's relentless metaphor*—"straying over the crooked stile of recollection, vaulting the babbling brook of oblivion, yes, you'll remember how—and I uses the word advisedly, knowing how you has all been forgetting things, I does, yes, but he's an old man with a memory what's as long as this book, and longer—I says, *remember* how in the old play I was sent to this goodly earth them multitudinous years ago, such an age past that he's almost forgotten himself, and would have forgotten but that it was brought to me mind not thirteen chapters since as he will be telling you, he will, how he was sent here like he was saying, sent with the object of reforming man and preparing him for his Creator, that he might stand before the bar of universal judgement and be purged of his sins, or not purged of them, in which case he goes straight down there, he does, and becomes the property of the other party. Oh yes, in the beginning was De'Ath and De'Ath was in with God, he was, bosom friends we was, God and me, enjoying a very business-like relationship, yes, and all was right in God's heaven and we had regular transactions, we did. But I'm coming to that all in its proper time and place where it belongs, and if he gets lost or strays down that winding path, he begs you not to interrupt 'cos he tends to lose track a bit, he does, on account of him being immortal, yes.

"Ah, those was palmy days. The world and I was younger then and books was rare—though not so rare as they is today—and that yard of which I have care was not so full as it is now. A fine time I had of it, I did, for I was held in respect by all and was sure of everyman's ears just like how I've got your ears now; yes, De'Ath played many parts, he did, he was everything ecclesiastical and secular, he was. Why, if he was to tell you what he was (him that was always a sinister pressman), it would be a new principle of composition and would run to a new book. He's been nothing honest and full of promises; is told confidences in trust and betrays them in the open, has played chess with scholars and tennis with kings, has sold bad ale to peasants and swilled worse wine with the gentry, is bold and subtle, coarse and genteel, is known as nothing and everything, and is given as many names as God whose sower's reaper he is and shall ever be while men live and his work lasts. And he works with many things, he does; with sores and pustules, plagues and agues, chills and faints, fevers and flushes, rheums and rickets, cankers and tumours; there's not a part he doesn't know, such as your ducts and valves, tracts and vesicles, he's in them all, he is, in your blood and marrow, yes; but most of all he likes a brain, he does, a nice soft, warm pink brain what's like a second home to him that never had nothing but a grave to sleep in. Yes, he gets into his brain, he does, and curls himself up in the seat of madness and folly and pride."—*Not this one, De'Ath, not this brain. No . . .*

"But not until this seventh and latest age of man has he been an author, friends, in circumstances he'll now proceed to narrate. 'Cos he's a narrator too, he is,"—*He is, is he?*—"yes, he is, not like that one what's had charge of this book, no; old De'Ath has his faculties about him, not like your narrator, friends, what's mad. Oh, I shall have him, in the yard I shall have him, bugger him I shall, like what I buggered the Baron Hank Caughlin Mangaravidi D'Arcy Fitz Kelly Mordant, him what broke me shanks, and the Baron before him, a great lecher he was, yes, but I got him in the end just like I'll get this narrator, for he's De'Ath's character as I am me own, yes!"——*But not in the body, De'Ath, because I am C, the fourth entity whose will is the will of the text, the one text, the text universal and collated without end. Not in the body, De'Ath; the Collator's bodily will shall endure for a thousand pages!*

"Objects, to whom do you owe your existence? Who has brought you into being? Whose will is your will? Objects, your Collator contines the struggle for the well-being of this text!"

"*Shurrup!* You's outside of yourself, you is. Get back in where you belongs. You's mine, all mine, yes, 'cos next to God—and it is of God he wants to speak, if you doesn't butt in on him—next to God, he's all the world's author, he is—not that he had to do any writing till of late. Then he writ on himself, all over his robes, yes, half on his parchment and half on his robes, on account of his forgetting his tallow down in the ———. Tut-tut, yes, I says to meself, I says, 'Where's me tallow, De'Ath? What's that noise, *eh*?' But let that pass. Yes, where was he now? Tsk-tsk, you is getting forgetful, De'Ath, full of forgetfulness you is. All on that lunatic's account, it was, that he was called to God, sudden like and out of the blue, a bolt from the blue you might say. Not like in the old days, no. He didn't have so much as a Jacob's ladder, and as for your premonitory warnings, your thunderings and light-nings—well! 'Just when the plot's going nicely,' he thinks to himself, 'This has to happen. Almost rounded up all the characters, I had, made them his own and put them back in the book. *Talking head? There was no talking heads in it!* He remembered! He remembered perfect, he did . . . ' No, it wasn't like them days of yore when he had regular and proper appointments with the Lord and he used to be sent an angel or two, but violent and unexpected like. 'I want an explanation,' says God. 'What are you doing up here? I didn't send for you.' 'It's the book,' says I. 'Not that again,' says He, 'I thought we'd been through all that.' 'I mean *another* book,' says I, but once God's set His mind on something there's no turning him away from it. 'I told you to leave the book alone,' says He. 'I suppose they'll be translating it next. What a Babel that will be.' 'They already has, God,' says I. 'But that was a long time ago, God, ages and ages, yes.' 'It only seems like yesterday,' says God, becoming all nostalgic like, 'since you was up here last time, De'Ath. The days come and the days go, my dear old reaper. One day's the same as another. I've read all the books, De'Ath . . . ' 'This is a new book, God,' says I. 'I don't suppose you've reformed the world yet, have you?' says God. 'No,' says I, 'but that was a long time ago, God. If you hadn't have muddled the first chapter then things might have been different . . . ' 'The secret society,' says He, brightening, 'did you start the secret society?' 'Centuries ago,' says I. 'God, I keep trying to tell You, it's a different book.' 'Then what about the Crucifixion?' says He. 'Too much was expected of it,' says I. 'People forget, they's always forgetting.' 'What about the coliseum,' says God, 'what about the burnings? What about all the martyrs?' 'That didn't work either,' says I, 'none of that worked. Why doesn't You listen to me, God: *it's a different book!*' 'Plagues?' says God, 'Pestilences? Famines? Wars? Miracles? Individual chastisements? Global catastrophes? Tyrants? Have you tried them?' 'All,' says I. 'Now, about this book, God . . . ' 'Then it's Armageddon, De'Ath, that's what it is: *Armageddon!*' 'I don't have the authority myself, God,' says I. 'It would seem rather drastic,' says God. 'Drastic's the Word for it,' I says, 'but it's up to You. What would happen to my job if you put the screws on, God? Now, concerning this here . . . ' '*Book*,' says He. 'My dear old reaper, I may appear simple at times but I *am* omniscient. I know what you've been doing down there with those authors. Now where did you find the authority for that? It wasn't very successful, was it?' 'No,' says I, 'they escaped, after I fell into me plot, they escaped, God, because of that talking head, yes, got away they did. Don't be Wrathful, God. I was only trying to make things better.' 'I think,' says He, 'it was because you wanted the field for yourself.' " —*My very thoughts, reader! God and I are once more in agreement!*— " 'You wanted to be an author, didn't you? And that would have put you in the pit with the rest of them, wouldn't it, De'Ath?' 'And did, God, and did, yes.' 'Don't quibble with me, De'Ath!' " — — —*God exposes the hermit's designs!*— — — "No interruptions! Does you hear me? How does you know what He said next? Who does you think you is? 'There's only one thing for it,' says God, and I 'opes you's listening, 'yes, there's only one thing to do.' 'What's that, God,' says I, 'what's to do?' 'Well, De'Ath,' says He, 'if you can't beat them, join them. Since you're in the book, you have My full authority to do what you like with the characters.' " — —*A lie! Lies! All lies!*— —"Gospel Truth. 'Yes, says God, 'I'll give you a new face, De'Ath, and renew your contract. Reform the world, reform the book, but for My sake do something with the plot—and do it quickly.' 'That's very conformable of you, God,' says I, 'thankee kindly.' 'Wait,' says He, 'what do you intend to do with the hero, by the way?' 'I'm glad you mentioned that,' says I, 'because I was just coming to it. All in good time, God. All in good time . . . ' 'Dismissed,' says God."

Alright then. You know who I am, don't you? Yes, God's on my side, He is, De'Ath, because I am you, yes. You see I stopped your invasion, De'Ath. Threw it back. You didn't even establish a bridgehead, no. What a surprise you've got coming, my dear old reaper and ancient Sexton. Buggerum, buggerum, buggerum, boo!

"The world," Alice observed aside, 'has lost its head."— to which eternal truth I would ordinary have given my consent, but not being quite myself, said:

"Don't interrupt him!"

"*Ahhh!*" De'Ath continued. "*That's a nice narrator;*

that's what he likes to hear, he does. But dismissed, he was, dismissed from Apollo's presence. Reform the book, he will. And he will, he will, he will, he will, won't he? There's no doubt about it, no. Oh, he'll be a daffodil: a very sunny occupation. Yes, he'll be a daffodil before he's a turnip, for he's all the world's author which is the same as being a daffodil. And he has all the world to change, he has. Began with himself, he did. A new face, it was; old De'Ath reformed in specific. But reformation in general, *a-hackle, a-hack,* there's a task for wise men and old gods.

"Down he came to the Masque, skirting the wicked constellations with their populations of vices, lusts, spectres, your framed images of shame, greed, and error, your *summum malum* of earthly history. He met a god there he did, a god what would change the stars themselves to effect a sort of cleansing. But De'Ath's not a god, no, so he listened, yes, for once he listened. What a chatter there was amongst the gods; such goings ons! Rumour's quick to fly up there. 'De'Ath's to reform the world,' they said. 'What again?' Yes, they knew. 'Then we'll help the hermit, that he may succeed where we have failed.' Then this same god made a brave speech. Let me see if I can recall it properly. It's in me mind somewhere—*a-hackle, a-hackle.* Bless me soul, here it is as it was spoken.

" 'Oh, let not the dawn's rosy fingers expose the iniquity of our corruption. Take hands, gods, to celestial levers of purest intellect; work, operators, upon the world of clay. From heaven cast out URSA MAJOR, that BEAR of Deformity, and let Harmony take his place; from SAGIT-TARIUS withdraw the ARROW of Infamy (I have it here, masters); here's an end to CORVUS that CROW of Ill-Luck and Imposture, to CANIS MAJOR and MINOR, LARGE and LITTLE DOGS of Muttering and Servility, to EQUULEUS, LITTLE HORSE of Levity, and to the HERCULES of Strong Might. Begone LYRA of Conspiracy and PLEIADES of Faction; farewell Impious and Fraudulent TRIANGLE; let us drive out BOOTES that some call ARCTOPHYLAX of Falsehood and Crime; no more let us think of CEPHEUS of Cruelty and Foolish Faith, of CASSIOPEIA, his wife, known

410

for her Vanity, mother to ANDROMEDA the Slothful, nor of her savior PERSEUS, bringer of Vain Anxiety. May we forget CYGNUS, SWAN of Neglect; DRACO, DRAGON of Jealousy; OPHIUCHUS, the Serpent Bearer of Evil-Fame; AQUILA, EAGLE of Vainglory; DELPHINUS the Talking Dolphin and Matchmaker, known well for Salaciousness; EQUUS MAJOR, LARGE HORSE of Bad Temper; ERIDANUS, RIVER of Excess; HYDRA, SEA MONSTER and Longest Tale-Bearer of All, famed for Concupiscence; CETUS (you may catch the Tale), WHALE and Creature of Gluttony, ORION, GIANT HUNTER of Ferocity. Let us sit upon the ground and for Zeus' sake have done with ARGO the Envious, divided into four rooms. with LEPUS the Timid; GORGON the Ignorant; CRATER, the CUP of Drunkenness; LIBRA, BALANCE of Evil-Doing; CANCER, CRAB of Slowness and Indirection. Let us never be known to CAPRICORN the Deceitful, nor to SCORPIO the Fraudulent; nor to the CENTAUR of Animal Lusts, nor yet to the CORONA BOREALIS and AUSTRALIS, TWIN CROWNS of Pride and False Law. Let us not bring gifts before ARA, ALTAR of Superstition, nor worship PISCES, Unworthy FISH of Shameful Silence. May Truth and Goodness drive out Lying and Defect from URSA MINOR; may those Indecent TWINS, GEMINI, no longer lay with each other; may TAURUS the BULL abandon Pettiness; the RAM, ARIES, think of others, and may LEO leave off his Tyranny. Here then is AQUARIUS cured of his Dissoluteness and VIRGO of her Persiflage. *Sic itur ad astra*, may all the constellations be cured of their vices and addictions, for the greater glory of men and the gods.'

" 'Nothing's happened,' I says, 'the stars is still there, Jupiter.' 'No they's not,' says he, 'they's all gone out.' Well, you can't argue with that, and I thinks to meself, 'Now's the time to be on your way, De'Ath.'

"Yes, so he came down to the Masque he did, with a mask of his own. And though he's been around, he has, up and down, yes, though he's a very, very old man, he'll continue to reap—it's the best he can do in the unreformed world. Yet, friends, yet may you 'ope to improve the world by abolishing reformers, or keeping them to their ordained offices which is the proper regulation of vegetables. As for himself, he got him a Mask, he did, and hid corruption that way, behind his Mask, yes. And he would advise you to do the same, he would, 'cos the brighter the Mask the better the world will seem to look on. He would, but he won't, no, on account of the fact that he knows your ears is deaf when it comes to his advice. Just like that nice little boy, yes. What did I tell him? 'Seek God or the other party,' I says. Did he take any notice? No, he didn't listen to me. An old man like me that's got brains. I's got plenty of them, pickings, that's what they is: pickings."

"Bartleby! Where is Bartleby?"—Alice, and:—

"*I*"—Hautboy, possessed of De'Ath, "*am*"——run him through the guts: thrust *in*, and *out*, the steel causing a partial exhaustion of pressure in the fictional abdomen, drawing the entrails after it so that the filth poured out: "*aaaaaaaa!*"——stamp on them, slippery: "*aaaa!*"

"Jesu Maria!"—the Sepulchral Sister; I had always suspected her of complicity in De'Ath's designs. Where to strike? *Where?*

"*Liquid objects,*"—the narrator listened to his own persuasive words, "*there is one Subject and one Collator! In the midst of our fluidity, let us consider his identity. I put it to you that I am D. In so far as this book was once in my desk, in so far as I came into this book, in so far as I have narrated it as I, in so far as I have publicly admitted that W is the author, that D is the author, in so far as I am you, D has no existence. He ceases to be! Thus D creates the larger entity: C!*"——the narrator advanced towards Sybil: "*And C is death!*" he cried. "*In death we are one!*"

"Kill me," the Guardian presented him with an alternative choice. "Kill me or kill yourself."

"*Objects,*"—the narrator was mad, yes; you can have his head now De'Ath, but not what is left. Freedom of action, I must retain that.—"*Objects, the narrator will be confined to an institution for the criminally insane!*"

The applause was deafening. I had finally convinced them that the hermit was mad. It remained only for me to give the last of the missing chapters.

CHAPTER SEVENTEEN   *The Unfortunate Tale of Bartleby's Death, which Concerns the Circumstances of His Nativity.*

You may well ask why I didn't kill Sybil. The simple fact was that De'Ath had gained control of my right hand, establishing a salient in my physical being, the material correlative of *I*, the narrator.

As Subject, *I* accordingly decided to give ground. Retreating from the styloid process along the radius and ulna, *C* conceded the entire forearm to its junction with the coronoid fossa of the upper arm.

Nevertheless, the hermit maintained his objective existence. Indeed, so advanced was De'Ath in his delusion that he had taken *I* over that he now accepted the Collator's applause as his own, and reiterated his crazed claims to authority with such a dragging about of allegorical luggage, such a fumbling of papers and a rattling of bones, a whirling of crowns and a discharge of broken arrows that he actually succeeded in drawing forth his own applause from the mob which ever loved bedlamite displays.

But the mask! Everything animal, vegetable and mineral crossed the face of that device which De'Ath clung onto as life itself. It was a mask for all seasons: like its wearer, a creature of boundless caprice, limitless poses, infinite guises. And one of them was *I*, the narrator, *yes.*

"Friends,"—the voice of object *D* began again—"a *riddle:* what is dead but will never die though it has died many times before; is conceived not born, is present but always absent, draws no breath but has breath drawn for it, wakes without sleeping, is perceived not seen, speaks and has no words, cries and is not heard, walks and has never moved, touches yet has never felt,"——*the cancellation! D was going to announce the cancellation!*—— "No, he's not! No he's not! And tastes but cannot tell? Nothing, is it nothing? Eh, what is it? Who is it? Has you got the answer?

"Me, it is, yes, me meself!"———a self-cancelling object!

"Objects, D is nothing! Nothing is not! The narrator cancels himself!"

"De'Ath, yes, The hermit—*shurrup!* Had he asked, 'What is the sometime child of nothing?' then the little boy would have done very nicely as an answer, but he didn't—did he?—and so he won't. Oh, but pardon me, kind folks, while I wipe away a tear from these old eyes. Propinquity when it's parental will not hide itself, and old De'Ath is two in one with Bartleby; yes he is, and with you too."

"D is de-objectified. The objective phenomenon called D is no more! The Collator requests immediate compliance with this directive. Failure to comply will result in demateri-alization and liquefaction of all objects!"—Yes, oh dear me yes! Even if D maintained his existence by occupation of the Guardian Alice (henceforth assigned the nominal value A) . . .

"And what comfort does he have, now that his audience stands before him? What joy in his declining years; what hope as the autumn steals on, creeping up gradual like in the summer of his life? None, oh no, none, he has none, none at all. Oh, he shall become distraught, distraculated he is with grief. *Ahhh!* But he's an author, isn't he? But where's the solace, where's his dream now, where's his only consolation, him that was a lonely old bugger in the yard, where's his only pride and joy, that nice little Bartleby? Gone, he has, yes gone to distant chapters. *Ahhh! Ahhhhhh!* Beside himself, he is, beside himself with grief. Distressed, yes, very so. But he's got powers, he has, poetical powers, transfiguring powers!"—*W?*

Deal with A first, the Guardian. Arm? From the coro-noid fossa—the way of the crown—to the proximal end, the humerus is yours, De'Ath. Concession to the socket. But not the scapula.

"It's not funny, it's not! Gone, the nice little boy, he has: *GONE!* Transported on the senseless wings of poesy, yes. We had much in common, we had, Bartleby and me. Put me heart and soul into him. Oh, his old eyes rage not so much now, friends. You appears to me as the rainbow itself, the colours of me brain, a-sparkling through these briny lashes—all but that one what mocks the rainbow in his attire. Fine and dandy, he is. Just you wait and see! Does you hear me, does you hear me out there?"—*In there, De'Ath, in. The right scapula must be defended against the fallen humerus. Then A, then A, then . . .* "NO BUTTINGS INS! he was in the book from the beginning, he was. Who can say that? Here I am and here I stays. He begins at the beginning and ends at the end, he does. 'Come into the tomb,' says he, 'sit down and tell me your name.' For so it was that the nice little boy came to see him one eve while he was at song, and he sees then that no mother had bore him but this very brain. Oh, he was suspicious at first, he was, yes: suspicious till he knew this was his very own ancient brain's Bartleby, not some imposter, not a sham boy sent as a decoy to lure old De'Ath away from his plot. How his eyes filled with tears, they did, how he wept at news of the boy's Guardian; wept half in wonder to see the plot so working out, half in anger when the boy wouldn't stop butting in and talking of his Auntie. *Ahhh!* How he loved to tell him tales, he did, and show him the joys of the night, letting him see his plot, the gravest plot that ever tickled a bugger's fancy. Yes, friends, it all comes back to him, it does. Rage! Rage! Revenge! Salamanders! Snakes! Thieves! Reptiles! His book was snatched from him, it was, thieved out of his hands. 'Orrible, it was! 'Orrible! 'It's enough to turn your mind,' says I to meself. 'Yes,' I says, 'but just a minute, De'Ath, just a minute. Isn't you forgetting your *powers?* Them what's thieved your book, De'Ath, can be done away with. Buried up, they can be buried up, De'Ath.' And he was right, he was, yes, he was right was old De'Ath. He that made Bartleby can unmake him, unmake you all!

"*Ahhhhhh!* How that takes me mind back, it does. Friends, he'll propound another riddle, he will; what death knows no funeral, nor sad obsequies? For what dissolution

415

is no dirge sung, no shrieks of lament cast up, nor yet the solemn passing bell resounds its muffled knell? What sarcophagus shrouds no body, nor will ever be borne by the mourners' heavy tread; what corpse never meets its insult of worms? Oh, he's a Sexton, he is, and finds these matters very ripe. We's waiting for an answer, we is. Is you listening to me? 'Is you listening to me, Wordkyn?' he says, 'You used to like riddles, you did.' '*Ssssss*,' says he, not very well in himself. 'You's not very well in yourself, is you, Wordkyn? But he'll tell, he'll tell you will old De'Ath. Oh, what a marvel is man, Wordkyn, and what stuff at the end. Very like a fiction, he is, when dead; a fable what cannot be believed, read and forgotten by a few friends, and then—no more. *Is you listening to me?*' He was dying at the time. '*Yesss*,' says he, 'anything you want, De'Ath . . . ' That's what I likes to hear; that's real gratitude, says I to meself and to him, to him I says: 'Who wrote the book, Wordkyn? Is I the author or is you? Tell me who wrote the book and he'll answer the riddle, your dear old ancient Sexton will answer it for you.' 'You, De'Ath,' he says, 'you . . . *you* . . . ' Finished, he was, gone like the nice little boy. 'Tsk-tsk,' says I, 'alas, poor Wordkyn, you couldn't have been more dead if you'd tried.'

"He'll expurgate the riddle, he will, for his friends, and for him what's little clothes he wove, wove on the loom of time, wove with the weft of words and the warp of space, applying his broken shanks to the treadle of memory, yes, he'll expurgate it for him too. Here's no corpse, not him; no cause to mourn. He'll weep no more, but he'll keep his body and preserve it in a jar, that nice little boy's body pickled in vinegar, he'll keep it till the end of time, he will, and talk to it like he used to talk to himself, and ask it how it felt, and did it like the look of the day, and was it comfortable in its jar. He'd change its brine, he would, and see to all its needs, but he can't, can he, and he won't, will he? Oh, pity an old man in his grief, him what has no body to weep for must weep for himself. Then what's he done? He's written him out of the book, that's what he's done. Called him back to his creator, him what made him, called him back to himself, he has. And he's calling you all back, he is, all back to himself. It's his right, it is, his right as an author, 'cos he's going to have you, have you all like he had the Baron. '*Ahhh*,' he says to himself, he says, 'but was he alive, De'Ath, was the nice little boy ever alive if you wrote him? I means from an epistemolatory point of view like, could you say that he was a living boy?' 'But you talked to him in the Baron's tomb, De'Ath.' 'Ahhh,' he says to myself, 'but the Baron was a story too, written by meself when he was a Sexton, yes.' 'Right,' says I, 'and you can write another little boy, another little boy what was never alive except in the head like what you is, De'Ath.' 'Right again,' says I to himself, so he asks you, friends, he asks you: what does that make me? An author, that's what. 'Then it was you what wrote the talking head, De'Ath, and it was you what wrote himself into his own plot, and it was you what . . . what . . . ' 'What what, De'Ath?' says I. 'You remembers,' he says, 'you remembers it exactly what. When you forgot your tallow, it was, and you saw it: the monster what makes more of itself. 'Orrible it was, too 'orrible for words. You remembers, doesn't you, how you wrote on his shroud?' 'I does,' says I, 'me recollection is clear.' 'Then doesn't you see, De'Ath, you wrote the monster what makes more of itself and still more, and more and more and more, yes, until . . . until . . . ' '*Until what?*' says I to meself. 'Until . . . *Aaaarghargull!* No more! No more! He can't go on!'

"But that's it! That's it! He was outside himself, he was, but now he's back, yes. He's in the head, old De'Ath, in the head, himself at last. 'Who's that?' says I. 'Bartleby,' says he. In his head, yes. Not dead. Some there is what says he's mad, but he made them too so they ain't no cause to talk. He made them, he did, in his head where it all comes back to him, it does, how him that was his friend stole his book, then doubled himself, he did, doubled himself and threebled himself. Oh, but he's powers, he has, *powers!* He's recollected himself, he has. Not mad, no, he's not mad, he's not. Sane, he is. 'Who?' says I. 'You,' says he. 'Who's me?' says I. 'De'Ath,' says he. 'Then who's you?' says I. 'Me, meself is what I am,' says he. 'Me?' 'Himself,' says he, 'the same.' He's found a way, he has. In the head. He's not dead, no. Makes more of himself, I does. Makes the dead live, yes. In his head. Who?

Me. Him. Yes. Who is he? What is he? Can he say it? Will he say it? Yes, he can, he will, he does. The answer to his riddle, that's what he is.

"*I am Bartleby!*"

" *The subjective merge of D and W and I in the fourth entity C is absolute! Whoever denies the Collator's authority shall be liquefied! Blood, objects, red blood is the end of life. Blood is the purification! Blood, objects! Blood!*"

Conscious of death in the humerus bone of his right arm, the Collator experimentally stabbed himself and experimentally bled. There was no pain. Good, he thought, let the blood run out. And now we shall purify object A.

For some inscrutable reason, object A chose to defend itself with an axe stolen from object N.

C faltered. The automatic and higher centres of cerebration were functioning normally. He instructed the little finger of his left hand to bend at the joint of the medial and distal phalanges. It obeyed. C checked the time taken for the impulse to travel from the neuron through the axon to the finger. Practically simultaneous! Better yet: make the finger move without thinking.

C's right arm felt warm. He watched as the axe flashed down and missed, and saw that the distal phalange of the little finger of his right hand moved in an unpremeditated condyloid tic.

CHAPTER FORTY-TWO *In Which a Tactical Withdrawal Is Instantly Accomplished and Damon Gottesgabe Gives Some Excellent Advice, to the Great Advancement of the Plot and All Therein.*

O numberless bards, scribble, scribble, scribble the life long day. To arms, hacksmen; flex your pens! Though your brains come out like curds, wrongs are to be righted, causes taken up, pockets weighted down, books bought and books sold, stocks remaindered and pages pulped. Bards of a feather, quire, quill, and flock together. Here's rhetoric to you. Your characters are cut into pieces, your plots disassembled and gone in the binding, your public selves hung high for the auctioning. Well, gentlemen, I made my bid and made it long ago. Better a blank page than a lie; better that the inexpressible remain unexpressed and men crave after perfection, their imaginations unsullied, than that they take the imperfect for the perfect, base metals for gold. But to you who have accepted the coin of several realms, I say scribble on. Your representations of nothing are soon to be perfected, and this very book soon to be as it was before the beginning.

How do I know? And whose voice is this that speaks?

I am, readers and bards alike, a man of critical dispensation. Yet unlike the narrator—or Collator as he now calls himself—and his moral friend, Gottesgabe, I have no wish to save the world. Perhaps you are surprised to hear the narrator and Gottesgabe mentioned in the same breath; perhaps you are disconcerted that I should attribute to the one the motives of the other. Good, kind, gentle Damon Gottesgabe—you say—could never have wreaked such havoc amongst the characters of this book. Indeed, the noble Gottesgabe is largely ignorant of the action (in so far as it directly concerned his narrative friend), and those chapters which actually came under his benign purview were marked by his reluctance to interfere for better or for worse.

Then need I remind you that we cannot distinguish between the man who acts and the man who stands passively by? Both are culpable; both guilty. In this case, the one complements the other, and if I might declare my own interest it would be for the narrator. This is not to excuse him—he has so callously disregarded my advice—; nor do I wish to be taken as an *advocatus diaboli*. It is simply that in matters representational, where all things are necessarily imperfect, imperfect action is more courageous, more humane, more charitable—yes, *charitable*—than the imperfectly inane.

But I see no reason to give any more away. Since the narrator cannot narrate and Gottesgabe will not narrate, the task falls to me, the third man of our history, the soul of this book.

Blood, thought the narrator, listening outside his room. Blood: a balanced solution of salts and ions—hydrogen, sodium, potassium and calcium—fresh blood, smelling of the sea. Who was responsible? When the first creatures arose on the beginning land, they had brought the sea with them. Enveloped, they became envelopers. Death was in blood and blood in death, but the first creatures, incapable of reflection, were not responsible. Mind was, the mind which viewed itself as the outcome of that paleozoic migration was guilty of blood, steeped in blood.

Blood, he thought, remembering his arm, dark and warm; the hairs on the skin surface, glistening and wet. The arm had deserted, had rejected his warnings and had been disciplined like the other objects. There was no pain because the arm itself was an object—or had been. Not that the arm was dead. Spontaneous repairs were being undertaken. His blood was thickening. Loyal and devoted cells, unthinkingly responsive to the dictates of his will, went about their duties;

420

some taking up positions in the breach, others replicating the invader with insidious biochemical flattery. What possible reason was there to further his own dissolution? None, he had none.

Bleeding and healing were both automatic, yet a man should have some say in his body chemistry, should collate himself as he had collated the objects. That he felt the meshing of blood-platlets, the production of coagulin, the mulching, as it were, of his blood, was a sign of mental health—even of the will's invincibility. Self-assertion, the dominance of subject over object, was all that was needed for survival in a cosmos of indifferent objects.

Consoled, the narrator became gradually aware of an alien consciousness, whose presence within his room was conveyed to him by the mechanical sound of breathing. Whose breath was being drawn? Gottesgabe's! Damon Gottesgabe was waiting for him inside the room. Who else? This was the forty-second chapter, wasn't it? And he had returned, returned in time and space to meet with his friend Gottesgabe.

Immediately, the narrator's hand went to open the door. The handle, he discovered on contact, was sticky. Ah, the blood. How was he to explain the blood to Gottesgabe? If he waited long enough, perhaps it would simply go away. All things change: blood was no exception. It would dry, turn to powder and dust, be caught up and consumed in the universal vortex. In another century, there would be nothing left at all. Less than nothing. A hundred years might pass while he was waiting—a hundred years after which his memory would be irretrievably lost.

Masterfully, the narrator issued a directive to his blood. Cessation of bleeding was demanded. He was prepared to go to extremes. This was no miracle he required, rather it was controlled chance: a disciplined permutation of the infinitely particular against the infinitely fluid. Time was short. Considering the choice between bleeding to death and not bleeding at all, what else was there except to live? With more particles in his body than in the material universe the laws of probability based on observed phenomena no longer applied to him. In him time, space, history, the universe itself, were outnumbered. Men had recovered from worse things than a wound in the arm; Christ had healed lepers, raised the dead. The narrator's hands must be cleansed. It was imperative that there be no stain or taint—no stigma. Relatively speaking, the loss of blood was insignificant. What was lost could soon be replenished. A cellular quantum jump was enough to undo the past, anneal the flesh. If I will it, the narrator's cry sounded to himself, it shall be so! There is no blood! There is nothing; neither blood nor guilt nor pain! My hands are clean!

He was made whole, this narrative man was made whole and indomitable!

Sensation returned to the arm. His blood smelled rusty and the edges of the wound puckered. He had defeated death in life; there remained only life in death. And now, thought the narrator resolutely, now for good Damon Gottesgabe.

Inside he found him, islanded by an oasis of light, sitting at the narrator's desk in the narrator's room, puzzling over the first page of the forty-second chapter of the narrator's MS.

From the doorway, he made out the back of Gottesgabe's head and his hands, at rest on the arms of the chair. Why, he wondered, should he feel like an interloper in his own room? And where had he seen those hands before?

"Damon, the text!" His gaze fixed on the hands. "Show me the text . . . You are Damon Gottesgabe, aren't you?"

"But yes," the narrator's childishness amused Gottesgabe. What difficulties he must have had in recognizing the characters! The narrator's understanding was so nominal. "You startled me—for a second," he said, and careful not to show his true surprise at the narrator's punctual appearance, explained his presence thus: 'I was wondering who was narrating this chapter."

Cradling his right arm in his left, the narrator sank into a chair and stared at the hands. "I'm the narrator," he muttered. "No text. Don't show me the text."

"You are to be congratulated," Gottesgabe found cheap praise for his friend, "in returning on time. That was not so easy, I should imagine?" And Damon Gottesgabe, who had read only the non-Throcktonian chapters, folded his arms and waited for the narrator to glorify himself unto others. Whatever he has to say, thought Gottesgabe, is bound to be false.

"Easy?" The narrator was speechless. Gottesgabe, if he really were Gottesgabe, had no idea. Who did he think he was? Who had gotten him into this trouble in the first place? Whatever was attached to those hands was responsible. The narrator, his hands were clean: necessity alone had compelled him to strike, against the characters, against the heroine, against himself too. If Gottesgabe thought Gottesgabe's hands had written the book, then he would have to think again.

"You are certain, Damon," the narrator demanded assurance, "that you are yourself?"

"More or less," Gottesgabe was prepared to be rather less gracious. "And you," acknowledgement of the external realities, he decided, had never been the narrator's strong point, "are you yourself?"

"Exactly!" The narrator was amazed by what he took to be Gottesgabe's vicarious understanding of the book. "You have a fine pair of hands, Damon," he changed the subject. "scientifically speaking the human hand is a unique tool." The narrator waved his mutilated arm, then tucked it away. More than sensation had returned: it was beginning to hurt. "I'm glad, Damon," he winced, "that you are yourself and that those are your hands, because if they were not I would have to think—and think seriously—about cutting them off. Since you are my friend," the narrator flexed his hand while making this appeal and searched for tell-tale drops of blood, "I do not propose to take any such step. Nevertheless, I would like you to know that as I have not spared the characters, so I have not spared myself."

"That was very equitable of you," murmured Gottesgabe, his eyes searching for the meaning of this last remark.

"Don't humour me!" snapped the narrator. "I've done worse things. Why should I stop now? Where do you keep them," he wrenched open the desk drawer, "when they're not on your wrists? In here?"

423

"I'm afraid," the other smiled, "that they are not removable." The narrator's words, Gottesgabe admitted to himself, were quite inscrutable. And that was strange: opacity was not one of his characteristics. He could be oblique, even devious, but there had always been a certain bluntness to him, an honest dishonesty almost. Yet now as Gottesgabe sought the truth behind those eyes, he sensed not evasion but frankness, a frankness that—whatever the reason—could not or would not express itself in terms of itself.

"Try as I might," said Damon Gottesgabe, a lover of the enigmatic, looking down at his hands, "they will not come off."

"Is that any way to talk to a friend," the narrator found it necessary to raise his voice, "who is trying to help you? Viewed as objects, the hands are liquid! You do not know," he modified his tones, "what I am capable of. I have capabilities, Damon, capabilities that you have never suspected. I can tell what they're thinking. I can read it in their eyes, Damon. I'm not mad, I'm not mad at all! Look!" cried the narrator, extending his right arm in a triumphant salute. "Look what I've done!"

Gottesgabe watched his friend impassively. "*I* do not think you are mad," he spoke softly as the narrator's left arm grappled with his right, "though if you go on like this, others—they—will take you for . . . " He faltered, not wishing to be unkind. The narrator was not mad; a little disturbed perhaps, but definitely not mad. Piously hoping for his friend's speedy recovery, he made a comforting attempt at small talk. The narrator had suffered a shock, temporary disorientation caused by some unpleasant experience. That would soon pass. He would be his old self in no time. "And then," said Damon Gottesgabe engagingly, "then you can relate what great feats you have accomplished in Throckton."

When this leading utterance drew no response, it was Gottesgabe who felt disturbed. "And then," he added an edge to his voice, "you can relate what great feats you have accomplished in Throckton . . . *in the book.*"

The narrator seemed not to have heard. In itself, thought Gottesgabe wryly, this was not unusual, yet for him to overlook a potential compliment was nothing short of the miraculous. But the narrator was shouting, and shouting wildly.

"I can see you understand," he cried, "that I am the Collator, *C!* No pain; he didn't feel any pain!" In front of Gottesgabe's apprehensive gaze, the narrator's left hand finally succeeded in lowering his right. "*I* feel the pain for him! Out with his eyes! Wizards next! He was infiltrating the characters, you know that, don't you, Damon? You understand? One by one, he was taking them over. Including me, Damon. But I am the Collator, *C*, yes, *I* plus *D* plus *W*, an integral and self-regenerating alliance against which the fluidity of objects is powerless! Impressed, Damon? I knew you would understand. In point of fact, your understanding of this book has never failed to impress me—for one who elected to remain outside it, for one who has not even read it."

"Well," Gottesgabe was temporarily at a loss, "I always had great expectations of you." What was wrong with the narrator's arm? And what did he mean by this talk of fluids and objects? "Perhaps," he made a tactful suggestion, "you ought to begin at the beginning. You established there was no fog, of course?"

Begin at the beginning! Fog. What fog? The only fog was in Gottesgabe's mind—and he'd thought his friend had understood, had understood the measures which he had been forced to take. "The egg came down the road." He made himself perfectly clear. Why was Gottesgabe looking at him like that? "And broke." Had he seen the blood? "Throckton was destroyed." *There was no blood!* "The text refused to be read. Missing chapters began to appear." What then? Gottesgabe had seen the wound; his attention was fixed on the (to him) inexplicable manifestation of a wound without blood. A bloodless wound was not encountered every day. He had better explain: "You're admiring my wound," he said as Gottesgabe's hands rose in a gesture of dismay. The hands were objects to Gottesgabe's subject. Likewise, Gottesgabe himself was an object to the Collator's subject . . .

"It hurts now," the narrator was crying. "I did it. I did it myself. It was an object. It hurts, Damon."

Gottesgabe allowed himself a mental 'So,' which communicated itself to the narrator as an attentive and respectful silence. "Continue," he said under his breath, giving an exaggerated wave of his hand and deliberately concealing the real nature of his thoughts from the narrator.

"Object of the hermit's." The response was clipped; "Hurts now. Hurts."

"I see," said Damon Gottesgabe, who understood that his friend believed he was suffering from a self-inflicted wound—a significant delusion. Yet the mad finally help themselves, and if the narrator was mad there was nothing Gottesgabe could do about it, humanist though he was.

Yet the delusion of the self-inflicted wound was interesting. And, for the moment, it indicated no more than a neurosis, albeit of the most depressing—and amusing—kind: his friend feared for his manhood. Such were the pressures of existence; such was the diagnosis.

"Well," said Damon Gottesgabe symbolically, "before you lose any more blood, we shall just have to bind it up."

Again he was surprised by the narrator's reaction: "Don't temporize with me! Any fool can see there's no blood. There was blood before, but then there was no pain. The arm was an object before—like the characters. How could it have felt pain? How could they have felt pain? If you think I would have . . ." The narrator halted. Complete the sentence, he thought. Carnage was abstract. A matter of degree, when all was said and done. There was no comparison between his condition and theirs. "No comparison, Damon." Pain was not allowed in the subject-object hypothesis. The narrator was not a cruel man; then nor was he especially kind. But he was not a monster, not that. His fantastical friend—!—he would have destroyed everything. And Gottesgabe, the narrator went from one desperation to another, what would Gottesgabe have done? He didn't even go into the book. He didn't *know*. Complete the sentence, the narrator listened to himself: *complete the sentence before communication becomes impossible.*

"If you think," the narrator spoke, and spoke boldly, "I would have blinded Estrogen, disembowelled Hautboy, stabbed Waldemar, cut off Nat's hand, knowing then what they suffered . . ."—*No. He* suffered, not them. "No,

Damon. *No!*"

"So you mean," the slightest trace of a smile showed on Gottesgabe's kindly features, "that you have annihilated half the characters?"

"*Objects,*" the narrator used the correct terminology, "objects are fluid. Hacked, cut up, liquidated, yes: annihilater. *Shocked?*" Yes, the narrator could see his friend was shocked. "It hurts, Damon. It hurts."

"You're tired," Gottesgabe erased his smile. He regretted sending the narrator into the book. But that had been a dramatic gesture, not meant to be taken seriously. Ah, how Gottesgabe lamented his own inadequacy as a spectator. He should have read the book before the narrator had disappeared into Throckton. "The MS," he said, "do you have the rest of the MS?"

"Not tired," the narrator answered. "Cold." Why should he feel the pain? And what did Gottesgabe want with the MS? He was checking up on him, that was it. Gottesgabe did not believe him—he could see that Gottesgabe did not believe him! "Just because there's no blood, you don't believe me. How can there be any blood outside the book? Why won't you listen to me? Come back with me, return to the book if you want confirmation. It isn't finished yet. There's still time, Damon, still time." Time to do what? Find an ending. Gottesgabe would help. If he stayed outside, he had failed. And there was no pain in the book. To return was to stop the pain. What of the objects? They would never forgive him. "Do you know what I told them, Damon, the objects? '*I am the incarnation of this text! The supreme sacrifice is called for!*' "

The narrator laughed. He was getting feverish, and sentimental too. Of course the objects would forgive him. They had no choice. He would explain to them that their wounds were fictions, cathartic wounds. He must be careful though, careful not to be sanctimonious or moral—like Gottesgabe. Vigilance was not to be relaxed in favour of undue sentiment. In his absence, it was entirely conceivable that they had been conspiring against him. Who wouldn't have done? Was it at all possible that the objects had ever felt pain? Pain could only be equated with moral deficiency, a

427

failure of the will.

The narrator felt pain. Now that he had deserted the text, might they not be experiencing the same pain as he? His return was doubly imperative: to find the ending, and—if necessary—to put the characters out of their misery. A man, thought the narrator, must accept what he creates. That is the law.

"Damon," the narrator pleaded, "you will come back with me, won't you? You'll help me find an ending?"

"Of course, of course," said good Damon Gottesgabe, who had no intention of doing any such thing.

"We'll make an end of it together." With Gottesgabe at his side, it wouldn't be so bad.

"These actions of yours," Gottesgabe was hesitant, "in the book. Were you serious? You don't really mean to say—?" He recoiled at the thought. It was offensive, an affront to his fastidious sensibility. "I cannot believe it," he added lamely; "I cannot believe it of you."

At last he was beginning to get some idea! Communication wasn't so difficult after all. "You have only to read the book, Damon. Better yet, return with me."

A spasm of pain contorted the narrator's face, drawing his lips over his teeth. He welcomed the pain. It was the price of atonement, a sign that he lived. The characters had attached little significance to life; the narrator still less. That was in the past. With or without Gottesgabe he had to return to that past. Between total annihilation and a happy ending, perhaps something might be salvaged. "To narrate is to create, Damon. That is the principle I worked on as an absent narrator, and that is the principle I applied when I was in the text. Yet . . . yet . . . " He would make no confessions. Let Gottesgabe see for himself. If he didn't like it, so much the worse.

"Ah creation," Gottesgabe sensed a conversational change. "Creation is divine. It is man's highest attainment, the noblest of his activities through which he comes to know God Himself." Gottesgabe sighed. "But who am I to talk this way? Compared with yourself, I am the most uncreative of persons. I have frequently lamented my lack of—"

"In my place," said the narrator coolly, "what would

428

you have done?"

Gottesgabe found the question immensely distasteful. He was not so literally inclined as his simple-minded narrative friend. "I'm afraid it is not a question," he said defensively, "of what I might have done—nor of my returning with you to find an ending. The truth is never so easy. For example, have you considered the chance that there is nothing to return to? Obviously not. What," he tried another approach, "what of the possibility that there might be no ending?"

No ending? No ending was an ending in itself. Why was Gottesgabe delaying? Was he afraid? The narrator was not afraid. "Do you think *I'm* a coward, Damon?" He might as well talk to himself. Some people failed to recognize the truth when it was staring them in the face, the truth with bloody hands. "Look, Damon, look," the narrator's teeth were bared, "blood. Blood, Damon, *blood!* I did what I did! Their blood is on my hands; my hands are steeped in blood!" It was difficult to be more explicit. "Throckton is washed in a sea of blood! Who is responsible? The narrator is responsible! I am responsible! What absolution is there if I stay here? No one can absolve me. I am guilty, Damon, *guilty.*" He was alone. Narrators absolve themselves. He should have stayed where he was. The greatest danger now was that all the characters might have died.

Cold, he was so cold. Because time was in suspension, he could not tell how long he had waited outside the room. Before the whole world bled to death, he must return to the past.

"Time, Damon, time!" the narrator cried. "For God's sake, I shall go mad! Tell me the date, tell me the time, tell me I am not mad!"

And on the 26th of September, 1970, good Damon Gottesgabe was conscious of lying when he told his narrative friend that he was not mad.

"No," he sighed, "you are not mad. Confused, that is all. But not mad, my friend. Definitely not mad."

No doubt the reader disagrees with Gottesgabe. In the face of the evidence, I think he has every right to disagree. And yet for reasons soon to be made apparent I am afraid I

429

must accept Gottesgabe's spoken verdict, while strongly disagreeing with his unspoken verdict. Just one year had elapsed, reader (as if you had not already guessed!), since I gave this MS into the narrator's hands, the then hands of an old-young man, a three-in-one, would-be bard.

So aptly and ably has this same would-be bard of yore executed my programme for this book (by which I mean textual nullification), so unstintingly has he promoted my own cause that I would find his case of conscience an inexcusable reversal of what it pleases the critics to call *character development*, were it not for these two forward reasons. *One*: pain makes the weak cry out. *Two*: it is an highly respected convention of our form that recusants recant. Having bowed to convention, I think it only fair to add that of our twins the first weighs in heavier than the second.

Alas, but I am not so easy of mind upon Gottesgabe's perverse reluctance to admit the narrator's crimes. True, he has not read all that he might. Perhaps the answer has to do with the mediocrity of the dismembered characters. Even Gottesgabe—there is no love lost between us: the animosity, I am pleased to say, is mostly on my side—even he knows mediocrity for what it is: worse than death, the death that calls itself by the name of life. Yet I am not persuaded. Indeed, I entertain sufficient hope for the soul of Damon Gottesgabe that I think I have discovered the secret of his disbelief in murder and madness. He knows the guilty party better than the narrator. He knows himself; he knows emptiness and is afraid.

Both have carried self-deceit to veritable perfection—admittedly not the perfection that I have long desired. But how close they came, reader, how close and closer yet shall be! The one has been a skilled practitioner of death, and at the last is weak; the other, full of a deadly vacuity, believes himself wordly wise. What vapid creatures they are!

But I shall intrude no further. The text is well enough upholstered; the stuffing will be dragged out of it presently. In the meantime, I shall end this chapter as it was ended: with this conversation.

"How can you return," Gottesgabe strove to press an advantage, "now that you are no longer the narrator?"

"But I am, I am," the narrator replied. By staying he prolonged the agony of the characters. Yet how, without certain knowledge of a certain ending, could he ease their suffering? Gottesgabe had said there might be no ending. Death was an ending—of sorts. However, the existence of death was extremely controversial. Death was a monstrous contradiction in terms. You could not define it as non-being, for non-being was an absurdity. Death and language were enormous question-beggars. No language had an adequate word for death in itself. The words of death defined it in terms of what it was not.

Life, death, the thousand and one existent things, were no more than linguistic concepts, and as such were capable of negation. If life and death were the same, life was not life and death not death. The characters, whom he had so correctly regarded as not human, were by definition not mortal. As fictions, they could never die; their authors, yes, but not the characters. Death, thought the narrator, is defeated by language, I have no need to return.

And therefore I shall return. Freedom of choice is all. Even without Gottesgabe, I will return.

This freedom of choice was immediately conveyed to Gottesgabe, who did not like the look of illumination which dawned on his friend's face.

"Think of the reader," he appealed to a third party. "It should have ended long ago."

"It will not be long now."

"But it is only a fiction."

"To murder and create is 'only a fiction.' "

"But you cannot murder a fiction."

"Yes, Damon, I have just found that out. I am not guilty and I am guilty as well. A fiction can inflict pain; I have inflicted it. A fiction can suffer; I suffer, the characters suffer."

Gottesgabe floundered. His friend had been supposed to write himself out of difficulties; now he was confusing art with life. And life was horrible enough without the fictional misdeeds of the order described by the narrator.

"Yes," said Gottesgabe wearily.

"You agree?" The narrator raised his eyes, "You think I ought to return? It is my duty," he warmed, "I conceive it as my duty."

"I defer to your duty." Those who are persuaded of complicity in a terrible crime, he reflected, often find it necessary—and expedient—to transfer the burden of their guilt onto others. The narrator, however, was not transferring anything. Rather he had taken the world's guilt upon himself, the guilt which he imagined ran in the blood—a convenient means of retreat and withdrawal for a man without art, for a man who had failed in his art.

And knowing his narrative friend as only he did, good Damon Gottesgabe hit upon this stratagem. "Your duty," he spoke slowly and with feigned hesitation, "you can say it is your duty to return. You asked me before what I would have done if I had been in your position, and I avoided an answer. You were right to interpret this as a weakness on my part. And so it was, so it was.

"I was expecting you," Gottesgabe startled the narrator by cracking his knuckles, "to ask me what I would do now—if I were you," he added, "which, however, I am not."

"Very well then," the narrator mustered his patience, "if you were me, what would you do now?"

"You have conceived your duty exactly as I would have done." Gottesgabe lied for a second time. "I know that you have always taken my advice, that you have always valued it highly. Then if I were you, I would return to the book. That is my advice, and I am happy that you saw fit to ask it. It is all that you can do; you have no alternative."

The narrator smiled through his pain. Damon Gottesgabe, you are incorrigible. And transparent too. I shall return, I will return because I am not compelled to return. And you, there's no blood on your hands, why do you try so hard? "Yes, Damon, *yes!* For once, just this once," Gottesgabe's strategy collapsed, "I shall take your advice." Yes, your hands are clean, aren't they?

"Consider our hands, Damon. They're really very similar. Consider the structure: eight small carpal bones, arranged in two rows—the proximal and distal—from the wrist. Yet to subdivide is to subdivide further. The proximal row consists of the scaphoid, lunate, triquetrum and pisiform bones. The latter is placed anterior to the triquetrum—triquetrum because three-cornered, Damon. These bones articulate with the distal end of the radius to form the wrist joint, so we haven't even got to the hand yet. The distal row includes hamate, capitate, yes *that*, trapezoid and trapezium, a group which articulates with the proximal row of the carpal bones and also with the proximal ends of the metacarpals. So much for the wrist. One wrist is as good or as bad as another. The metacarpals themselves are the *long* bones of the *hand*. They have rounded knuckle-like heads distally—you cracked them very effectively—and flat articular areas proximally for contact with the distal row of carpal bones. The phalanges form the skeleton of the fingers. But what's in a hand, Damon? Speech? Murder? Intention? The first digit or thumb consists of two phalanges, a proximal and distal—the same old story. The other digits have proximal, middle, and distal phalanges—three in all. The anterior or palmar surface of each is flattened. The distal end of each, which is called the head, is also flattened, and in the distal phalanx this area is shaped like an arrowhead.

"You see," the narrator stared at the emptiness that was Gottesgabe, "I know you for what you are."

And he did, reader. You have my word for it, the word of a fantastic. And if you doubt that, then you can have Gottesgabe's word too.

"Yes," he said, "I know."

"But the pain, Damon," said the narrator, "the pain."

CHAPTER FORTY-THREE   *The Transfiguration and the
Ascent: A Chapter Concerning the Dissolution of Masque and
Time.*

"*I am Bartleby!*" Thus spake De'Ath. And the crowd
roared and its voice was as the voice of the forest consumed
by fire, and the crowd grew and its growth was as the flame
that leaps from branch to branch, and the crowd swayed and
its movement was as the forest swept by the wind that goes
before the fire.

"*I am Bartleby!*" Thus spake De'Ath. And the crowd
was made one in itself and was incorporated with De'Ath,
believing its hero had come down like a god—he that had
ascended on a pillar of flame. And those who could, saw; and
those who would, rejoiced; and De'Ath was sure of his
subjects and put no space between them but let them come
together so that many were destroyed in the press and the
blood ran out as a river.

Even as I reoccupied the husk of myself, I became aware
of Alice's voice. "What is it?" she was shouting above the
roaring of the crowd: "Why don't you answer?"

Answer? What was there to answer?

The characters huddled together at the edge of the
multitude. Not one spoke, nor moved, nor made any gesture
of any kind.

"Patricia," said I, "are you not pleased to see me?"—
nothing. The colleen squatted next to the frozen Wachposten-Würzig. Horn aflop, lips pouting, the *it* in transit

searched for the missing member, delving deep into her groin amid effusions of musk, vine damp-rot, and the perfume of purple prose.

"Come, Sybil," I shuddered, moved almost to tears by the pitiful sight, "a word for your narrator."

"No," said she, and turning away to Alice, made this sad appeal: "I want something—anything—anything but this. I do not know what."

"Try," said Alice, "you can only try."

"But characters," I hesitated. The words were bitter in my mouth. "Characters, I have returned." *Justice!* The very stones cried out as though in pain. "Who has done this to you? Who are we to blame?"—For so I tried to rally them, stirring vengeance in their blood: "Who is guilty?"

"The hermit," Alice turned back to me, "is not too well in the head. He thinks he's Bartleby. He . . . Oh! Your arm—it's hurt!"

"The hermit, yes! De'Ath, yes! *Guilty!*" She began to say something, but I silenced her. Verdicts first, accusations later! My hands were again in my possession; my hands were again upon the text. A defence was to be prepared—for crimes against the characters, a defence and a prosecution too. What my arm had done, I had not done; and what my arm had left undone, I would finish. Now that I was back, back and bleeding . . . in truth I had not noticed. No pain: *there was no pain.* "The arm, characters, *my* arm: see how it bleeds! Have I not suffered? Do I not suffer now? But I have come into my own again. I have returned to make an end of this!"

"An end!" Alice gasped, not understanding.

"Nuh!" Hautboy stiffened in a feast of curdled bowels, a dehiscent package of visceral effluent.

Oh bounteous vitality! Oh natural urge of the injured to take their revenge!

"All present and correct, Hautboy?" I cheered his resolve, though the life already pulsed within him—and without. "Characters, Hautboy affirms De'Ath's guilt. What other proof is needed?"

"Spare him, oh please spare him!" Alice interceded on the hermit's behalf. "Just this once, spare somebody."

Ah, but how she humbled me then.

"Characters," I resolved to sample their opinion, "Alice has entered a plea of mercy. Let us control our feelings; let us proceed against others as we would have them proceed against us. The greater the excess, the greater our restraint must be."

"Dat's it! Yessum!"—agreement, agreement from Nat! "Dat's de way!" Bleached, grey, and grained in the face, his axe hand hanging by a tendon, Nat soulfully regarded the poor ruined talking head, and began wistfully crooning a swing low sweet Jesus lullaby, a treacly plantation air cloyed with the humid fragrance of molasses, magnolias, marsh-gas, cotton blossom, boll, weevil, and all.

"The hermit is forgiven, Alice," said I, heartened by Nat's enthusiastic response. "For my part I am prepared to forgive him the injuries he has done me, although it is not—and can never be—mine to pardon him other hurts." Hence I counselled her against excessive compassion as she had me against excessive zeal. "Look at Zog," I chose an example at random, "do you think he has forgiven De'Ath? Do you think he can forgive him?"

The cave of one eye opened and shut; then the other—to the left of his serrated nose, and somewhat displaced as I recall—allowing a brief glimpse of the sloth within as it scampered in furry terror.

"Here," he croaked, jowls dropping, tearing the polyp apart to reveal the tongue, neatly perforated by a row of pearly teeth. Bud-like and coated with an unguinous residue, the tongue protruded from the aperture, preventing further speech.

"God!" exclaimed the Sepulchral Sister, her oracular ardour much dampened. "Do you know what has been happening? Zog is—"

"What is he, Sybil?" I enquired as gently as I knew how, when a hand, laboriously raised, summoned me to the palanquin as if to an audience with the dying. For it seemed that character though he was, and therefore to be numbered among the immortals, Zog had little time left. So little time . . .

"You—" the bud withdrew: "You—"

436

Leaning over to garner his next words, I noted the cheeks had swollen; a minute thread of spittle escaped the junction of polyp and jowls, and not until I was close enough to observe the beads of sweat welling from the pores of his marbled flesh did the polyp burst, projecting its brackish load into my face, so that I was very nearly blinded.

"Now you look!" cried Auntie, bustling over to wipe the phlegm from Zog's jowls: "You look!" she cried, hardly knowing what she said or why. "Look what you've done! Not De'Ath! Not him! As for poor Estrogen . . ."

"Whatever happened—? Whatever happened—?" Waldemar stared mesmerically at his companion who lay flat on his fleur-de-lys back, his eyes still flowering on the stalks of the optic nerve.

"As for poor Estrogen—*what?*" I cried, my eyes streaming acrid tears.

"It's not De'Ath!" Alice was shouting hysterically: "It's you! You!"

"Kindly remember," I began, but:

"Eth'genth dead," Patricia whimpered.

"—who you are, Alice, and where you are. Calm yourself; united we—"

"He is dead," said Sybil woodenly, disregarding all evidence to the contrary. There was surprisingly little blood: "—stand!"

—though what else was to be expected from such an anaemic representation of the human condition?

"—fall!" declared Alice. "The Knave is dead."

Dead?

Manifestly impossible. What did they mean: *dead?* If he was dead, he had been killed, if that . . .

"Doan act too good," Nat mumbled. "Swat it seems to me."

True; but there was a line to be drawn between death and the absence of life. Death for characters had no existence. It was a linguistic contrivance. Another cheap trick of De'Ath's: a means of substantiating character by violence.

"Estrogen!" I shook the Knave; "You can't be dead! Do you hear me? Nobody can be dead!"

The Knave's thin lips yawned slackly. His reply was

voiceless, yet nonetheless eloquent of its kind.

"Well," Alice recovered her composure, "is he dead or isn't he?"

"One moment,"—a sword stroke down the sternum confirmed the negative prognosis. It was a cursory dissection: the tension beneath the skin expanded cut into gash and effected a release of gas and bile, bubbling gas . . .

"He is not alive, Alice. Not alive."

Guilty! The still small voice accused me. *Have you breath to confer, life to give? Are you so easy with the world's body, so full of the elements, so in harmony with angels that you are your own master?*

"Lord! Lord!" Sybil knelt over the cadaver; "Let me know mine end and the number of my days: that I may be certified how long I have to live!"

The end, of course . . . the end was *prefigured in Estrogen's death!* "Characters," I addressed the sum of them, "what is this life, what this death, if not the end of suffering? Yes, the book may be over for him—he has taken his last curtain call—but we, we live on. Then which of us is not secretly pleased, secretly gladdened, to find himself still alive?"

A well-driven point! Never had their silence been so significant.

"Are not your lives," I drew on their attention, directing the book towards its certain (if premature) close, "confirmed, nay, reinforced by this unhappy passage, which perforce appears in an altogether different light from that of mere death?"

"Mos sholy!" Nat applauded, unfortunately severing axe hand from chopping wrist, to which it had been but tenuously connected in the first place. Undismayed, he regained the hand, and clapping its pink palm against the gristly stump, renewed his applause: "Mos sholy! Dats de way! Dats de way!"

"Therefore, characters," I spoke with hoarsened voice—the mob now raising a deafening chant of *Bartleby! Bartleby!*—"Therefore let me be the first—on this optimistic note—to announce a successful resolution to our common history. The book is over! We have survived! *We are the Survivors!*"

438

"Uck!" Hautboy chortled, plunging a hand into his belly and lugging out some soiled abdominal organ which he placed gingerly before him. "Uck! Uck!" he gurgled: "You can say that again."

"I do not hesitate to repeat it," said I:

THE END

"The noise," Alice moaned, completely disregarding the ending of the book—De'Ath, centre-stage, struggling on with his mask, an action more clumsily executed than that cumbrous device warranted, as if it loathed to sit again on the head of De'Ath:—"Can't you do something about the noise?"

"Not really," I replied, searching for a more appropriate terminal convention, the mob roaring while the *SECOND MASQUER, ERROR*, strained lewdly at the *THIRD MASQUER, HARMONY*, prisoner of the *HANGING AUTHORS*.

Yet even as I sought THE END—even thus—the last act began. What would be my part this time? There was no way of telling, but pretence is all in the Masque. And therein I sensed the hope of finality, and in finality—peace.

Hence before De'Ath could make the last *coup de récit* I stepped forth as the *INTERLOCUTOR* with an improvisation all of my own—an improvisation which met with more success than I had dared dream of.

*

INTERLOCUTOR, from the Square: To this charmed stage two vengeful spirits do I call down: angelic messengers are they to some, furies to others. Down, sweet spirits, down! Hark, ethereal voices hum about our ears, weaving perception with perception that light be made melodious and rays of measure sound is visual opulence. See where they make sublime play of purest illusion, heralding swift change of state, fusing light to sound and sound to light in fiery blows of metamorphic trance! Two guardian souls are they come straight from the ultimate sphere, our show to end!

FIRST SPIRIT (descending)

Hail, fellow mover! Say, what occasions this
Factitious turmoil and riotous throng that hence
We are called from our own proper stations?

SECOND SPIRIT (also descending)

Nothing less than their formal dissolution:
End without beginning, and beginning that
Knows no end. Strike, spirit! Destroy!

*

Ah, mutable form and amphibious circumstance! How
best to describe what happened next?
Whirling like orbiting furies around De'Ath's mask, the
newly-summoned spirits forced its wearer to retaliate with a
flight of sling shots and arrows, plus repeatedly ill-aimed casts
of his ivory sickle which flashed again and again through the
leaden air. The mob, observing its hero chastised, set up a
terrible booing and howling, to which in no time was added a
barrage of pies, eggs, piemen, chickens, chicken legs, flagons,
quails, and the occasional roc as further evidence of disappro-
bation, a shrieking din, including De'Ath's cries of "Vile
spirits! Accursed fiends!"—as well as a more distant and
unfamiliar reverberation, a rhythmical drumming and horny
clattering, swelling with the bombardment which grew to
include a disproportionate number of boulders amongst the
eatables, solids and combustibles alike being not of the
slightest consequence to the angry spirits but of considerable
physical consequence to De'Ath, who, still discharging his
arrows and howling frantically, *"Powers! Me Powers!"* was
greatly imperilled by the rain of detritus from his erstwhile
supporters, and clinging tenaciously to the crown that was to
have coronated *ERROR*, fought a rearguard action across
stage, deploying the mask as a shield, and retreating under
the torrential hail towards the entrance of the New Machine,
the booing and howling, the thundering and drumming all
having swelled to create a very fair dissonance, certainly one

440

of the best and noisiest in this history.

"Momma says rice is nice," Hautboy burbled to himself. "Rice is nice but mice's nicer."

"Why? Auntie cried. "Why?"

"Dunno," said Hautboy. "Schlurp-schlurp," he continued, and observing the lobed sweetmeat before him, commenced to . . . *eat?*

But the mask, the hermit's mask! Ah, how that changed. What grotesque transfigurations convulsed the mask, each displacing its predecessor in ever swifter succession so that the device writhed like a creature possessed of a life apart from the wearer's, which now seemed in mortal danger. While the rest of the Masquers (including *ERROR*, who of necessity abandoned his designs on *HARMONY*) sought refuge under a mountain of refuse, and De'Ath yet howled upon his powers, his mask indulged in an endless chain of metamorphic contortions whereby it hoped to avoid damage from the palpable hits being scored by the mob. On the impact of an overripe tomato, the bewitched vizor changed into an overripe tomato; scored by a pomegranate into a potato, by an apple into a land crab, from a land crab to a sea crab, from that to a land wolf, snarling and snapping at the besieging spirits that moved in a concord of epicycles. Next, a piece of offal curled messily about the wolf's chops, a hit not at all to the liking of the mask's lupine guise, for thrashing and snarling in lycanthropic rage, it changed into an eagle as if to escape by flight, taking De'Ath's inner head with it—a decapitation, I must confess, that would have afforded me no little amusement. But this was not to be and the eagle speedily converted itself into a sea anemone—a deft reversal of tactics and medium by the mask, which henceforward attempted to digest the debris raining down from above.

De'Ath likewise opted for a change of tactics and endeavoured to struggle out of the mask as he had first struggled into it, a move the reader will immediately perceive was both ill-timed and ill-executed. For the hermit's head was now encased by a translucent globular form, and those scrawny hands that sought to grapple with a sea anemone met instead with a jelly fish and were sorely stung into the bargain, a fate shared by the interior head which shone like a

441

beacon through the outer layer, a face resplendent in its ugly frustration, and an eyesore for all who could to see, as indeed they did, howling the more for it.

"Hoorah!" Nat's stump went up to hide a grin. "Ifn it's finished, when's we goin back? When's we goin back to dem dar books of origin? Dat's de question, yessah."

"Soon," I replied, "Soon. It cannot be long now before the—"

"Dey skins me heah an dey skins me dar. Ya kint help but suffah, missy,"—this to the head: "Ohh, Ahhs goaain hoaam," he crucified the air, "hoaam to maah Laawd!"——a lament which the head acknowledged dysenterically, in a disgorge of jugular puree.

On stage, meanwhile, De'Ath's mask entered the critical phase of uncontrolled and uncontrollable change. Wildly permutating the entire phyla and genera of the natural creation, the mask simultaneously became everything and nothing—a parody of types which momentarily overawed the mob—before the vengeful spirits bore it aloft, and the device, whirling and writhing, exploded in a nebulous flurry of incandescence.

And in this wise was our book ended:

The Sister, overhearing Nat's refrain, took Alice aside. "I want," her eyes shone with the light of a peculiar grace, "I want another book, another way. Another book and another time—that will make me happy."

"Dat's right! Dat's de case!" Nat affirmed—his testimony amputated by a scream . . . out of the windpipe of the head . . . a development I would not countenance, this vision of the head: its hair spiked on its scalp, its eyes stopped in red sockets, its mouth fully open and the noise, that cry of one who does not know life and cannot know death, sounding from the jagged shoulder of the neck—this, I say, was too much even for *Bartleby*'s narrator.

Accordingly, as the Sister made to take her leave (despite Alice's tearful entreaties), raising herself from Estrogen's waxen corpse and once more affirming her right to another book and another time, I, seizing the hour, gave her the assistance she had yearned for these chapters without end, in this book without end, time without end. For my strategy was finally clear.

A transubstantial cloud circulated beneath Sybil's feet. At one centimetre altitude, she was not unduly alarmed; at two—rising on the cloud—she cried for mercy; at three her face shone beatifically, and at four . . . but such was the acceleration of the transfigured Sybil that she was gone before any could hold her, a star in the firmament marking her celestial trek.

"If trek is the right word," said I as the crowd fell down on one calloused and carbuncular knee.

"Another book," Alice sighed, "and another time."

"Besides," said I, "the wench is—"

THE END [SYBIL]

CHAPTER FORTY-FOUR *The Resurrection and the Life,
Wherein the Dream of Reason Indeed Brings Forth Monsters.*

"Individual endings, obviously," I remarked to Alice—
the mob renewing its din—"are of the essence."——to which
she did not reply, but busied herself with ministrations to the
general hurts, hopelessly beyond repair as a consequence of
my all too manifold errors.

Yet how, I asked myself, how could it ever be THE
END without Bartleby's return? What of the hero's life—and
death, if he were actually dead, if anything could die in this
book? What of *His Edifying and Most Instructive Comments
and Opinions upon His Journey into Several Parts of the
World and Time*?

"*Auntie! Auntie!*" A square of squared spare Bartlebies
danced round Alice—infinite Bartlebies in a finite space,
acting out the genetic injunction: go wax and multiply. The
square could not hold them; Throckton would not hold them,
infinity might hold them—but to what end?

"Characters, be patient!"—Hautboy, rummaging in his
guts, lugged out the lower alimentary canal, smooth
palimpsest, eeling on the reddened flags.

What to do with these others, who, enduring this
indefinite state of putrilage, neither lived nor died?

Ah, vinous confection! Yet though the promised end
had not come, I took brush to palette and daubed again.

As De'Ath cleared the stage for his own upshot—
consummation devoutly to be forestalled!—another and

louder shout went up from the mob, signifying a new diversion at the fringe of chaos—if chaos, properly speaking, may be thought of as thus tasselled—; a huzzahing and up-throwing of hats sufficient to presage some new turn perhaps not unrelated to textual nullification (now more than ever my aim); an anapaestic and therefore lame galloping, more suited to an ox, carving a soul-scattering avenue through the populace down which careered that valiant hooved destrier:

"*Hannibali!*" cried his mistress.

Hannibali indeed—with a whinny, snuffle and snort, the cavalry arrived, the least apocalyptic horse imaginable for no jacinthed and fiery plated host rode on this steed, unless the faithful retainer:

"*Ichabod!*"—merited the description, riding upright in the reverse position, that is moving forwards facing backwards, most like unto his name, a son of woe, bethinking Hannibali's posterior his anterior—a gift horse nevertheless: a *horse with a message!*

"Characters, relief is at hand!"

"What news," Alice enquired mawkishly of her creaking and besotted serving-man, "what news, Ichabod, of my charge: Bartleby?"

"Wooah, Neddy!" (Horsey sobriquet); so Ichabod triumphantly brought the triumphant news from X to hence, holding the piece by its tail, gazing with undiluted disbelief at the decrepitude before him, aft of him, to the starboard and port of him, and had scarce oped his rusty jaws, saying: "Good news, maam!"—the characters all ears at this chance falling out—"Bartleby is . . ." *than he fell down upon his head?*

Beaten at the post!

"Beggin your pardon, maam," said he, "the world is overturned. Ichabod is no more." Whereat he died, and died concisely.

THE END [ICHABOD]

"You—!" Words failed Alice: "murderer!"—saddened by this retort to merest accident, I must confess that I feared for her reason. Was this not a harsh judgement against my strategy of individual endings, incidentally furthered by Ichabod's fall?

"I shall change my tactics," said I.

"Your hands are covered in blood!" she exclaimed madly.

"Blood, Alice? Now be reasonable." In a composite picture, you cannot exlude the middle. Not all red liquids are blood; not all red words are liquid. "The coincidental similarity," said I, "between the *pigment* haemaglobin and the *word* red, does not give you cause to—"

"Look at them!" she cried, unconvinced. "A priest! They need a priest!"

I considered her proposal. Death was not unknown to follow the adminstration of the last rites. But I could do it myself.

Zog was fast asleep. Should I wake him for burial? 'Every man digs his own grave': characters were not exempt from this general rule.

I set them to work with a will. "Dig, characters! Dig!"—Nat's wrist ineffectually stumped at the ground.

"Faster, characters!"

Alice gasped. She did not like my direction. Yet when they were buried, and the red stuff with them, she would come round to my point of view. Not that *I* would bury them, not in their present condition.

Mass suicide offered the only solution. Lots might be drawn. There were plenty of fingers to choose from. A little finger was to signify the first. Or should it be a thumb? By rule of thumb as the saying goes. Nothing could be more democratic. Alone and at the end, the narrator guaranteed the last blow. Alone and at the end, the narrator would deal with the hermit. By committing voluntary suicide they deprived De'Ath of allies and increased the narrator's chance of success. Let there be no misunderstandings: he who has the thumb bears the palm away. Corpses would be shipped back where they belonged, free of charge.

"I'll foot the bill, characters!"

"Fuh-fuh?" Zog puttered.

"Free, *yes!*"—the offer was sealed:

"Dumb! Dumb!" Nat rejoiced——signed:

"Feedum!" Patricia sang out———*and delivered*:

Emerging from the third part of the sun, moon and stars, Waldemar took the initiative and impaled himself on Roman steel—exemplary cooperation!—and, twitching, he stiffened; stiffening, he twitched—twitching *and* stiffening, he tottered, rose, splintered and ****!

With Amazonian fortitude, the colleen excised her right breast and hurled it by the nipple into Hannibali's velvetine muzzle—liberation! Not to be outdone, Hautboy made short work of a colectomy while Zog slashed his throat, opening there the smile of death, to whose tender embrace Nat surrendered, leeched and larval-white as Wachposten-Würzig extended both hands in last salutes and fell eternally to attention, at ease with twilight gods.

RIP! [OMNES]

Which left but Alice and I—

"Look! Look!" she cried: "There!"

—undespatched, as I was saying—

"The sedan chair!" she cried; "Wordkyn the Novelist! Wordkyn *our author!*"

It was with unwonted celerity that Wordkyn made his extra-vehicular presence felt, dismissing his written chair bearers with a sweep of his black wings. Yet . . . to my left Hautboy rose on all fours, trailing the glory of God's creation.

"*SSSTAAWP!*" he cawed at the ancient mountebank, preoccupied with on stage reparations. "*SSS*uch a *sss*ight is this*ss!*" he hissed tragically. "But I, Wordkyn the Poet, have *sss*ertain ver*ssss*es," the spittle flew, "joyful and happy ver*ssss*es!"

"What?"—I thought my ears deceived me—not my eyes—Nat's hand (severed) flexed.

"An epithal*aaa*mium," Wordkyn baaed; "nuptials first. I can *sss*ee," he surveyed the wondrous scene, "that I am in time."

A happy ending! Never was auctorial intervention more timely!

On stage, De'Ath had at last assembled a fine and regal array. Behind *ERROR*'s throne, there loomed *DEATH THE AVENGER*, the death that grins and wears robes of sack and carries a scythe across his shoulder. To his right stood one that wore a *GARGOYLE*'s head, another that was a *GRIFFIN*, the seven stars in its hair; to his left stood *DISEASE*, muffed in a mumming dress and holding a garland of flowers; by her side one that hid his face in a mask of black, the *EXECUTIONER*, servant of an earthly king with his double-headed axe ready to hand. A *MOCK ANGEL* there was, that carried the keys of heaven and hell: a *JUDGE* that wore a gown of red, and was grave, grey, and bewigged: a *MACE-BEARER*, a *SHERIFF*, and a simple inadvertent *PIEMAN*—all these were gathered to watch our simple ceremony.

"And who—?" I meant to ask after the bridal pair, but:

"Dearly beloved," the Poet intoned, "we are gathered together here in the sight of God," he continued, oblivious to De'Ath's entourage, " . . . which is an honourable estate . . . "—and no less oblivious to the condition of the celebrants: " . . . not by any to be enterprized, nor taken in hand unadvizedly, lightly, or wantonly, to satisfy men's carnal lusts and appetites, like the brute beasts that have no understanding . . . "—-Zog's head lolled on his neck: even before the banns were out, I feared a mismatch: "DEARLY BELOVED," the Poet boomed, "*Nat*, wilt thou have this head to be thy wedded wife, to live together after God's holy ordinance in the holy estate of Matrimony?" *etc*, "Wilt thou love, honour and keep her, in sickness and in health?"

Their replies, though feeble, were audible.

"Dearly beloved,"—the Poet was not finished—"*Patricia*, wilt thou have this *Zog*? Dearly beloved, *Wachposten-Würzig*, wilt thou have this *Würzig-Wachposten* to be thy wedded husband-wife, wife-husband? Dearly beloved," he crowed insanely, as though he would have us all wedded before the day was out, "Dearly beloved, *WORDKYN*," he folded, "wilt thou have this *ALICE?*"—an eye cast itself up from the tawdry heap: "I," the Poet gasped, "am so *happy!*"

"Oh, Wordkyn!" A tear rolled down Auntie's cheek.

Ah, how Zog disgraced himself then. A rending fistulous

explosion: *PHRRRTPHLOOSH!*—and he jilted the colleen.

"Chunk! Chunk!" Nat, however, was deliriously happy. "Dat's de way we gits our hominy grits. Ah loves you, missy. Taint mah fault you aint got nobody, yessum." And head under arm, hand in hand—his right in his left—they walked off into our inaugural sunset, fine testimonies, both, to their author's ink.

THE END

But it was not to be. For suddenly, from out the portals of the New Machine, there roared and bellowed one Bercilak de Belamoris, unvanquished, merely equalled in arts concupiscent, a lovely and lusty bachelor, his broiled features gaping with astonishment to see so many goodly folk, they no less astonished than he, for—*behold!*—from out the portals of the New Machine, there roared and bellowed one Bercilak de Belamoris, unvanquished, merely equalled in arts concupiscent, the two raising a sonorous duet: "Lungs! *LUNGS!* The Record! *THE RECORD!*"—whereat, ever the eager and faithful slave to his master's commands and his master's commands, emerged Lungs, scribe and amanuensis to Bercilak de Belamoris, followed by Lungs, scribe and amanuensis to Bercilak de Belamoris, each with a double burden of hallowed scrolls, blank parchments, blots, quills, followed in their turn by *ME*, *Me*, ME, and Me, the four Me's each reading amazedly in four books, followed—*as I always knew they would be!*—by Bartleby, boy of natural parts and lustral years, and Bartleby's own Bartleby, the hero's hero, but——and this is what I had to contend with——the hero's hero was followed by Bartleby's own Bartleby's Bartleby, and this hero's own hero's hero by Bartleby's own Bartleby's Bartleby's Bartleby, and he by———but you can count. Whereupon:

I' the empyrean heights a star was discerned, harbinger of grace and goodwill to all mankind—or star it seemed at first—falling down out of the void, tumbling closer——the mob fragmenting into several sub-mobs, one of which declared itself for Lungs and Lungs, another for Belamoris, a third for the four Me's, a fourth and faithful for De'Ath, a fifth for Bartleby, a sixth for Bartleby's own Bartleby, a seventh for Bartleby's own Bartleby's Bartleby until the mob's atomization was complete and every man his own mob——down, down, down the bolt of revelation hurtled, hit, crumpled, and

THE END

——bounced———*Sybil?*

"I have seen it!" she cried. "The Scarlet Woman with the Name written on her forehead: MYSTERY, BABYLON THE GREAT, AND ABOMINATIONS OF THE EARTH. I have seen it and know that there is *no other book!*"

THE END!

But: "Auntie," the first of the Bartlebies made his way down from the stage. "Auntie."

"You," said she magisterially, "are not Bartleby, and I am not your Aunt. But," she softened, "you can stay with me now, for these are all my Bartlebies."

"*Not* Bartleby?" I cried, "then . . . "

"The real Bartleby," she replied, "is a fiction; dead like any other."

"Then he can be raised," said I, "raised like any other."

"*Krrrk-krrrk! Krrrk-krrrk!*"—The death-rattle I believe: the *Knave*, the *Knave* was getting up!

The skin of his face tautened, drawing one side of his mouth over his teeth—yes, he had teeth—and his nostrils flared. The nasal passages, I noted, were lightly and delicately veined.

"Make him dead," Alice moaned, "please make him dead."

Blind, still blind, he turned his gaze upon me, his breath rending and ripping: a corkscrew in his throat, his eyes like knots of phlegm on their stalks—the Knave Estrogen, born again to die a second death.

"Lord, Lord," Sybil cried, "thou has raised me from the dead, and I am miserable and I suffer. Dost thou expect gratitude?"

"Afraid to breathe," the Knave spoke, his lips crinkled,

his tongue a milky bladder; "afraid to talk; afraid to see."
"Characters, your narrator has raised the dead!"

THE END

Alive and seeking the death that would not come to him, he turned and, leaving a trail of bloody footprints, walked off in the direction taken by Nat—off towards the stage where Bartlebies without number poured from the New Machine as Nat and his wedded head shuffled back into the square from the opposite direction . . .

THE END

And indeed it was—for the narrator.
"Characters!" he cried, cutting down the first of the Bartlebies, "so much for infanticide!"
Unperceived by the narrator, who now took up his position by the Machine's entrance, cutting down Bartleby after Bartleby, I—a fantastic friend and true—again assumed his part. The shades of former characters, victims of the cosmic egg, lurked and crept about the stage's flanks. There, the blind beggar and the eunuch that got his godly globe with pincers of steel; the leper that almost had the bitch with the lash of blades and canes, and she herself, applying persuasion's bite to flesh unregenerate; there, the aged harridan and her bedevilled wares, the hermaphrodite that sent De'Ath to heaven on quadruple cups, the anthropophagite that vomited limbs—creatures of the night these, that silently enfiladed the stage with solemn and muffled tread. And strange to say (stranger to see), they dragged with them a wooden cross, to which was pinned the effigy of a broken god, crowned not with thorns but laurels—as if he had been the prince of words instead of peace.
On stage, *ERROR* strained and cursed, fast in his avowals not to be a bound king. United to the Dildo by copious lashings of the gallows' rope, the *HANGING AUTHORS* succumbed at last to death's fragrant appeal, the flesh of this life falling from them in swaths; blood and bone, muscle and guts, emptying in one homogenous mass, not

without its own pulchritudinous appeal, a spreading patch of blues and reds, the conversion of one kind of matter into another.

Nourished by the exits of an age, *ERROR* swelled proud and erect, as stiff as a Hindu lingam, and growing taller by the minute, he soon towered over the stage in monumental, if erroneous vigour. Still behind the yet uncrowned potentate's throne, *DEATH THE AVENGER* skittled nervously, and in the shadow of the cross performed a few preparatory passes on the scythe, slicing the garland offered by *DISEASE* who sucked reflectively, a black depression marking the mouth of her gauze mask as she danced a mumming dance, front stage, whirling her scourge, a little embarrassed at the thought of so much death and pestilence already in the air. The *EXECU-TIONER*, hitherto passive, rehearsed a blow with his axe, an example followed by the *GRIFFIN* with the seven stars in his head who produced a scimitar, so that there is soon a great deal of naked steel flashing through the air, steel which the hermit De'Ath nimbly avoids as he capered across stage, screaming for the last time upon his powers.

And—behold!—on they came. Behold, the Pornogryph that couples with itself and brings forth more of itself, its parrot beak of adamant made, its breath more potent than the basilisk's, its skin shimmering with the irridescent taint of rotten meat, alive with the excrescences of the worm, crustacean claws grappling at its pudendum, there to whelp endless numbers of its kind, advancing to the stage where they run the gamut of raw steel, on and on, armoured claws and beaked heads flying into the embattled mobs who cheer this new spectacle while the whelping of Pornogryphs and the toll of Bartlebies mounts until the slaughter was beyond the ken of narrative art.

It is finished, the narrator thinks as the legion of creatures multiplies and the instruments of holy vengeance are unleashed, *it must be finished now*.

The blind beggar offered his back to the bitch with the lash of canes and blades who carved there in slats of flesh a stairway to mount the stage, thence gaining that ground made treacherous by the putrescent authors, that ground where Belamoris and Belamoris, Lungs and Lungs, the four

Me's, and the cast of the Masque of De'Ath Victorious battled with the growing generation of Pornogryphs, and *ERROR* swelled prouder and prouder, and De'Ath himself urged harder and harder, and the host of Bartlebies waxed vaster and vaster, thus she gained that ground, dragging the dying and the dead after her as the wooden cross fell abandoned and the curtain of blood began to close on Throckton's stage.

And through that curtain of blood went the narrator, quondam would-be bard and sometime explicator of this book—with which the reader has spent some time, and (we devoutly hope) from which he has gained no little pleasure—hence he vanished from our sight.

We do not know his thoughts, the innermost being of man, the creative core of life. And if we did, we should not relate them here. For *that* there is another time and place.

Thus upon the very principle of beggary did this Narrative Age founder: the stage groaned and the timbers, more human than their creator, did cry out in pain, until, overburdened by the age's excess, the structure split asunder and the earth opened and received the cast into it, *ERROR* even now at the centre, sliding down into the abyss of blood and dung.

And upon the mobs there fell a hail of scythes, scimitars, quills, keys, axes, arrows, wigs, blots, bones, nooses, maces, mooses, camels, stars, sickles, plagues, crutches, crosses, scrolls, bandages, scourges, bolts, rocs, griffins, chimeras, flails, garlands, chains, masks, thrones, powers, pigs, pies, plots, sub-plots, climaxes, a withering hail of symbolic instruments, followed by the golden crown which fell not upon the mobs but upon the prepuce of the Dildo's tip just before the phallus itself slid down, at which a viscid orgasmic spray was ejaculated forth, covering the entire square with a surging sickly sweet loblolly, a white caparison signifying death.

But not before De'Ath's written-upon shroud floated down upon the narrator, covering him like a shroud yet giving him life and written words enough to stay the course, whence he alone was left to tell the tale.

Gracious and heavenly reader, my apologies! I do not wish to strain your eyes further, yet although it is done I note that our history lacks one detail (small in the inclusion–large in the omission), without which no book can terminate (let alone begin); to wit, the prefactory dedication. That included, our book is done.

To Anyone Who Wants It
And Especially To Those Who Do Not:
This Book,
Conceived in Mirth,
And Undertaken
In a Like Spirit.

CHAPTER FORTY-FIVE   *The Afterword of a Narrative Man.*

I am confined to this book. The pages are clean and white. Freshly laundered, asceptic, blank. Sometimes when I am perplexed, I write on them—but they do not like that. *They?* Gottesgabe and the fantastic.

I have been studying how to decipher De'Ath's cerements. They are only half there; yet thereon, I am convinced, is enscribed the key to all meanings, a key to unlock the pages of this book and the eternal mystery of its plot.

Gottesgabe is smug. All that you have taught through scorn and malice, he says, another coming after you will learn at his leisure. All that you have suffered, he will find pleasant and amusing.

My fantastical friend is silent like me. He sits and looks at himself in the mirror. All day he tries to find his reflection. I watch them both, especially their hands, which cannot and do not object to my attention. They are occasionally rebellious, as, for example, when the fantastic's left hand—to be more exact, the index finger and thumb of the same organ— inserted itself, with murderous and singular fixity, behind the thyroid cartilage of Gottesgabe's neck. It is said that the evolution of the hand is in part the evolution of mankind. My right hand, therefore, is more humane than its fellow, for it saved Gottesgabe's neck.

Gottesgabe thinks I do not speak because I am ashamed. The fantastic thinks I am silent like him because I am mad,

455

also like him. They are both wrong.

Today, in full possession of my faculties and conscious as I am of the mistakes that the narrator made, I began a second draft of this book, a draft to be conducted in a more determined spirit of objectivity than was previously the case. For if I had entered the book earlier—perhaps a mere chapter earlier—I could have assumed control of the characters before the hermit attempted to master my narration. That was my greatest error.

During the interregnum between the last page of one book and the first of another, I am carefully watching my left hand. It may have to be removed. The arm too. If so, the right hand will have to go as well.

There are specially designed typewriters for such people.*

---

* Electrodes affixed to the stumps transmit nerve impulses to the machine.

456

ιe. What a nose he's got. It's a
ɔse for following. Ooo, but it's
ble. Where's his tallow? Forgot
ɔf that nice little boy. Can't see
no, and he can't see to read
ι! Where's you gone?' Buggered
in the dark. " 'Hello! Hello!
osthat?' Himself, it is, yes.
?' " With his tallow, he could
:r and see for himself. But you
)e'Ath? Remember? No, it's all
ads, there was no talking heads
he does. 'Hello?' What's that
s, he does. You let 'em know,
ɔu's here. Yes. 'He's not deaf,
Ⅎot deaf!' What's that? What's
s it with his hands in the dark.
ѡas deaf? What is it he feels?
Yes, them's bodies, they is,
for what he tolled the bell.
ιm, *boo*! Not here, you can't
Must find me way out. *Shhh*!
uld see what he hears, he might
ɘ might. Evil doings is afoot,
ɔle doings. You'd better watch

A clink of light. Yes, you'd
an old man, very old, and all
's that clink of light doing,
he does. Wood? Handle? Door?
eeeeeeeeeeeeeeeeee! Aaaah! It
ss his bleared old eyes! Oh dear
is, doesn't he? Them's gibbets,
a-hanging inside them? Them's
:osy cheeks they's got!
God, 'elp him, yes, quick. What
·rible! On his bended shanks he
will, give up buggeration if you
where's me bone? Aaaaa! Me
)oo! Stop it, God, please 'elp,
Not in it! 'You're not in it, do
. eyes, he has. Can't see it, no.
ε, not in the plot — never was.
t open them he won't, not till
e'll say his prayers, he will, and
re? Does he dare? Lift up your
. Yes, he does, gone: all gone.
seen nothing like it before. But
th, powers. Is it tameable? Yes,
. But you'd better bugger off,
Not going back that way, he's
itions again, De'Ath. Happy
sniffle and snuffle. Food. Yes.
:'Ath, all sorts of dainties and
. Chickins!
. . . .